UNDERSEA

BY GEOFFREY MORRISON

Morrison, Geoffrey
Undersea / Geoffrey Morrison — 1st ed.
ISBN 978-0-9847779-2-1

Cover designed and illustrated by Clara Moon

Spine and back cover designed by Betty Abrantes

The sans-sarif font used on the cover, spine, title page, headers and elsewhere is called Telegrafico, designed by ficod

Edited by Dennis Burger

UNDERSEA

PART 1

I

In the darkness of the deep, Thom Vargas slept.

The damp, cramped, cold cockpit pressed in around him, a dormant barrier to the sea beyond. At their dimmest, the backlit buttons on the console before him normally wouldn't have looked lit at all. But at this depth, they pierced the darkness like suns.

A new crimson beacon flared up near the top of the panel, just below the blackness of the depths outside. It started to flash, brighter and brighter with each pulse, faster and faster, with a sense of urgency all its own. The cockpit was lit, then dark, lit, then dark, bathed in blood red light then near total darkness.

Still, Thom slept.

He slept as the platter-sized central screen came to life, adding a new, steady, bluish glow to the tiny cockpit. He slept as the rest of the panel came to life, buttons, levers, more screens. The new hum of equipment masked the quiet gurgling of the sea, and after a moment it too was replaced by the louder drone of engines.

"Wake up!"

Thom's body convulsed, his right leg jabbing out, kicking the hard underside of the console. His head jerked forward, narrowly missing the roof of the sub, but connecting with the viewscreen. He groggily tried to rub both new aches at once. "Thom! Are you at your quota yet?"

Thom hit the comm button on the well-worn arm of his seat.

"You're killing me, Tagger. Killing me."

"Quota. Yes or no?"

"Yeah, pretty much. I'll get the rest on my way back in."

"You will, or..."

"Or..."

Tagger let out a sound that seemed half growl, half exasperated sigh, and said nothing else.

A white-green blob on the edge of the screen grew in size rapidly as it inched toward the center. Its real life counterpart suddenly appeared out of the darkness, its running lights adding their own mix to the illumination of the cockpit. The keel was so close, had there been no canopy or sea, Thom could have reached up and touched it. His sub pitched forward in the wake, dumping Thom forward towards the console and half out of his chair before the autogyros reacted, dumping him back in his seat as his sub righted itself.

Tagger's craft quickly faded back into the black while Thom went about waking his sub—and himself—the rest of the way up. The cockpit illumination rose enough to make visible all the non-backlit switches and toggles. The engines made their presence even more known. Satisfied that everything looked correct, Thom edged the throttle forward and he was gently pushed back into his seat. Aside from the motion on his screen, that gentle force was the only indication he was moving forward. Outside, through the panoramic viewscreen, everything was still black.

He pulled back on the stick, and watched the depth bleed away. After a few moments, the sub passed an invisible layer, and everything started to get brighter. More objects started appearing on the central display. Then even more. He nosed off his ascent, made a minor course correction, and throttled up even more. The sub shuttered against the strain of the engines. A school of fish darted past him, reminding him to reel in his net with the tug of a lever near his left knee. He felt the engines strain against the pull.

And then the main console display was taken over by a new sight: at the top of the screen, a single, enormous white-green blob stretched from one side to the other, crawling slowly down the display, consuming smaller blobs as it moved. Soon it occupied the entire top half of the screen. Thom throttled back.

It was hard to make out at first, just water against water. Then, a darker area in an otherwise uniform ocean. From the blacker than black, details began to emerge. Then there it was, stretching as far as the eye could see in either direction: the citysub *Universalis*.

Thom aimed for the keel and soon the larger ship towered over him. Its oblong form bulged in the middle, and as the small fishing sub neared the hull, it entered the ship's gigantic shadow, bathing the cockpit in darkness again. Above him, two parallel rows of amber lights blinked along the hull, leading him towards a glowing opening near the bottom of the larger sub. The lights turned red as he approached and Thom throttled his sub to a stop. He keyed the comm.

"Fishing Sub 2439 requesting docking and offload at bay 224."

"Request granted, 2439. Have a good nap, Thom?"

"Take a swim, Pol."

Thom used the thruster controls on the top of the stick to nudge his way towards the beckoning bay. The amber lights that led him this far continued along the edges of the rectangular bay. They converged in an "X" on the far bay wall. Thom lined up, and brought the sub in right on the target. Looking up and out of the viewscreen he could see his sub in the reflection in the underside of the surface of the water. There was a metallic *thunk*. The sub jerked downward for a moment, and then rose steadily upwards.

The rectangular bay had a dozen fishing subs like Thom's lined up along its white-paneled long wall, parallel to the pool. Ahead was an empty cradle with myriad hoses—small ones along the sides, and a large one underneath—awaiting attachment. Thom started powering down the submersible as it made its way up out of the pool and towards the awaiting offload and refuel cradle. Streaks of water ran down the viewscreen. By the time the sub was seated, he had already popped the hatch and was heading down the ladder that hung from the rolling crane above.

A dozen people hooked up hoses, checked the sub for damage, and cleaned parts that needed cleaning. Notes were made on whatever it was the blue uniformed technicians needed to take notes on. Water streamed off the sub into grates on the floor below.

"Thom."

"Pol," he said to a short man with long brown hair and a headset. Pol had the build of a man that could drag one of the fishing subs across the deck with his own bare hands, if he wanted.

"You should have heard Tag on the comm after he found you."

"My question is, why was he looking for me?"

"OK, I guess you have a point there." One of the technicians with a clipboard approached the pair, and handed Pol a sheet of paper. "Made your quota again."

"I always make my quota."

"Maybe your quota should be higher."

"Then I'll still make this quota, and everyone will think I'm lazy. Then they'll assign me this quota again, and everything will be back to where it was. So... what's the point?" Thom said with a bit of a smirk. Pol made some notes on his own clipboard, and handed it to Thom for his signature.

"Here, take your receipt. I'll see you tomorrow."

Thom left the bay and caught the beige tram just before it left. The five brown vinyl benches, torn in places and marked with graffiti in others, were little more than half full as the car scraped along the bowels of the ship, passing bay after identical bay. The floor and walls were permanently damp, causing an odd mixture of rust and growth that required non-stop maintenance. The tram passed a team of engineers, one of many, whose fulltime job was to scrape off the rust and make repairs just to this boulevard. The lighting, as far as could be seen, was barely adequate. Occasionally they passed a bay with an open lock, creating a trapezoid of cool light glistening on the wet floor.

The tram came to a stop in front of a bank of elevators with an unhealthy screech. The seven other tram passengers entered one of the elevators as it arrived, none paying attention to each other or Thom any more than he did them. As they rose up into the heart of the sub, his communicator vibrated on his ear as he suspected it would. He tapped it.

"One message from 'Olly' received at 'oh-nine-thirty-two.'" The machine voice cut out and Olly's voice cut in.

"I don't know how you do those early shifts, T. I'm meeting the boys at this place called Waves up on 8 for lunch if you're interested. Figure we can get an early start on tonight. Kidding. Sort of."

The elevator doors slid aside to reveal a wide open courtyard, and the flood of light caused all aboard to squint. The vast space was called the "Basket." The far end was obscured by rows of stores in the foreground and some trees in a small central park area beyond. Around the elevator, the well-worn deck tiles continued to a path along the outer edges. It would have taken Thom a good ten minutes to run to the opposite side of the Basket. Lengthwise it was even longer. This was the rearmost central communal space on the *Universalis*, and second largest.

As the others from the elevator scattered, indifferent to the sights, Thom took it all in. Maybe it was because he was cooped up for hours each day in a tiny sub, but he enjoyed strolling through the Basket. That he had so many memories here didn't hurt.

The walls of the Basket looked like the exterior hulls of a few dozen different ships, which is exactly what they were. Along the deck level were the exteriors of a pair of full-size submarines, with doors cut into them at different access points. Further along were the blank reddish metal of the hulls of three tankers. Their double hulls housed several "secret" forts from Thom's youth. Thom realized there was far more rust on those hulls than there had been when he was younger. Or maybe he just never noticed it before. At the far end was the bulbous nodes of a former (well still, technically) under sea laboratory. These former vessels were matched, more or less, on the opposite side for some semblance of symmetry.

Stacked above these were predominantly cruise ships, their porthole and balcony bedecked hulls looking something like a bizarre themed hotel. Above these, squeezed in close to the roof, were elaborate yachts and streamlined sailing vessels. Thom spotted one of these yachts about halfway down the Basket where his first girlfriend lived. She still might, he realized, not that he had any interest finding out.

Every former ship was wedged, fused and patched together to create the Basket—a clumsy patchwork of vessels precariously clinging together to form the walls of the great open space. The ceiling was painted light blue, with a picosun in the middle, too bright to look at. The whole courtyard was lit like a park at noon, except without the skin-tingling warmth of a real sun. The air was an assaulting mixture of mildew, wet steel, and humanity. Sensitive noses could try to pick up, underneath, the subtle aromas from the nearby cooking stalls.

Cables crisscrossed between the opposing walls, and from these, as well as from every available window or porthole, were hanging gardens of fruit and vegetables, their frail aromas masked by the scented noise.

Thom's work boots clinked softly as he crossed the simple metal deck tile. A clock across from the elevator, crudely attached to the blue-black hull of a former submarine, read 10:22. Running his hand through his dirty, matted black hair, Thom made towards his cabin, knowing he had time for a desperately needed shower.

II

"But that doesn't make any *sense*," Ralla pleaded with the Council. She brusquely pushed her light blond curls out of her face, a nervous affectation she'd developed in her youth when she felt she needed to look older. She quickly dropped her hand back to her side, knowing the men here knew exactly how old she was.

"Miss Gattley, please remember your presence here is a courtesy," Council Proctor Jills said coolly. His salt and pepper crop followed the angles of his skull, making him appear, if not menacing, at least very serious. From the Council's collective looks of patronizing amusement, Ralla realized they saw her as a child and a daughter, not the educated young woman she had become. OK, she thought, if a petulant child is what they expect to see, that would work too.

"Fine, then I'll drag my father out of his bed so he can tell you how stupid you're being," she replied. The looks of horror among the eight Council members had the desired effect. "I may be here just as a courtesy, but that doesn't mean what I have to say isn't relevant. If my father had brought up these concerns, there's not one of you who wouldn't be listening."

"Maybe so, *Miss* Gattley, but he isn't here," Council Junior Larr said, tipping his gaunt face forward and resting his bony elbows on the conference table. "Perhaps we should take this time to adjourn for the day? Proctor?"

"Agreed, Mr. Larr," Jills replied. Ralla could feel herself flushing red. The white and beige conference room emptied, each Council member passing her without a glance as they left. She walked around the long black glass table and stepped onto the patio overlooking the Yard.

The Yard was a smaller, squarer version of the Basket. The floor here, though, was alive with greenery: grass, bushes, flowers. Blossoming trees grew around the edges. Enormous vines climbed the aligned hulls of the ships and yachts that made the interior walls. The foliage had gotten so dense, it was nearly impossible to see the ships behind them. In the park below, children were playing under the watchful eye of an adult, though they were all small from Ralla's height. Ralla took note of several cabins, visible from this vantage, that weren't tending their vines. She wondered if their neighbors had noticed the shabbiness.

The Council Chambers were near the ceiling. The picosun, though still bright, wasn't overly so thanks to a ring of filters built around it like a lamp shade, shielding the upper ships from too much light. She smoothed out some imagined creases in her delicate and elaborately decorated green frock, and sighed.

It was a short walk to her father's cabin. The lushly carpeted corridor curved gently to mask its extensive length. Just this section, primarily for the Council members and their staff, would take 25 minutes to walk from end to end, and that didn't even cover the entire Yard, or the bow where the bridge was. Aft of the Yard was the Garden, and of course the Basket. She had never walked from one end of the ship to the other in one stretch, but had heard some people did it for fun. Then there were the annual races, one of which was a lap around the entire ship. She couldn't imagine how people could do that.

She entered her father's cabin without knocking. As she expected, he was standing at the balcony, his burly frame backlit by the picosun's radiance.

"Get back into bed!" she said with a mixture of annoyance and insistence. If he was startled by her entrance, he didn't show it.

The cabin wasn't overly elaborate, at least compared to some of the other Council members' rooms she had seen. The large bed took up most of one wall, and draperies hung from the others. The floor was wood, something she had never seen anywhere else on the ship. She strode across it, not noticing. Mrakas Gattley turned at his daughter's approach.

"You nag like your mother."

"What a surprise," she reached quickly for his arm, but grasped it gently. With his weight off the balcony railing, he seemed to wither. He shuffled towards the bed, and half fell into it with a stifled cough. "I told the Council that if they didn't listen to me, I was going to drag you to the next meeting."

"I'm sure that went over well. I don't suppose Larr had anything to say about that?

"No, of course not," she said with a smile.

"Well, not much we can do about it now," he pushed himself up to lean against the soft brown headboard. "If it comes to it, you'll just have to go public with what you know."

"I don't think that will force the Council's hand."

"You're probably right, but if they won't listen, we're at a dead end," he said. Ralla sighed and sat on the edge of the bed. She smoothed out more smoothness in her frock. "I know you don't like it when I talk that way. It's easy for me. I know it's hard for you, and I'll be more careful."

"You're not dead yet."

"True. But it seems I might as well be," Mrakas said, taking his daughter's small hand in his bulky ones. "You'll get my seat when I go, and I'm sure you'll win in the next election. You'll still be a Council Junior, but at least they'll have to listen to you. Next week you can visit the mining dome, and poke around to see what you can find out. Until then... come on, I know that look. Let's put on an old vid and get our minds off all this."

III

Thom Vargas had a moment to smile as he flew though the air. Landing hard on the gangway deck, he slid face first into the thin glass separating the gangway from the precipitous drop to the floor of the Basket. Olly, tall, bald, and less than a year older than Thom, landed a moment later, squishing Thom even further into the glass.

"Don't come back. You hear, you bastards? Ever. If you do I'll lock you myself," said the proprietor of Waves. Clearly stronger than he looked, he glared down at them from the entrance of his bar. Behind him, two other young men looked on, using every bit of their willpower not to break out in laughter. "OK, you two as well. Get out!"

The two other men mocked a look of innocence as they made their way out to the gangway. Thom stood, looked over the railing at the drop, and laughed.

"Can't say I understand what *his* problem is," Thom said, his voice rather slurred.

"Back to The Landing?"

"Lead on, Hett," he said to his bearded friend. Yullsin, the diminutive fourth member, had succumbed to the giggles. The boys made their way along the gangway. Barely wide enough for three of them, Yullsin followed a step behind. More than once they had to go single file to let someone pass. Each time they received dirty looks.

"They're just jealous," Thom said.

"What," Olly asked. "That they're sober and we're not?"

"Exactly," he answered with a grin.

They leaned against the walls of the elevator, and fell out when the doors opened at B1, one level below the floor of the Basket. Some light from the picosun far above trickled through clear panels and open grates placed in the ceiling of the corridor.

Featureless metallic corridors continued ahead and behind, branching off into countless side corridors as far as the eye could see. Light fixtures tucked in with various pipes along the walls played tricks on Thom's blurred eyes, seeming to get closer and closer together as they disappeared into the distance. The crew staggered down the hall, slipping on the moist floor, and entered a hatch with a hand-painted sign above that read "The Landing." Inside, the lighting was better, the floor drier, and the dozen or so patrons smiled knowingly as the boys made their entrance. The bartender placed four drinks on the bar.

"No puking inside this time, OK?" he said jovially.

"No promises!" Thom said as a salute, downing the drink in one gulp. An older man at the bar looked over with a scowl.

"Don't you boys have to be in school?"

"School?" Olly said after downing his drink. "How old do we look to you? Even Yully finished school four years ago."

"Then this is the best thing you can think of to spend your money on?"

"Umm, yeah!" Olly said, raising his empty glass to the bartender. Thom smiled, but didn't seem as enthused. The old man noticed, and nodded stoically at him.

At night, as it were, the ship slept. The picosuns automatically dimmed, their color cooling to mimic the blue cast of moonlight. There was some life, though. Cleaning crews made their rounds. Floors were buffed, lightbulbs changed—all the daily, or in this case nightly, activities to keep entropy at bay and the aging ship in fully working order. As every school kid knew, there were 16,950 windows facing the Basket alone. Those that weren't personal cabins (most of the higher ones) were washed from the deck with powerful jets of seawater and cleaner.

Take, for example, the section of the ship that was once called the *Ocean Voyager III*. Its starboard side, all 12 levels from waterline to weather deck, from stern to roughly the bow, now occupied one of the center positions in the port side wall of the Basket, bordered on the bow by the similarly sized *SeaWinds* and on the stern by the smaller *Sea Spirit II*. Underneath the *Voyager III* rested a *Contentent*-class tanker whose name no one remembered, and above were four personal yachts that had changed names too many times to count. Where one ship ended and another began was difficult to determine, as so many welds, patches, paints, and repairs had been done over the years that it all blended into one hodgepodge of a wall. And that was just the middle of one wall. The *Voyager III*, being one of the larger former ships, could fit end to end four times along the wall of the Basket where it now lay, and nearly two times port to starboard.

The interiors were mostly intact, though families and/or shop owners had taken down non-structural walls over the years to create larger spaces. Carpets had mainly given way to the bare deckplates.

On the far side of these ships was a maze of corridors, trams, and elevators designed to keep people and goods moving from the Garden or docks to storage areas or shops. The widest of these, known simply as Port Street and S Street depending on what side of the ship one was on, were the longest open areas on the ship, running unimpeded from just shy of the bow to just ahead of the engine bays. Only late at night were these thoroughfares not busy with tram, cart, dolly, and person traffic.

On the other side of the Streets was a ring of even more ships, still mostly intact from their former lives. These more or less matched up in terms of size to their inward counterparts, but while the inward former-vessels were predominantly housing, the outer ships held storage, manufacturing, and all the machinery needed to keep nearly 200,000 people breathing, eating, drinking, and not living in their own filth.

If you knew where to look, or were on one of the maintenance teams assigned to the area, you could get through one of these ships, and exit the other side. This was one of the few places where you could see the sophisticated superstructure of the *Universalis*. Mostly you'd just find ballast tanks, watertight bulkheads, and the triple-redundant cells between the ultra-hard carbon-composite exterior hull and the still-watertight hulls of the outer ring of ships. But in a few places, for access and maintenance purposes, you could see the extensive latticework that held the hull to the hulls and the ships to the ship that made the buoyant city possible and a home for so many, so far beneath the surface.

The lights were off in Thom's cabin, but enough leaked through the porthole past his dirty towel curtain to let him know that it was barely dawn. His mouth tasted like his body felt. Rolling over and standing up in one motion, he paused with a knee on the bed, one foot on the floor, and his hands bracing the opposite wall of his cabin. Eyes closed, he took a breath, then entered the head. Not much larger than the toilet that occupied its center, he was able to do his morning business, brush his teeth, and shower all at the same time. None were done well.

Thom removed the towel from the porthole, dried himself off, and dressed slowly in his gray-blue uniform. There were orange-red patches on the left elbow and right knee. The brown bottom-most button on the shirt didn't match the other clear ones.

The Garden was by far the largest space on the ship, though it was hard to tell by looking at it. More than double the size of the Basket (itself half again as large as the Yard), the Garden was exactly what its name implied. Row upon row, tier upon tier, hanging garden from hanging garden, every cubic inch of the Garden was maximized to take advantage of the three picosuns that lit the space. A semi-permanent haze imparted a softness to everything. The plants that could thrive in just water were housed in clear containers so they could be placed over something else. Mirrors were used to give light to plants tucked away underneath overhangs. Fruit vines covered every wire and support. It was bright, hot, humid, and had more co-mingling smells than any nose could deal with.

The only pedestrian walkway ran the length of the Garden in the shape of an "I." Recessed as to take up as little growing space as possible, it was covered by an open grate intertwined with vines. Along here, dozens of shops and restaurants offered produce from farms in the Garden, or from any of the small personal gardens maintained throughout the ship.

There were also stalls selling the fish that Thom's employers (or one of their competitors) had caught earlier that morning. The hectic floor was in constant gridded shadow from the grate and the vines.

Four gigantic locks, one each at the corners of the "I," were designed to keep the Garden's weather in and the ship's weather out. This time of morning, they were temporarily kept open, as the traffic was so continuous that the door wouldn't have time to open and close anyway.

The tram ride from his cabin took its usual ten minutes, and Thom stood in the lock looking out over the part of the garden he could see, and promptly sneezed like he normally did. Then it was down the ramp, out of the bright light, for the five-minute walk to breakfast.

The restaurant's patio was empty, an eddy of calmness in the constant stream of pedestrians. He seated himself with his back to the wall of the restaurant, looking out at the people passing by. It wasn't long before an older, overweight man brought out a plate of smoked fish and fruit, placed it in front of Thom, and slumped into the chair beside him. He looked to be a little more than twice Thom's age. He watched the flow of the crowd with sunken and puffy eyes and flushed jowls. Thom's own brown eyes were puffy, though not from age.

"I think I'm gonna try to get out of the fishing corps," Thom said, breaking the silence they both seemed to enjoy while he ate.

"Yeah?" the older man said non-committal. His voice sounded like he needed to cough.

"This guy at the bar last night..." Thom said, taking a bite out of a green piece of fruit. At this comment, the older man turned to look at Thom. "I don't know. It's not like he said anything, but he did, you know?"

"No."

"I suppose not."

"It's a good job. You're outside."

"I know. Look, I know it's not like there's a lot of jobs, but maybe something that's just a little different. I'm not trying to be Captain or anything."

Eerre snorted a laugh and said, "I get it. How about this. I've got a buddy that's the number two over at Logistics. We served together. His wife cheated on him with me. They divorced. So he owes me. With your piloting skill, I'm sure he could find you something."

"Thanks, Eerre. That would be great."

"He'll probably have you driving sewage scows or shuttling rich kids around or something."

"That's not the same thing?" Thom said with a smile. Eerre tipped his head back and let out a bellowing laugh, the chair creaking under the strain.

They said nothing else for several minutes, silently watching the market patrons.

"I like being able to run stuff by you," Thom said quietly into his plate. Eerre's face visibly softened, and he turned away from Thom as he struggled with what to say.

"I'm glad you do. Or, you're welcome. Or, whatever." The two avoided eye contact at all cost, and focused instead on the fast moving crowd. "Roo wanted me to invite you over for dinner this weekend. Nothing major. She's just got some fine cut of something and wants to make a big meal."

"Just tell me when, Eerre. I'd love to," Thom said with a smile, glad the awkwardness had passed. Glad he had spoken his feelings. He wasn't sure why it was hard to do with one of his oldest friends, but it just was. Eerre nodded then stood up, using the table and the back of the chair for support. The older man made his way past Thom, and patted him on the shoulder, the last pat lasting longer than the rest. Then he disappeared inside. Thom finished, yelled a goodbye into the seemingly vacant restaurant, and started off for the 20-minute trip down into the bowels of the ship and the docks.

IV

"But you have to. Don't you see how important this is?" Ralla pleaded. She had pulled her light blond curls back in a bun, thinking it would make her look more serious. Seated in the small office of the editor of the *Uni Daily,* she was now convinced it hadn't worked. The newsroom outside the office, really just a cluster of a dozen or so desks with terminals, was busy with people. Inside, there was silence. The editor, a middle-aged man with dark brown hair and a soft demeanor looked down at the papers strewn across his desk.

"What I see is a bunch of maintenance reports."

"Which all show..."

"...which all show repairs and maintenance. What do you want from me?"

"The ship is falling apart, don't you see it?" Ralla said just below a yell. "Here. Here, look at this one," she said, grabbing a sheet off the pile and waving it in his face. "We almost had a hull breach!"

The editor's eyes darted out to the newsroom, scanning for signs that people had heard her. Satisfied no one did, he looked back at her, his calm face taking a darker turn. He reached out and lowered the paper in front of him without giving it a glance.

"Look. I know who you are, which means you already went to the Council with this, and they ignored you. I don't know why, and I don't care. All you've shown me is a bunch of reports..."

"That show..."

"That show nothing. What is it you expect me to do? Run a story implying the ship is going to sink and we're all going to die? I don't think so. What good would come of it?"

"But it would force the Council to act," she protested, but she had already lost her nerve.

"I'm sorry about your father, I really am. Maybe if this was his fight..."

"This *is* his fight."

"So you say. This is an old ship; problems are bound to come up. All you're trying to get me to do is incite panic. No."

"But these reports are being repressed. No one below the Council would be able to tie all this together," she sat back down in her seat, visibly deflated. "They're hiding it. Don't you see that?"

"Miss Gattley, in tonight's edition, we interview the oldest person on board. She's 143, and doing really well. She still does her own shopping, and finishes every meal with a beer. It's a feel-good story; people will love it. She remembers being on land. Remembers the Waves. Remembers both wars. In her years, she's seen every possible catastrophe. She's seen this ship go through far worse than scattered maintenance reports from techs no doubt trying to justify their jobs. I believe that you believe this is all part of some larger eminent disaster, but I'm sure the Council has a reason for ignoring you, and that's good enough for me." He slid the scattered papers together and handed them across the desk to Ralla. She looked on the verge of tears. "I met your father once, at an event a few years ago. He was a great man. He did a lot of good for this ship," the editor said. Ralla nodded.

"Is."

"Sorry?"

"You said... never mind. Thank you for your time." Ralla turned and left quickly.

Eight days later, Ralla was in the back of a small transport, about to leave *Universalis*. There were six seats, three facing three, in the back of the sub, with the pilot at the front. The usual survival gear was stowed, rather sloppily she noticed, above and below the seats. Everything was clean, but worn. The clammy air didn't help. She hesitated to touch anything.

The sub was released from its loading crane, and it accelerated out of the dock. Turning to look out the tiny porthole between the seats, she briefly saw the starboard hull of the *Uni* before her own sub turned and all she saw was sea.

"Is this your first time going down to a dome?" she asked the pilot. He turned and looked at her. Ralla was surprised to see he didn't look much older than she, handsome, though rather unkempt. He was unshaven, and his black hair was either too long or too short, she couldn't decide. He cracked a great smile, and Ralla was shocked that this made her heart do a little jump. OK, she thought, that smile makes up for a lot. She hoped she wasn't blushing.

"Actually, yes. You?"

"Oh no, I've been to a bunch," she replied. A lie, a flat out lie, she thought. Why did I do that? He didn't seem to notice.

"Well, then you'll have to tell me how this one stacks up. My name's Thom. I guess I'll be your pilot for the day."

"Thank you, Thom. I'm Ralla."

"Well Miss Ralla, if there's anything I can get you, let me know. I have a full stock of the finest alcohols and treats."

"Really?"

"No, sorry. Stale rations?"

"Sounds lovely. And I'm not a Miss."

"Missus?"

"Oh, no, no. Ralla. Just call me Ralla."

"Ralla it is, then." This time she knew she was blushing.

Dome M3324 was a mining facility, nestled into a narrow canyon, home to roughly 3,000. The standard duty rotation was three months in the dome and three months back on the *Uni*. Generally, the workers were single, not because the work was especially dangerous, but because it was tough on families. A 50/50 split between men and women was the goal, though it usually ended up being more like 60/40. This occasionally led to problems, but not often.

Before long, Ralla noticed a yellow glow coming from the front of the sub, and tried to sit up in her seat so she could see above the raised console. Thom dipped the bow as he cleared the edge of the canyon, and the brightly glowing dome came into view as the walls of the canyon rose to envelop them.

"Better?" he asked,

"Thank you." She realized this probably wasn't what someone who had been to "a bunch" of domes would do, but it was too late now. They skimmed the surface, passing ghostly abandoned structures and massive equipment left to decay after the dome was built. Thom brought the transport around the front of the reinforced transparent hemisphere, slowing their approach as they neared the giant lock at its base. It made the sub seem minuscule by comparison. They moved along a path lit by lights in the sea floor towards a smaller open lock built into the larger door.

The sub settled with a clang onto the metal floor off to one side of the cavernous lock. The water drained quickly, and no sooner had the pumps cycled off than a well dressed, gray-haired gentleman with a boxy build stepped through a door set into the wall. He stood just inside; his posture implied some sort of military background.

Thom powered down the sub, and keyed the toggle to drop the back stairway. Ralla gathered up her things, and disembarked. The still-dripping hull gave her a bit of a shower, and she tried not to appear flustered as she approached the gray-haired man.

"Proctor Wenne?"

"Yes, Miss Gattley. Welcome to Thirty-three Twenty-four."

"Thank you, Mr. Wenne," she replied. His gaze drifted over her shoulder, and she turned to see Thom exit the sub. He nodded at them.

"Will there be anything else you need from me, Ra... Miss Gattley?" Thom's voice echoed in the open space.

"No, thank you, Thom. I believe we're scheduled to leave at 19:30. Will you meet me back here then?"

"Will do," he replied. Proctor Wenne led Ralla through the door he had come in, through a small foyer with two technicians sitting lazily in front of the lock console, and into into the dome beyond. Thom waited for them to get out of earshot, and then looked over to the techs.

"Where does the help get drunk around here?"

All three left immediately.

Ralla tried to hide her shock at the size of the space. It probably wasn't much bigger than the Basket, all told, but it seemed larger. The geodesic dome itself was clear to the sea beyond, giving it the appearance of night despite being late morning. The top portion of the lattice shell was embedded with lights, enough to make the interior of the dome as bright as daylight. The floor was packed with square buildings. Near the edges these were no more than a single story, shops from what Ralla could see, but as they approached the center the buildings got taller and taller in scale with the dome—blocks on top of blocks on top of blocks. The center building stood like a 15-story monolith surrounded by buildings that seemed to step down away from it. The top was less than a story from the apex of the dome. Each wall of each building, save the central tower, was painted a different color: reds, yellows, greens, and even some purple and magenta mixed in with the mostly white. Wenne followed Ralla's gaze.

"That's the main administration building in the center. We try to keep all the governmental stuff in one building so the workers can have the rest of the facility to make their own."

"That it's the tallest building of course carries no significance," she said with a smile.

"The colors aren't the original design," he continued, ignoring her comment. "But after a few years of the drab base composite color, people started procuring paint. My predecessor tried to put a stop to it at first, but it became like a sort of color mutiny, with everyone doing it." Wenne smiled to himself, remembering the incident. "Now my only rule is to keep whatever color you want well maintained. As long as it's kept up, I say go for it. My wife thinks some of the mish-mash is an eyesore, but the workers love it, so it stays."

They continued walking towards the mass of buildings. As they moved slightly counter-clockwise around the dome, a narrow street revealed itself between a few of the buildings. They entered and soon much of the light from above was blocked by the ever-growing urban canyon walls. They passed workers, all not much older than Ralla. The men eyed her slowly.

"You have a higher population here than most mining domes. Why is that?"

"We also have a refinery on site, so a lot of the crew is here for that."

"Ah."

"It also means we have two ball teams that compete in the Uni Cup each year."

"That doesn't create tension among the workers?"

"You'd think, but by the time they get to the finals, everyone is just cheering to bring the Cup back to 3324. Some begrudgingly so, I imagine," he said, smiling again. Ralla realized it was from pride. "The *Uni* Gov is our biggest client, of course. Their demand determines what we charge for what's left. We do well, though. As you can see, we have to import all our food, but we can do that without having to go through *Uni* Gov, so that's a plus. No offense."

"None taken."

They were almost at the central building, its height towering over them. The radiance of the dome beyond caused Ralla to squint.

"I heard your father isn't well. I'm sorry."

"I'm more than his proxy," Ralla replied.

"I'm sorry. I didn't mean to imply..."

"It's all right. I've just been hearing that a lot."

"Of course. My mistake. Up ahead is the entrance to the mine shaft. We'll need ear protection and hard hats. Both are through that door over there."

Ralla and Wenne emerged over an hour later from the mine, ears ringing and covered in sweat and filth. They returned their ear protection and hard hats, and freshened up in restrooms adjacent to the mining office.

"I was told you wanted to see some of the apartments?" Wenne said as they resumed their tour.

"Yes, please."

"I assure you, we treat all the workers well here. Many have larger accommodations than if they were shipside."

"Please understand, Mr. Wenne, I'm not here trying to get some exposé or to shake anything up. You run a tight operation here, and I am sure I'll relay that to your superiors," Ralla said as she eyed a restaurant with food on display. Her stomach growled. Wenne seemed pleased with her statement. "I do have one question for you, though it may seem odd."

"Please."

"How many people do you think this dome could hold?"

"Sorry?"

"In a pinch, how many people?"

"Well, we run pretty close to capacity as it is. I can't say more than 3,500. Maybe 4,000."

"If it were an emergency. Maybe 5,000? 6?" Ralla did her best to seem nonchalant, but caught Wenne staring at her and realized she had failed. He stopped. Thankfully the street was lightly traveled.

"Miss Gattley, what are you saying? What are you trying to ask me? Is there something I should know?"

"Mr. Wenne..." she said, setting off the way they were headed. Wenne jogged a few steps to catch up. "I am not here under any official capacity by the Council. I am here on a fact-finding mission for myself and my father. Please don't read into my questions any further than that," she was pleased with her official sounding tone. Wenne seemed to relax somewhat.

"Well, OK. As long as this is just a thought exercise or something."

"Yes, that's perfect."

"Then I guess 6,000 would be possible. If we convert the roofs and a few of the common areas, maybe a bit more." This time it was Ralla's turn to stop. She smiled at the older man.

"Mr. Wenne, thank you."

They continued on, making their way out of the building canyons to the open space that looped around between the outer edge of the city and the inner edge of the dome. They approached it, and Ralla marveled at its size as she twisted her head around to follow the web of the structure all the way to the glowing top. She followed it back down to inspect one of the giant clear panels in front of her. It was much taller than she was, and showed the black sea beyond.

"May I?" she asked, motioning towards the dome.

"It is fine with me, though I'm sure one of our cleaning crews won't be thrilled about the handprints," he said with another smile. She reached out and touched the panel. It was cool to the touch. "I have to admit, I often do the same, late at night. There is just something about being close to the pressure and the deep. Is it not? All that motion outside, yet the dome sits in stillness," he said. Ralla nodded, transfixed. She placed her other hand on the panel, and leaned in squinting. It was nearly impossible to see out into the dark water.

"Mr. Wenne, do you have any mining going on outside the dome?"

"No." Wenne turned as he replied, as if something caught his eye. He looked back at Ralla, her hand still on the dome.

"So, nothing going on outside. Nothing at all?"

"No, I..." he turned again, this time like he had heard something.

"Are you in contact with your staff?"

"My staff? I have a secretary. She knows where I am. Why?" Wenne's face had taken on an air of worried confusion. Ralla removed her hands slowly from the dome.

"I suggest you call her immediately," she said with obvious urgency. It was then they both heard it, like a quiet, distant, arrhythmic bass drum.

"What?... I..."

"We need to go to your office. Right now," she said, grabbing him by the arm. He nodded and allowed himself to be pulled back into the city. They weaved briskly in and out of the pedestrian traffic, and as they did, Ralla kept talking.

"Mr. Wenne, I went to school just like everybody. And then I came home every day and got a wholly different sort of schooling from my father." They were hurrying now, as the distant booms were increasing in volume. Wenne frantically turned his head trying to figure out where it was coming from. Some of the people they passed were starting to take notice. "You see, he was grooming me, almost from birth, to take his seat on the Council. My afternoon school was about Council politics, government, ship systems, leadership, ship agriculture. And war, Mr. Wenne. My father served in both wars, and he made me watch countless vids, documentaries, even take part in simulations." They entered the center building, strode past the elevator, and jogged up two flights of stairs. As Wenne put his hand on his office door, Ralla reached out and held it shut. Wenne was out of breath and sweating, and all the color had drained from his face. He had figured out what she was going to say, but she said it anyway.

"Sound travels father in water than it does in the air. And the sound of a submarine imploding after an explosion is unique. A unique two-part percussion unlike anything in nature. I've heard it in vids, I've experienced it in countless simulations since I was a child. Right now I need you to get me in contact with Captain Sarras and the *Universalis*. I need you to activate the city's main alarm. And I need you to stay calm. There is someone out there blowing up submarines, and from the sound of it, they're headed this way."

V

The music in the bar was loud. Thom's view was horizontal, from bar level, his face resting in a warming puddle of alcohol. He saw himself in the mirror at the end of the bar and smiled. Then he noticed the comm on his reflected ear blinking. Maybe that was what had woken him up. Maybe it was the cute girl he had driven down here that morning. Maybe she was done early and wanted to get some drinks. He raised his left hand quickly, and rapped it against the underside of the bar. In the din, no one heard him swear profusely. This time, slowly, watching his progress in the mirror, he reached up with his right hand and tapped the comm. It burst to life.

"Pilot, where are you?" It was the girl, all right. Man, she sounded pissed.

"Hi there, Ralla. I'm at..." he turned his head around to try to look at the bar's entrance behind his other shoulder and twisted his way completely off the barstool and onto the floor. "Well, I'll tell you, Ralla. I'm on the floor." He heard what sounded like alarms in the background as she spoke. He liked her hair. It was bouncy. Wait, he thought, did she just call me "Pilot?"

"OK, I'm a few levels above you in the command center." He didn't think she understood what he had meant by... "I need you to—"

Over the loud music, over the loud patrons, and cutting through his obvious internal haze, was the unmistakable sound of an explosion.

Thom sat up.

He looked around to make sure it wasn't just in his head, and from his vantage point, all the legs had stopped dancing, and the music was quickly muted. There was another explosion, this one louder, and he could feel it in the floor. Adrenaline did the best job it could sobering him up. He made his way to the top of the bar stool as everyone started to file out into the street. Alarms started going, and everything took on a new urgency.

"Thom, can you hear me?" Another explosion, this one shaking the ground enough that he had to grip the stool to keep from falling. Bottles of alcohol fell from shelves shattering on the floor.

"I'm in a... restaurant," he finally replied. "I think they call this area B-Block. It's on the far side of the city from where we came in. Where are you?"

"I'm in the central tower. Meet me here. We have to get back to the shuttle."

"On my way," he said, tapping the comm off. As he made his way down the bar, he downed two half empty glasses of water before polishing off a shot that someone had left at the end. "Well, that probably wasn't a good idea."

He exited to the street into complete pandemonium. People were trying to move in every direction, blocking others trying to go in the opposite direction. He was bumped, shoved, and eventually pushed stumbling into a dead end and empty side alley. He promptly threw up. Twice.

The alley spun only slightly, but he noticed boxes stacked up a wall. Climbing these, he was able to make it to the roof of the single story structure. Above him he could make out little flashes of light in the darkness outside the dome. He never wanted to be sober more in his life. He jogged across the roof, leapt a narrow alley, and jumped onto the next roof. The corrugated steel and composite rooftops made an unhealthy clamor as he scurried across.

It was easy grabbing onto the roof of the next building, and hauling himself up. Then there were ladders and no more alleys. He made good time, and was soon at the central building, roughly twelve stories above ground level. The city spread below him, and the dome seemed very close. Below, the mine was emptying out and the streets were wall-to-wall people, trapping themselves in their own traffic.

He jogged across the last rooftop, and crawled through a window in the central tower. The exercise was doing wonders for his head. As he entered the stairwell, he keyed the comm again.

"I'm here. What floor are you on?"

"Five, they have a tiny command center with... No, No! Didn't you hear me?!" she barked to someone else. "Get up here quick, pilot. We need to get out of here." The comm clicked off. Up. *Ha!* And what's with this pilot crap again? In the stairwell, he touched the middle step in each flight, the landings, and that was it. He pulled the door open to the command center to a scene of slightly more organized chaos than what was going on outside. He spotted the diminutive Ralla, her curls with a mind of their own as she pivoted this way and that. Terrified-looking personnel jostled around her. Thom looked behind Ralla at one of the dozens of screens set around the room. There was a mass the size of the *Uni* bearing down on the dome, but from the wrong direction. Another burst of adrenaline, this time brought on by pure, unadulterated panic. Ralla saw him and pushed her way to him through the swarm of people.

"We need to get out of here. Now. Are you... are you *drunk*?"

"Well, I'm not going to say *no*," he said as carefully as possible. She pushed past him and headed down the stairs. He followed, and they made it two landings before the worst explosion yet knocked them off their feet. A new alarm sounded in the distance. Ralla stood and was about to start down the stairs.

"Stop!" Thom shouted. She looked at him with distain, and then looked back down the stairs, about to go. "No, wait," he said, and grabbed her by the arm. She tried to fight him off, but he half dragged her out of the stairwell into the office space at that level. They made their way past the desks, and as they neared the windows she wasn't fighting him, but pushing past him. They got to the windows, and had a clear view down the street towards the main lock. Above and to the left, just over the top of the far buildings from their view, was a gaping hole in the dome, a steady torrent of black and green water flooding in. Already there was water in the streets, and people were running *en masse* away from the lock. Thom and Ralla stood in shocked silence for a moment, then Thom turned away from the window.

"Come on," he said with as much authority as his slightly slurred speech would allow. They got to the stairs and he started to go back up. She came to a halt. "Trust me, I know what I'm doing." She took one last look down the stairs, and then followed him up.

They made good time back up to the twelfth floor, both out of breath but running on panic. They went out a different window, and then down the ladders, dropping from roof to roof across the city. They tried not to look at the deafening surge from the dome or the accumulating water on the floor.

By the time they reached the one-story buildings closest to the lock, the water was nearly roof level. Thom turned to look at Ralla, who was looking at the water.

"The lock is probably still dry," he shouted over the noise. "We can operate the outer doors from the sub. All we have to do is get down there and open this door. With any luck, we'll be able to walk over to the sub with the water around our ankles as it fills up." He turned back towards the area where the entrance to the lock supposed to be, now submerged under churning dark water. The city now looked to be surrounded by an ever-growing moat.

"And without any luck?" Ralla replied.

"We swim and hope the sub will let us open the hatch when it's submerged." Thom looked back at Ralla, and wasn't expecting the look of fear. He took her by the shoulders. "Look, easy swim to the wall, then I'll dive down and open the door. Then you just have to go with the current. We'll be safe inside the sub in no time." She nodded, but looked terrified. The water crested over the top of the roof, reaching its tendrils out to their feet. The thunder of the waterfall was all encompassing. They were close enough to feel the spray.

They jumped and were almost instantly numb. At this depth, the water was near freezing. They both knew they had minutes. Maybe less. There wasn't much of a current preventing them from getting to the dome wall, which they reached with ease.

"OK, you can stay here. I'll get the door open," Thom shouted to her. Her lips were blue. She grabbed his arm before he submerged.

"We go together," she said definitively. He nodded. They took a series of deep breaths, and pulled themselves down the dome wall. The outer door to the foyer was open, and they were able to pull themselves across the bulkhead towards the console. It was still lit. Beyond, they could see the shuttle lit and dry in the bay. Thom looked across the console, but couldn't find anything. Ralla pushed past him and hit a series of buttons. Half the console lit up red, but she continued. They could hear a new siren gurgling to make itself heard underwater, and then a rotating red light came on above the lock door. Thom's lungs burned. Ralla looked back at him, eyes wide at the moment they both realized their folly.

The lock doors snapped open, creating a vortex sucking in water and two people into the bay. They were launched halfway across the open space before the amount of water that had entered with them became spread too wide to be deep. They gasped for air for a moment, and then started towards the sub, shivering.

The water level was increasing rapidly. By the time they stumbled their way to their sub, it was already lapping around Ralla's waist. The rushing water from the entry lock was nearly as loud as the waterfall had been outside.

Thom reached the panel first, and slammed his fist against it when the sub denied him the ramp. Ralla shuffled up next to him. As Thom struggled with the panel, the water neared her neck level, a full head lower than his.

Finally, an override worked, and the rear hatch lowered, partially flooding the inside of the sub. Thom turned just as Ralla, eyes closed, face blue, sank beneath the surface. He grabbed her and hauled her on board. The sub automatically retracted the hatch and started pumping out the water. Within moments, it was quiet, dry, and starting to warm. Ralla's eyes were open now, and she watched Thom pull down towels and emergency blankets from the storage areas above the seats. He did his best to dry her off, and the color started to come back into her face. Her wet hair stuck awkwardly to her face. She gave him a small smile, then blacked out.

VI

Ralla awoke, shivering slightly. The coarse fibers of the emergency blanket scratched her skin. It took a moment to register that this meant she was not wearing her clothes. She looked around the sub, and saw them draped on the seats across from where she lay, along with the clothes Thom had been wearing earlier. She looked towards the cockpit and saw Thom hunched over the terminal, wrapped in the other blanket. Past him, the bay was flooded, and the lights created an eerie greenish-blue murk.

"How long was I out?" she asked as she pivoted upright.

"Not long. Less than a half an hour. I promise later you can see me in my underwear so we're even." She fought a losing battle with a smile, but quickly regained her composure.

"What have I missed?

"I can't raise the *Uni*. From what the dome computer is telling me, there's one hell of a shit storm going on outside."

"We'll get to that. What's happening in the dome?"

"Seems like your early warning saved a lot of people. By the time the water started coming in, most people were already inside. Seems like a few saw us, and did the same to get to higher ground. Their central tower has most of the survivors, huddled around office space and such. It seems like the air pressure is pretty intense, but there are no other leaks so the water has stopped rising."

"Casualties?"

"Most are listed as MIA, but they know there's still a few hundred in the mine. Seems like the shaft door sealed shut like it was supposed to when it sensed water, and now there's too much water above it to get it open. Dozens probably got swept away by the water, and just couldn't get to a building. I activated the pumps in the lock here, and that seemed to have bought them a little time, but there was nothing I could do."

"Who's attacking us?"

"Well, that's the scary bit. From its size and general shape, it can't be anything but the *Population*."

"Seriously?!" she asked rhetorically as she bolted from the floor to look at the terminal. It had a feed from the dome's central computer that showed an enormous mass hovering just above the canyon, directly over the dome. Size and shape were almost, but not quite, a dead match for the *Uni*. She slumped down into the co-pilot seat.

"OK, I have some good news and some bad."

"What?"

"The *Population* is sitting right on top of the canyon. So we can't go up. Apparently they've been shooting down every shuttle and transport in the area, so we can't go back out the way we came in."

"No one's putting up a fight?" Ralla asked. Thom stifled a laugh.

"Seriously? I worked with a guy who joined the marines. He told me most days they just sat in their barracks drinking and playing cards," Thom said. Ralla's eyes went wide.

"Well, what do you expect? There hasn't been war in decades. We haven't even heard from the *Population* for, what, 20 years?"

"But why? Why now?"

"Don't know, don't care, and at the moment neither do you. Here, look." Thom leaned to one side so she could get a better look at the terminal. "If you continue past the dome in the direction we were headed to get here, the floor drops out and there's a thermal layer. We have about this much open water to cover before we can sneak down into that other layer. Then we churn it through the canyon and hope they don't have anything fast enough to catch us. Then at top speed it's half a day or so to the rendezvous with the *Uni*. As long as no one sees us while we're in the open, we'll be invisible under that thermal layer. I can't imagine they won't have plenty else to do."

Ralla leaned back and closed her eyes.

"I know you're…" Thom started, but she waved him off.

"No, you're right. We can't stay here. We have to at least try to make a run for it and warn the *Uni*. Think we'll make it that far?" she asked him. He shrugged. "Captain Sarras you aren't."

"Clearly. There are some drysuits in the foot lockers. I think we should put those on so we can move around."

Ralla looked down at her blanket as if noticing it for the first time. She had a fleeting and, given its timing, rather inappropriate thought that she wouldn't mind seeing Thom out of his.

The door imbedded in the main lock pivoted upwards, as the transport rose slightly from the deck. It slid sideways while rotating 180 degrees, and was soon positioned just at the edge of the lock, with the open sea just beyond.

"I'm strapped in. Go for it," Ralla said, closing her eyes again. Then she thought better of it and turned to look out the front viewscreen. Thom pushed the throttle forward hard against its stop. As the little sub rocketed forward out of the lock, Ralla caught a glimpse of the battle still raging overhead.

Small fighter subs battled it out in the distance. Often a brief flash was the only thing that would mark the resolution.

The hull of the sub rang as if struck by a hammer. The stern sank several inches before the computer corrected for it.

"What the hell was that?"

"I think the *Pop* is shooting at us. Hold on," Thom said, and immediately jerked the joystick. The transport turned sharply to starboard, then to port. Another hit; this time they rolled clockwise. "They hit an engine pod." Thom struggled to right the craft. Another hit, this one dead center. Ralla looked up and could actually see where the hull was now convex from the impact.

"How are they doing that?"

"I don't care. We're only..." but he was cut off. Another hit on the opposite side, spinning them again. This time, with no way to correct, the little sub augured its way into the sea floor, digging its own shallow grave in the silt.

Thom was aware of cold across half his face. The right side of his face was cold. He tried to open his eyes, but only the left responded, and he soon realized why. His face was pressed against the viewscreen, ground zero for a web of spider cracks radiating outwards. The other side of the viewscreen was mud. Bluish mud.

His body was contorted such that his face was pretty much the only point holding his weight. He righted himself, and rubbed the chilled half of his head. As he stood, he noticed he was knee deep in water. Even through the suit it was frigid.

Ralla hung from the safety harness, arms and legs dangling in a way that was almost humorous. The sub on its side, gravity was doing its best to pull her towards the "floor," which had been the starboard bulkhead. The harsh emergency lighting cast long, sharp shadows. Thom sloshed out of the water and patted Ralla on the hand.

"Ralla. Ralla!"

She awoke groggily, and looked around the sub. Her eyes focused on the damaged viewscreen. Then the water. Then at Thom.

"OK."

"Yeah. I'm gonna unbuckle you. Hold on to my shoulders," he clicked the release, and she dropped to the slanted floor, slid a little, and then braced herself with one foot on the floor and one on the side of a footlocker.

"Do we have any power?"

"I don't know, I just woke up. I think my head did the damage to the viewscreen," Thom said, aiming his right temple at her.

"Seems like," she replied, surprising herself with how little genuine concern was in her voice. Using the seats and armrests, she pulled herself to a porthole that was now effectively the roof. "I can see the bow of the *Pop*. I don't think she's moving."

Thom pulled himself up to an adjacent porthole, and surveyed for himself.

"Can you see anyone coming our way?" she asked.

"No, but we're further out than I'd thought we'd be. We're probably pretty close to where the floor drops off."

"Well maybe if you hadn't been drunk we would have made it," Ralla said coolly. Thom turned around. Ralla had dropped back to the now-bottom of the sub, and stood defiantly.

"What?"

"You heard me, pilot. You were drunk. You probably still are. And because of that, we're trapped here."

"Whoa, whoa. Are you being serious right now?"

"When I get back to the ship I'm going to do everything I can to make sure you spend the rest of your life washing dishes or cleaning toilets or whatever else a drunk can do without causing anybody any harm. You're not even fit to be a mechanic on a sub like this, you shouldn't even touch a ship like this. You…"

Thom's face went hard, and his voice went eerily quiet.

"Perhaps before you say anything else you should realize that I'm the only other person in the sea that knows you're alive."

"Was that a threat? Did you just threaten me? Do you know who I am?"

"The better question is if I'd care even if I did. Now you can continue to squawk at me like a privileged little bitch or you can sit down, shut up, and let me see if I can get us out of this muck."

"Good. Do that."

"I don't like you anymore. You are not cute when you're scared," Thom said as he reached for the helmet for the dry suit. Before she could respond, he had sealed and pressurized it, muffling all sounds down to below a whisper.

Three days had passed. The helmet had only lasted on his head a few hours, but they hadn't spoken since. Ralla had tried to siphon power from the emergency batteries to run one of the radios. Just getting the wiring run had taken a day and half, but the end result was just draining their dangerously low power reserves.

Thom had tried to get the thrusters working. There was access to several of them from inside the ship, but two were buried in the mud and another had been blown off in the attack. The remaining thruster, after two days of work, would only run at 2% speed, doing nothing.

The emergency blankets had stayed dry, so at night or when they got too cold to work, they were able to bundle up. For sleep, they took turns bracing themselves on the one set of seats that wasn't hanging from the ceiling. The other slept on the floor.

Thankfully, the water level hadn't risen, likely due to the leak being buried in the muck.

Their clothes had dried enough to put them on as another layer. The air in the sub was warm enough to stave off hyperthermia, but not by much. The *Population* hadn't moved, but they could see nothing else from their viewpoint.

At the end of the third day, while they ate another dinner of emergency rations, Ralla broke the silence.

"I don't want to die here, Thom," she said it softly, just above a whisper. They shared a look in the cold and the wet. He nodded. The silence stayed, but much of the tension had left.

"Well, at our current rate of power consumption, the air processor will let us breathe for two-to-three weeks after the food and water gives out," Thom said dryly. Ralla closed her eyes and smiled.

"Thank you."

"Look. An idea came to me yesterday. Let's get some sleep, and we'll talk about it in the morning."

"OK. You want the bed?"

"You can take it; the sofa's just fine."

The next morning, over a breakfast of mealbars and water, Thom laid out his plan.

"I assume you agree we can only go back to the dome as a worst case scenario."

"So you heard the same stories from the war that I did growing up."

"Right. I like the number of fingers I have now. Without better knowledge of the dome, I can't imagine how we'd get back in other than the lock or the hole they created, which I hope is patched by now."

"OK, well, that's about as far as I got, too."

"Well, there's another possibility. Can we assume there are a similar number of people on the *Population* as there are on the *Uni*."

"After all this time, I don't know. I couldn't even guess."

"More than 100?"

"Certainly."

"More than 10,000?"

"Sure."

"More than 100,000?"

"Yeah, I guess. What's your point?"

"OK, how about 100,002?"

They tore up the emergency blankets, and insulated their drysuits the best they could, then ate a few more ration bars and stowed the rest of them and the remainder of their fresh water into a waterproof satchel. The rebreather gear was still strapped in behind the seats. They helped each other suit up and strap weights to their ankles.

"Comm check."

"Comm check," Ralla replied. "Look, what if we miss or the *Pop* moves while we're floating?"

"Then we rise to the surface and die of compression sickness or radiation poisoning."

"How do you know we won't get CS when we get to the *Pop*."

"I don't."

"I think I liked it better when we weren't talking."

"Well, we'll be in the suits in the water for the rest of the day at least, so you can not talk to me then. Ready?"

"No," she said as she nodded. Thom dialed in a series of commands to the pad next to the hatch and almost immediately, water began rushing in. Even through their suits, the water was frigid, the sound deafening. They shared a look through the glass faceplates of their helmets, and as the water passed their knees, Thom could see the distress in Ralla's face. By the time it reached mid-thigh she was in full-blown panic, torn between fight and flight, pawing at her helmet erratically. Thom wrapped his arms around her, pulled her tight, his own rapid breathing not any example of calm.

By the time the water had reached their heads, she was still shaking. But as the last of the air left the sub, he gently pushed her away from him so he could look into her faceplate. It was partly fogged up; she was breathing too fast for the rebreather. He rapped his knuckles on the glass, and she focused on him in between breaths. With his other hand he pushed his own helmet backwards, and at the same time pushed his head forwards so his mouth touched the glass. Making a seal, he blew out a breath, revealing all his teeth and flapping tongue.

After a moment's stunned silence, Ralla's still-ragged breath turned to laughter. She caught her breath, hugged him, and keyed her comm.

"OK. I'm OK. Let's go."

Thom activated the hatch, and it opened, revealing the seabed, the dome in the distance, and the looming submarine *Population*. They stepped out of the transport and onto the canyon floor.

VII

It was slow going. The seabed had a layer of silt that swallowed their weight-laden feet. They stopped twice in the first hour, but pushed on. The dome didn't seem to get closer, and the abandoned transport barely got smaller.

It took them the better part of the day, but they were finally somewhat below where they could see some open bays, visible as tiny squares of light in the otherwise black hull. They decided they would risk it from here, and removed the weights on one of each of their legs. While they had stood out slightly against the lighter colored silt, as they ascended they disappeared into the murky sea. The canyon walls, featureless in the dark and distance, offered little sense of movement. Occasionally, the running lights of transports would ascend or descend close enough to seen, but not close enough to see them.

It was excruciatingly slow, but rising any faster would have been too risky. They also didn't mind the respite. The ship got larger and larger, soon occupying their entire field of view. The black hull stretched off in every direction as far as they could see.

Then, suddenly, they cleared the canyon. The sea floor extended in every direction, a vast barren wasteland. The *Population* loomed, a solid near-black cloud over a gray landscape of nothingness.

It was well into the night, their time, when they touched the composite keel of the *Population*. They had drifted away from the few open bays on their ascent, so they pulled themselves along the hull headed aft in search of them. As they approached the first open bay, they froze. A transport sub was rising, all lit up, from the dark crevasse below them. They remained perfectly still, no more than a few body lengths away from the lit hole in the bottom of the *Pop*. The transport passed them, breaking the surface of the water in the bay, and floated for a moment on the artificial surface. Then it rose out of the water and disappeared. Thom activated his comm.

"This is our best chance. Follow my lead," he said. Ralla nodded, and Thom immediately started inching along the hull. He paused at the edge of the bay, his chest flat against the hull, helmet out into the opening. As slowly as he could, he bent his head around, broke the surface, and peeked inside the ship for the first time.

The bay layout was very similar to those on the *Uni*, with subs lining the walls and a crane to remove craft from the water. There was no one near the opening, but what looked like maintenance personnel were attending to the recently arrived transport. The sub's hatch opened, and people started filing out. Their dress was obviously a uniform, not totally dissimilar to those found on the *Uni*. This offered no help as to whether or not their casual clothes were similar or not to what Thom and Ralla wore. After a few more minutes, the sub was apparently empty, and the techs moved out of sight on the far side of the bay.

"Slide down a bit with me," he said over the comm. She tapped his leg, and they shuffled down the edge of the open bay. When they were positioned better behind the resting transport, Thom slowly pulled himself around the edge, and rolled out onto the bay floor. Ralla did the same. They crouched behind the transport. It was one of theirs, from the dome.

"We should just take this."

"Even if we could get it in the water with no one noticing, it's not speedy enough for us to get away. No, we'll have to figure out something else. Take off the suit."

They removed their dry suits, wrapped them around the helmets, and pushed them into the water. They sank out of sight.

"We should at least see if there's anything on the shuttle we can use," Ralla said. Thom nodded. They checked around for any other people in the bay, and then moved quickly up the ramp. The inside was similar to the one they had left that morning, though this was a larger model meant to transport 18 people. They sat in the seats, ate a few of the emergency rations, and drank packets of water. Otherwise, there was nothing of value.

Voices. They were headed towards the shuttle. There was definitely an accent, but it was at least the same language. Thom jumped up and sat down next to Ralla and started kissing her. Her eyes went wide, but seeing the terror in his, she went along. The voices stopped as the group of three men stood in the doorway of the sub.

"You really need to do that here?" one of the men said. He was rather lanky and gaunt, but stood tall in a way that implied authority. The dialect had vowels that sounded longer than Thom was used to hearing, so he tried to mimic it the best he could.

"Sorry, sorry," Thom said as he pulled away from Ralla. She was doing her best to smile and play along. The man eyed them suspiciously. Thom stood, and helped Ralla to her feet. "Sorry, sorry," he said again, this time with a smile. He started moving towards the three men, holding Ralla's hand as he moved. The men said nothing, and parted as they approached. Thom and Ralla stepped down from the sub, and walked quickly, hand-in-hand, toward the exit. They waited for the lock in front of them cycle, and by extension, the one they had come in to close. Thom kissed Ralla on the cheek, and out of the corner of his eye, he looked back at the sub. The lanky man still stood in the doorway, watching them, but the others had moved further into the sub.

Thom and Ralla stepped out into a long corridor, almost a twin for the one of the same purpose on the *Uni*. As the lock slid shut, they released each other's hand, and moved quickly down the corridor.

There was a track for a tram, but no tram was in sight. The lights were set low, and it was difficult to see.

"I think we may have lucked out. It seems to be really late or really early."

"Or they're calling security."

"Nothing we can do about that now. We need to find a change of clothes." They kept walking at a fast pace, but soon slowed as they came across no one else.

"Is there anything even down here?"

"Well, on our ship I worked down here. So did my father and just about everyone I know." Thom said it without malice, but Ralla didn't say another word for some time. "There should be an elevator up into the ship up ahead, as long as they followed roughly the same design as our ship." They soon arrived at a bank of elevators. One arrived with a disconcerting bang, and the doors scraped open.

When they opened again, both Thom and Ralla stood in shock for a moment. Unlike the *Uni*, whose interior was broken up into three sections, with substantial cross bracing and bulkheads in between, the *Pop* was an open tube, bow to stern. From their vantage point near the bow, they could see almost all the way to the other end of the ship. Fog obscured the far end, and along the roof there seemed to be tiny clouds. There were gardens everywhere, different levels, angles, and sizes. Walkways crisscrossed the open spaces. Instead of picosuns, a single lighted strip ran the length of the ship, dead-center along the roof. It wasn't very bright, further evidence it was night local time. The walls were ships, just like on the *Uni*, but in addition, there were ships placed in the open areas as well, sailing in a sea of gardens and walkways. Even the area near the elevators was impressive, an enormous open amphitheater that gently sloped towards the forward-most bulkhead. Thom closed his mouth.

"This is only the third place I've ever been," he said quietly.

"Me too," Ralla replied, equally impressed.

They found some uniforms in a bin near some kind of store a few minutes' walk from the elevators. They were all the same orange color, and a similar design as the uniforms the men down in the docks wore.

Thom and Ralla, now clothed in local attire, found a secluded corner behind another shop, and passed out.

The next morning, what felt like only a few hours later, Thom and Ralla woke to the din of people streaming past their hiding spot. Most wore uniforms similar to those they had borrowed the night before, but of a variety of different colors. Others wore clothes that wouldn't have looked too out of place on the *Uni*. Simpler, perhaps. Everyone was headed in the same direction, and all were talkative, even jovial. After checking themselves for wrinkles or anything else that would seem out of place, Thom and Ralla joined hands, and stepped into the flow of pedestrians. The few who saw their exit gave them a good looking over, but soon went back to their conversations. The crowd was headed towards the amphitheater.

All the seats were filled by the time Thom and Ralla got there, and as the crowd continued to build everyone moved as far forward as they could and just stood there. There was a genuine friendliness to the greetings, the waves, the exchanges that perplexed Thom and Ralla.

Applause started near the stage and spread quickly to the back of the standing crowed. Thom and Ralla joined in. The clapping was more salutation than excitement, though there were some in the crowd that had noticeable enthusiasm.

A man stepped out onto the stage from a space in the front wall. Many in the crowd immediately clapped louder, though most remained rather neutral. He waved out at the audience. His hair was a wavy light brown, and as much as Ralla and Thom could make out, he had a sharp jaw and a defined chin. While older than either of them, he didn't seem to be into the age where either of them would really call someone an "adult." Maybe old enough to have a young family. His first words, though amplified, were drowned out by the applause. He paused as it died down.

"Good morning, *Population*," he greeted with a smile.

"Good morning, Governor Oppai," the crowd replied in unison. Thom and Ralla mumbled along, but still got a few odd looks from the people near them. Oppai looked amused.

"You know, that really makes me laugh when you do that. All right, let's get down to it. A few morning announcements before we get to the good stuff. Food production shipwide is up 4.6% over last month. Let's hear it for the farmers," he said, motioning with both hands out into the audience. There was heavy applause. "Tram 2 is going to be down for maintenance. When I asked them when it would be ready, the crew said 'when it's done'." There was some mild laughter. "We also had 87 births last month. Let's hear it for the new moms and dads!" The applause was much louder this time. He waited for it to fade, then started again. "OK, now on to the good stuff. And this is real news: I just found this out a few hours ago. We have fully reclaimed our stolen mining facility!"

The applause was immediate and thunderous. Shock hit Thom and Ralla as if the clapping had brought it.

"Did he just say..."

Ralla grabbed his hand and squeezed it tight. The citizens all across the amphitheater seemed thrilled. It took several minutes for the applause to die down.

"We did lose a few of our people, but you all know that we couldn't let this attack on our solidarity stand. We offered free passage or asylum to the miners who had taken over. It pains me to say they chose to seal themselves in the mine and flood it. Sadly, such is their way, I suppose."

The color drained from Ralla's face. Thom wrapped his arm around her, pulling them close like a couple would and supporting her as her knees began to wobble.

"We expect to resume mining operations within a few weeks. Tomorrow, we head for New Unstalla, and liberate our people there. We will not let them take our fair share anymore! We will not let them take our mines and our farms anymore!" The applause nearly drowned him out. His face beamed out onto the crowd. He waved them quiet.

"OK, that's it for today. Now I have to get back to work..."

"And so should you!" the crowd and he said together.

He waved at them all again as they applauded. He left the stage the same way he came in, and almost immediately the crowd started to disperse. Thom and Ralla went with the flow. Passing the series of shops where they had slept, they were able to break off and sit on a bench. Ralla's hazel eyes were moist, and her nose was running. Thom took her hand in his, and she squeezed it tight.

The shops had started to open, and some from the crowd stopped and took seats. Thom watched them as casually as he could, both to see how they interacted, and to give Ralla as much privacy as he could without leaving the bench, or her hand. People passed them without a second glance. They all seemed jovial, and most seemed in a hurry. A few of the shops nearby started to spawn lines of patrons.

The closest shop, a cafe not unlike Eerre's back in the Garden, opened its doors, and there was a semi-organized rush for seats. As he thought of Eerre's cafe, he suddenly felt very alone, very small, and very far away from home. He watched the customers for a few more moments, and then turned back to Ralla. Her eyes were clearing. She pulled her hand from his to wipe her eyes.

"There's no money," he said quietly.

"Huh?"

"I've been watching these shops. People walk up, ask for something, they get it, and then they walk away. There's no hard credits, there doesn't even seem to be a scan to charge an account."

"Maybe they tell them their name or their cabin or something."

"I guess so, but I can kind of make out what some of the people are saying and it doesn't sound like they're even saying that."

"You know what this means?"

"I know what *you* think it means, but *I* think it means we're going to be able to eat," Thom said with his eye on the cafe. Ralla made like she was going to object, but was too hungry.

The meal was uneventful, and though they were ravished, they came away unimpressed. At the end, the waiter thanked them in the same accent the whole ship seemed to have and they went on their way. An older couple at the table behind them was finishing up at the same time, and caught up to Ralla and Thom as they headed back towards their bench.

"Your water out?" the gentleman asked politely. Ralla turned and smiled at him.

"Sorry?" she asked, doing a far better job mimicking the accent than Thom. For a moment, the man seemed uncomfortable, but his wife took over.

"My husband was just asking if the water was out in your house, because, you know..." she said, bringing her hand discretely up to her nose.

"Ohhhh," Ralla said with a laugh that Thom mimicked. "As a matter of fact it is. I'd wish I could say 'how'd you know', " Ralla's eyes flicked between the two.

"We had the same problem last year. If you'd like, you can use the shower at our place," the woman said, her smile never wavering. Thom squeezed Ralla's hand, but Ralla squeezed back.

"Well I'll tell you, we'd love to. If it wouldn't be a bother," she replied. The older couple looked very pleased. As a group they headed up into the superstructure.

The "house" was just a small cabin a few decks up and away from the main central area. Thom was tense the whole walk, but followed Ralla's confident lead. He did his best to look calm by taking in the sights as they went. The corridors were smaller than on the *Uni*, and almost uniformly wetter and rustier. Many lights were out, creating areas that were in deep shadow. Paneling was missing or broken in places. The moisture pooled in places, causing the threadbare carpet to squish beneath their feet.

The cabin itself was clean, but only about twice the size of Thom's cabin single. The bathroom was larger, though, and the older couple made it rather obvious that they expected the two of them to shower together. Not wanting to engage in potentially dangerous small talk, this suited them both. They turned on the water, a low pressure trickle, and then awkwardly undressed back to back. They stepped into the shower in the same unspoken arrangement. While washing off several days of grime, they spoke as quietly as they could.

"Before you say anything, we needed this and you know it. How long before some less-polite people would start to take notice?" Ralla said over her shoulder.

"OK, fair point."

"Any ideas what to do next?"

"We should get the lay of the ship, and wait till tonight to see if we can steal a sub from somewhere."

"You think they'll just let one of their subs leave on its own?"

"No, probably not. Let me think about that."

"Do you think they killed everyone in the dome?" Ralla asked, even more quietly. After a moment's pause, Thom replied.

"Yes."

They finished showering and wrapped themselves in towels that hung nearby. They redressed—no small feat in the cramped quarters. Thom didn't feel bad sneaking a glance at Ralla, as he didn't miss her do the same. When they exited the bathroom, the cabin was empty.

After a cursory look around the cabin and finding nothing of interest, Thom and Ralla wandered out into the ship. The layout and overall build wasn't radically different from the *Universalis*, alluding to their common ancestry. The *Population*, though, was in visibly worse shape. Ralla pointed out key structural members that had noticeable decay, while they both marveled at the rust apparent on all surfaces. They came to a park area with monitors set up on tables. There were a handful of people, but several of the tables were empty. They sat next to each other at two adjacent computers and tapped the screens.

After a few moments, Ralla said to Thom, "Do you want to find the ship layout and I'll go over the news?"

Thom nodded, and turned back to the public terminal. They sat in silence, searching through whatever information they could find. After a few more minutes of searching, they started talking.

"I think I have an idea how we can get out of here. We'll have to wait till we're underway though."

"So, the guy we saw yesterday is Herridki Oppai. He won the governorship about six months ago. From the articles at the time it doesn't look like he had much opposition; he won in a landslide. This talk about the mining dome only started a month or so ago, and *man* is it vicious. They blame us for their lack of resources. For... well, for just about everything. That was going on for a while before Oppai took office and it has really intensified since then." She looked up from the terminal and at Thom. "How can they do this? They're just lying to these people. We're not the bad guys. They're the ones that attacked us."

"Let's not call it 'us,' OK?" he said quietly. She nodded.

"We've always tried to help," she mouthed "them" and motioned with her head vaguely to the rest of the ship.

"Have we?"

"Are you serious?" Ralla said, looking shocked. "Why... how? Why would we do any of this?"

Thom shrugged.

"I'm just saying, I drove *you* to that dome. I have a feeling I have a different perspective on the ship than you do."

"What's that supposed to mean?"

"It's a big ship, Ralla."

"Not that big."

"I'm just saying I've seen some, well, *optimistic* stories in the Daily."

"That's not the same thing."

"Maybe. Maybe not. How would I know? But we can worry about that later. Keep going."

Ralla, visibly riled, was unsure what annoyed her more: his flippant insinuation about her father and the Council's honesty, or that he had moved on so casually. Or that he was right. They could deal with it later. She finally turned back to her console.

"There's a lot more. I wish I could just send it to my storage on the *Uni*."

"Remember what you can. There's not a lot of technical info I can dig up, mostly just maps and stuff, but enough for us to find our way around." Thom leaned over and put the palm of his hand on the deck. "I think the engines are starting up. We may be moving already, which is good. We should keep wandering around, seeing what we can see. We'll get some dinner later and then hide out when everyone goes to bed. Sound good?"

"What's your plan?"

"Well, it's a little complicated.

VIII

They explored the ship, taking mental notes on anything that was remotely interesting. They listened to nearby conversations. The food, being free, kept them eating throughout the day. Each time they ate, they stored what extra they could in their clothing. No one paid them any attention. They were careful not to loiter too long in any one place, and always made it look like they had some place to be. They had a late dinner at the same cafe where they had breakfast, then wandered arm in arm through the nearby park as the area slowly emptied. The shops closed up, and Thom and Ralla took temporary refuge where they had started the day so many hours before. Ralla fell asleep leaning against the back of a restaurant.

Thom woke her several hours later, and in silence they retraced their steps back to the elevator, back down into the long corridor that connected the bays on this side of the ship. Thom checked the identification panels on the doors. Finally, he stopped at one and pressed the adjacent button to open the lock.

The bay was longer than the one they had entered from. Instead of a pool at one end with a gantry crane to remove the subs, this one had a gentle ramp into the water which got progressively deeper until it met a vertical, fully submerged lock on the far side.

There were small craft shaped like arrowheads lined along all the walls and in cradles hung from the ceiling. Those on the floor sat on wheels extended from flush mounts integrated into their hulls.

"I thought we were going to take one of transports?" Ralla asked as the lock sealed itself shut.

"This will be better. They're missing some of these already because of the attack, so when they go down to clean up the mess we're about to make, they won't know one is missing."

"A little cramped, don't you think?"

"I do think that, yes."

"It looks like there's barely room for the two of us in there."

"Technically, they're one-seater attack subs," Thom said, eying them closely. He missed Ralla's glare. Thom continued to scan the bay, and found what he was looking for. He made his way over to the tool bench and grabbed an oversized wrench from a hanger on the wall behind it.

"OK, go get in..." He looked around at the stable of subs, and chose the closest one to the pool. "That one. There's probably a single glowing button. Press it."

They moved in different directions, their footsteps echoing though the quiet bay. The air smelled like seawater and grease. Thom moved towards the lock they had entered and opened it. He stuck his head out into the corridor, looked both ways, then looked up and down the jam where the door sealed itself against the bulkhead. Holding the wrench over a certain spot, he hit the button again. The door slid back, pinning the wrench between the jam and the door. The door motor whined.

He jogged across the bay, past the sub where Ralla sat. He heard it making noise, its systems coming alive and its engines spooling up. Near the outer wall, next to the pool, there was a small console. Thom stood over it and looked from the pool and closed lock back up at Ralla. She had the cockpit canopy open, and gave him a thumbs up. Thom pressed a button on the middle of the console, and it was as if he lit off a war.

Alarms pierced the silence and echoed into cacophony. Blue strobes flashed from locations all along each wall. Thom pressed the button again, and sprinted toward their new sub. Jumping up towards the cockpit, he half pulled himself in and half got pulled in by Ralla. The water in the pool started to churn.

The seating position in the sub was severely reclined, and Thom and Ralla squeezed into it the best they could. Thom took up most of the seat, and angled himself so his left side was partially against the bulkhead on that side. Ralla folded herself into what was remaining of the right side, nestling rather uncomfortably into the space between his arm and his torso.

Thom scanned the controls and within a few moments got the craft moving. The electric motors in the wheel hubs provided minimal speed, but got them around till they were facing the ramp at the fore-most corner of the pool. The water was getting increasingly turbulent. Waves had formed and water had started spilling over the top of the pool and onto the deck.

The lock started opening slowly, but rapidly increased its pace. Due to the speed of the *Pop,* water surged up and over the stern-most edge of the pool. As the lock reached its fully open position, a continuous wave of water inundated the end of the bay. The surge crashed into the far wall, and started echoing back, bringing once parked subs with it like toys. The wave, now not much higher than knee height, hit the forward wall, completing the flooding of the bay. Air screamed out of the bay though the braced-open lock, seawater rapidly taking its place. It wasn't more than a few moments before the water level was at the bottom of Thom and Ralla's sub.

"Hang on," he said. Ralla braced herself against the cockpit and Thom as he throttled up the dry engines and eased the craft into the water using the electric hub motors. The turbines behind them screamed in the open air. The second the bow touched the water, the current took it, jerking them sideways and pulling them deeper into the water and towards the rear of the ramp. The port turbine submerged first, spinning them around so they faced back the way they came. Thom swore, throttled into reverse just as the starboard turbine caught. The end of the pool loomed large in the viewscreen just as the powerful engines shot them out into the ocean. Thom cut the engine and powered down the ship immediately, floating in silence along the dark rippled hull of the *Population*. Looking out the cockpit to the left, they could see their sister subs being ejected from the bay and slowly sinking to the bottom.

Thom looked the other way, at the stern of the *Pop*. Ralla had relaxed her grip. Sensing he had no time to explain, Thom braced his feet against the sub, pulled Ralla tight against him, and closed his eyes.

The *Population* had six propellers arranged roughly in a "U" shape. Each eight-bladed propeller was just over four stories in diameter. As the tiny attack sub cleared the stern of the ship the massive suction of the props sucked them into the wake, tossing them around like a bit of paper in a hurricane. Thom and Ralla were thrown violently about the cockpit, impacting each other and every surface in the sub.

They awoke to find themselves bruised, battered, and uncomfortably tangled up with one another. A single button was glowing warmly on the console. The backup mechanical dials showed them to be at neutral buoyancy and in a slow spin. As he and Ralla adjusted into the seat the best they could, Thom looked around them to see if there was any trace of the *Pop*. Nothing but empty sea. He powered up the sub. The main screen showed a thermal layer not too far above them, and no craft in the vicinity. He set the sub to rise slowly, without using the main engines. Once through the layer, and again showing no other ships, he powered up the main engines. Everything appeared to be in working order.

"OK, Dome F211 here we come. Two days in here won't be too bad, right?" Thom said with a smile.

Ralla scowled.

It took them two and a half days to get to the farming dome, F211. From there, a transport got them to the *Uni* in just under a day. The transport, designed for short trips hauling grain to the *Uni* when it was parked nearby, was modified with extra seats, supplies, fuel. Its only cargo, besides Thom and Ralla, was the attack sub stolen from the *Pop*.

Something had changed between them. Silence was the norm during their cramped voyage, but the close quarters had somehow diminished the animosity. During the last leg on the transport, they said nothing, but sat next to each other despite a choice of seats. She fell asleep with her head on his shoulder.

F211 had signaled the *Uni*, so when Ralla and Thom stepped off the transport it was to a hero's welcome. Everyone they knew, and everyone those people knew, filled the large forward bay and the corridor beyond. Cameras broadcast their arrival throughout the ship.

Of course, it was predominantly for Ralla. Her father did his best to look regal as he greeted his only child, back from the dead. The tears were real, though his standing was not. He was supported by no less than two aides and a hastily made brace hiding under his robes.

Thom spotted Olly and the crew, but before he could wave, he saw something out of the corner of his eye. Ralla had released her father and was now kissing a tall, handsome young man, much to the delight of the crowd. Thom was glad the cameras weren't on him. To their credit, Olly and his friends either didn't notice the look of disappointment and jealousy on his face, or said nothing if they did.

As the mass of people slowly made their way out of the bay, Thom received more pats on the back and handshakes than he could count. The crowd moved with them and in front of them, as if a single entity. Thom started walking slower and slower, letting the bulk of the crowd—and the cameras with their built-in spotlights—follow Ralla, her father, and Mr. Handsome. Thom caught glimpses through the crowd of the two holding hands. After a few more minutes, Thom just stopped, and his friends stopped with him. They all understood what he was doing, and he motioned for them to go the other direction down the corridor. They were able to disappear through a lock in the Dockyard.

The Dockyard was the largest bay on the ship, running down the keel for almost the entire length of the Garden. This was where the largest ships were able to dock, and even be lifted from the water if the need arose. With the reduction in the average sizes of the ships in the *Uni*'s small merchant fleet, it wasn't used much anymore.

At least, it hadn't been. The amount of activity surprised Thom as they made their way across the huge space. Subs hung from cradles. Groups gathered around long tables all around the pool, which had its lock closed. People with carts drove trailers of parts big and small all over. Sparks flew from grinding. Searing bright pinpricks of light denoted welding. There was activity everywhere. Seeing his confusion and his pace slow, Olly nodded to the lock on the far side.

"I know it's only been a few days, but a lot has changed. We'll explain at the bar," Olly said over the din.

It took them a few more minutes to cross the space, then a few more to make their way down the main corridor on that other side of the ship. A short elevator ride later and they were at The Landing getting utterly annihilated. Thom drank for free.

Ralla exhaled slowly to the silence of her cabin. Behind her, Cern closed the door, and as soon as his hands left the door controls they were on her shoulders. Suddenly he was this abnormal presence in her space. She smoothly slipped away and stepped further into her quarters. Things were different.

"I cleaned up a bit while you were gone. I couldn't think what else to do," Cern explained, sensing her confusion. She didn't know what to say. The bed was made with her favorite pale green sheets. Her glass desk was empty of its usual clutter. Gone were the piles of clean and dirty clothes, presumably in one of the closets. Even the curtain that had fallen and been forgotten was rehung. It was all very sweet of him, so why was she so uncomfortable? He tried rubbing her shoulders again, and his soft touch was grating. She ducked away from him again.

"I'm sorry, Cern. Please. I just need some time alone."

"OK, sure. I understand," He held his hands up and gave his patented disarming smile. "Can I see you later?"

"I don't know. Maybe."

"OK, well, I've got dinner planned for us with some of the Council members tomorrow. I'll send you the info."

"Cern..."

"What?"

"Nothing. I'll talk to you later."

He stepped up and kissed her on the forehead, then left. She fell backwards onto her bed, hoping for sleep, but got nothing.

IX

"At some point, do any of you actually want to listen to what I have to say?" Ralla said rather loudly over the varied conversations. The conversations continued.

The Council chamber was full. Each of the eight other Council members plus her father sat at their seats, while their various aids behind them jockeyed for position amongst each other. Mixed in were the Chief of Mechanics, Chief of the Fleets, and for good measure, representatives of the Farmer's lobby, the Fisherman's lobby, and the Dock and Bay Workers' Union. Captain Sarras sat stoically in his seat at the end of the black glass table closest to the door. Ralla stood at the other end, her back to the balcony and the Yard. Sarras was a tall, thin man with black hair, angular features, and a piercing stare. His body made no unnecessary movements, which made him an odd person to look at. He rose slowly from his seat. The room silenced immediately. His eyes focused sharply on Ralla.

"Miss Gattley. Please tell us of the *Population* and your time there," he said, before sitting back down as slowly as he had gotten up.

Ralla stifled a smile, and told the silent room of the previous days. When she got to the part of the flooding and the presumed murder of the personnel in the dome, there was hushed surprise and concern from the room. She took a moment to drink some water from the table, mostly to give her a chance to gather her own composure. Cern Hennorr caught her eye, and gave her a wink. She pretended she didn't notice, lowered the aquamarine glass to the table, and continued with the briefing. She finished with the escape and the journey back to the *Uni.*

"There were a few other things that Thom and I noticed. Their ship is in bad shape. Really bad. Worse than ours. Things were rusted, corroded. They seem to be doing fine with food—we didn't see anyone wanting for anything—but it was as if none of them could see what was right in front of them: how much danger they were in by letting their ship fall apart before their eyes." Her comments were not lost on the Council members, but not in the way she had hoped.

"Miss Gattley, were you able to discern their overall military strength?" Council Junior Larr said, interrupting.

"No, we didn't have time."

"How about overall fleet numbers, sizes, that kind of thing?"

"No, that information wasn't in the terminals we found," she replied with a sigh. Larr nodded and leaned back in his chair, as if done with the entire proceedings.

"Let us adjourn for the day and go over what Miss Gattley has said. We'll meet back here tomorrow and discuss our next plan of action," Council Proctor Jills said, rising from his seat opposite Sarras. The Captain also stood, nodded once at Ralla, and left with his two lieutenants.

The room started to empty, and aides came up to her with questions their bosses didn't want to ask in front of the room. Her father nodded at her as he was wheeled out in his cart, and she nodded back. Cern stood off to the side, patiently waiting. One by one the aides got their answers, and left quickly to report back. Soon, the room was empty, and Cern and Ralla were able to step out onto the balcony overlooking the Yard. He wrapped his arm around her, and kissed her on the top of her head.

"We all just figured they were holding you for ransom. When we hadn't heard anything after a few days, I started pressuring the Council to organize a rescue party."

"I'm sure that went over well," Ralla said, turning towards him and freeing herself from his arm in one motion. She looked up at his face. He really did have some amazing eyes, she thought.

"After hearing all that you were going though… it kills me I wasn't there for you."

"Well I did do OK by myself."

"And this Thom guy. I'll have to thank him personally."

"I'm sure he'll love that." Her sarcasm was completely missed as Cern nodded, looking out into the Yard.

"Is everything OK? I didn't hear from you last night."

"Everything is fine. I just needed some time to myself."

"I missed you, that's all," he said, hugging her.

"I missed you too." After a pause, she returned the hug.

This time, Mrakas Gattley was in bed when Ralla arrived, and he looked grateful for it. The bedcovers were pulled up to his chin, and he was pale, gaunt, and shivering. She sat down on the edge of his bed and he took her arm in his hand. She leaned over and curled up next to him, like she had done since she was a little girl. He rested his hand on her head and, the world temporarily forgotten, she fell quickly asleep.

The next morning, Ralla and Cern met for breakfast at a restaurant halfway up the starboard wall in the Yard. It had a terrace that stuck out from the wall, offering unmatched views of the greenery through the hanging vines. The food was mostly fresh vegetables, with some fish, and for the more flush patrons, even fresh eggs. The owner seated them at the best table, at the apex of the terrace, and made it a point to bring them two omelets, on the house. Even Cern was impressed, and he thanked the owner profusely.

Cern was almost as well known around the Yard as Ralla herself, though perhaps not shipwide. His parents had been extremely successful turning his father's fishing business into a small empire, with a few dozen ships and their own processing facility in the outer ring. They supplied fish to half the restaurants in the Basket. While neither of his parents had aspired to politics, they might as well have, as there were few decisions made by the Council that didn't involve input from one or both of the Hennorrs. They owned an entire shipsuite on the bow side of the Yard. Tenncy Hennorr and Mrakas Gattley had known each other, and were often friends, their whole lives. When the Hennorrs had Cern, many within the families and throughout the Yard, secretly hoped for a daughter.

They inevitably grew up together, but ended up going to two different schools for most of their education: Ralla at the leadership school Ahead, while Cern attended the larger business school that was part the ship's college. Though their families lived only a few minutes from each other, after adolescence they ended up seeing each other only in passing and on holidays. After school they reconnected, and much to the delight of their parents, started dating. That was five years ago.

Ralla knew from his silent wince that he wasn't enjoying his omelet. She reached across the table, jabbed the remainder with her fork, and swung it over to her plate. He scowled, but said nothing. She hadn't taken more than a few bites when she noticed a young man nosily making his way across the restaurant. She recognized him as an aide assigned to the council, but couldn't remember his name. As he approached the table, his eyes couldn't leave the double stack of omelet on her plate. He addressed it as he spoke to her.

"Miss Gattley, the Council requests your presence immediately."

"Uh..." she said, motioning towards the plate, even though his eyes still hadn't left it.

"I'm sorry, Miss Gattley. They said I needed to find you and bring you down to the Dockyard immediately."

"The Dockyard?"

"Yes. I was told to say to you, 'Sunlight.'"

Ralla was out the door before her dropped fork settled to the floor. Cern nodded at the aide, and then motioned at the omelet. The younger man's eyes went wide.

The Dockyard was empty, save for a dozen or so people gathered around Ralla and Thom's stolen attack sub. There were four Council members including Jills and Larr, their long maroon robes a stark contrast to the wet gray steel of the deckplates. A handful of techs and mechanics poked at different areas of the sub. A half-dozen aides and two very out of place and armed marines hovered nearby. Standing and slightly swaying, facing it all, was Thom. He turned as she approached, then turned back to the sub. Jills and Larr separated from the group and approached Thom and Ralla with the marines in tow. Jills raised his hand to silence Ralla before she spoke.

"Miss Gattley, you are not to speak. If you say a word to Mr. Vargas, you will both be confined to the brig until the current crisis is resolved. If I am clear you may nod."

She did as he instructed.

"Mr. Vargas, would you please tell us exactly how you escaped from the submarine *Population*."

Thom shook his head like he had just woken up, thought about the question for a moment, and then started to tell them about the previous days, starting with the escape from Dome M3324 and how they got on board the *Population*. When he started talking about their theft of the attack sub, Larr raised his hand.

"Stop," Larr said, his eyes darting between Ralla and Thom. "Now I want you to tell us what happened, starting at the point you landed here and working your way backwards. Spare no detail."

"Ummmm..." Thom said slowly. He started to turn around to look at Ralla.

"Do not look at Miss Gattley. Do not move at all. Marine, garnish your weapon."

Without hesitation, the marine did as he was asked. Thom froze for a moment, resumed swaying a bit, and then turned back towards the Councilmen. It took him a moment, but he relayed the story starting with their celebrated return, then the farming dome, back to the sub, the escape, and the rest of the days back to Dome M3324. The whole time, Larr's eyes continued to dart between Ralla and Thom. Once finished. Jills looked at Larr, who seemed satisfied. Jills nodded at the marines who saluted and left.

"I apologize, Miss Gattley, Mr. Vargas," Jills said, placing his hands into his robe.

"There was something on the sub," she said.

"Yes."

"Is it leading them here?"

"We don't think so, not exactly. The technicians are pretty sure it can't escape the *Uni*'s hull, but it's powerful enough to transmit for hundreds of miles in the water."

"Leading them right to F211."

"Correct. We've already notified the dome. A full evacuation is underway and we're sending transports to assist."

"How long will that take?"

"Days, if we're lucky."

"You didn't really think..."

"We needed to be sure. I wanted you down here, with the sub, without a chance to talk beforehand. I needed to hear if your story was true, and it seems to be." One of the techs who had been waiting somewhat patiently finally got Jills' attention and waved him over. Larr followed, leaving Thom and Ralla a brief moment alone.

"Are you drunk?"

"And asleep, I think. You?"

"What? No. What the..." she said, flustered. She was sure she saw a slight look of amusement on his face. "So is this a thing for you? To get drunk when people need you?"

"To be fair, I get drunk when people *don't* need me. I just happen to *be* drunk when you need me."

"We."

"You. I'm good here. I was pretty sure that guy wasn't going to shoot me and I haven't paid for a drink since I got back. So far, I'm doing all right."

"Are you serious?"

"Are you?"

"That's... stop talking to me."

"You started it," he said, still not looking at her. She walked, half stomped, towards the sub, arms crossed, wanting nothing more than to let out a scream.

Jills looked up at her, then over at Thom, and waved them both over.

"We want to try to lead them off the chase for a while. We're going to send someone out in this sub, along with an escort, then ditch it. Someplace away from us and the bulk of our facilities on the floor. It's going to take some time to get everything up to war-ready status, and hopefully this decoy will buy us some of that time. Thom, we'd like you to drive this sub."

"A minute ago you were going to shoot me."

"Mr. Larr says you are telling the truth, and I've never seen him wrong. You obviously have the most experience in this craft and while I don't think one of the ship's marines would have difficulty figuring it out, I wanted to offer it to you. Your ship needs your help; will you give it Mr. Vargas?"

"Nope. Can I go now?"

"Absolutely. Thank you for your time," Jills said, turning back to the tech who was pointing at a portable readout.

Thom turned around immediately and headed for the closest lock. Ralla caught up with him in the corridor beyond and grabbed his arm. He stopped but didn't turn, so Ralla moved around in front of him.

"What is your problem? You just had the Proctor of the Council ask you personally to do something for your community. How can you say no to that? Have you no thought for your future? Don't you want more than piloting a transport for your whole life?"

Thom's face went sour.

"More? Are you kidding me? More? Come here." Thom grabbed her arm and started for the nearby bank of elevators. She followed without protest, but he didn't let go. Once inside, he slapped the touchpanel for a level several above them. He steamed, staring impatiently as the level indicators lit up, then faded out. Thom didn't wait for the doors to fully open before pulling Ralla out and down a dank corridor crowded with pipes and wiring. Within moments they entered a door, the shoddy sign above revealing the establishment's name as "The Landing."

She immediately felt self conscious as every eye turned to her, and stayed transfixed.

"You want to say that again? Tell me here, in this place, what more is. Don't you think everyone in this place wanted more at some point? What more is there? I was nine years old when I watched my father drink himself to death. The best he could do was Mechanic 3rd Class. He had never been inside a cabin above Deck 12. You people talk about wanting more. Look at you! Have you ever worn clothes that were dirty because you had already spent your water ration? Have you ever been told that you can only get a promotion when one of your coworkers dies? How about eating the same crap from the same place every day, because that's all you can afford?

"Look at you: your hair is perfect, your clothes are new, handmade. You want to talk to me about more? What more is there? This is what life is for us. We all know what you people are selling in the news and on the vids is just propaganda, but we want to believe it, so we do. We want to believe we'll do well and get a better place to live and a better job. But what more jobs are there?

"We've been in this coffin for almost three generations. The people who had before have now, and the people that didn't, still don't. I know how it is, so does everyone. We just don't need some well-dressed, condescending Yarder telling us we should work harder or do more for the community. We *are* the community. I don't come down here and drink all day because I like doing it. I do it because *there is nothing else to do.*"

"I'm sorry. I didn't mean..."

"It's not your fault. You just don't know any better."

Thom sat down on a stool and the bartender slid him an ale. Ralla, still overly aware of all the eyes, sat a few stools down. When the bartender looked at her, she pointed at Thom's drink. He poured her one but kept his hand on it. Ralla understood, and took out a few credits.

"Here's five. Keep the change."

"It'll be 20, actually," he said coldly. She looked about to protest, but silently handed over the money. The other patrons at the bar turned back to what they were doing. Ralla knew she should have been upset with how Thom had just treated her. Passive acceptance had never been her thing, but here, in this place, who could argue with him? Everything he said had been true. Everyone knew it. No one said it. That was how their society functioned. Thom hadn't exactly opened her eyes to that fact, but his impassioned speech had certainly reminded her of something she often chose to ignore.

"I'm sorry I offended you," she said over her beer. Thom said nothing. "I am not going to disagree with you. I won't patronize you like that. Please let me just say two things, and then I'll leave you alone." Again, Thom said nothing. "I won't pretend I know what it's like to be someone down here. But please believe that what you said had meaning for me all the same. Maybe someday I can show you that. So if I can empathize with you, at least on some small level, let me say this: Your father, everyone your father knew, and everyone in this bar now, never had the opportunity you passed up. I can't speak for any of these people here, but unlike them, you just made a choice to be here. They haven't. Maybe none of these people will own a cabin overlooking the Basket. But you. You just turned down the Council Proctor, the Council, and the entire *Universalis*. And if you don't think *that* would lead to more, well Thom, you deserve to be stuck down here."

Ralla stood and downed the remainder of her beer. The bartender watched as she pointed at Thom's ale and slapped another 20 credits on the bar. Flashing a half-smile at the bartender, she left.

X

Thom braced himself against the swaying cockpit. The attack sub hung in a sling just above the Dockyard pool. He motioned to the tech, and suddenly he was weightless. The bow hit the water first, and he pushed the throttle to its max. The engines hit the water a moment later and the sub shot forward, pushing him back into his seat. The hull loomed over him like a menacing dark cloud. A transport sub, his escort, lay motionless ahead. Thom throttled back as he approached.

"Comm check," Thom said into the headset in his drysuit.

"Comm check," a voice answered back. He got close enough to see two men inside the larger sub. "Lead on Vargas. Heading 078."

Thom found the heading and throttled up to 60 percent, about what the techs had figured would be the maximum speed of the escort transport. He watched the monitor, and noted the sub was falling a little behind, so he dialed back on the throttle a little more. The *Uni* slowly shrank on his screens, and soon it was just the two subs moving at a good clip away from everything. The open sea beckoned.

After nearly half a day's travel, the sea floor dropped away rapidly where the continent-less continental shelf ended and the deep ocean began. It was rare anyone came out this way. There were fish, of course, but they were larger and there were fewer of them, making them harder to catch. The sea floor may have had materials galore, but at such a depth, even the *Uni* itself couldn't get near them. It was, for all intents and purposes, a wasteland. And the perfect place to set up a decoy.

The sensors in his suit told Thom his sub was broadcasting its message, and not for the first time that day, he hoped it would be a while before anyone would come to check it out.

They continued out into the open ocean, the two subs tiny specks in a vast sea of nothing. Every few hours they rose and sank to check if anyone was following or approaching them in the different thermal layers.

As designed, by the third day Thom was running low on water and rations, and the recirc pumps in his suit were in need of a recharge. He signaled the transport.

"OK, let's call it. I think this is far enough. There's a current here that'll keep dragging the sub away from the *Uni*. I'm gonna slow up here and head over to you."

"I think we should keep going. Are you really out of your rations already?" a voice returned on his comm.

"The longer we stay out here the more likely it is they'll get to us before we can get back. Also, I've been in the same seat and the same suit for three days. I'd like to get out."

"So... you're going to jeopardize the safety of the entire *Universalis* for want of a bath and a nap?"

Thom could hear the tone in the marine's voice. Contempt mixed with amusement. For a brief moment, he had the feeling the marines were going to leave him there. Thom started to make a mental calculation if he could make it back to the *Uni* with the water and supplies he had remaining. Probably not.

"Stopping here," Thom responded. He throttled back and killed the engine. The current was fairly strong, and he felt the sub immediately start to move with it. He flooded the cockpit, and he immediately felt the cold of the water pressing in on him, even through the suit. He released the canopy and his restraints.

The transport sub had passed over him and was now drifting in formation with the attack sub, just a short swim away. The rear hatch opened, revealing amber light from the flooded lock—a bright oasis in the otherwise featureless dark of the sea. The lights were warm and the space looked inviting to his weary eyes and cramped body. He pushed off gently from the sub, and started to swim towards the transport.

Suddenly, panic. The transport shot forward and full speed. They were actually going to do it. They're actually going to leave me here, Thom thought. He was close enough to get tossed slightly from the wash. The attack sub had drifted further away. He keyed his comm, making a mental note of the words he probably shouldn't use, when three attack subs, identical to his own, shot down from above, narrowly missing him. Their wash pushed him even further. Now he just floated, spinning slightly, watching as the attack subs pounced on the transport. They must have come from the layer above. Perfect timing; they hadn't checked the layer in hours. Careless. The marines deftly tried to avoid the incoming fire, but could only do so much. One of the marines had taken his time to get to the turret on top of the transport and had just started firing back.

Why had it taken him so long to... Thom froze in mid thought. They weren't in their suits. They had gotten lazy, gotten out of their suits. Why not? It was dry, the sub was big. In order for the marine to get to the turret he would've had to pressurize and empty the rear lock to get to the turret. Getting into his suit would have taken too long. This would mean the death of them all. They'd have no way of picking him up now unless they beat all three of the attack subs. And if anything happened to their hull, they'd drown instantly.

Thom spun around and started pawing his way towards his derelict sub. He could feel explosions in the water as the torpedoes detonated near the hull of the transport. The current and drysuit conspired to make for slow going, but he finally pulled himself into the cockpit and closed the canopy. Pumps automatically started draining the water, and the console started to light up. Before the water level was halfway down, he could see the main screen and the battle unfolding around him.

The transport was still alive and seemed to have taken out one of the attackers; one enemy sub looked adrift and powerless. Pulling hard in circles at full power, the transport was kicking up a lot of wake, both masking its location to the three torpedoes hunting in the water and giving it a somewhat better shot at the following subs. Oddly, they weren't taking advantage of their better maneuverability, just trying to keep up with the transport and avoid shots from the turret when possible. The turret's mini-darts left visible trails in the water, convenient for aiming, but at enough distance they could be dodged.

Thom got a ready readout from the panel and slammed the throttle to its stop. The sub leapt forward into the fray. The transport was spiraling down towards the thermal layer below, and Thom dove to follow. He avoided the wakes of the transport and following attackers, choosing instead to head down the center of their descending corkscrew. He timed it just right, pulling up and placing one of his sub's drychem rockets directly into the side of the trailing enemy. No guidance, no maneuverability, the rocket was a motor and a warhead that went in a straight line from one sub to another. The explosion caused the enemy sub's port engine pod to rupture and tear off. The sub immediately entered a violent spin, careening off and down into the dark depths, trailing debris and bubbles.

The other sub took notice and broke off its attack in an attempt to get a bead on Thom. It pulled away from the corkscrew course, pulling up and around. Thom, instead of aiming up to meet it, turned the opposite way and cut his throttle. Now stationary, he used the maneuvering thrusters to spin the sub. His gamble worked, revealing the port side of the still-turning enemy sub. Thom fired off the other three rockets, along with its two small torpedoes. The rockets and torpedoes gained speed, impacting the enemy sub before it had a chance to pull away. There was a brief white explosion, which collapsed in on itself, leaving just debris to fall to the ocean floor, and bubbles to rise to the surface.

Thom signaled the transport. No answer. He signaled again. It was still spiraling downwards. Thom throttled up and nosed his sub over. It was only a moment before he was next to the transport, mirroring its course on the outside of the curve. He could see into the lit cockpit of the sub. As he suspected, one of the marines was hunched over the controls, bloodied and unconscious. He signaled again. External pressure warnings started lighting up orange on his console. He signaled again. This time, the other marine answered.

"Vargas?" the voice said over the comm. It sounded confused and disorientated.

"I need you to get to the cockpit and stop the sub. Can you do that?"

"I... I'm kinda hurt here. There's this piece of... wow. Hey, I'm kinda hurt here."

"MARINE! I need you to get control of the sub. Can you do that?"

"I think so."

Looking up, Thom could see the other marine enter the transport's cockpit. There was blood coming from his ears and his right arm hung limp at his side. With his left arm, he pulled the other marine off the controls. The body slid off the chair and onto the floor. The sub righted itself.

The one-good-armed marine pulled back on the throttle, and the transport came to a stop. Thom could see the marine clearly now, looking very pale as he slumped into the seat that had been holding his partner. The marine looked at Thom and there was a brief moment like he knew what was going on, as if his head was clear. He toggled a few switches on the dash, then slumped back into the chair, unconscious.

The pressure warnings had switched to red, well past what was advised. Thom paused. His sub was fine. At full speed it wouldn't take more than a day and a half to get back to the *Uni*. Part of him could see the value in getting back soon. He could warn them the *Pop* had patrols out this far. That they were probably closer to the *Uni* than anyone thought. Opening the canopy, in all reality, could kill him. There was just way too much pressure at this depth. His hand was on the button before this thought was even fully formed in his head.

The pumps couldn't work fast enough, the water was under such pressure that it pushed itself past the impellers as fast as the escaping air would let it. Within moments the cockpit of the abused but intact attack sub, formally of the citysub *Population*, was full of water. The main screen and dials cracked from the pressure. It pressed on Thom like a blanket of lead. Instantly, every warning light on the inside of his helmet started flashing red. It was impossible to breathe. His suit was tighter than skintight. The pressure crushed his diaphragm and throat. His only option was to take short, shallow breaths, as quickly as he could. His suit switched over to pure oxygen, which made the shallow breaths a little more tolerable. Knowing what was going to come, he hoped his time on pure O_2 would be enough. The suit tried to equalize the pressure somewhat—he could hear little else aside from the whir and whine of the pumps—but the strain was too great, and soon his suit's processor shut down to avoid frying completely.

After opening the canopy, Thom unbuckled himself and kicked away from the sub and towards the transport. He looked down as he drifted upward, and had the first attack of vertigo in his life, staring down at nothing. His ears hurt, his chest hurt, the pure oxygen was already making him nauseous. He swam clumsily to the back hatch of the transport and breathed a tiny sigh of relief that the panel indicated the back of the sub was clear and ready for flooding. He keyed it to do so. He could hear pumps working to keep the sub buoyant as several tons of water crashed into the rear of the transport. A few minutes later the door opened, revealing the seawater-filled rear cabin. The water pressure had crushed the seat cushions and several of the bottles containing drinking water.

Thom pulled himself in, his eyesight starting to tinge red. Keying the door closed, the wait as the sub cycled out the water and pressurized was agony. But it did so, and he sank to the floor as the water drained. The suit auto-equalized, and he removed his helmet. For a moment he just lay there, wheezing.

From his vantage point on the floor, Thom could already see the damage the craft had sustained. The bulkheads were bulging and bent in odd directions, cross beams twisted. Shelving had been ripped away, dumping supplies everywhere. There was blood on the deck.

He opened the door to the cockpit, and checked the pulse of the two marines. They were alive. Thom took one last look at the various screens, aimed the sub towards their rendezvous point with the *Uni*, and throttled up, slowly. The transport shuddered, let loose a cacophony of creaks and pops, but got underway. He slowly trimmed off their depth.

After dragging the two marines into the rear of the transport, Thom settled down for a long, hopefully boring, trip back to the *Uni*. The console would announce any nearby ships, so his last thought before he passed out was to hope sleep found him before the inevitable decompression sickness had its way with him. It did.

XI

It was well into the fourth day before Thom was able to make contact with the *Uni*. The two marines had regained consciousness a few hours after Thom had. One had medic training, and was able to diagnose himself and his copilot with severe concussions, and bandaged their other wounds the best he could. The concussive blasts from the battle had done substantial damage to the transport, but not to any of the main systems. They became enamored with their hardy conveyance as it brought them home.

The *Universalis* was running, and running hard. At top speed, the transport was just able to creep up on them. Had the big ship started off earlier, or the transport any later, they wouldn't have caught up before the transport's food ran out.

"Say again, Traffic Control?" Thom said over the comm. The *Uni* was making such a mess of the water running at full speed it was affecting the communications.

"Transport 53A, we are unable to open any of the normal docking bays. You are instructed to proceed to the rear landing deck and dock manually with the airlock there."

"They want us to do what?" Diier, the marine with the medic training said to no one in particular.

"Have either of you ever done that?" Thom asked. The others shrugged.

"They stopped using that part of the ship years before either of us joined up. I thought they decommissioned it with the rest of the war fleet," Tegit, the other marine, said.

"TC, this is 53A. We are not sure how you expect us to do that," Thom said back over the comm. There was a pause, then a new voice came over the transport's speakers.

"53A, we are aware of your situation. We are currently running at full emergency power for reasons that will be made clear when you are aboard. We cannot slow down enough to open any of the bay doors without risk of damage or flooding. Approach from above; when you enter the lee space behind the hull, the microcurrents will pull you to the deck. Then all you have to do is maneuver into position near the airlock. Please get on board as soon as possible. TC out."

Thom looked at the two marines, and they back at him. The *Uni* had come into view, and they looked out over the back of its hull. The propellers were making a churning mess of the water. Above the rounded stern of the ship, the arc of the back of the *Uni* sloped down smoothly, except for a small notch, where it dropped down straight then flat out till it continued the curve. In the war, this little notch was used to launch and recover attack subs at speed. Thom wondered if there was anyone alive on board who had ever used it.

The transport started to descend as soon as Thom had lined them up over the landing strip. He matched velocity the best he could. The *Uni* seemed to slowly rise up to meet them. As they got close, the turbulence from the hull tossed them around. The transport shook violently, then suddenly it dropped hard into the deck and was still.

Ever so slightly it scraped along the landing strip towards the lock. Thom increased the throttle, edging them closer.

Just before he reached the lock, in the lee of the hull, Thom spun the craft around, and mated the rear of the sub with the lock. Diier and Tegit took turns patting him on the back as the lock cycled. They left the transport tired, hungry, smelly, and in all cases in need of some kind of medical attention. It would have to wait. Two young aides to two different council members near dragged them to a waiting cart which shot off down the narrow passageway that ran along the spine of the ship. After a few minutes, they were shuffled down a side access tunnel.

What followed was a blur of staircases and corridors that ultimately led them to the main Command Bunker, one level below the bridge. It was a long space, but not very wide. Thom had never seen so much new tech in once place. It was as if the entire room had been taken out of some vid and brought to life. There was a pair of rectangular tables positioned longitudinally, each with embedded screens and terminals. Along the walls were stations with more screens, terminals, and controls. At each station sat a busy crew member. The room was dark, lit mostly blue and red by the glow of the terminals and the tables Even if he was a more hands-on kind of guy, each station was clearly just a newer version of equipment he'd used before. Thom identified his unease as not so much intimidation, but more the complete lack of a place to sit.

Everyone in the room was busy enough not to have looked up when Thom, Diier, and Tegit entered. Gathered around the closest table were several council members that Thom recognized, but whose names he couldn't remember. Closest to him were Larr and Jills. Across the table, standing rigidly like every picture he had ever seen of him, was Captain Sarras. The two marines next to Thom stood up a little more erect. Sarras nodded to Diier, who rattled off a report of what had happened. Tegit filled in where Diier was either unconscious or had a lapse in memory. Thom shuffled on his feet, growing uncomfortable as important people did important things around him. The only one to notice was Larr, who said nothing.

Before he could finish, Diier was interrupted as everyone's attention focused on the door behind him. Leaning heavily on a cane, Councilman Gattley filled the entrance of the bunker. He stepped inside and made his way haltingly to the table. Despite his obvious illness, he still carried a quiet power that commanded the respect of everyone in the room, including the Captain.

"The marines here were just telling us..." Larr started, but Gattley waved him silent.

"It doesn't matter. Captain?"

"Councilman Gattley, we are currently running at flank speed due to the skirmishes with the enemy corvettes."

"Show me," he said, moving around the corner of the table, forcing Larr to concede his space. Thom looked at the marines, who were clearly just as puzzled as he was. The portion of the table closest to Gattley changed to a map of the seafloor around them. It showed the *Uni* in the center. It zoomed out, showing a smaller version of the ship and larger area. It zoomed out again, and showed a red silhouette of a small ship.

"This is where we made contact," the Captain said, motioning towards the red shape. "Then again here, here, and here," as he said it, three more silhouettes appeared. Each was staggered, with the *Uni* seeming to follow a zig-zag pattern bouncing between the enemy ships. The captain looked quizzically at the display, as if seeing it for the first time. Gattley stared at him.

"You see it now, don't you?" Gattley asked. The other Councilmembers saw it as well. "Captain, I spend a lot of time in bed. More than I should. We all are so used to the way the ship feels. How it vibrates, how it moves. Lying in my bed, it feels different. I can listen to it. I can *hear* it. I knew we were running. Everyone could hear the engines. But I could feel when we were turning. I could feel by how much. How many watch changes have you made? Two?"

"With a third coming up."

"With all the commotion of the attacks, with no one person navigating or driving, I can see from your face that this is the first time anyone has looked at the course.

"We were just running to put distance between us and them," one of the Councilmembers said.

"That's where you're wrong. We're not running. We're being herded," Gattley said. The Captain nodded distractedly, already on to the next steps in his mind. "Jills, we're not going to have the time we wanted. We need to mobilize now, with whatever we've got."

Jills, still fixated on the screen, agreed. Gattley looked up at the Captain, who made eye contact, and nodded definitively.

"Chief of the Watch, sound General Quarters," Sarras said. From behind him, Thom could hear alarms reverberating down the corridors of the ship. "Navigation, I want charts and maps for everything that's ahead of us, no matter how small."

"Sir!" one of the crewmen acknowledged from a nearby terminal. The screen in the far corner of the table switched to a new map, and Sarras hunched over to study it. Gattley turned to Jills.

"Janner, I'm going back to my cabin. The boy here..." he said, motioning over his shoulder at Thom. "...is going to help me. Then he's going to come back here and be my eyes and ears."

"OK." Jills replied, looking up from the table for the first time in several minutes. "Mrakas, we're going to need you on this."

"That's what scares me." Gattley turned and motioned for Thom to exit ahead of him. The two walked side by side down the corridor for a bit. As the passageway curved out of sight of the Bunker, Gattley reached out and put his weight on Thom. "I'm sorry, Thom, you're going to have to help me back to my cabin."

"Of course, sir."

"Don't *sir* me," Gattley said. His voice sounded raspy. Thom turned his head, and the older man seemed to have aged a decade since he entered the Bunker. Their pace slowed but they made their way down the corridor.

"I have a feeling Ralla doesn't know you're out of bed."

"Let's keep it that way, OK?"

"You got it."

"My daughter told me how you two escaped the dome."

"I would have figured that was old news by now."

"No, I mean she told me personally, not as a report or something. She's really fond of you, Thom. And having rescued her like you did, I am as well."

"Sir..."

"Mrak."

"Mr. Gattley, we did what we did. There was no other way to do it or we wouldn't be here. So I guess I just did what I had to do, and so did she."

"Maybe so, but you did it and I'm grateful. I'm putting in with the Council for you to get a battlefield commission and commendation for your actions."

"Mr. Gattley I don't want..."

"Thom," Mrakas said, cutting him off. "I don't really care what you want. Events are unfolding that will have no outcome but bad. There are things you don't know yet. This is far bigger than you understand. I'm having you commissioned as a Lieutenant. For now that will give you access to information and let you get a fighter out in this inevitable war. I know it's strange to want to put you in harm's way, but I've heard how you handle a sub and we need people like you right now. Past that, I don't know."

They had reached Gattley's cabin. After toggling the door open with the wall switch, Mrakas shed himself of his human crutch and shuffled across the floor to his bed. He hunched over further and seemed to age another decade in the process. He waved Thom away.

"For now, go back to the bridge and keep me informed for as long as you can," the elder Gattley said as he reached overhead and pressed a button that closed the door.

Thom stood outside the door for a moment, stunned. Not till he was running back to the Bunker did his brain register that the floor had been made of wood.

The *Universalis* lit up its active sensors, sending out ultrasonic pulses that bounced off the sea floor and any ships nearby, and returned to be picked up by microphones spread all over the hull. The turbulence the ship created at maximum speed affected the resolution, and by extension, the range. So the results were less than optimal. Worse, the massive wake created a cone-shaped deadzone behind them.

What was clear, to the crewmen manning the sensor stations, to the navigator, and to the Captain, though, was that the seafloor was rising. They were running out of maneuvering room. They tried deviating from their current course, and each time the sensors would pick up a handful of subs of varying sizes either on a parallel or converging course, just out of weapons range.

"Proctor Jills. I'm afraid we have no choice but to engage," the Captain said, after his countless checks of the navigational charts.

"With what, Captain? Have you been secretly building up a fleet that I don't know about?"

"We still have ammo for the defense batteries. That will have to be enough. I wish we had had the time you and Councilman Gattley had requested to get an attack fleet up and running, but we don't. Hopefully we'll have enough firepower to get us on a different course. If we don't..." he looked down, and slid the chart displayed on the glass table in front of him across the console to be displayed in front of Jills. "We'll either run aground, or be forced to surface. Personally I don't like the choice of defenseless destruction or being irradiated. We'll need to go on the offensive, such as it is."

Jills stroked his narrow jaw as he stared at the navigation chart. Thom, who had been standing silently near the wall, stood on the tips of his toes to see the chart. Out of the corner of his eye, Jills saw him and waved him over.

"If you're going to be Gattley's eyes, then put them on this."

Thom studied the chart, and nodded knowingly, knowing that he had no idea what the chart meant. To his credit, Jills moved on.

"How well are your men trained, Captain?" Jills asked.

"They're trained, but on simulators. Since we sounded General Quarters, there have been teams on the guns getting them loaded. Most are in working order. It's the best we can hope for right now."

"How big are these other subs?" Thom asked. There was a pause as all eyes went in his direction.

"Big. Bigger than anything we've got," the Captain responded. "They look corvette size mostly, with what we think may me some frigates."

Thom's eyes went wide.

"Did we ever have anything that big?"

Larr's face flashed a momentary burst of annoyance, and then back to his usual stoic expression.

"Not since the war," Larr mumbled. "Proctor, Captain, I would like to recommend we launch the few attack subs we have; perhaps they can buy us some time."

The Captain shook his head.

"A dozen single seat subs wouldn't even bother a corvette, never mind four. It would be a waste of men and equipment. No, we need to do this now. All agreed?"

Jills nodded immediately. Larr and the other Council members followed suit.

"Chief of Arms, notify all batteries to be ready to fire. If a craft comes within range, they are to destroy it."

A man standing near a pair of terminals acknowledged and started talking to the two crewmen at his station. The Captain stood upright and pressed a button on the edge of the table.

"New heading. Come to starboard six-zero."

"Starboard six-zero, aye," came a voice from over the speakers imbedded in the ceiling.

At speed, a ship the size of the *Uni* changed direction at an agonizing rate. But when passenger comfort wasn't a concern, as now, it could turn much harder. Everyone in the bunker was forced to grab a hold of something nearby to steady themselves.

Far down and back in the Garden, hanging plants swayed against the turn. Plates and glasses slid from tables, a few people out in the open stumbled. Having heard the alarm for General Quarters, most had thought it was some drill for the military. Now people started to get concerned. Restaurants emptied. Public areas were vacated as people ran to their cabins.

"Captain, new contact!" shouted a crewmember excitedly.

As the *Universalis* made its broad sweeping turn, the sensor deadzone shifted as well. The area previously hidden became exposed, revealing the submarine *Population*.

All eyes in the bunker went to the sensor screen as a huge glowing blob revealed itself out of the noise.

"How'd they do *that?*" Thom asked, trying to hide his anxiety.

"They must have snuck up behind us when we were running, and were already in the cone before we starting popping active," the Captain replied, still staring at the sensor screen. They watched as the *Pop* turned sharper, trying to cut the corner. In doing so they started gaining.

Suddenly, the huge single blob on the sensor split into one single large section with two arms spreading out from either side, each of which then broke into separate dots.

"New contacts. Sir! They were hiding in close to the *Population* so we couldn't see them," the crewman said, not noticing that all eyes were on his terminal.

"Noted," said the Captain.

Subs of different sizes and shapes continued to break out from the overall bulk of the blob that represented the citysub *Population.*

"Sir, the computer is registering them as Wave class corvettes and Rapid class attack frigates."

"Keep tracking, ensign."

"Sir, yes sir... Captain!" the young ensign said as he looked from his computer screen to the sensor screen. He saw what the rest of them did. The enemy fleet was spreading itself wide, and the starboard arm was accelerating, trying to come up on their starboard side.

"Come to port, two-seven-zero degrees," Sarras said over the comm.

"Port, two-seven-zero, aye," the voice came back.

They all leaned as the big ship canceled its hard right turn and started left. The left wing of enemy ships disappeared on the screens as they entered the cone behind the *Uni*. It reemerged as the *Uni* turned, having spread itself out, matching the arm-like formation on the opposite side.

More ships started appearing on the monitor. Smaller ships, filling in the gaps between the others. Soon, the wings of enemy ships were wider than the *Population* was long, and resembled a massive claw attempting to pinch down on the *Universalis.*

"Depth under keel?" the Captain asked.

"110 and rising," a crewman responded.

"Sir, they are no longer gaining. They are holding at 80," said the sensor crewman, seemingly exited by the news, but Thom could see the concern in Captain Sarras's eyes.

"Active sweep forward, full power. Go." the officer did as he was told, and one of the monitors showed the result of the sweep. There were gasps of horror across the bridge. The Captain looked out past the monitors as if he could see into the darkness of the sea beyond. As if trying to see the ridge they were imminently going to impale themselves on, at flank speed. For a moment, just a flash, Thom saw defeat in the Captains face. Then it was gone.

"Options. Go," he said briskly. The room was silent. They all could see that turning meant destruction by the *Pop* fleet, and surfacing meant a vicious, painful, and horrifying death from radiation.

"Comm..." the Captain started.

"Captain," Thom said. All eyes went to him. He didn't flinch. "What's at the front of their boat?"

The Captain thought for a moment.

"Sensors, the bridge..." The Captain's eyes went wide. He stabbed at the button on the table.

"Bridge, full reverse," he nearly shouted.

"Sir?" came the response.

"Full reverse, and sound collision. Gentlemen," he said, regaining his composure and turning to the Council members. "I would suggest you hold on to something."

XII

The signal took just a fraction of a second to get from the bridge at the front of the ship, along the torso-thick bundle of wires that ran along the Spine to the engine bay. It only took a moment longer for the house-sized electric motors that turned the propellers to switch direction. They fought against the propeller shafts, which took a moment to spin down. Slowly at first, then gaining speed, the shafts started turning the opposite direction.

The propellers, though, started cavitating immediately and viciously, causing noise and vibration that spread throughout the ship. But as they gained purchase in the water, the ship slowed with fervor, as if someone had pulled an emergency brake—which in a way, they had.

Instantly, tens of thousands of people were knocked off their feet and thrown violently into forward bulkheads. Every hanging plant in the garden swayed hastily forward, many coming loose and crashing to the deck below. Plates, glasses, chairs, tables—everything not bolted to the deck crashed forward, striking people on their way to piling up on the bulkheads. Metal joints between the various ship's hulls in the Basket and Yard creaked deafeningly and ominously. Cracking, popping, and an infinite symphony of other sounds were heard throughout as the stern grabbed hold of the rest of the ship with huge invisible arms of force, and said "STOP."

The slow pulse of the collision klaxon sounded, causing panic. People struggled to get to their feet as the ship tried to accelerate in the opposite direction. The alarm rose in pitch and speed. Everyone who hadn't made it to their cabins tried to get somewhere safe, while others just tried to get somewhere where they could brace themselves in. In the bunker, only the Captain had remained upright among those who weren't seated. The Council members picked themselves up off the floor, and looked at the monitors. They told what they all could feel: the combined colossal power of the *Uni*'s engines and thrusters had rapidly ground them to a halt, and were now driving them backwards. With the wake now flowing in the opposite direction, they had a clear look at the *Population*, now rapidly approaching.

"Right about now, I'd say their Captain just soiled his uniform," Sarras said with a wry grin. He braced himself against the table, and subtly gave it a gentle pat with his left hand. On the screen the *Population* was starting to turn and dive away, but she was moving too slowly, and there as just too much mass. He tapped the button on the table one last time, "Stay with her, Mr. Pallee."

"Yes, sir."

Sarras' body became rigid. The crewman at the sensor station did his best to stifle the panic in his voice,

"Impact in 5...4...3...2..."

The bulbous middle of the stern of the *Universalis* impacted the *Population* just above Deck 12 on the former, and Deck 4 on the latter. The rear of the *Uni* started crumpling immediately as it scraped up and across the bow of the other ship. The carnage was limited to the storage space and the fighter deck at first, but as the powerful motors on both craft continued to drive them into each other, bulkheads started to collapse and water started stabbing into the inner hulls. Water cascaded into corridors and cargo holds. Locks slammed shut sequentially, but as each shut, the bulkhead around it crumpled from the impact, flooding still more space. The loss of buoyancy drove the back of the *Uni* down with the descending *Population*.

On the *Population* the damage was worse, water pouring in immediately, flooding the forward-most parts of Decks 2, 3, and 4. The *Pop* continued to turn and dive, and the impaling *Uni* started to slide down the port side, opening up swaths of Decks 3 through 9. The outer hull tore away like paper under the mass and pressure of the *Uni*.

The tangled mass of bulkheads and hull from both ships ground away, tearing more and more from each other. The nose of the *Population* finally got forward and low enough to snag the starboard-most propeller of the *Universalis*. The blade's edge dug into the ship, slicing the hull ribbon-like. With a deep clang it dug in hard on a main support frame. Instantly its rotation stopped, tearing itself and its shaft sideways out of the side of the *Uni*. For a moment, the two ships were attached, then the force became too great. The prop freed itself from both ships, and started its free fall to the bottom. The gouges left in the *Population* were deep, and had done enough damage to the front of the ship that the watertight bulkheads were no longer water tight. Ocean filled the bow of the ship, and it started to nose over even faster.

The hole the shaft left in the side of the *Uni* was no less catastrophic. The entire starboard engine bay was quickly flooded, killing hundreds and shorting out the adjacent engine. The abundance of power on the port side of the ship, still in full reverse, sent the nose to port and the tail to starboard, pivoting the ship around and separating it temporarily from the diving and retreating *Population*.

Chunks of debris fell to the depths as the two behemoths shrugged each other off.

"Damage Report!" Captain Sarras yelled. On the bridge there was pandemonium. Alarms were sounding at every station, people were yelling to be heard over the din. Adding to it all were the sounds of the ship dying around them.

"Flooding on Decks 12, 13, and 14, sir," an officer yelled from his station. "I have reports of water on Decks 15 and 16. We have lost Shafts 5 and 6; 4 is badly damaged."

"Ensign," Sarras yelled over the comm, "all ahead, flank. Now!"

"Sir!"

"Engine room reports heavy flooding and fires, Captain. Water is flooding in from the damaged shafts. I have lost all communication with Engine Room 6."

"Ensign, bring us about and out of here."

"Sir!"

"Chief of Arms, those batteries had better be firing."

"They are, sir."

"We have structural alerts throughout the ship. The Basket is reporting five craft are loose and are dangerously close to breaking free."

"Hold together..." the Captain said under his breath.

The two ships gradually began to put distance between then, trailing debris floating up or falling down to the sea floor. As they continued their turn, the defensive batteries started to fire on the left arm of the *Population*'s fleet. Drychem rockets lanced out, impacting the enemy ships. They scattered immediately, diving down to rendezvous with their stricken and sinking mothership. The *Population*, veering starboard, revealed her broadside to the fleeing *Universalis*. All along the side of the ship, portals snapped open.

"Captain, weapons warning. Enemy sub has gone hot. Correction, enemy sub has launched torpedoes. Weapons are active and tracking." The officer's voice had taken on a fever pitch.

"How many weapons, ensign?"

"I... dozens, sir. Impact in 20 seconds." The ensign looked away from his station to look at the Captain, and every eye in the room followed.

It was subtle—Thom didn't think most would notice it—but something had changed in the Captain. The look of fire was gone. He knew he had lost.

Sarras stood stoically for a moment. He hastened a glance at Jills, then back to the console.

"Mr. Lindl, fire countermeasures. All hands, brace for impact." Head sinking to his chest, Sarras closed his eyes and gripped the console with both hands.

PART 2

PART 2

I

Thom Vargas sat in a cramped, dark cockpit. None of the varied indicators, switches, buttons, or screens were lit, save the main one, and even it was set so low as to be barely visible. Off to his left, out the side viewscreen, a boulder loomed like a vertical cliff. He watched as a transport and two diamond-shaped escort subs cruised silently past just above him.

Tapping a button on the roof of the cockpit, Thom activated an invisible laser that pulsed straight out into the darkness. A moment later, his dimly lit console registered that it had sensed a return pulse. Instantly, Thom pushed the throttle forward hard, and the little craft burst from its hiding place, stirring up a cloud of gray silt. In front and beside him, four other attack subs of the same streamlined design all revealed themselves from cover and converged on the transport. All his dials and screens were now lit and feeding him information. The escort subs veered off from the transport, and came around to engage.

Thom pulled back on his controls and shot straight up at full speed. As he passed the thermal layer he rolled over, keeping his speed but now going parallel with the transport. His screens went blank as the battle below became obscured from his sensors by the thermal layer. The water-jet engine, nearly the entire back portion of the tiny sub, bucked and whined loudly in protest. After a moment he nosed the front of the craft over. His screens lit back up, and Thom saw that the escort subs had taken out two of his compatriots while taking minimal damage of their own. Of the two remaining attack subs, one was clearly in distress, with gasses escaping from the engine compartment.

Directly ahead of Thom, or below him, depending on your perspective, was the transport, cavitating hard in an attempt to make a getaway. Thom adjusted his angle of attack so the nose of his craft was aimed slightly in front of the fleeing transport. Gravity now assisting, Thom's sub became a missile, slicing through the water at speeds that would have made a less experienced pilot panic. As he got closer, it looked like he had lined up perfectly, with the transport moving forward into his sights just as his weapons came within range. He turned on his weapons systems and fired off a series of shots, all impacting along the spine of the transport a moment later. The transport slowed to a stop, and Thom shot by, buzzing the cockpit and showering it with a cloud of silt. Dialing back the throttle, he keyed his comm.

"Good work everyone, back to the barn for a debrief. Last one in has to swim in the pool."

Behind him, the three stricken attack subs powered back up, and came around to follow him. The transport and escorts formed up and did the same.

Twenty minutes later they came across a meandering undersea canyon, like someone had taken a knife and drunkenly carved a line in the sea floor. The mini fleet dove over the edge and twisted through the canyon at high speeds, as if daring each other to go faster. After a few minutes, the canyon broadened out and the floor dropped down and away. There in the center was the *Universalis*, partially buried in silt.

The little light that reached this far down showed the carnage of battle. The aft section looked as if some massive beast had crushed and ripped away at the fragile hull, pulling structural girders, bulkheads, piping, wiring, and flooring with it. Exposed decks collected the same silt to match the rest of the hull. Tiny bursts of bright light shown like stars all around the damaged sections. Dry-suited welders, doing their best to hide the telltale signs of their profession, chopped and cut at the carnage. The bow and most of the forward sections were deep into the sea bed.

On closer inspection, small valleys, too smooth and regular to be erosion, had been dug into the sea floor leading underneath the giant sub. Occasionally, a small sub with no running lights would enter or exit the *Uni* via one of the small valleys.

Thom extricated himself from the cockpit of the attack sub, the hull still dripping onto the white bay floor. Around him, the other pilots were doing the same. The larger escort subs, with their crews of three, were waiting with open cockpits for rolling stairs to be brought over by the bay crew. After a few minutes, everyone was assembled in front of Thom. No one looked pleased.

"OK, what could you have done better?" Thom asked, pointing to a young pilot on the left of the group.

"I think I needed to get closer to the deck when someone was on my tail," he said cautiously. Thom nodded and pointed at the next person over, a middle-aged recruit from the maintenance corps with graying hair and a lanky figure.

"I drystalled my motor in a turn. So... not that, I guess," he replied. Thom nodded again and moved down the line. Each of the pilots listed his screw-ups. Thom said nothing until they were all finished.

"All true. There were larger failures. Two, really. Anyone know what they were?" Thom scanned the group for an answer. He pointed to a tall, burly pilot of one of the escort subs. "Deebee, think you have an idea?"

"We lost the transport?"

"Exactly. In your effort to get the attackers, I was able to sneak past you and take out the target. He was so far away there was nothing you could have done even if you had seen me, which you didn't. Mark your targets. That's why there are three of you in there: one to drive, one to watch, and one to shoot. Transport," Thom said, scanning the group for the transport pilot. "When you're trying to flee, don't just go in a straight line. Veer off. Weave around. Drive like a fish would. I knew exactly where you were going to be. But that's not the other big failure—just wanted to mention it. OK, what's the other one? One of you guys?" he said, pointing at the attack pilots.

"Don't die?"

"Thank you. Don't die. That's pretty much the first rule around here, as far as I'm concerned. Now cheer up. This was just your first of many combat exercises, and you did a lot better than most of the other classes. The vids of the battle will be on the shipnet for you to watch. I'd advise watching everyone else's too. And what's our motto?"

"Sure beats fishing," they all said in unison, not altogether unconvincingly.

"Sure does. See you next week."

Thom changed out of his drysuit and made his way to the Garden for some lunch. He found Ralla waiting for him at a table in front of Eerre's cafe, digging through a pile of papers as she sipped at a thick-looking black beverage. She looked up and smiled as he approached the table. He liked how her eyes squinted a bit when she smiled.

"How'd class go?"

"Each group seems worse than the last."

"Well, give them some time. A few months ago these guys were farmers and fishermen."

"A few months ago *I* was a fisherman."

"You know what I mean."

"Sadly," he replied. Thom scanned the cafe for a moment until he made eye contact with Eerre, who nodded at him and headed back towards the kitchen. "Anything new?" he asked, motioning towards the papers.

"They think they'll be able to finish a new landing deck in a few weeks, but only because they're flattening out the whole area instead of rebuilding it. The corridors and hull repairs are coming along more slowly. It seems like every time they patch one leak they find a new one." She dropped her hand to the table, obviously weary and agitated, splattering the papers on the table with a bit of the black liquid from the glass she was still holding "The ship is old, Thom. It was old before this mess. It was old before we were born. I don't know what..." Thom interrupted her by putting his hand on hers. It was as if his hand had opened a valve that let the aggravation flow out. She sighed, and smiled at him. "Sorry. Thanks."

Eerre arrived with their food, plates of fruit and vegetables with strips of grilled fish in a thin bread wrap. After clearing a space, the two ate ravenously.

"Are you around tonight?" he asked between mouthfuls. "Want to catch a vid? I think they're showing *It Came from the Surface 2*, and I know how much you loved the first one."

"I hated the first one."

"Everyone hated the first one. I thought that was the point?"

Ralla smiled apologetically.

"I wish I could. This," she said motioning to the covered table, "is just part of what I have to make it through today. Another time?"

Thom raised his hands in defeat. "Another time, Councilwoman," he said with a smile. She opened her mouth, full of food, and then stuck her tongue out at him. He replied in kind.

Out of the corner of his eye, Thom could see Eerre smiling and shaking his head.

"I'm actually headed to one of the elementary schools after this. Want to come?"

Thom cocked his head in question.

"I've been doing it for a few years now. The teachers like having guest speakers. Give the kids ideas about what they want to do with their lives, that kind of thing. I love it. This will be my first time as a real Councilmember. Who knows, maybe I'll inspire one of them," she said with a smirk. The joke was lost on Thom, who shrugged.

"I don't think I'd give them the message you're hoping for," he said into his sandwich. The atmosphere at the table suddenly cooled. Ralla nodded and finished her food. She stood and gathered up her papers in silence.

"Ralla..." Thom said finally. She waved him silent, then put her hand gently on his shoulder and left.

II

Ralla took the elevator up four levels, and made her way to Starboard Elementary 3, or See3 as they called it. The "school," one level outward from the innermost cabins, was really just a collection of cabins opened up and connected to fit the dozen or so students from each grade. She was not surprised to see a classroom nearly identical to the others she had visited, and to her own almost two decades earlier. The teacher saw her in the doorway, and quickly wrapped up her lesson. Ralla had a brief moment of panic as she forgot the teacher's name, then almost laughed out loud at herself when she noticed it written above the front board. Ms. Itters started to introduce her, and Ralla noticed with no amusement that the teacher was actually younger than she was. That was a first. She felt oddly old.

"OK, kids. Say hello to Councilwoman Gattley," Ms. Itters said in the same voice teachers have spoken to young children since the dawn of education. The kids parroted Ralla's name after saying "Hello."

"Hi, kids. As Ms. Itters just said, my name is Ralla Gattley. I'm a junior member of the Council. Can someone tell me how many Council members there are?" A few hands went up. Like she always did, she picked a girl.

"Eight plus the Proctor?"

"Correct. Good job. I take it Ms. Itters has taught you some of this already." The children nodded. "OK, how about a tough one? How old is the *Universalis*?" This time, only boys raised their hands. She picked one that looked especially enthusiastic.

"93 years next month."

"Very good. And why did our ancestors build this ship?" This time the same girl raised her hand. She had a mound of blond hair that spilled out from no less than five hair clips. Ralla called on her again.

"Because of the floods and radiation?"

Ralla looked around the room and saw the stock pictures of what life had been like before their civilization had fled under the sea. She nodded at the girl who had answered, who looked pleased.

"It's important to learn history," Ralla said to the class. "It may seem like a whole lot of stuff that doesn't mean anything now, but if you don't learn what people did before, how will you know what works and what doesn't in the future? OK, do you have any questions for me?"

The same girl raised her hand, Ralla tried to hide a smile as she called on her.

"What do you do on the Council?"

"Well, I am the main liaison... um, I'm the person who talks with the new pilot training program and the Council. I also represent the people of District 1 in voting when the Council needs to make decisions."

"How long have you been a Councilman?" one of the boys asked. Ralla felt a lump in her throat, but was able to swallow it.

"A little over two months. Before that I assisted my father, who was also a Councilman."

"Council*woman* Gattley," asserted the same girl. "How old do you have to be to become a Councilmember?"

Ralla couldn't hide the smile this time.

"Well, there's no rule that gives a specific age. It all depends on the people in your district. If you can convince them that at age 25 you're the right person to represent them, then they'll vote you in. Or 20, or maybe even 10." The young girl beamed. There were a few more questions, and soon the teacher stepped in and wrapped things up. The students and their teacher thanked Ralla, and she left in the best mood she'd had in a long time.

Another elevator ride, another corridor, and she got to her next meeting just as it was starting. She took a chair near one end of a long table of older men. She looked down at her notepad and grimaced. The bi-weekly commerce meeting. There were few things more boring in her schedule. The men droned on and on about the skyrocketing price of fish and minerals and the effects that had on the farmers and by extension, the restaurants and grocers. They spoke of setting prices, offering service subsidies, and on and on and on. If her father hadn't drilled into her how vital this committee was to the survival of their micro economy, she would have signed up for pretty much anything else.

Her father. It had been two months since he stepped down from the Council. There had been ceremonies, parties, banquets, and on and on. She half suspected he had done it to get people's minds off the battle. The other half figured he wanted to exit before he died in office, with all the disruptions that would go along with that. He named her as successor and the Council, surprisingly, voted unanimously to her appointment for the rest of her father's term. From the voices of support, both verbal and electronic, she didn't figure reelection next year would be too much trouble. The one three years later, on the other hand, she'd have to win on her own. That is, if the ship even lasted that long.

By the time they landed, or more or less crashed, on the bottom of this trench, there wasn't a single part of the ship that hadn't sustained damage. They were taking on water at such a rate that, even with every bilge pump and vertical thruster going at maximum, they were still sinking. The countermeasures had set off enough of the incoming torpedoes that the resulting compression waves had detonated the others some distance from the hull. Those same waves, though, wreaked havoc on the aft third of the ship. Ironically, the damage already sustained from the impact with the *Population* acted as a sort of buffer, absorbing much of the energy.

The *Pop* fleet apparently wasn't so lucky. The ships closest to the blast crumpled and imploded, as far as the sensors could tell. The others took enough damage that they didn't pursue as the wounded citysubs limped away from each other. With so many of the hull microphones damaged, destroyed, or ripped away, it was difficult to detect what damage the *Pop* itself had taken. They could hear bulkheads bursting, metal creaking, and other sounds buried beneath the roar of the ship's engines. It had taken the techs weeks to sort out all the data. They were still going over it. That's a meeting tomorrow, she realized.

Her father had been instrumental in figuring out the *Pop*'s plan of trying to get them to ground themselves. Then, of course, he had been the one to find the perfect hiding place. It had taken them two weeks to get here. Only able to go deeper, never shallower, thermal hopping was out of the question. She doubted anyone slept as the ship changed direction every half an hour for six days to see if anyone was following. It seemed like they hadn't been. They had to coast the last half-day as they lost two more screws, and navigating the narrow trench would have been too hazardous with power only on the port side.

The landing had knocked loose two entire cabin ships, both overlooking the Basket. These were evacuated successfully, and the ships secured before they fell to the floor, a disaster narrowly averted.

As it stood, they had lost just under a thousand people. The single biggest loss was E6, the starboard-most engine room. Torn open to the sea, 223 crewmen and women were killed instantly. Pressure change like that was a quick death. Others in the aft of the ship hadn't been so lucky. Dozens drowned, unable to outrun the advancing carnage and influx of water. She had attended several of the mass funeral ceremonies as one of her first official duties. Not that it was a "duty"—she probably would have gone had she not taken her father's job. There were a few dozen that had fallen or been crushed in the impact. The worst, she thought, were those that had been trapped in a tiny oasis of air, surrounded by flooded compartments. They had found many of these too late. The thought made her shudder.

She focused on the table. No one had noticed. She was still being ignored at most meetings she attended. Even when she asked questions, the responses showed a poorly veiled condescension. This was one meeting, though, where she was glad to be invisible. She would get the transcript of the meeting later that night, and look it over then. Understanding the numbers wasn't hard, but trying to understand them as they were being spoken was next to impossible. She was half certain no one else in this room followed any of it either, a shared mutual deception.

Overall, the crew and inhabitants of the *Universalis* were handling it all fairly well. Updates on the repair progress were broadcast every night on the news, unfiltered by the Council.

Her father had been implicit on that. It warmed her heart that the number of volunteers actually outnumbered the jobs and equipment available to them. Most were told to continue what they had been doing before the start of the war. That's what most people were calling it. There was a near palpable camaraderie across the ship that she had never seen before. People seemed genuinely more friendly and helpful.

It hadn't been easy, though. Most difficult was resources. The Garden had suffered relatively mild damage, and was back up to 100 percent within a few days. Fishing was harder. Only a select few fishing businesses were allowed to leave the ship. This had the other companies on the verge of rioting. They were given a subsidy, or their workers given other jobs, in the meantime. The fact was, the Council only wanted certain pilots outside the ship: those they could train, or had trained. It was still a pretty well-kept secret that all the current fisherman were actually marines or one of the new batch of navy pilots. Their main job was to fish, that was true, but they were also scouts, and served as an early warning system if the *Pop* managed to find them. Not that it would do much good. They were still months away from having a working navy like they did in the last war, nearly forty years earlier. The designs had been modified, both for efficiency in manufacture and to reflect four decades of sub development. Even the weapons were upgraded. Drychem rockets with better range and explosive potential, microtorpedoes, and some new weapons that she hadn't been briefed on yet. Later in the week, she thought. Those meetings were always fun.

The biggest problem had been raw materials. They had sent out messages through emergency channels: a tightbeam to the nearest facility, which relayed it to another and that one to another and so on. The message warned of possible aggression, and asked that whatever supplies they had be delivered to certain rendezvous coordinates. After a brief quarantine in the middle of nowhere to be sure they weren't followed, they were escorted to the *Uni*. This took time, and also meant there weren't steady shipments. Each dome was told to send what they could, and to hunker down and be prepared to defend or surrender. That decision was left up to each dome. She found it odd that not too long ago she had been sizing up a dome as a possible permanent habitat in case something went wrong on the *Uni*. Now dome refugees were looking for a home on the crippled ship out of fear of attack from the *Population*, and they simply weren't prepared for the influx. That didn't stop them from coming, though.

Eight domes in the past six weeks had gone silent. One, near where the Battle of the Shallow Sea had taken place (as her father insisted on naming it), had broadcast distress, and then the signal went dead. She had seen on a map the domes that had stopped responding to messages, and they were sequentially in a line starting from that first. Though small consolation, the *Pop* seemed to be travelling roughly away from their current location. It pained her to think what may be happening to the poor people in those domes, but there was nothing they could do. They had barely a skeleton of a fleet. Not to mention they were buried in silt, hiding. It was frustrating, to say the least.

The meeting broke up, and she said goodbye to each man by name. The next meeting was right down the corridor, and she was the first one there. She took a seat in middle, and went over her notes from the previous week's meeting. This was her committee, so to speak. She didn't run it—she was too junior for that—but she was the sole member that brought data; everyone else was there to keep apprised of the situation. Throughout the week she met with the heads of the training programs for pilots, damage crews, marines, and so on. Then it was just a matter of compiling the info on recruiting and progress. Nothing too major, but she was the liaison and it was her first real important duty as a Councilmember. Also, it gave her an excuse to see Thom.

This presented a bit of a challenge. She wasn't sure what it was about Thom... wasn't sure what she felt towards him. They had been spending a lot of time together, and not just in an official capacity. If there was one thing, it was how he spoke to her: like she was one of his drinking buddies. An old friend. She couldn't remember the last time someone did that. But then, it wasn't just one thing. She wouldn't go so far as to call it a crush. Even the thought of the word made her feel like she was cheating on Cern.

Cern had been so good through all of this. He had been the first one to congratulate her on her nomination. He had helped her get her schedule sorted out, and had been by her side at every party, every banquet, every funeral.

But there was just something about Thom. He was funny. Unpredictable. And he looked at her in a way sometimes... But other times he was distant. And, in all honesty, he was a bit of a Basket loser. She was sure that if her father hadn't forced a commission on him, and handed him the role of pilot trainer, he'd still be a drunk fisherman in some below-decks bar. No one said no to old man Gattley. Still, Thom did step up into the role, and well.

People started filing in. There were four other Councilmembers on the committee, along with two representatives each from the Fisherman's and Farmer's unions (there to be sure their ranks didn't get too pilfered); the last member was the Proctor of Manufacturing, in charge of the several divisions tasked with building their new fleet. This should go fairly quickly, she thought optimistically. She stood, and clasped her hands behind her back.

"Good morning, gentlemen," she said in her most official-sounding voice. The seven men looked up at her, expectantly. Her meeting. Her show.

Mrakas Gattley lay on his bed, covered in blankets. From the doorway it seemed he was even thinner than the last time she had seen him. He had always had a look of strength, of power, about him. As a child she remembered him being a giant. While others lost this feeling as they aged and grew, she had not. It wasn't just physical size, but a presence. And though he had been sick for some time, it wasn't until the last few weeks had he started to emaciate. His skin had taken on a pallor. He smiled as she entered. She took a breath and pushed down her fear.

"Hi, Dad," she said smiling.

"Today was your committee day, right? How did it go?"

"Good, very good."

"Tell me what's been happening," he said, struggling to push himself upright in the bed. She hurried over to help him. Sitting on the side of the bed, she went over her notes with him from the other meetings that day, and the afternoon of the previous day.

"I spoke with Manufacturing like you asked, and they said production is on track."

"They're lying. They always lie. They don't want to lose face in front of the Council, for fear that you'll try to butt in and run things. Next time, ask him what he needs to increase production. He'll know you're really asking what he needs to maintain the current pace, but he'll appreciate you letting him look strong."

"Good information for this morning, but I'll keep that in mind for next week."

"And training, how's that going? How's that kid working out? Thom."

"Both are doing fine. We're on track. Thom is doing good work," she said, glancing away. He noticed. His eyes were still good. "Some of the recruits, like those coming from the fishing fleet, take to the subs pretty well. Most pick up the tactics fairly quickly, and their instructors have no problem graduating them to full pilot status. On the other hand, those without previous experience haven't done as well. Most have struggled with even the basics of sub maneuvering, and have failed completely on tactics. I and their lead trainers recommend that we have a higher failure rate for pilots, but instead of kicking them out of the program, require them to complete a secondary training program predominantly on simulators."

It was clear his attention had wavered.

"I hear you're having lunch with Cern. How is he?"

"Well, you seem to have talked with him today; why don't you tell me?"

"He's a good boy. Man. A good man."

"Yes, Dad. He is."

"You know, as a Councilmember, you don't have to participate in the lottery."

"Dad!"

"You don't."

"I wasn't… I am aware of that, Dad, and if at some point Cern and I decide to have children, we will have a discussion about the lottery. Personally I don't think we should have any different rights than everyone else on this ship," she said, slamming her notebook shut. The sound it created was less than satisfying. When she looked up, her father was glaring.

"Maybe so, but that's the way it is," he said coolly.

"Can we talk about something else?" she pleaded. It never ceased to amaze her how easily she could slip back into adolescence when she was with her father. Mrakas nodded, and seemed to relax.

"There is something else. I need you to do me a favor," he said. Before she could respond, he continued. "I need you to get your mother."

"We sent out an emergency recall message to all the research domes. She ignored it."

"I need you to do it."

"Dad, if you want to see her, just call her. I'm sure she'll come," she said, a lump rising in her throat. Mrakas shook his head, and from the look on his face immediately regretted it.

"That's not what I mean. She knows what condition I'm in, I've spoken to her enough. That's all fine. I need you to go out there and put her on a transport. Her and all her research. She's close to something. Something important. Something that can't be destroyed or lost. She needs to be here. She's going to fight you, but you need to do whatever it takes to bring her here. Am I clear?" he asked, gripping her forearm.

She nodded. "You need to act quickly. *Pop* isn't going to wait."

She wondered if he meant that both ways.

Proctor Jills had long ago commandeered her father's office, which was fine with Ralla. It would have been unprecedented for someone of her tenure to have an office of that size. After some shuffling around, she got one conveniently close to both her cabin and the Council Chambers. There was no doubt in her mind that at some point in the far past it had been a closet. An actual closet for one of the staterooms that made up this part of the ship. Those staterooms were gone, split into smaller rooms, but this closet had remained as someone's idea of a reasonable space. Oddly, she liked it.

It was lined with wood veneer, giving it a certain warmth that much of the *Uni* lacked. The desk half filled the tiny space. Above it were shelves, the highest of which she could only reach by standing on the desk. The other wall was open, but her desk left no room for another table, or even chairs. So she used what little empty space there was to spread out papers, or to lie down when her back ached from too much sitting. Out of nowhere, the thought occurred to her that if Thom lay with his head against one wall, his feet would touch the other.

She wrote a short mail to her mother, as a final plea, but deleted it. Instead, she logged into her terminal and accessed the part of the system only Councilmembers could view. After searching for a few moments, she got the info she was looking for, and headed out.

If there was a time to appear sober, this was it, and Thom was failing miserably. He wasn't sure what she had said, but he was sure the entire bar had gone silent to hear her say more. She stood at the end of the bar, fuming. Her eyes were wide, her nostrils were flaring, her fists were clenched... actually, she looked kind of silly. He put down the drink in his hand, and wobbled to his feet.

"Ralla, I have toomorrrrow..."

"Forget it," she spat, and stormed out. He thought better of following her, and thought better of not finishing his drink.

As Ralla entered, she noticed Cern smiling at the waitress, politely declining another refill of water. As she moved aside, he saw Ralla and waved to her. Ralla dropped into the chair, slammed her notebook on the table, and sat with her eyes closed, soaking in several deep breaths. Cern said nothing, but she could feel him waiting patiently for her to finish her mini-meditation. When she did and her eyes opened, he smiled patiently. Ralla composed herself and returned the smile.

"I'm sorry. I'm so late."

"It's OK, I know you're busy. From the look on your face, I get the feeling I need to punch someone."

"No, no. Someone just really let me down when I needed them. Again."

Cern nodded, not really understanding.

"Are we still on for dinner tonight?"

"I'm not sure. I'm just so *busy.*"

"OK, OK. I don't mean to push. I just hardly get to see you anymore."

"I know."

"Maybe there's something I can help with?" he asked.

"No. It's OK. Look, I don't really want to talk about it. Thank you, though. Thanks," she smiled, and reached across the table, taking his hands in hers.

"Dinner, then?"

"Can we have lunch before we figure out dinner?"

They were sitting on the terrace, overlooking the Garden, in one of the few restaurants with such a view. There was a breeze, which made the soggy air more tolerable. She closed her eyes and let the smells and the light wash over her. Calming her. For that moment, the biggest decision pressing upon her was what to order for lunch. For a moment, she was alone in the breeze. In the air. Soaring around the Garden. Wind fanning her face. Exhaling. Exhaling. Exhaling. Then slowly she was aware of the sounds of utensils on plates. Of glasses clinking. Of background chatter. Of the seat below her, the table under her arms. Of Thom's hands in hers.

Cern's hands! She opened her eyes with such jolt she was sure her hands flinched. Cern didn't seem to have noticed, reading the menu between his outstretched arms. She let his hands go, and opened her own menu.

That little mistake, perhaps confusion, was what did it. Cern had been a beautiful companion for years, but with that one jolt, she knew it was over. Ralla still wasn't sure what she felt towards Thom, but she knew what she didn't feel towards

Cern. Food was ordered on autopilot. She didn't listen as Cern spoke about his day, about his father's increasingly vocal desire for him to take over the family business. In other words, the same conversation they'd had yesterday and all the other yesterdays. But now she didn't care. Suddenly she couldn't be done with lunch fast enough. Ralla knew there was nothing he had done wrong, nothing specific, but any residual feelings she'd had for him drained away over marinated fish and vegetables.

More than anything she just wanted to be free of it all. Of him. Of their relationship. To be on her own. Maybe Thom, maybe not. But for now, free. Her life had progressed to someplace new with the Council, much as the ship itself had moved to a new stage with the coming war. Even so, this was going to hurt. Better fast than slow; she owed him that at least. She waited till they'd finished their food.

"Cern, I can't do dinner tonight."

"Tomorrow, then," he said, obviously not getting it.

"No, Cern. I think we're done."

"Huh?" he replied, taking a moment to register what she had said. "What? Are you serious?"

"Yes. Please, I'm sorry. I don't want to hurt you, but... I need to be on my own."

"You're breaking up with me? Here?"

It occurred to her suddenly they were still at the restaurant. She'd been so focused on what to say, she hadn't really considered where she was saying it.

"But we're so perfect for each other," he continued. "I've always taken care of you. My family thinks of you as one of their own. Have you discussed this with your father?"

Exactly the wrong thing to say at exactly the wrong time. This was getting out of hand.

"Cern, I'm sorry. You're not what I need anymore."

With that, she left. On her way back to her cabin, emotions swirled. Sad, partially, more than she had expected to me. Unhappy she'd had to hurt Cern. Remorseful at throwing away so many years with someone who had never mistreated her. Had always cared after her.

By the time she reached her cabin, though, the melancholy was obscured by the invigorating relief of freedom. Hope, for the first time in a long time. It felt like she was shedding off the last hook holding her to her former life. The life of being someone's daughter, of being someone who needed to be taken care of.

And as that thought occurred to her, she realized what she needed to do next.

III

Somewhere into the first hour, Thom stopped apologizing. The apologies started the instant he opened his cabin door and saw her standing there, the afternoon after their little one-sided spat in the bar. He continued apologizing the next morning when they met at the bay. It was as lopsided a conversation as their last: him pleading forgiveness, her offering nothing but cool, detached instruction in reply. As she sat in silence in the back of the transport, his mea culpa finally came to a quick halt. The trip was over a day and a half, and if she wasn't going to forgive him for having fun on his first real day off in months, then so be it. What was worse was that she seemed distracted as much as pissed. Well, whatever. He called up a vid on the computer, sent the audio to some headphones, and leaned back in the cockpit chair. It was going to be a long trip... for some.

There was a strict quiet-running rule in effect for the entire fleet, so they had to proceed at partial power and spend time moving between different thermal layers, occasionally zig-zagging to throw off any potential followers. Full speed, in a straight line, the trip wouldn't have taken more than sixteen hours. Knowing that somehow made the long and winding trek that much more unbearable. Despite her current attitude, Thom knew the trip was important, even if the explicit reason behind it was a mystery. Heading out alone to some research station in the middle of nowhere, even if the *Pop* fleet seemed to be halfway around the planet, was not something that she would do on a whim.

By mid-afternoon on their second day, they started seeing light in the murky distance. Less than an hour later, they were almost blinded by it. The official name of their destination was Ocean Research Station 24, but to those who worked there it was called Vertigo or Verti. It was built 22 years earlier, and if its existence hadn't been classified, it would have been considered quite a technological marvel for the citizens of the *Uni* to be proud of. It was perched atop the Grengen Crevasse, a near bottomless gash in the sea floor that ran north-south for nearly a quarter of the hemisphere. Vertigo was above the deepest part, straddling the east and west cliff faces. Like a giant glass slug, it formed a bridge across one of the deepest depths of the planet.

It was mostly a metal framework, a hump-backed, flat-bottomed, tube that arched over the Crevasse. Most of the floor was, thankfully, standard metal deckplates. The designers, though, apparently oblivious or psychologically deviant—Thom couldn't decide which—had built several areas where the floor was the same transparent permiglass as the walls and ceiling. Staring past your feet into the seemingly infinite void was something that only amused a certain sort of person.

The station was fairly narrow, and not that long given its location. The Grengen got wider as it meandered south, but this point was close to its narrowest. It probably wouldn't take more than 10 minutes to walk from one end of the station to the other, and maybe 30 seconds from side to side. It was blindingly bright in the otherwise black surroundings, casting long shadows on the sea floor on either side, but the light vanished in the long black darkness below.

"Yep, creepy," Thom said aloud. Ralla had leaned into the cockpit a moment before to watch the approach.

"Yep," she replied.

There were two small bays at either end of the station where the arches of the frame lanced out and buried themselves deep into the bedrock. Thom threaded his way between them, looking out along the bottom of the station. It wasn't far before the station continued, but the sea floor didn't.

The pool wasn't much larger than the transport itself. Calling it a bay was a bit of a stretch, as there was no crane, no real support equipment. It was open to the rest of the station. From the cockpit of the sub as it floated on the surface of the pool, he could look down the length of the station. If it weren't for the low stack of orangey-yellow buildings in the middle, he could have seen the pool at the other end.

There was a metallic clang as stairs were pushed against the hull, serving as egress and to secure the sub to the station. Ralla was already at the door, and Thom could see as he left the cockpit a look of disappointment on her face as she looked out from the open hatch. Thom stepped out and watched a young tech offering a hand to Ralla as she stepped down to the deck. Whoever she was expecting to see, it wasn't this guy.

She uttered a question that Thom couldn't hear, and immediately headed towards the buildings with a purpose. Thom nodded at the technician, who gave him a blank stare and said nothing.

All of that purpose that Ralla exuded, Thom himself completely lacked. He had nowhere to be and nothing to do.

"Got a place to eat around here?"

The tech pointed towards the buildings.

"Thanks. Wouldn't have guessed that."

The lab was a square building in the exact center of the station, with an open space in the middle that could almost be called a courtyard. Instead of grass or benches, the space had a permiglass floor surrounding an elaborate rig of winches and whirring boxes at the very center. The lab was open to the courtyard on all sides, and techs came and went from different areas of the lab, some checking the rig, others carrying samples in large vials.

The young woman who had led her in from the door—Ralla wasn't sure of her position—pointed across the courtyard to a long table packed with equipment tucked into the far corner. There was one person in the center of this table, hunched over a microscope, back to the world, surrounded by esoteric equipment that seemed almost comically, stereotypically "scientific" to Ralla, like set dressings from a bad science fiction vid.

Ralla kept her head up as she strode across the courtyard, doing her best not to look down. She couldn't help herself when she got to the center. From below the rig a thin filament dropped down from the station far into the distance. Farther than she could see, which somehow made the whole thing worse. She fought back a wave of nausea and kept going.

"Hi, mom."

The figure remained hunched over the microscope, and for a second Ralla wasn't sure if the other woman had heard her. Finally, her mother spun in her chair and opened her arms wide. They embraced, and for a moment Ralla felt safe and relaxed.

"Give me just a second to finish up some notes," she said, turning back around and scribbling on a notepad. Ralla stood awkwardly behind her mother while the rest of the lab continued at a seemingly frenetic pace. "You know, I only got word you were coming this morning. Why the surprise visit?" Ralla's mother asked, still hunched over her notes.

"Dad asked me to come."

"Did he?" The question sounded almost rhetorical.

"Mom, can we go somewhere and talk?"

"We can talk here, sweetie; my people are far too busy to care about what we're talking about."

"That's the thing mom: why aren't you packing up? We have to get away from here. There's a war going on and you're defenseless out here."

"Nope, that's not it. Try again."

"Huh?"

"That's not why you're here," she said to her notepad. Ralla made a face at her back.

"I'm here because Dad asked me to come get you."

"Has he gotten worse?"

"Yes, but…"

"Well OK, then," the older woman turned. Her long gray hair was tied back in a ponytail, which seemed to move on its own. "Sweetie, I made peace with your father's illness a long time ago. I made peace with your father long before that. This is where I need to be. You can't imagine how important our work is here."

"Actually, that is why Dad asked me to come get you. *Because* what you're doing is so important. He wants you to be safe."

"Sweetie, don't worry your head about this," her mom said. Each time she said "Sweetie," Ralla got a little more annoyed. "You don't understand, we can't do this work on the *Universalis*. If your father is having a fit of nostalgia and wants to see me again, that's sweet. But it's also selfish. I need to be here, and he should know that."

"No, mom..."

"I'm sorry you came all this way, but we're not leaving. I'll be taking a break for supper, if you want to join me in the Mess. Always good to see you, Sweetie. It's been too long. But I need to get back to work. I'm sorry." And with that, Ralla's mother buried her face in her microscope, leaving Ralla standing very alone in the crowded and busy lab.

"You want a drink?" the bartender asked Thom. After the briefest of pauses, he shook his head.

"Yes, but just some water, please." The bartender put the glass of water on Thom's tray, and he made his way to a table in the middle of the low-ceilinged common area. He noticed on the wall opposite the entrance a sign that read "MESS" in big letters, then "Leave it like you found it" painted carefully in red underneath. Thom hadn't gotten more than two bites into his sandwich before he saw Ralla enter. She also got a tray of food, but ordered two tall, though skinny, glasses of beer from the bartender. As she sat down across from him, he could tell her mood had clearly not improved since arrival. She seemed more annoyed than anything.

"Well, cheers, Thom. This has been a complete waste of time," she said after depositing one of the glasses on Thom's tray. They hoisted their glasses, but Thom took just a sip while Ralla downed the whole glass. After a moment's hesitation he put his glass on her tray. She angrily bit into her sandwich. Thom thought better of asking her what was going on.

"So, what is it they do here? I'd never heard of this place before yesterday."

Between bites, Ralla answered.

"It's an ocean research station, though that much I'm sure you figured out. What they're testing is the water from the surface, water at this level, which is roughly the depth the *Uni* cruises at, and from several different depths below, all the way down to the bottom."

"OK..."

"The wind on the surface churns up the water. Waves are the obvious result of this, but it acts like a blender. Air gets mixed in with the water on the surface, so immediately the water on the surface is contaminated by the air up there."

"Mmhmm, that much I remember from school."

"The radiation might do different things at that point. It may just stay at that depth, and in that general area. Or it may drift with ocean currents. The radiation in the air is pretty uniform, so we can't tell if what we're reading was mixed in the water directly above, or on the other side of the planet. Regardless, the water eventually makes its way to the north, and as the surface water cools, it drops down towards the bottom. Now the radiation has gone deep, but there is so much more water down there, the radiation gets rather diluted. So even if it starts getting moved around with other currents, it's not strong enough to cause any threat to us. That's why we live so deep. One of the concerns with the attack a few months ago wasn't just that we may have been grounded, but that in our carelessness trying to escape, we entered shallower waters and picked up more radiation than we would have in 50 years traveling at depth." As she took another bite, she waved off the question that Thom was obviously about to ask.

"Don't worry, we're fine. All that is the conventional wisdom. But up until 25 years ago, we had no idea if this was a set, stable system. As in, if the radiation in the atmosphere would continue to poison the ocean, and eventually we wouldn't be able to go deep enough to avoid it. Not to mention destroying what little life is left down here."

"So what happened 25 years ago?"

"There was a group of scientists, one in particular, who led a campaign to convince the Council to build this station. It needed to be near a trench so that they could sample the water at many different levels. We had no baseline readings, you see. So the background radiation the ship, and our drysuits, are easily able to cope with, well, we didn't know if there was actually more 50 years earlier, or even earlier than that. By the time our forefathers built the *Uni* and the *Pop*, they were more concerned with survival than scientific tests, and then more concerned with killing each other than with science at all. So we needed a baseline, and going deep was the only way to establish one. So it came down to that one scientist, who had the theory and the confidence to fight against the conventional wisdom at the time."

"Which was that everything was fine."

"Right. That scientist was also conveniently married to an influential Council member," Ralla said, taking the final bite of her sandwich. It took Thom a moment, but he leaned back in his chair and nodded.

"Oh."

"Exactly. So my mom spearheaded the project, came up with the design for the labs and even some of the equipment, and was the natural choice to lead the team that would stay out here collecting data. I was four when my mom left, and every time it would look like she'd be coming home, there would be some new theory, some new test she would have to oversee or try out. Testing water isn't the only thing they do here. That water you're drinking? My mom and her team came up with a way to purify it in half the time, using half the energy as the old way. The harvests in the Garden doubled in less than two years because of that."

"Wow."

"Yeah. For a lot of years I'd look at a glass of water and think, *you took my mom away from me*. But I've come to terms with how she is. And she and my dad don't seem to have any resentment about how it all played out. I don't know, sometimes I wonder if they ever..." She looked up at Thom, casually scratching his stubble with his thumbnail. "Most people look at me different when I tell them what it was like for me growing up. But not you. Why?"

Thom shrugged. "You knew your mom, and could talk with her when you wanted, for the most part. That's better than I could do, so I guess it makes you seem a little more normal to me, not less. Not sure who you all hang out with, but among my friends, my story is a lot more common than not.

"I'm sorry."

"Hey, if growing up didn't suck, how would we know what good a time we're having now? I mean, wasn't that the best cold sandwich you've had in a remote isolated research station?"

Ralla smiled. "Thank you, Thom." It was irritating how much she wanted to kiss him right then. And like that, her animosity from the night before vanished. He may be a drunk sometimes, but he really did try. "Want to take a look around? We came all this way."

"Why, are we leaving?"

"Oh, sorry, right. Well my dad sent me here to get my mom. Her work is critically important, and we couldn't let her be killed or be captured by the *Pop*. She thinks he just wants her there to take care of him now that he's close to dying."

The casualness with which the words left her mouth surprised even her.

"How about this: lets walk around, check this place out. See if we can not throw up standing on one of those insane clear walkways. Then you can have another run at your mom. If she still shoots you down, we can kidnap her."

The little spark in her eye when she heard that scared him a little.

"Ralla, I was kidding."

"I know you were."

The building walls were all paper-thin, no more than an orangey-yellow plastic membrane stretched between black metal and composite support frames. Somehow this was strong enough to create multi-storied structures. The tallest was three floors, its roof about two stories below the ceiling of the station. As Ralla and Thom walked around, they found mostly dormitories, one other eatery (a café), and a large room labeled "Theater," with a screen hardly bigger than the personal vidscreens found in many cabins on the *Uni*. No bars, no real entertainment, nothing superfluous.

"People come here for three to six months at a time, then head back," Ralla told Thom as they were walking. "About 20 percent sign up for another stint, but the rest continue the research back on the *Uni*. The longest, other than my mom, have been here about nine years."

"I think I'd go insane in a place like this."

"Me too."

As they reached the far end of the station, Thom eyed the pool.

"It's so weird they just leave it open like that."

Ralla stomped on the floor. Thom, took a step back, and looked at it as if for the first time. The deckplates they were standing on were fused together, with a defined line running in an arch shape behind them. The shape and length of the fused plates were such that if it pivoted up from the end closest to the pool, it would fit snuggly with the ceiling and walls. It reminded Thom of draw bridges he had seen in vids as a kid.

"Well, that's rather genius."

"They needed a way to lock off the pools in case of an emergency, but they had no real walls or ceiling to hide the door."

"As I said: genius." They were alone, standing side by side, looking back on the cluster of buildings at the center of the oblong dome. They soon found themselves sitting on a pile of shipping containers lining the wall. Ralla's feet dangled, so she tapped the hard plastic with her heels. Ralla felt she should say something, but Thom beat her to it.

"I'm sorry about the other day. It was my first off in weeks and I hadn't seen my friends in forever."

"Thom, stop. Don't apologize. I had no right to be mad."

"Yeah, but..."

"Please. It's fine."

"Fine like it's fine or fine like you'll yell at me later for it."

"Thom..."

"OK. "

The echoes of Ralla's random tapping thundered in the silence that had appeared between them. He really didn't have anything to apologize for, she thought. Why did he even bring it up? The quiet got the better of her, as it often did.

"I don't think I could work here. It's so damp and creepy," Ralla said, surprised at the nervousness in her voice.

"It's because I'm afraid I'll turn out like my father," Thom answered. There was only a moment while Ralla adjusted to the new direction of the conversion.

"I'm afraid I won't," she replied.

The station creaked beneath them. Water lapped against the edges of the pool. Thom lifted his right arm up, and after a moment's hesitation, she slid over and under it. She hadn't realized she had been cold. He always smelled so good. She could hear his voice resonating in his chest before her brain focused on the words.

"I think we could make it work," he said. Ralla stiffened, the conversation progressing much faster than she had anticipated.

"Make what work?"

"This place. If you and I had to work here," he said, motioning towards the station with his free arm. She relaxed with a short laugh.

"Sure. A few colored lights."

"Exactly. Some trees."

"Maybe a dance floor?" Ralla said with a smile.

"Absolutely. Techs love a good dance. Me too. I get some of my best standing-around done at dances," Thom said, his face deadpan. Ralla elbowed him playfully. She tilted her head to look up at his face, her hair falling to partially bock her view. His eyes were locked on hers. His head moved almost imperceptibly closer.

Then suddenly his grip relaxed, and he let his arm drop from her shoulders as he leaned back.

"Man, all this talk of not dancing has gotten me wondering what these techs do in their spare time," Thom said, carefully looking away from her down towards the rest of the station. Ralla sat up, and pulled her hair behind her ears. "When did your mom say she'd be done? he asked, looking back at her, though not as piercingly as just moments before.

It came to her suddenly: He's worried about Cern! That made her want Thom more than she had when she leaning against his warm chest.

"Thom," she started, but it was too late. Thom slid himself off the crate. Everything that she wanted to say welled up into her throat and stuck there. Her mind focused on what he had said.

"She didn't. We can start back home now if you want, or we can see if we can stay the night and start back in the morning."

"Let's stay. It will be like a mini vacation."

"Ha!" Ralla snorted, not saying in the single syllable how pleased she was for the extra time.

"A pseudo-vacation?"

"How about a night away from home that doesn't involve sleeping on the floor of a sub?"

"Perfect, just want I always wanted."

Perfect, indeed, she thought.

IV

Thom awoke on the floor, his face just barely not smushed against the wall. It took a moment for his brain to warm up and register the fact that wasn't where his face was when he fell asleep. He rolled over and looked at the bed along the other wall, and definitely remembered crawling into it last night. Had he rolled out of it? That would be a first; he usually woke up in the same position he fell asleep in. The clock in the wall said it was 03:20. Ralla said she had wanted to talk to him later, but hadn't returned from talking to her mom. So he had called it an early night without even a drink.

As he crawled to his feet, his brain registered the sound of the explosion at exactly the instant the floor beneath his feet failed him. This time he hit the floor hard, his head clanging against the deckplates in a way that would have been humorous under different circumstances. He dressed quickly.

In the alley outside, people were emptying out of their rooms wearing expressions that ranged from confusion to panic. He knocked on the door to the cube next to his, the one where Ralla had put her things. No answer. Opening the door, he found a nearly identical room to his own: sparse, stark, empty.

There were no alarms, but he could hear shouting in the distance. It was faint, but unmistakable.

Then weapons fire. Thom's blood ran cold. In the tiny plaza, really just an open space where several buildings had their front doors, techs and scientists milled around trying to decide what to do. Thom took off at a fast jog towards the main lab. Bursting through the front door, he made his way to the middle but found it empty. Turning to leave, movement caught his attention. Through the glass floor he watched a submarine pass silently under the station. It was not a sub from the *Uni.* He left at a full sprint.

There was more weapons fire, louder this time. Either he was moving closer to it, or they were moving towards him. Or both. Wails of panic filled the silence between the bursts of weapons. He hit the Mess door at full speed, finding Ralla pleading with her mother as they crouched behind an upended table. Both looked at Thom as the door boomed into the wall. Ralla's mom looked from one to the other, and then walked briskly towards Thom.

"Thom Vargas, I'm Awbee Fratl Gattley," she said, like it was a greeting at a fancy dinner. "Please get my Daughter back to the *Universalis.*"

"Mom, NO!" Ralla begged, getting to her feet. Awbee strode past Thom and headed directly towards the lab.

"I'll see if I can get the sub ready; you get *her,*" he said, motioning over his shoulder. Ralla ran out the Mess after her mom. Thom ran other way and burst out the back door of the building. His momentum plowed him directly into an armed and uniformed man who was caught so off-guard he hit the metal deckplates and was knocked out cold. Thom didn't recognize the uniform, and didn't care.

He picked up the rifle, which was not similar to the one he had fired in training. The sidearm, though, was a dead ringer. Slinging the rifle over his shoulder and readying the sidearm, he continued through the alleys in the general direction of the transport.

His pace was slower, not figuring he'd be so lucky twice. Peeking around the edge of the last building, he saw a clear path to the transport, bobbling in the water untouched.

Around the pool he could make out heaped drysuits and handprops, at least a dozen. He started back towards the lab.

As Thom forced his way through the panicked frenzy gripping the inhabitants of the station, it occurred to him how poorly people, in general, handled crisis. Around him, with no thought other than "escape," they ran in every direction, clogging logical escape paths and ignoring others.

Fish, he realized, for all their lesser abilities, at least knew how to react. Danger! Flee! Stay together! All with a purpose. All without speech. Well now Thom had a purpose, and for it he didn't need speech either. But first, he had to get back to the lab.

Hearing voices from around a corner, he pressed himself against a wall. The door beside him was open, and he slid quietly into what must have been a small office, judging from the debris covering the floor. The struggle to get whoever was in here out must have been substantial. He crouched in the corner, gun aimed at the door. He watched as a rifle barrel nudged the door back open.

"How are we going to get all these people back to the ship?" one of the voices asked. He sounded young—not much past school, if that.

"Probably take them in shifts. Or maybe they'll send another sub. What I want to know is why all these people are way up here. There's nothing around here for half a hemi." The other voice sounded to be the same age. They started speculating as to the purpose of the dome as they walked away. When he could no longer hear them, Thom sprang from his spot, peeked out from the door, and continued inexorably towards the center of the station.

In the otherwise abandoned lab Ralla was yelling at her mother. To her credit, Awbee seemed to be gathering files from her terminal and saving them to memsticks.

"There's at least a dozen of them," Thom said, startling Ralla. "They're spreading out through the station. It doesn't seem very organized. I'm not sure they expected to find the station here."

"Can we get to the sub?" Ralla asked.

"I think so, but we need to go now while they're still trying to round everyone up."

"I'm not leaving my people. You two take the data and get back to the *Universalis*."

Ralla stepped in front of Thom and pulled his head down so she could speak in his ear.

"Getting her off this station is the *only* priority. Get it? Last night she showed me what she's been working on, and it's more important than you could imagine. We *have* to get her back to the *Uni*, no matter what." Ralla released him, and he looked over at Awbee.

"Let me be clear, Mrs. Gattley. I'm leaving with both of you, and that is the end of the discussion. How soon until you're done?"

"I'm as done as I can be. If they destroy this station..." said Awbee, looking around the lab.

"I don't think they have any idea what this place is, though I suppose that could go either way. We're going straight to the sub; you two need to stay right behind me. OK?"

The two woman nodded.

"Thom, give me the rifle. Or the pistol, either one," Ralla said flatly. Thom looked at each weapon, then handed her the pistol.

"Sweetie," Awbee said, resting a hand on her daughter's shoulder. "What if he needs that?"

"No, mom, what if *I* need it." Shrugging off her mother's hand, Ralla clicked off the safety and checked the charge, all in one fluid motion. She nodded to Thom to proceed.

They moved as a unit from edge of building to edge of building though the narrow "streets" of the station, making it to the Mess in no time. There was no one else around. Behind them, in the distance, they could hear voices and occasional screams. Then it was out though the Mess, retracing Thom's steps back towards their sub. While moving along the edge of the building across from the Mess, they encountered a patrol of two uniformed men.

It took Thom just a moment too long to duck back behind the wall, and all hell broke loose. The soldiers immediately started firing and shouting for backup. They backtracked along the wall to try to go around, and came under fire from another patrol. Cut off from their sub, they crouched down against the wall, Thom shooting blindly around the nearest corner, Ralla down along the building the other way, keeping them covered.

The rifle made a "blump" noise as it accelerated its charge out its long barrel. The ammunition spread out on impact, punching holes in the orangey-yellow plastic walls, but creating a small explosion when hitting the metal support beams. The pistol sounded like a higher pitched version of the rifle. Above them, the plastic ripped and tore as the soldiers tried to fire at them through the walls.

Suddenly, Awbee cried out in agony and slumped forward onto the floor, hitting her head hard on the deckplates.

"Mom!" Ralla yelled, diving to her side. Blood gushed from Awbee's left leg. Ralla handed Thom the sidearm as she went to work making a tourniquet out of her belt. The older woman was alive, but unconscious.

Thom entered full adrenaline panic mode. The noise of the tiny explosions, the shouts from soldiers—all the chaos of battle seemed far away. They couldn't go forward, and going back meant they'd be trapped. He peered the best he could around the corner, and still couldn't see where the two soldiers had taken cover. He did see the effect his firing had on the wall he'd hit. Ralla looked up at him, terror in her eyes. He handed her back the pistol, swung the rifle over his right shoulder, and picked up Awbee. He put her over his left shoulder, unslung the rifle, and fired a stream of shots into the wall in front of them. The plastic tore away under its own tension, half melting in the process.

Thom made eye contact with Ralla, then stepped through the hole he'd made in the wall into a tastefully decorated living room. Thom stepped on and crushed a low green plastic coffee table, lost his footing, and crashed over the sofa behind it. He shot out the next wall, and then they were out onto the next street. He spun as he saw the two original soldiers and fired a few shots in their direction. They dove out of the way and out of sight down an alley.

Two more paces and a few more shots and they were through the next wall littered with terminals and desks, apparently an office. He stepped up to a solid jog. More shots and they were through the next wall. He could smell the burnt plastic as it clung to his hair and clothes each time they passed through one of his gun-made punctures.

It didn't take long for the *Pop* soldiers to figure out what he was doing, and soon they were firing at them through the walls. The shots impacted around them, causing Thom and Ralla to duck involuntarily. One more building, a storage area, mostly empty. That next wall gone, and then the transport was in sight.

They had barely made it out of the final building when the alarms finally started to howl, red lights flashing along the walls. With a sinking feeling in his stomach, Thom realized this wasn't an alarm for the invasion. They were sealing the station. Ahead, the lock was closing. The forward lip jerked up a few inches from the deck around it. It wobbled for a moment, the internal gearing and motors struggling with their first motion in two decades.

"Go go go *go!*" he shouted over his shoulder. His legs were weak from the running and the extra weight of Awbee hanging across his shoulder. He threw away the rifle and got ready to do whatever he had to do get the elder Gattley on the other side of the lock. The watertight drawbridge was already at knee height. More steps, he thought. Keep running, keep running.

By the time he reached it, it was at waist height. He flopped Awbee onto the rising surface, and pushed her down below the line of gunfire. As the floor rose, her limp body started to slide down the increasing incline towards the pool. One problem at a time. He turned around and felt his heart stop.

Ralla was still in the building. She had been covering them. Thom looked frantically around for his discarded rifle.

162 | U N D E R S E A

It had slid against the wall. Screaming for Ralla to hurry, he dove for the gun. The charge was nearly depleted. Ralla heard him and started running; Thom fired into the hole he had created in the building wall, and then towards the spaces between the buildings and the outer walls as he saw soldiers appear there. The rounds hit the permiglass, scoring it and causing a puff of smoke, but little else.

Ralla was running. Running and shouting. With the noise of the gunfire, the alarm, the grinding of the lock behind him, he couldn't make out what she was saying. Then she pointed. The lock door was now head height. His head height. There was no way Ralla would be able to reach the edge by the time she got there. He leaped up and hung with one arm. The mechanism struggled for a moment, and then started to lift him off his feet. He motioned with the rifle for her to hurry. He fired off the remaining shots, wildly hitting the dome and buildings. Useless now, Thom dropped the empty rifle, holding out his hand ready to grab Ralla. Just a few paces away now, almost there. *Almost there.*

The look that crossed her face when she was shot was unmistakable. Thom took solace in the fact that it was a look of surprise for now, but he knew the pain would follow. The impact from the round knocked her forward, face first onto the deck. As she fell, she shouted, "GO!"

He wasn't sure how he didn't immediately run to her. It would have been so easy. He only held on with a few fingers, but he was already higher than he could jump even before she had gotten hit. To let go now would mean all three of them would be captured. She looked up at him, face bloodied. He could tell by her look. In the clamor he couldn't hear her, but her mouth formed two words: "Save her." Her face showed no fear, no pain, just resolve. If he let go he knew she would hurt him. Worse yet, she would hate him. Rounds started to impact the underside of the lock as it lifted him farther and farther away from her.

He nodded once, then swung up, getting a leg on the edge and pulling himself over. As the door passed 45 degrees, he stretched his neck up to peek over. She was surrounded by soldiers, grabbing her and pulling her to her feet. Her eyes locked on his. He knew he only had a moment, knew that he had to tell her something. That he'd come get her. That he didn't want to leave her. More rounds started impacting around his head, hitting the lock and the ceiling above. He said the only words he could say, the only words that would sum up what he needed to tell her. Three words: *I love you.*

She closed her eyes as Thom slid down the lock door.

Awbee lay in a crumpled, bloodied pile at the bottom of the lock. One arm dangled over the edge into the water. After failing to find any controls to the lock, he carried her into the transport, kicked away the stairs, and sealed them in. The sensors told him there were just two other subs in the area. One was docked at the other end of the station; the other had been patrolling, but was now holding just above the station, waiting to pounce. It seemed like the enemy pilot figured that was the best place to cover any escape. He was mistaken.

Thom blew the ballast and the sub fell away from the station like it had been dropped. Instantly his console lit up with warnings that the other sub had locked on and was eminently firing weapons. Before his craft hit the seabed,

Thom pushed the throttle to its maximum, launching them forward like a rocket. The supports for the station flashed by, close enough to touch. Then he was in the open, still accelerating. He blew the rest of the ballast and dove straight down.

By the time the other sub caught onto his tactic, the transport had disappeared into the Crevasse.

V

The forth punch put him on the floor. By that point, he wasn't sure why he had remained standing for the two previous. There, among the stickiness and the stench and the filth, Thom decided that if this guy wanted to beat him to death, he'd be OK with it.

It had taken Thom and the unconscious Awbee three-and-a-half hours to get back to the *Uni* using full emergency speed. They weren't followed; his depth and course had seen to that. A medical team was waiting for them on arrival, as he had requested. While Awbee was brought down to MedBay, Thom was rushed to the Bunker to brief the Captain. He told Thom he would personally brief the Proctor and the Council in the morning. It was little consolation to Thom that the Captain felt he had done the right thing, and congratulated him on making the right choice.

He made it all the way back to his cabin before the weight of what he had done hit him. He sat on the edge of his bed, shaking. As if in a daze, the world around him disappeared as he relived the moments over and over. Her face. Her face as she fell. Her face as it looked up at him. He couldn't come up with any reason why he hadn't let go. She was right there, just a few strides away. He could have picked her up...

But no, even then. Even with the haze of shame and regret, some part of him knew that he had been too high. There is no way he could have jumped back up. Then they'd all be captives. That was so nearly a better option. But it didn't matter. Not in the least.

He slid off his bed and sat on the floor, knees to his chest. He wanted to yell and cry and scream and weep. He wanted to go back to that moment they had been alone at the far end of the station. To touch her hand. Tell her that they should leave then. Now the tears came.

He staggered down to the bar a few hours later and buried himself in booze. He didn't see the guy enter who hit him. Just the fist as it landed on his right eye. But as he fell off the back of the stool, mostly standing, he saw who it was. It was the blond guy. The guy who kissed Ralla. The guy she wore on her arm like a big dumb genetically engineered accessory. Thom knew Cern Hennorr, by look, reputation, and now by feel. The second punch was on the other side of the face, and he staggered back a step. The next was the gut. The one that put him on the floor was to the jaw. The guy was screaming at him, face flushed with furor and wrath. That part, at least, felt good.

At least they put her arm in a sling. It hurt brutally. She wasn't sure what was in the ammunition they'd been using, but the pain it created was mind-numbing. That was probably the point.

From what Ralla could tell, and from the opinions of the scientists surrounding her, her wound wasn't deep, though it would probably leave a scar across her shoulder blades and down her arm a bit. Surprisingly, she didn't care.

There were eight of them in one room of one of the dormitories. The bed had been removed and they all sat on the floor, shoulder to shoulder. There was a worn cyan carpet that did little to insulate them from the icy steel deckplates.

She leaned forward the best she could, having nearly blacked out the one time she'd leaned back against the wall.

The others had tried to move so she could lie down, but she wouldn't have any of it. There was barely enough space for them to be sitting as they were.

Over the next day they were allowed turns in the bathroom, supervised by an armed soldier, and served meals of whatever packaged food had been found by their captors. They could whisper, but if the soldiers heard them talking they'd be threatened at gunpoint. She heard shots down the hall at one point, and figured the threats were probably real.

The biggest problem was her layered linen indigo blouse and black cotton pants. She explained away her dressy clothing saying she was new to the station and had wanted to make a good impression. It was a bad lie, but under the circumstances no one thought to question it.

The second day they were ordered out of the room and down to the lock she and Thom had entered. She felt a twist in her stomach, hoping he had gotten away OK, that he had gotten her mom away OK. She was sure she would have heard it had the sub been destroyed near the station, that unmistakable sound of a sub imploding. But still, she wondered.

They entered a transport, which left and immediately docked to the side of another sub. She was unable to get a look at its outside, but from its cramped quarters and state of interior, she was pretty sure it wasn't the *Pop*.

The hallways were narrow and the walls were covered with bare tubing and wires. The lighting fixtures were unadorned filaments that had gone out of style on the *Uni* decades earlier. It was a strange mixture of old and new. The deckplates had patches of rust, but they passed several rooms adorned with new looking equipment and terminals. Some bulkheads were even shiny. The best she could tell was that it was an old ship—or at least one hobbled together out of other, older ships—that had been refurbished.

They made it to this ship's small mess, and were handcuffed to brightly polished benches. It surprised Ralla that they hadn't seen anyone other than their captors. She was sure a ship of this one's apparent size would have to have a crew of at least a hundred or more. Other captives filed in and were placed around the other five gleaming tables. She wasn't sure the complement of the research station, but it would have to have been more than this. Maybe there was another sub, or this one was making multiple trips. She had no one to share her curiosity; their captors made it very clear that there was to be no talking. So they sat in silence on the cold benches, smelling food they weren't having.

Then for the better part of a day, they sat. No food, no water. Bio breaks were done in shackles. She was glad she had used the facilities on the station. From what Ralla could guess it was in the evening when they finally made it to their destination. There was a disconcerting jolt that the four guards in the room must have been expecting, given their lack of surprise. As a group they were herded off the way they'd entered, but now exiting down a set of stairs where the transport sub had latched before. She concentrated on not losing her balance as she descended the soaked and slippery metal stairs. When she reached the deck, she took in her surroundings. It was awe-inspiring.

From what Ralla could tell, given the height and the curves, she was in the front portion of the interior of the *Population*, roughly where she and Thom had slept and seen the speech so many months before. It had been completely transformed into a portal for war. They stood on what had been the bottom deck. A colossal pool occupied the center, larger than anything on the *Uni*. There was an unobstructed view clear to the ceiling, more than twice the height you could see at any open part on the *Uni*. Every few stories, there was a "U" shaped floor with maintenance bays, launch bays, and rows upon rows of submarines. Attack subs, escorts, subs of different sizes and designs she'd never seen. She counted fifteen of these floors, with a least fifty subs per floor. And those were just the small ones.

Getting her first real glance of her "transport," it seemed to be roughly corvette sized, with a crew of maybe 50 to 70, and that was the smallest sub she saw on the floor around the pool. There were half a dozen frigates, 100 to 150 crew, and a pair that were even larger.

None of those compared to the menacing submarine at the far end of the shipyard. It was all hard angles bristling with guns. Ralla guessed two rows of five corvette-sized subs could fit into the pool at the same time. The sub at the end of the shipyard looked almost too big to fit in the pool at all. Fear mixed with awe caused her to stop walking, and she was jabbed hard in the back by one of her captors.

Everywhere there was work being done on the subs, on platforms, but the space was so open, so cavernous, it was all faint and far away. At the end of the shipyard, where once there had been a view clear down to the other end of the *Pop*, there was now a bulkhead, floor to ceiling. The amount of metal, minerals, energy required for all this, in such a short time—Ralla could hardly fathom it. They were marching them across this space, in front of all this, for a reason. And it was working.

Ralla's group entered a small elevator in the bulkhead that separated the shipyard with the rest of the interior of the ship. It rattled as it rose, and quickly lurched to a stop. The doors opposite the one they had entered opened to reveal the interior of the ship. As she suspected, it was as if a giant patchwork of metal had been sliced down into the *Pop*. Walkways just ended. Shops were split, the bulkhead as a new wall. Ralla could see cabins bifurcated high above by this new end to the living space. The light was bright, but there were oddly few people about. And that wasn't the only thing that had changed since her last visit. New floors and platforms jutted out into the open down the length of the ship. Light squeezed past their staggered placing, casting sharp shadows that blanketed the floor.

Supports extruded out from bulkheads and hung haphazardly to any flat surface seemingly able to hold them. These arched up, connected with the new levels, then arched back down to the other side. She couldn't see what was on the closest of these new levels, but those farther away appeared to have some greenery and what could have been tents.

They crossed the park where she and Thom had done their research, the terminals now blank, and continued to the starboard side. Then countless corridors, all damp and poorly lit, before the group arrived at a space that was likely a ballroom in its previous life. Now, though, it was littered with cots. Rows and rows of cots. Worse, there were more people than cots, so the floor was covered in sitting, sleeping, and obviously distraught bodies. Ralla had her first moment of panic. Her breathing quickened. Her heart pounded. Her face flushed. These were *Uni* citizens. These were her people. And this was a jail. The faces nearest her were gaunt. Uniforms and clothing were soiled and torn. Some in the cots had blood on their clothes; others had more obvious injuries.

She saw few blankets, most covering unseen figures too still to be sleeping. Her sharp intake of breath went unnoticed as the others around her all processed the same thing.

For a brief moment, she had wished she had run to Thom when she had the chance. She saw him, hanging from one arm, being lifted from the deck. The anguish on his face as he was pulled away. Not for a second had she wanted him to do anything else. More than anything she hoped he understood that. Then she wondered, not for the first time, what he had said before he slid down the gate.

VI

Marines had found him still on the floor of the bar, bloodied, bruised, and unconscious. A med team had picked him up, cleaned him up in the Medbay, and sent him home. No sooner had he changed out of his sticky, bloody clothes than there was a knock on his door. One of Jills' assistants, after giving him a confused once over, informed him that the Proctor wanted to see him. The assistant neglected to say the entire Council would be there as well.

The entire Council, save one. A wave of guilt and pain washed over him, but he fought it back down, such was its familiarity. During his walk to the meeting, a few paces behind the rushing assistant, he hoped Ralla's father wouldn't be there. On that, at least, he was lucky.

The rest of the Council—plus Cern, Thom was almost amused to see—was seated at the black glass table, and all eyes turned to him as he entered.

"I was told you were uninjured in your escape," Jills asked, looking genuinely surprised. Thom's eyes had already started to blacken, his nose was taped, and there were lacerations down the side of his face.

"I fell," Thom replied. After a moment of silence while they waited for him to elaborate, he looked around for a place to sit. An assistant appeared, as if decloaking from the wall, and wheeled him over a chair. He sat at the end of the long table, facing Jills, in the spot normally reserved for the Captain. Cern was at Jills' left, and if he felt shame or regret for the damage done, he didn't show it.

"The Captain briefed us this morning," Jills started. "But we would like to hear it again from you. Please don't take this as a trial of any sort. Dr. Gattley backs up your story to the extent she can remember it."

Thom told them step-by-step what had transpired, every detail he could remember. The firefight at the end he told in exacting detail, including what Ralla had mouthed to him as he was pulled away. He left out his reply.

"Mr. Vargas... sorry, I guess *Lieutenant* Vargas is more accurate," Jills began. "I have no doubt the decision you made concerning our Councilmember and her mother will be a difficult one for you to live with. I have decided, against the judgment of several elder Councilmembers, to allow you to stay and hear Awbee Gattley's report regarding her work of recent months. Then you will at least understand why Ralla chose her mother's life over her own."

Jills motioned to one of the assistants, who left the room and returned a few moments later with Awbee. Despite a cast that covered her entire left leg, she looked ready, willing, and able to throw Thom and everyone else out the window. Thom slid his chair aside, and another was brought for Awbee. While she looked at everyone in the room with contempt, Thom saw her eyes narrow as they fell on Jills and the wiry and oddly silent Larr.

"Mrs. Gattley..." Jills started.

"Doctor," she corrected flatly. He ignored her.

"I get regular reports from you and your team, and the Science sub-council and I have, to this point, kept them secret. Your, shall we say, colorful..."

"Vehement."

"...disagreement with that decision is a matter of record, one that will be irrelevant soon. Your most recent reports are exciting to a degree that I don't think should be kept from the people of the *Universalis*. For those here not on the Science sub-council, and our invited guests," Jills said with a nod towards Thom, "please tell us of your work, from the beginning."

Awbee remained agitated for a moment, but as she collected her thoughts, she seemed to calm. Her tone of voice changed, like she was teaching a class of young students.

"Our world, such as it is, has two problems: One of water, and one of radiation. The impact spread radiation over much of the globe. What didn't spread from the initial impact was circulated by the wind. It would have killed everything on the surface within a few months, had it all not been dead already by problem number one. The asteroid, despite our best efforts to knock it off course, hit at the very roof of our world, instantly vaporizing all the ice and snow there. What the floods didn't take care of, the endless rain did, and that's how we ended up down here.

"I tell you all of this," she continued. "Because I know what kind of science grades some of you got," she said, looking at Larr, "and I want us all to be on the same page for the rest of this. There wasn't much research done post-impact. Everyone was either dead or trying to get to whatever safety they thought would work. What we've determined, using methods I'll get into in a moment, is that the impact didn't significantly alter our orbit or rotation. So with time, the ice caps will reform, the waters will recede, and eventually there will be land again."

Awbee was about to continue, then paused when she noticed what was to her a rather mundane fact was obviously a bombshell to the rest of the room.

"At the current rate we're seeing in our tests, this will take around 30 years. Though, that's not our only problem. The radiation from morons like you trying to knock the big rock out of the sky flooded our world with something else. The scientists of the day estimated the fallout wouldn't last for more than 20 years. They were wrong."

Awbee seemed to be enjoying being the center of attention and was really getting into her presentation.

"My lab, what I hope won't be my *former* lab, was perched over one of the deepest trenches on our world. My team and I could take infinite samples from any depth all the way down to the bottom, and all the way up to the surface. We did this so we could compare 'old' water and 'new' water. What I mean by that is the water at the bottom of Grengen is relatively stagnant. The currents are slow, so the water there has been there for a while. By comparison, the currents near the surface are such that any given molecule of H_2O could travel around the world in just a few months. The fact is, there's still a lot of radiation on the surface and in clouds above. But here's the thing: it's decreasing."

"How quickly?" Jills asked.

"Very. We could see livable levels of radiation within ten years. Negligible amounts in another five after that."

"I'm sorry, are you saying we could be living on the surface in 15 years?" Thom blurted out. He expected to be chastised for overstepping his bounds, but from what he could tell, most were glad he asked what was on their minds.

"If everything continues as it is, yes. And possibly on some tiny speck of mud within another 15 after that," she replied.

Larr had been silent and still the entire meeting, but now he leaned forward and looked right at Awbee.

"Is there a way to... accelerate this process?" he asked.

Jills simultaneously raised his left hand to stop Awbee from answering, and placed his right on Larr's arm.

"Thank you, all," Jills said, rising to his feet. "We will keep you informed of further developments. For now, if you would like to tell your constituents there is a chance we'll be living on the surface in our lifetimes, that would be fine. But do not give them details or specific deadlines."

The Councilmembers thanked Awbee as they left the room. She remained seated, as did Larr. Thom had no sooner stepped out of the chambers than Cern stepped out behind him and grabbed his arm, leading him forcefully down the hallway.

"You know, I was going in this direction already," Thom said. The grip tightened. When he saw their destination, he didn't try to fight, but he did get a bottoming out feeling in his stomach. The door opened, and it was worse than he imagined.

Ralla didn't think it was possible, but the crowd compacted itself even more so that the new arrivals, herself included, had a place to sit. Aisles had been maintained, so some of her group wandered through the crowd in search of familiar faces. A young woman seated near the door, a tech from the looks of her uniform, wrapped her arms around her knees and rocked a little. She looked at Ralla.

"They do feed us, once in the morning, once at night. Vegetable paste, mostly. There's not a lot of it, but it's something. There's water and bathrooms in the corner over there," she said, pointing with a tilt of her head.

Ralla looked where she had indicated and saw a few dividers and a pair of water fountains. Both had long lines. There were at least 3,000 people in this one room.

"Are there other rooms like this?"

The tech shrugged her shoulders.

"Can't say. There were 2,000 people in my dome, and I've only seen a few people I know. I hope they're all right, wherever they are."

"Hasn't anyone tried to overpower the guards. There were only a few that brought us in."

The tech looked on the verge of crying, and her eyes darted to a nearby cot with a blanket covered shape.

"I'm sorry, I didn't mean..."

The tech shook her head, and wiped her eyes on her sleeve. She continued to rock a bit.

"My name is Ralla."

"Dija. Dija Yunner. I'm a Technician 1st Class in Dome F511."

"A tech in an F dome. What did you do there?"

"Repaired the farm equipment, mostly."

Ralla smiled at her, and Dija smiled back. Ralla extended her hand, and the other woman looked at it for a moment, released her knees from her own grip, and shook Ralla's hand.

"What do you do, Ralla?"

"I recently took over my father's business."

"Oh." Dija said, then looked unsatisfied when no further explanation followed.

"I'll tell you, I could really use a shower," Ralla said with a smile.

"I like your dress," Dija replied.

"My dress thinks I could really use a shower."

That did it. Dija smiled a big smile, and seemed to forget about the room, the ship, the world around her for the barest of moments.

"Di, I'm going to go have a look around. Will you watch my stuff? Don't want all the riff-raff coming by and stealing all my nice furniture."

Dija smiled wider and nodded.

The room only had two doors that weren't barricaded, each attended by two guards. As she passed one, the door opened, and she saw several more well armed goons outside. Looking up, she noticed a few missing ceiling tiles (spy holes maybe, should couldn't tell). She didn't see anyone she knew, which was probably a good thing for now, and after doing a full loop she ended up back at her spot with Dija.

"Some guy tried to steal your dresser, but I beat him with a stick and he ran away," Dija said with a bit of a forced laugh. Ralla smiled back and slumped into the tiny little spot she was already starting to think of as her own. The people around her and Dija were either sleeping or just lying down for lack of anything better to do. It smelled of humanity.

The room was much as he saw it last, though the man in the bed was a fraction of who he used to be. Mrakas Gattley was limp as a nurse attempted to pull him upright in the bed. The old man's eyes burned as he saw Thom.

"You couldn't have had the decency to tell me yourself?" he bellowed. His voice filled the room. "Don't stand there staring at your feet like a child, get over here."

Thom did as instructed. Cern followed, and took a seat by the balcony as the nurse left the cabin.

"Well, I can see someone gave you a good working over," Mrakas said, his eyes falling from Thom to Cern. Thom tried to explain what had happened, but Mrakas stopped him.

"The fact of the matter is, you left my daughter with *them*. And because I'm stuck in this *damn bed* and can't do anything about it, *you* will. I don't care how you do it. But you must do it." He meant this as a statement, but there was a tinge of pleading in it as well. Thom was caught off guard. The thought had never occurred to him that he would be in a position to fix the problem he helped create.

"Cern is temporarily sitting in on the Council in Ralla's absence. He is going to convince the Council that a rescue mission is required. The details of which can be worked out after you get their permission. They'll understandably question his motives. They all know his relationship with Ralla; that's why he's there. So it will fall to you to convince them that getting her back by force is possible, and that you're the natural choice to lead the assault."

"Me? This week was the first time I've ever fired a weapon at anybody."

"Congratulations, you have more combat experience than every marine on this boat, and you've been on the *Pop*, something else that makes you uniquely qualified. We'll make sure you have the best team we can muster, but it's up to you."

"I can brief them on what they need to do. I don't need to be there."

"So they can get in harm's way to clean up your mess. Is that what you're saying?"

"No, I'm not..."

"Thom," the old man interjected. He shot a glance at Cern, who stood and left the room without a word. Mrakas' demeanor changed dramatically: he softened, letting his age and illness show. "I need you to do this. There is no way the Council will sanction a mission to get back one person. They have no interest, and most of them never liked me or my daughter to begin with. You and Cern are the only two that can convince the Council that this isn't madness, and you're the only one mad enough to actually make it work. Cern is a good man, but despite his looks, he's quite soft."

Thom resisted the urge to touch his face.

"I see a fighter in you Thom," Mrakas continued. "I see the potential for greatness. Had you been born up-bulkhead, you'd be where Cern is now. Probably higher. You've handled every challenge I've put in front of you—all except bringing my daughter home safely, and to be fair, I only asked you to bring my wife back. But you can do this, Thom. You need to do this. Get my daughter back. Go to the *Pop* and bring her back. If she's not there, tear the seas apart until you find her. But whatever you do, find her."

Thom let those words rattle around for a bit as he drifted towards the Council chambers. Cern was waiting outside. Thom let the silence between then grow nearly intolerable before breaking it.

"I would have hit you too."

That seemed to do it, and Cern relaxed a little.

"Cern, let me try something."

The Councilmembers filed back in and took their seats while Thom remained standing.

"Thank you for hearing me again and on such short notice. I have some understanding of our situation here. The buildup of our fleet and personnel is going slower than we'd hoped, and I can assume the *Population* continues to strike and occupy our mining and farming domes throughout the hemisphere." Thom saw a few subtle nods and kept going. "I have been thinking for a few weeks now of a plan that could delay the *Pop*, hopefully long enough for us to get up to full strength."

"Go on, Lieutenant Vargas," Larr said, legitimately interested.

"In the time I spent on the *Pop*, I saw enough to lead me to believe the sub would be extremely susceptible to sabotage. A few well-placed explosives would be enough to cripple the vessel, at least temporarily."

"And who would plant them?" Jills said, his tone neutral.

"I was able to get aboard the *Pop* once, I see no reason I couldn't do it again. Given some of the equipment I've seen being developed down below, I imagine it would be easy for me and a small team to sneak aboard, plant explosives, and get back out before anyone knew we were there."

"Does this have something to do with the... disappearance of Ms. Gattley?" one of the other Councilmembers asked. Thom didn't know his name.

"Insomuch as it's motivated me to bring my plan to your attention. The enemy is obviously getting bolder, and it's only a matter of time before we're discovered either by chance or on purpose. We need to put them out of the game long enough to build up our defenses." Thom stood tall, felt himself puff out his chest a little, only to be deflated by the throbbing ache of his face and the loose tooth his tongue couldn't help but pester.

Jills deliberated for a few minutes, and without consulting the Council said, "Coordinate with the marines for equipment and whatever men you need. Keep in mind, Lieutenant: I want every precaution taken. They must not find their way back to us should you be discovered. Do you understand what I'm saying?"

"Yes."

"And you still wish to proceed?"

"Yes, only because I don't think it will be as risky as you think. Getting onboard will be fairly simple. Getting back out again, presuming we have the right equipment, will be just as easy. I'm not suicidal, Proctor Jills. I believe I can do this."

"Then work out the details and report back to me. We'll proceed from there."

"Proctor Jills, I would like to request to be a part of Lieutenant Vargas' team," Cern said placing both hands on the table.

"No. Thank you, Thom. Please start your preparations."

Cern, startled, looked about to object, but it was clear Jills had ended the discussion. The meeting broke up as quickly as it started.

As Thom waited for the elevator down to the marine barracks, Cern caught up with him.

"That was pretty impressive back there. Were you really working on that plan for the past few weeks?"

"Of course I wasn't."

VII

It had been two days and Ralla could tell the tension in the room had built to a peak. What must have been squalid conditions weeks ago grew only worse as new prisoners were added to the mix twice a day. Groups started to congeal out of the crowd. Voices were raised. Angry glances were aimed at the guards. It wasn't long before the number of visible guards doubled. Then tripled. When soldiers came with food the next morning, the air was thick with the potential violence as people shoved their way towards the vats of gruel.

That evening, the guards with food came with shocksticks, and tapped out anyone who got too animated. This had the opposite effect as was surely intended. After the soldiers left, people became apoplectic. Ralla and Dija watched as a shoving match ensued. The tension was palpable, even among those too weak or too scared to get involved.

"I wish they would calm down," Dija said, sounding terrified. She had tucked her knees into her chest, and had resumed rocking. "I wish... I wish someone would say something." She rocked harder, gripping her legs so tightly that her fingers went white.

When the fight broke out, Ralla didn't see who threw the first punch. Fists flew, people tripped over others, who quickly joined the brawl in agitation. The fight spread like fire through the room. Ralla watched in horror as the guards fled, sealing the doors behind them. Dija buried her head between her knees and rocked violently as the room devolved into full-blown riot.

Ralla was only a few paces from the knee-high stand that only moments ago held the vats of food that triggered this mess. She closed her eyes and took a slow breath. After giving

Dija a comforting pat, she got up, walked to the stand, and stood on it.

She stood there, took another deep breath, and for the first time in her life exorcized a piercing, terrifying scream—not a scream for attention, nor one borne out of excitement. This was a scream of high-pitched, unadulterated terror. She took a moment to mentally thank her middle school acting teacher. The room stopped. No less than 6,000 eyes, all on her. She looked back at Dija. Across her gripped legs, she flashed Ralla an astonished smile.

"Can everyone hear me?" she said, projecting to the back of the room. She heard murmured affirmatives. "My name is Councilwoman Ralla Gattley. I represent the people of District 1. I took this role after my father, Mrakas Gattley, stepped down from the Council five months ago." As she suspected, she could hear her father's name whispered through the crowd.

"We need to stop fighting each other. Our enemy is outside these doors. So from this moment on we work together to help our wounded and to help each other. We will stop this fighting. The men and woman you see around you are in the same situation as you and I. We are prisoners, but we will not behave as such. We will not behave like any less than we are: Citizens of the *Universalis*. Now, I want everyone to sit down. Sit!" She stifled a laugh as the brawlers immediately plopped down where they stood, like obedient school children. "OK, now I want everyone with any medical training to come up here and make yourselves known. Everyone else, introduce yourself to your neighbors. The only way we'll be getting though this is together. OK, medical training, up here. Let's go!"

Ralla stepped off the stand and stood in front of it. Dija gave her a quick thumbs up. She saw people making their way through the seated crowd. Thanks Dad, she thought.

"It's a semi-rigid drysuit," the tech said, taking one off the rack. It hung in his hands like the carapace of an insect roughly Thom's size. The suit itself was black, while the armor pieces were a dark gray. It looked like scraps of a cut-up hardsuit grafted onto a normal wetsuit. Fitting, since Thom knew from a brief he'd read a few weeks earlier, that's pretty much exactly what it was. The tech rapped on the chest armor with his knuckles, proud of its apparent strength.

"It's non-conductive," he continued, "so if they hit you with any electrical weapons, you're safe. It's ablative, so you'll take the impact, but not the round. It's coated with light-absorbing paint, so it should take a few hits with laser weapons, no problem. All the angles were designed by computer to reflect the lowest amount back to the enemy's sensors. A squad of you guys in these would look no bigger than a shark. The suit underneath is pressurized, so you're good down to shelf depth, without a sub." At this Thom's eyes widened a bit. That was new. The tech spun the suit around. "The rebreather and pressurization unit are integral to the suit, obviously, and here at the lower back, under the breathing gear, are two small impellers to aid in swimming. Should be a little faster than swimming with fins, but for any real speed you're going to want one of our upgraded pullers. Would you like to see that?"

Thom shook his head. "What about the helmet?"

The tech showed a flash of personal pride and placed the suit back on the rack. From the shelf above, he brought down one of the helmets. It was of a similar angular aesthetic as the suit. The front was permiglass, as expected, but it was oddly rectangular on the sides, the top the only curve. With a final check to make sure he had Thom's total attention, the tech pressed a large flat button near where the ear would be. Instantly the face mask and entire front portion of the helmet retracted back into itself. The permiglass went up, the side pieces and bottom slid off to the sides. The tech was obviously pleased at Thom's amazement.

"It folds back so it's almost completely out of your peripheral vision. The whole helmet sits on watertight rollers, so you can turn your head while you wear it. It's about as close to not wearing a suit as we could figure out how to make." The tech hit the button again, and the mask snapped shut like the mouth of some freakish three-jawed beast. "It won't open without a voice override if it detects any pressure, so don't worry about bumping your head and popping it open."

"I have to tell you, Koin, this is amazing. How did you come up with this so quickly?"

The tech let out a little laugh that sounded like a small burst of air escaping from his nose.

"We've been working on the designs for years. Something we did in our free time, when we were bored, that kind of thing. There are some parts of this suit my father came up with when he had my job. There just hasn't been any need for it."

"Glad I could give you the need."

"Yeah! Well, no. I mean, you know what I mean."

"I do. How many of these do you have?"

"Seven is all we could build so far, but we're getting access to a manufacturing bay in a few days, so we should be able to equip two platoons' worth in a few weeks."

"Seven is good; I'll only need five. Let's talk weapons."

The tech motioned him into the next room of the lab cluster. When he looked past Thom to the door, Thom turned to see Cern standing in the doorway eyeing the suits.

"Koin, can you excuse us for a moment?" Thom said, not looking back at the tech. The man nodded unseen, and closed the door after him.

"I need to go with you."

"I don't think so, Cern."

"I can help. I need to go."

Thom looked him over, as if sizing him up for the first time. Cern was tall and well built. It was the kind of well built that showed he exercised and lifted weights. But there was a softness about him, not the kind of high muscle/low fat build someone would get as a byproduct of hard work. He moved with the relaxed manner of someone who had never been near any sort of danger.

"On the whole," Thom said finally, "I have to tell you, you're not much worse than the marines I'm paired up with. They all have this strutting macho attitude I'm positive is just show. I'm sure they'll wet their suits if we get into anything serious."

"Does the suit not handle that?" Cern said, nodding at the armor behind Thom.

"If it doesn't already, I'm sure Koin and his team could come up with a way to make piss into a weapon."

"That's comforting."

There was an uncomfortable silence again. A little piece of Thom wanted to be the one to rescue Ralla. The little boy inside him told him to say *no*. He recognized this as a little crazy, and a lot selfish.

"Thom, I'm sorry I reacted the way I did before. I understand now the situation you were in. Can I ask you to let me plead my case for a moment?"

"OK."

"Before you left, Ralla ended things between us."

Thom's heart jumped a double beat. There *had* been something there on the station.

"So you see, I need to come with you. I need to show her she was wrong. I know she needs me, Thom, and it's killing me. I have to save her."

Thom tried to mask his frustration. Of course he didn't want Cern to go, but clearly it was because he wanted to do exactly what Cern claimed *he* needed to do. If he said no, would it be on purely selfish grounds? On the other hand, if he said yes and Cern did save her, would that ruin whatever chance he might have with Ralla? He couldn't say no just because of that.

This was asinine, Thom realized. Ralla was incredible because she was a strong, intelligent woman. The core of the matter was that she needed rescuing; the rest they could work out later.

"I don't suppose you'll be officially going," Thom said rhetorically.

"Of course not."

"As far as the marines know, our mission is to poke some holes in the *Pop*. That's not why *I'm* going, of course. I guess it'd be smart to have someone back me up while I find Ralla."

"Any thought on how you'll do that?"

"Well, the plan is two groups of two, with me tagging along as an 'observer.' While they do what they do, I'm going blunder about calling her name. How's that sound?"

"So I'm in?"

"Why not? But we're going to need one more person in on our insanity."

"Who?"

"Koin, can you come in here for a second?"

The door opened and the tech entered. His long face showed suspicion.

"Koin, why don't you close that door and talk to us about your two extra suits."

Koin was a small man, but unlike many of his colleagues, he was kempt. His clothes and uniforms were always neatly pressed and he kept an antique brass comb with him. He would run the comb through his salt and pepper hair so often it had become something of a joke in his lab. He played it up, in on the joke, but even when no one was looking, he did it anyway. Such was the comfort it created. He stood by the heavily modified transport as a squad of men wearing his armor crossed the empty bay. He couldn't help but smile. They stood before him, mostly because he was blocking the rear ramp of the transport.

"Lieutenant Vargas, I just wanted to be here to see you off, and to say 'good luck'," he extended a hand to Thom, who shook it, the gray armored hand making Koin's seem like a small child's. "Your two packages are already on board," he said, motioning over his shoulder. "It's going to be a little rougher than we figured originally. We had to rip out most of the insulation and paneling so it would be buoyant with all the extra fuel and supplies."

"Thank you for all your help," Thom said, placing his gloved hand on the small man's shoulder. Koin moved aside and Thom followed the five marines up the ramp, closing it behind him. As he suspected, Sergeant Tegit had found one of the packages and was already livid.

"Who the hell is this?" he barked at Thom. At the beginning of training the Sergeant had thanked Thom for saving him in the sub a few months earlier. That thankfulness had lasted no more than a minute as the machismo and pride in his service took over. He hadn't been unpleasant, but that wasn't saying much. Right now his round face was flushed with anger.

"He's coming, end of story. You can complain about it when we get back." Thom pushed pass Tegit and the other four marines on his way to the cramped cockpit. There were two seats, but one person could easily touch the opposite side of the cockpit with his outstretched arm. The transport was meant for extended range missions, but that didn't mean the crew got any comforts. With all the modifications on this sub, the cargo wouldn't either. Flipping the toggles for the engines and systems, Thom hoped Tegit wouldn't notice the over-stuffed black satchel under Cern's seat.

The dead had been their first demand. When the soldiers ignored them, they lay the bodies by the door. As expected, the guards made it a priority to remove the corpses.

It had taken the rest of that night and nearly all the next day, but their ballroom prison was starting to show some levels of organization. The wounded were clustered in a corner, near one of the entrances and the water. There were only a few cots left over, so Ralla had Dija organize a lottery where each winner would get a night in a cot instead of the floor. If the winner wanted to give up the cot to another, they got extra rations for the next two meals. Ralla was surprised by people's enthusiasm. Making the ballots was the hard part, not least of which finding enough material to write on, and then wading through the room to collect all the names. It took Dija and a dozen helpers nearly the entire day.

New aisles and spaces were rearranged by a young math wiz research tech. Everyone got a little more space and it was easier to navigate. What had been sheer chaos was now starting to move toward some level of civilization. Ralla continued to be approached by people with useful skills, and kept a log on the faded wallpaper of who could do what. Throughout the day people would come to her with disputes or problems, most of which she resolved by shuffling people around. Two mornings after "the incident," the mood began to lighten a little. No one was *happy*, of course, but Ralla felt they had stared down the wall of the crevasse and taken a step back.

Then she was taken.

It happened fast. Four soldiers came in, walked right up to her, and marched her out. There wasn't enough time for anyone to register what had happened until she was already down the hall. She could hear shouts and commotion from the ballroom as the doors shut.

From the gentle curve of the hallway Ralla figured they were headed towards the bow. They took an elevator up a few floors before coming to a double door flanked by armed guards. The walls were plain white, the deckplates bare. This was a space built into the superstructure of the *Pop* itself, not a room on one of the ships-upon-a-ship. Ralla only knew of a few such spaces at the front of the *Uni*: the bridge, the command bunker, and a few small rooms that held comm equipment, computer mainframes, and such. In fact, across from the door they faced was the closed door of the *Pop* bridge. The door before them finally opened, and she couldn't help but marvel at the lavishness of the space.

The room was easily six times the size of her father's cabin. The floor was covered in thick cream carpeting. To her left was a seating area complete with soft fabric couches and a stone table, the wall behind covered in old books and various relics from the old world. To her right was a small bar with fancy blue and green colored lighting. The middle of the room held a long conference table made of what looked like wood. It was a little more than half the width of the room and could have easily held maybe 20 people, had there been that many chairs. There were only two.

Past the table there was a step up to a raised area at the back of the room. The left side held an enormous bed, the other side a pair of doors that led out to a balcony. She could see the lights and activity of the shipyard beyond.

Governor Herridki Oppai stepped from the balcony into the room. Ralla caught her breath and her escort gave her a nudge. Without thinking, she stepped in, and the door closed behind her.

Oppai stood silently, partially backlit from the bright lights of the shipyard. He wore a fitted dark green suit. His wavy hair was looser than when she had first seen it. There was something piercing about the way he looked at her, she felt, even from such a distance. Without taking his eyes off her, he made his way to the bar and starting making a drink.

"Can I fix you something?" His voice, even without amplification and a crowd, was still powerful. She shook her head no, but he poured them both a glass of wine anyway. Holding it in her hands, she watched him drink. For a moment, she considered pouring it out on the carpet.

"I'd prefer you didn't," he said, his smile broadening. She realized she had been focusing on the wine and looked up quizzically. "You look like you're thinking about pouring it out on the carpet. I'd prefer you didn't. It's rather fantastic wine, and if you don't want to drink it, I will. I also have a white, if you'd prefer."

His smile was disturbingly disarming. She took a sip and was annoyed to find that he was right. She took another sip when he turned away.

"Would you please join me?" he said, motioning towards the table. She didn't see him press any buttons but no sooner had he said it than a hidden door opened and two men carrying silver trays with bowls of soup and plates of food entered. The seats were facing each other across the narrow width of the table.

Oppai had already gotten around to the other side of the table when Ralla's legs started moving. It was the food, she kept telling herself. He waited for her to sit, then seated himself. On the plate was rice, some vegetables she couldn't identify, a roll, and a piece of something that looked like bird meat. It didn't hold up to what she could have found in any restaurant in The Yard, but at that moment it smelled positively gourmet. A piece of the meat—actual meat! she thought—was halfway to her mouth, when her brain got the better of her. She put it down, much to Oppai's disappointment.

"Governor Oppai, I would like to take this opportunity to insist you increase the rations to the hostages."

Oppai let out a small laugh between bites.

"No."

"The conditions are deplorable and unacceptable. I demand that you supply us with the food we need and return us to the nearest available dome."

A flash of something flickered across Oppai's face. Ralla couldn't make out what it was, but it hinted at anger. His demeanor had changed, the smile had gone. He placed his fork next to his plate and slowly finished chewing.

"Ms. Gattley, your people are being given no less than what the people on this vessel are eating. Are you saying that your people should dine better than mine?"

"No, I'm...wait, what?"

"It is sadly typical of people like you to expect such luxuries, when the regular people do with so little."

"Ummm..." she said, stabbing the fillet and holding it in the air.

"If I had known you were going to take my hospitality with such a lack of grace, I would not have invited you here."

"Invited? Are you kidding? Two armed guards dragged me here."

"Did they force you to drink my wine as well?

"That's not... That's not what happened. You're trying to..."

"Tell me, Ms. Gattley, how long did you think we were going to allow the *Universalis* to monopolize and horde the few resources left on this planet?"

"What? Our facilities barely cover one hemisphere."

"Are you sure of that? How many have you been to? How many have you seen on maps? How many were taken by force by soldiers from your ship?" Oppai had become visibly agitated, his face had flushed red. He pushed back from the table and stood. "Do you know who ordered innocent people killed on stations all across the hemisphere? Entire domes flooded, full of woman and children from the *Population*?"

Ralla said nothing, justifiably confused. Oppai seemed to change tactics.

"Your father, a great war hero, yes?"

"Yes," she conceded hesitantly.

"Have you ever asked *him* how many he killed, and why? How many people did he force to flee as he took their homes and jobs, taking it all for the *Universalis*?"

"No, that's not right. That's not what happened."

"How can you be sure? Who told you?"

"My father."

For a moment, it looked like Oppai smiled. It decayed hastily back to anger.

"Your Council has been systematically and surgically trying to eradicate the people of the *Population* for decades."

"No, that's not true!"

His anger turned into fury.

"We have tried war, and you crush us. We have tried peace, and you crush us. Well, no more. No more will we stand by and let you purge us from this world. Now we fight back. Not on your terms. Not on fair terms. You have taken fair and obliterated it. We will take back what is ours with the overwhelming force and might of the *Population* Fleet. And when we have taken what is ours, we will make you pay! Pay for every citizen of this great ship you have slaughtered. Then you will live by our rules. This world will be ours. Not yours. Not anymore. Not ever again!"

Oppai was near apoplectic, his whole body shaking. Ralla leaned back in shock. She looked around, but she was the only audience. Then, like a flushing out of a bay, the rage drained out of him, his face returned to its normal color, and he sat back down, as it nothing had happened.

"Good wine, yes?" he asked, taking a bite of the meat. Ralla couldn't think anything else to say.

"Yes."

"Sorry?"

"Yes," she answered more forcefully. This time she definitely saw the hint of a smile cross his face. A hint it may have been, but it was still the most unreadable, most unsettling smile she had ever seen.

The next morning, Ralla had Dija and her helpers start planting the seeds of a plan among the people. It was simple, and word was spread by whispers. When the soldiers entered with the vat of food, a wave of silence washed over the room. It was eerie how quickly everyone hushed. As the soldiers made their way to the stand, Ralla stood up, and in almost perfect unison, so did everyone else who was able. The rustle of clothes and shuffling of feet were the only sounds. Everyone turned to watch the soldiers.

Ralla took a peek at the rest of the room, and even she found it creepy, everyone standing, watching in silence. The soldiers there to deliver the food did so with spooked haste and made for the nearest door with almost comical expediency. The guards near the door kept their hands on their rifles, eyes nervously darting from silent face to silent face without locking eyes with any of them. The eyes definitely looked back, though. Only a few minutes had passed, but it was clear from the rapidly increasing anxiety of the guards that to them it seemed much longer. Finally one of the guards freed his shaky left hand from the barrel of his rifle and banged his palm against the door, which subsequently slid open. Still facing the crowd, the two guards on that door stepped outside. The guards on the other door almost immediately did the same.

Everyone near her cracked smiles, and Ralla bounded over to the stand with the food, and rose her arms in triumph. There was thunderous applause.

That evening, four guards took her again. She tried fighting them this time, as did a few others, but all were met with the butt of a rifle to the head or a fist to the gut. It was clear they were headed to the Oppai's cabin once again, and once again she saw no civilians, only soldiers.

After one of the guards pushed her out of the elevator, her temper flared, and she punched him—not in the face she was aiming for, but straight in the neck. The taller man staggered back into the elevator clutching his throat while the other three crowded around her menacingly, but no one touched her. She pushed one of them back, and from the way his eyes burned, not killing her was obviously a matter of some effort on his part.

They're under orders not to hurt me, she realized. The thought was fascinating, though somewhat confusing. She held up her hands, and motioned for them to proceed. They kept a tight cluster around her for the rest of the walk to Oppai, but they didn't make any further physical contact. By the time she entered the cabin, she was rather amused with herself.

The door slid shut, and she immediately went on the offensive.

"I demand to know what your plans are for the citizens you're holding against their will."

Oppai was pouring himself a drink and barely noticed that she had spoken. He wore a different fitted suit, light brown in color.

"Wine? I'm afraid we finished the one from last night. This one is, sadly, not quite as good."

She said nothing, but glared at him. He poured her a glass anyway.

"Shall we sit? Can I call you Ralla?"

"Councilwoman Gattley will be fine."

"Ralla is shorter. You may call me Herri."

He moved from the bar to sit on one of the sofas, and motioned for her to do the same. He placed the wine intended for her on the table.

She begrudgingly obliged to the sofa, but let the wine sit. He lounged in silence, sipping his wine, his eyes never leaving hers.

"Are you going to answer my question?" she finally asked.

"Well, for the moment, you're all fine and I don't see much reason to change anything. It won't be long before we've taken control of the *Uni*. After that we'll undoubtedly have work for you to do."

Ralla scowled at him.

"What else did you expect? Letting you go is not an option, and it's not like I can have you swim home. I need the resources you and your people had, and the prisoners below impeded that effort. You should be thankful we just didn't kill them all."

"But that's just it, why can't you let us go? Why are you doing this? If you were doing so badly, why didn't you ask for our help? We could have worked together."

"My people feel that you would sooner kill us than help us."

"They feel that way because *you* tell them to feel that way, with your pep rallies and propaganda."

Herri looked puzzled for a moment. "How would you know that...?" but even as the words came out of his mouth, his eyes widened. "It was you. It was you who got onboard and stole our sub, wasn't it? Do you know how long it took to clean up that mess?" There was no malice in his voice. If anything, he seemed amused. "I am impressed. You come across like this privileged Daddy's girl. I guess I'll have to keep that in mind."

Ralla said nothing.

"Well, it's too late for that now," he said, shrugging his shoulders.

"Why? Why is it too late? We can contact the *Uni* right now. I can talk to the Council. We can stop all this tonight and start working together. There's so few of us left."

"For starters, you know that's not true."

"What's not true?"

"You'd never be able to convince your Council to work with the people of this ship. There have been too many generations of hatred."

"What are you talking about? Most people on my ship hadn't even heard of the *Population* before you attacked our dome. I hadn't thought of this ship since my grade school history classes. Even the people of my father's generation that fought in the last war haven't held a grudge."

Oppai looked like he hadn't expected this. He quickly recovered with another shrug.

"You don't understand what it was like here barely a year ago. There were food riots at least once a week. Many of the cabins were so unsafe as to be uninhabitable. People were being murdered for their ration chits. What food we could grow, half would be stolen. A chunk of the other half would end up on the black market. We didn't have the manpower to police the population, and the police we did have were corrupt. We were *this* close to complete anarchy."

Herri stood, and swirled the rest of his wine around in his glass.

"Then I stepped in. Before I ran for office, I..." The statement just sort of hung in the air. And when the words stopped, Ralla noticed that everything about him stopped. It wasn't until he started talking again, having sorted out his thoughts, that he even appeared alive at all. "I have a certain knack. A gift, if you will, of explaining. A gift of getting people to listen, to believe. People have always looked to me for direction. So running for office was a natural thing; it just became a matter of timing. To win, though, to be sure of a win, I needed to promise them something. Something big. So I promised them you. You were the cause of all their problems. The old regime had been hiding the facts. You were stealing all the resources. You were waging a war of attrition. It was easy. People *wanted* to believe. The violence stopped overnight. We started putting people to work building the new fleet. We tore out all the old ships from inside the hull and converted them to new subs.

"But it's all lies. There have to be people who realize that."

"Is it? Is it a lie? Your people control the resources that my people need, for reasons too complex for most people to understand. I've merely taken that truth and... simplified it. My predecessor took over our only media a decade ago. The government has all the mainframes. We inserted reports, stories, testimonies dating back years to show the *Universalis*'s treachery. Within a few weeks, the citizens of this great ship were united. It's easy to get people to rally around a common enemy, wouldn't you agree? "

Ralla grimaced at his obvious reference. Oppai smiled his eerie smile, and continued. "My people have pulled together in a way they haven't since the last war. They're happy now, or as happy as can be. They don't care that they have no food and live in squalor. They're willing to make sacrifices because they know it's for the greater good. And that greater good is the destruction of the people who put them in this situation."

"But you're lying to them. You're creating this conflict, this animosity. You're killing innocent people."

"*Your* people."

"*Our* people! It's just *people* you maniac. We all come from the same place. You have to stop this." Ralla stood and leapt over the table. She knocked the glass out of his hand and grabbed him by the tailored suit. "Stop this. Stop all of this. You created this mess, this insanity. You can stop this. Please, you must stop this!"

Oppai gently but firmly removed Ralla's hands from his suit and held her by her wrists.

"Hating you was the best thing for my people."

"You couldn't possibly believe that."

"I took the rage of a populace on the brink of annihilating itself and turned it somewhere else. If you honestly think there's any way to calm that sort of rage without giving it an outlet, then you are every bit the naive girl I first thought. Look. *Look at them.*" He took her by the wrist and walked her out onto the balcony. The briny air was thick with the smells of metalwork and construction. The war machine in the shipyard hadn't abated, subs of all sizes being built, modified, armed and readied. He made a sweeping motion with his free arm. "These people live with purpose. An energy and a purpose and *I* got them here. *I* saved them from ruin. So no, Ralla. I'm not going to stop anything. This is better than anyone could have dared dream just a year ago. We have jobs, we have food, we have mining and farming domes."

"Which you stole!"

"Which my people needed. Still need. But soon we'll take the *Universalis* and our needs will be met."

"Killing thousands of innocent people as a consequence."

"Their innocence is known only to myself, my Cabinet, and you. My Cabinet I trust implicitly."

"Was that a threat? Are you going to kill me?" Ralla asked, surprised at her lack of fear. This close to the railing of the balcony, she figured she could bring him with her if he tried anything. Seeming to notice where she was looking, he led her back inside. The smile returned.

"No, Ralla, I have no interest in killing you. The guards will see you back to your, shall we say, accommodations."

Thom was tired of sitting in the dark. They had struck out at the first dome they'd snuck up on, its docking bays empty. The second was perfect timing. From the thermal layer above, they could see a transport being loaded through the permiglass dome. The place was lit so brightly, they had joked they could have seen the thing from the surface. They waited for a few hours for the sub to leave, then shadowed it.

It kept a straight course for the better part of a day, then on the long range sensors Thom made out a blip. They slowed, cut power, and dropped beneath the thermal. Sure enough, the *Pop* loomed in the distance. They determined its course, and rose above the thermal. This time, there was no one else around. They sped off for their intercept position.

The intercept was a planned version of how Ralla and Thom had gotten on the *Pop* in the first place. They cut all power to their sub, slowly descended to the sea floor, and landed softly on a bed of gray silt. Then it was a waiting game. They calculated that if *Pop* continued on the same course it would pass over them in six hours. Plenty of time to eat and drink their rations and get in a short nap.

If all went according to plan, they would flood the rear compartment and float up to the passing sub, all but invisible. Finding a way in would be the tricky part, but they were prepared to hang on for a little over two hours for the ship to stop and open a bay. If it took longer than that, they would let go, return to the transport, and start over at a different location. Thom didn't relish that idea, as the tiny suit motors could only propel them at a fraction of the speed the *Pop* moved. Worst case it would be nine hours in a suit in the dark.

The main sensor screen, set to its lowest brightness, showed a mass moving in their direction exactly at the calculated time. Thom switched it off and put on his helmet. The others did the same. He sealed the cockpit behind him. Tegit activated the pumps that would store the air in the compartment, replacing it with water. In the dark, with just the glow of their helmet readouts, Thom would have been surprised to find a single man in the bunch who wasn't terrified. He looked over at Cern, whose ghostly face looked ready to snap. Thom grabbed Cern by the shoulder and locked eyes with him. Cern closed his eyes and let out a long slow breath. His eyelids rose slowly, but he seemed stable, if not relaxed.

The cabin fully flooded, they opened the hatch and stepped out onto the dark sea floor.

VIII

This time, after they stood in unison, they started to chant "food," quietly at first, but with quickly escalating volume. Stomping feet soon followed, a few at first, then a few more. Soon the noise was deafening, the shouting, the chanting, the banging of the feet.

Two more soldiers entered carrying a large square device between them. They set it on the platform where the food was usually set. One pressed a button on the side, and a projected image filled the wall above and between the two double entrance doors. The image was of the room they were in, from a camera somewhere above the projector. The noise slowly abated as people tried to see what was going on. The image of the room was replaced by a new image, and the near explosive energy in the room was extinguished as if by open lock. The image was of Ralla, with a plate of food, glass of wine in her hand. Murmured confusion rippled through the crowd. Those near Ralla looked in her direction, their faces looking for explanation. Then it got worse.

The image was actually a video. Speakers hidden in the walls supplied audio. It cut to Oppai, looking resplendent in his dark green suit. This must have been recorded at a different time, she though, as he was in mid paragraph explaining who he was. Then it cut back to her, just her face. This was from the night before, where she had said her name and title. Then it showed the wine glass in her hand, mostly empty. There must have been cameras all over the room. The next shot was Oppai, starting one of his bizarre rants.

"Do you know who ordered innocent people killed on stations all across the hemisphere? Entire domes flooded, full of woman and children?"

Then it cut back to her.

"My father."

The shock hit her entire body at once. All she could do was collapse to her knees. Her mouth agape, her whole body paralyzed with the horror of it. Yet she couldn't look away.

"Your Council has been systematically and surgically trying to eradicate the people of the *Population* for decades."

"Yes," her projected avatar responded, forcefully.

The video continued with Oppai's questions and her with either a dismissive look, or worse, one of her many yeses. The video ended with Oppai's grand tirade that had seemed so confusing two nights before. The video went black, then Oppai appeared again, this time with the backdrop of the shipyard. He wore an outfit similar to what he wore when he addressed the crowd months earlier; neat, but not as showy as the suit from the video.

"Men and women of the *Population*, the video you have just seen was recorded on the security cameras in the Dignitary Dining room. I had invited a representative from the *Universalis* here to see if we could come to some peace between our two peoples. As you can see, I was met by condescension and disdain. When I asked her up front about their role in our troubles, she didn't deny it. She didn't even try to hide it. It is clear to me that we mean nothing to them. They would as soon have us die as to lend us a handful of grain. It saddens me, but we will be proceeding to the next stage of our action against the *Universalis*. It is our only path to peace, and our only path to survival. Thank you, everyone." The screen went dark.

Ralla couldn't move. She kept her eyes shut, but could feel all the others in the room burning holes in her flesh. They would have no way of knowing it was cut-and-pasted lies. It would be her word against a video. And with the food and wine, why would they believe her? She had failed. These people would never listen to her again. She had failed them, and she had failed her father. There was a part of her, a familiar part, that just wanted to hide, have her father fix it. But as this thought fully formed in her head, she rejected it. He wasn't here. But she was.

No. If they wanted to believe him, that was their choice. But not without a fight. She wasn't going to sit back and let this psycho twist the minds of *her* people with her own twisted words. Eyes still closed, she stood and started walking towards where she knew the platform was. She opened her downcast eyes and watched the worn red and gold carpet pass under her feet. People moved out of her way. She could hear whispers, but couldn't make out what was being said.

At last, she reached the platform and stood, facing the room. At last, she opened her eyes. She didn't focus on any of the faces, but they were all looking at her. Then, off to the side, her eyes focused on Dija. The tiny young woman stood rubbing her hands together. On her face wasn't anger, or even astonished disbelief. It was confusion. Ralla looked at other faces. Some were clearly angry, but most were like Dija. Confused. Waiting for... Waiting for...

Then it hit her. It hadn't worked. His plan had failed. They were waiting for her to explain. To explain what they had just seen, because they didn't believe it. She lifted her right hand high over her head, and put her left hand over her heart.

"On my life, and on my father's life, everything you just saw was a lie," Ralla said in so serious a tone that she didn't recognize her own voice. A few in the audience motioned to their neighbors in a *"See?"* gesture. The rest remained unconvinced.

"I was taken from this place each of the last two nights against my will. I drank the wine Governor Oppai gave me the first night and had you smelled it, let me tell you, you would have too. I thought we would be having some sort of meeting to discuss our situation, but when he brought out such a lavish meal, I suspected his motives were otherwise. I was hungry, as we all are, but I didn't have the stomach to eat. Not when none of us has eaten real food in a week or more. What you saw on that video, as I hope many of you suspect, was an edited version of several conversations between myself and the Governor. Now, if you want to believe him over me, that is your right. All I can say is that I know many of you have met my father. If you've met him you know he could never do the things he stands accused of. As far as the Council goes, no current member of the Council was in office the last time we had contact with the *Population*. The longest serving current member has been in office less than 10 years. And if you think any policy or doctrine could survive the changeover, well, I know all of you see how little the Council agrees on; how could you expect them to have held one policy together for decades? Sorry, I don't think so." She looked around the room now, and knew she almost had them back on her side.

"You shouldn't be surprised by a stunt like this. We are organized, we are angry, and that makes our captors nervous. If you want to believe him and go back to the way we were, fine. But I'll tell you right now, I won't give up on us until you tell me to. You trusted me once, and we are all better off for it. Please, trust me now. I would never say those things. I would never have betrayed you, my father, or the *Uni*. If you don't want me leading you, fine. But I'm still going to help in any way I can. You just let me know what you want. And if you still don't believe that I'm on your side..." She stepped off the platform and walked directly towards the two soldiers, who eyed her with caution. She walked up to the right one, punched him in the neck—this time on purpose—and removed his sidearm as he stumbled. This could be tricky, she thought. But as she turned towards the other solider, she realized she needn't have worried; his rifle was already up, the butt about to slam into her face.

It was an eerie silence that accompanied them as they ascended to meet the *Population*. As they drifted up through crushing darkness, the *Pop* moved forward, its ominous dark shape looming malevolently above them.

Tegit's men had their weapons strapped to their thighs. A collapsed carbine rifle on the left, and a pistol sidearm on the right. Cern and Thom had just the sidearm. Cern, though, clutched to his chest a black satchel, one of its handles wrapped around his wrist. A thin cable made out of some fiber Thom had never seen connected them all by the waist. Thom was at one end, Tegit the other, but the group lacked any real formation. They swam up, not wanting to use their suits' motors out in the open. The neutral buoyancy gave them better control over where they landed on the hull. It had all seemed smart in the briefing, but in practice it turned out to be exhausting.

Thom felt a hand on his leg and looked down. They were observing comm silence, but the suits had short range line-of-sight laser transmitters. From below, he could see Tegit staring at him. His voice came over Thom's helmet's speakers, tinny and echoey.

"They're moving too fast to have open bay operations. I think we should go to plan 'B' and just latch on where we can and wait for them to stop."

"Sounds good," Thom replied, knowing that it didn't. Any decent fisherman could tell you that bigger the fish was, the slower it appeared to swim. And the *Pop* was a big fish. As fast as it seemed to be moving, Thom knew its actual speed would be brutal. Within moments they were close enough to see the error in their optimism. The textures of the hull, so distinct mere moments ago, became a blur in the blink of an eye. And somehow, they were going to have to get ahold of that blur.

They activated their suits' propulsion units, and tried to minimize the difference in speed they best they could. Thom was the closest, with each member of the team down the line farther from the sub. The *Pop* appeared to slow as he accelerated, and he pushed upwards into the turbulent water churning around the hull. Thom nearly pulled his fingers out out of socket grabbing hold of the outer lip of one of the small bays near the keel. He couldn't hold on, so he readied a magbolt as the hull slipped past him. Koin had confidently hung from the ceiling in his office using a single magbolt, made from the same material as the ship's electric motors. Thom had his doubts, but jabbed it against the hull, closing his eyes as the line went taught.

Being simultaneously accelerated to the speed of the *Pop* and slapped against the hull knocked the wind out of Thom.

Down the line, each man hit with greater and greater force as the bolt held strong and the line went taught. Thom turned in time to see Sergeant Tegit, the last in line, slam violently into the hull knee first, certainly shattering it. He took small comfort in the fact that no one could hear the scream he saw through Tegit's helmet. His relief was short-lived, though; the other men turned in time to see Tegit rebound and slam back into the hull, again and again. When the bouncing stopped, Tegit's body was limp.

Thom felt every impact though the hull, and was worried that someone inside would have heard it as well. There was nothing to be done about it, though. The hull stretched out in every direction, like a sky, just darker than the world below it. They hung there, the sound of the water rushing by their only reminder of the world, buffeted by the force of it, like a piece of seaweed caught on the keel.

More than anything at that moment, Thom wanted a drink.

He must have passed out; when he came to, the clock inside his helmet said close to two hours had passed since they had left the transport. That meant he had been unconscious for almost an hour. Thom tilted his head down, and saw the row of men behind him, all trying to be as streamlined as possible, hanging onto the rope that secured them at the waist to the ship above. They were coming up on decision time. He used his right foot to tap the man below him, who looked up after a second, disoriented. He had passed out too. Thom used his tongue to activate the laser transmitter.

"Send down to Sergeant Tegit, see if we can rouse him, find out what he wants us to do. We're coming up on no return."

"Copy," came the reply. With the dark suits and poor audio, Thom had no idea who it was and he couldn't remember the order in which they'd strapped themselves together. The man mimicked Thom's procedure to the man below him.

It was several minutes before the reply came back up the chain.

"Tegit is still unconscious. He may be dead for all we know. What do you want to do, Vargas?"

The adrenaline came on in a wave, being carried in from his chest by panic. He looked at the clock. If they didn't leave soon, they wouldn't have enough air to get back to the transport. Even if they did sneak on board at this point, without the *Pop* stopping, they'd be as good as trapped on the ship, stuck too far from their transport.

"Hey Ralla, I'm here to rescue you. By the way, any idea how to get home?" he said to the inside of his helmet. He shouldn't have come. He shouldn't be here. He was perfectly happy being a fisherman. He was good at it. The hours were good. The responsibilities were negligible.

No, that wasn't true. But this? Tegit could be dead, and the lives of the other five guys were in his hands. He was the only one who could disconnect the magbolt. His body ached from the swim and the constant hammering into the hull. He could pull the bolt, and get back home in a few days. Only two people had expected him to do this. Cern was here; he must know what had happened. The mission was a failure. They already had a man down. They had planned wrong from the beginning with this open water assault. It was stupid. Some other team could come next time, to get in when the ship was stopped. They could send someone else to get Ralla. Someone qualified. Someone competent.

Ralla. He saw her face. Not the face he saw last, covered in blood and taken over with *the look*. The face he saw was laughing at one of his idiotic jokes. Her eyes pinched closed when she laughed. His mind drifted to one of their walks through the Yard, to giving him a hug after he had said something sweet. Her hair smelled of some fruit he knew only by scent, but really wanted to taste. It was how she looked at him. Not as some lazy fisherman, not as some below-decks nothing, but as a person, as someone who could be with someone like her.

Then came the memory of her bloodied on the deck. Of the fear behind her eyes and the men surrounding her. Something started to form inside him. It started deep in his chest, like he could reach in and hold it in his hand. It was unfamiliar, this thing. But he knew it by its name, and its name was *rage*.

Thom looked back down to the marine below him, who was still waiting for an order.

"I have to stay. I'm staying. There is someone on board this ship I have to rescue. This has nothing to do with your mission, so you can go if you want. If you leave now, you can get back to the transport and back to the *Uni*. If you come with me, I have no idea what will happen. But I promise I will do everything I can to make sure we get home and before that, mess up this ship something good."

There was a pause.

"This someone a she?" came back the tinny response.

"Yes."

"You're risking all this for a girl?"

Before Thom to respond, the marine continued.

"When I meet her, she better be worth it. I take it you want me to ask Hollus and the rest to come with us?"

"Yes, and thank you."

The marine turned to face the person below him. Guilt now entered the mix of emotions as the water rushed noisily by. He couldn't remember the marine's name.

Her head throbbed worse than she could would have thought she could tolerate and she could feel her face had puffed up. It was already sore; doubtless it would only get worse. Smiling was the worst, but she was thankful for reasons to smile nonetheless. A steady stream of supporters had come over to tell her they believed her. She lay propped up against the wall while a makeshift receiving line of people filed past, shaking her hand, thanking her, comparing her to her father.

Others, though, still sitting throughout the room, looked at her with distrust in their eyes. No malice or hatred, at least not directed at her, that she could see. But certainly no warmth.

Perhaps the biggest change had been in Dija. The quiet bookish introvert had completely disappeared. She had been replaced by an effective and efficient organizer, taking over Ralla's role as unofficial leader, making sure the wounded got what they needed, that food lines stayed organized, and disputes were mediated.

There had been no new arrivals for several days, but Ralla was sure Dija could have found places for them and made it all work. The younger woman was a natural, and her new confidence had had an almost physical effect on her. She looked people in the eyes, stood up straight, and spoke with authority. She still asked Ralla questions throughout the day, but it seemed like she had everything under control. Dija had insisted Ralla rest a bit, and with the flow of people all wanting to voice their loyalty and support, Ralla had little time to do anything else.

But as she sat there, thanking people and shaking hands, her brain had shifted from plans of mere survival of these people—her people—to a plan of escape.

Thom and his team had passed the three-hour mark, and all six of them still hung from the bottom of the *Population*, now committed to getting aboard. After that was anyone's guess. Thom was starting to question his decision; electric jabs of fear tried to chip away at his new-found drive. Each time he would picture her face, and his purpose would be refreshed.

Perhaps there was some way to force the lock open.

Suddenly, they were blinded by light. The bay lock they were dangling from started to open, the light driving their eyes closed after so many hours in the near total darkness. The *Pop* must have slowed down enough to begin operations. A few moments passed before a cargo sub dropped into the water and without delay descended away from the hull. There was no time to worry about what may lay inside the bay. They had all trained for this next step, and would do what had to be done. He looked back, and the marine behind him gave Thom the agreed upon hand gesture to show that everyone was ready. Everyone but Tegit, he was sure.

Thom activated his suit's thrusters using the pad on the back of his left hand, and it was enough to push him forward under the opening. It was like lying on his back at the bottom of a pool, the view even more distorted by the moving water. From what he could see, there were no people in the immediate area around the opening, though he knew he couldn't see far. He bent at the waist, letting the thrusters in the suit and the current of the water push him past the lip of the hull and propel him up enough to get his chest out of the water. He hit the lip hard with his stomach, the armor of the suit absorbing enough of the blow that it didn't knock the breath out of him. Thom struggled to swing a leg over, but as soon as it was out of the water, he was able to roll on his back on the bay floor and remove his pistol. The bay was empty. One by one the men exited the water. They helped Cern with his satchel, and hauled the lifeless Tegit onto the deck.

The bay was similar to the one Ralla and he had entered months earlier. There were two other subs nearby, both cargo subs, their rear holds open and awaiting goods. Thom motioned to the men, and they silently carried Tegit into the nearest one. They all toggled their helmets, the sound of the masks slamming open echoing through the bay.

Tegit was in bad shape, but alive. His face was caked in dried blood, and he didn't respond to repeated attempts to wake him.

Thom was unsure what to do at this point. They couldn't bring his body with them as they searched the ship. But could they risk leaving him alone? He looked around at the men, all visibly exhausted.

"Options? Go," he said, motioning to the marine whose name he couldn't remember.

"One of us needs to stay with him."

Cern's face wrinkled.

"What would that accomplish?" Cern replied. "So both of you can be captured? We strip him and leave him somewhere where someone will find him. They won't know he's not one of theirs who had an accident."

"We can't leave him here," Soli snapped back. Soli! *That* was the marine's name. Soli was small, but moved fast and seemed all muscle. The hulking marine Lo just shrugged his big shoulders.

The last, the taciturn Huth, said nothing, but continued to prod Tegit.

"Huth?" Thom said, getting the man's attention.

"Well, my two weeks of medic training I guess make me the most qualified here to make a judgment. His left knee and right femur are totally busted. My guess is, his ribs are cracked or something, too. If you listen to his breathing, there's a pretty creepy wheeze going on. His pupils are different sizes, too. I don't remember what that means, but I'm pretty sure it isn't good."

"Is there anything you can do for him?" Cern asked, though not with much apparent empathy.

"No idea. I can reset the leg. We can make a splint on top of the armor. For the rest, I don't know. If he's bleeding internally or something, I don't think he'll make it back to the *Uni.*"

"All right, look, we're not leaving him here," Thom said, surprised at his commanding tone. "Even if we dump him in their med bay, at some point they're going to figure out he doesn't belong here, and I doubt that'll end well. And we have to assume this cargo sub is going to be used for something. If not, we'll use it to get out of here. That is, if we don't find something better. Huth, make up the splint. Lo, Soli, I want you to scout around, quietly. See if there is some place nearby we can store these two for a few hours. Cern and I will look too. We'll meet back here in 15 minutes.

It only took ten. Lo discovered that the next bay over was storage for old subs, their hulls stripped of all useful material. In the corner away from either door, there was even a pile of hatches and deckplates. It took them another 20 minutes, working as quietly as they could, to fashion a makeshift fort out of the parts. They carried Tegit into the metal and plastic cave. From anywhere but right on top of the shelter, you couldn't tell it was anything but a pile of garbage. Thom, meanwhile, found a storage locker filled with soiled ceil blue coveralls. He took four of the cleanest that looked to fit the members of the team.

"If you're compromised, use your best judgment," Thom said to Huth, who didn't need to be told he was staying with Tegit. "I'd say shoot first, then alert us. This room is pretty defensible, so I figure you'll be able to hold out till we come running. To be honest, if any of us is discovered it's pretty much game over, so let's try to be as quiet as possible. Enable channel jumping algorithm '1.'"

Each of them checked the controls on the back of his gloves and nodded. Huth did the honors for Tegit.

"Lo, you and Cern are going to proceed with the mission that brought us here. We're going to need it as a distraction if we're going to escape. Start with the engines, then work your way forward. Set the detonators for 12 hours from now and on remote. We're going to stagger check-ins; the first will be 45 minutes from now."

"I'm coming with you," Cern said, his tone leaving no room for argument. Thom knew he was right. It was risky having him go with Lo, given his lack of real training. At least searching for Ralla had less chance of accidental explosion. There was a huge part of him that didn't want Ralla to see Cern until after he had a chance to talk to her. To rescue her. He recognized this as childish, didn't care, but still decided it was crazy.

"OK. Soli, you go with Lo and Cern will come with me."

They piled their armor with Huth, each taking just a sidearm. They set the thin trapezoidal communicators to vibrate, removing them from their gloves and placing them in their pockets. Soli and Lo took all the compact packages of high explosives. The multiple pockets in the coveralls swallowed everything, and looked no more bulky then when they were empty.

"OK, remember your accents, always look like you know where you're going, and we should be fine. Gentlemen," Thom said, looking each man in the eye in turn. "Thank you again, and good luck."

When the elevator door opened, Thom and Cern exited and stood slack-jawed at the sight of it all. Cern marveled at the differences between the interiors of the *Pop* and the *Uni*. Thom, was staggered by the differences between the *Pop* he remembered and the one before him now. He quickly looked around to see if anyone had noticed the two men in coveralls acting so surprised. To his relief, there was no one in sight.

There was no one in sight. Odd. The concourse food stalls were all closed and there was no foot traffic on the walkways. Even in the gardens he couldn't make out any movement. The light was bright enough for mid-day, but it seemed the place was deserted. Cern was still taking it all in.

"This space is amazing," he said, face to the "sky."

"It was even bigger before; that whole wall is new," Thom replied, still trying to find a trace of the *Pop* citizenry. Cern turned his gaze down the length of the sub, and took in the new wall for the first time.

"They built that in just a few months? Out of what?"

"Good question. Come on, we need to get out of the open."

Cern looked around at their level and noted the absence of people.

They kept to the edges, the cliffs of former ships towering over them, makeshift balconies and patios keeping them in shadow. They passed a few people, who smiled politely on their way to somewhere else. Thom relaxed slightly, knowing they could pass for natives. Cern started to get jumpy, though.

"How are we going to find Ralla? What if they're keeping her some place we can't get to? There's thousands of rooms on this thing. What if they just stuck her in some random cabin? How would we know? What if..."

Thom grabbed Cern's arm as they continued walking, silencing the taller man.

"We've been looking for minutes. Someone knows where she is. If it's not obvious, like a brig or a holding pen somewhere, we'll just have to be creative."

"I don't understand."

"Look at what you're wearing. How many times a day do you see someone dressed like this?"

"I don't know."

"Exactly. We're invisible. We make it look like we know where we're going, and everyone will assume we're off to fix an engine or patch a leak, or whatever it is that people dressed like this do. The people we've passed haven't given us a second glance. As long as we're careful, we'll probably be able to walk right into wherever they're holding her."

"And if that doesn't work?"

"Then we start shooting. I don't know, we haven't got there yet."

They continued in silence, making their way towards the new wall. They could hear the low rumble of heavy machinery as they approached. Thom reached out to touch the patchwork of deck and hull panels that had been fused and welded together to form the surface.

"They must have torn up half the ship to build this," Cern said, following a weld with his finger. "It's a wonder they have living spaces left." He stopped short as Thom froze.

"The domes. All the people. They're in our domes," Thom said, the weight of it all hitting him. "They're converting this into a pure warship and dumping the civilians into our domes."

"No... Why would... Can you imagine? We don't exactly under-populate. It must me horrific down there. What do you think, doubling, maybe tripling the inhabitants of each dome?"

"That's if they didn't displace our people," Thom replied somberly.

"Oh..." Cern said, going slightly pale. "What if Ralla's in one of the domes? How would we find her then?"

Thom took a moment to consider this.

"If they don't know who she is, and she's down on some dome, then she's as safe as anyone else. If they know who she is, she's here. If she's here, we'll find her. Let the Council figure out the rest. Come on, let's try the elevator in this wall, I want to see what they're doing on the other side of this thing."

"Lo, this is Thom," he said as the elevator doors sealed themselves shut behind him. His voice held fear. There was a pause, then the communicator buzzed with an incoming signal. Thom double-checked to make sure the transmission was scrambled, then put it to his ear as the doors opened again and he and Cern stepped back out onto the concourse.

"Go ahead."

"After you're done in the engine room, I'm going to need you to head forward."

"Why, what's going on?"

"The entire bow of the ship has been converted to some sort of shipyard factory. There's hundreds of subs in there. Hundreds."

"Wow. OK, Soli and I are finding a few choice spots, then we'll head that way. Is the rest of the ship as empty as it is down here?"

"Yes."

"Why?"

"We can talk about it later. This is close enough to our check-in time. Let's talk again in one hour."

"Got it." Lo's booming voice still sounded huge from the thumbnail sized speaker in the communicator.

Thom turned to look at Cern, who was bracing himself against an abandoned food stall. He was the palest Thom had ever seen him, his normal healthy patina replaced with a sickly pallor. He was visibly frightened. Vomit erupted from him, covering the side of the food stall. He dropped to one knee, shaking.

"I agree," Thom said.

Ralla was sure that her captors viewed her stares as contempt. In truth, she stared because the guards were consuming her thoughts at the moment. They had returned to their posts the night before, and while jittery, they were no more aggressive than they had been before. More importantly, they were still armed. That was the mistake. Ralla was sure none of the young men—they all looked even younger than she—would enter the makeshift prison now without weapons. The irony was that those weapons endangered more than protected them. With enough people—no, the right people—her band of refugees could overpower these four, take their weapons, and advance on the unsuspecting soldiers in the hallway. With any luck, before any of them could signal for help. With a lot of luck, they might be able to do it without anyone getting killed.

A lot of luck, and that was the problem. Poorly trained as these guards were, their lack of training made them unpredictable. They might give up, or they might just spray the crowd with fire. There was no way to be sure. She tapped Dija on the back.

"Yeah?" Dija said, rolling over.

"Can you make me a list of everyone who's had any sort of combat training? I know we don't have any military people, but even if it's just workout stuff, a hobby, anything."

"Yeah, give me a few minutes?"

Ralla nodded and leaned back against the wall, her eyes still on the guards. She was going to have to lead it, whatever they ended up doing. Not out of any need for leadership; a bar fight is a bar fight. But if she was going to risk these people's lives, she needed to be at risk too. There was no way else to stomach it.

Unsurprisingly, the thought of bar fights turned her mind to Thom. It was odd how in just the past few days, her perception of him had completely changed. What had started as an innocent crush on this guy—a new and exciting fascination with someone so unlike any she had ever met— had evolved. Now when she thought of him, she saw his strength, even if he didn't see it himself. It was odd: thinking of him now warmed her. She knew she was glamorizing him a bit, but she let herself have the fantasy. She wished for a moment that he were here, so he could take over.

No, she laughed to herself, if he were here she'd still be in charge. She played back that thought in her head, and it ceased to be a joke. She thought it through again. Of course she'd be in charge. She'd be in charge not because of who her father was or for the lack of someone better, but because that's what she did. She led. She was good at getting people to follow her, and to inspire people to do more. Not because of her last name, but because of her.

It was the kind of thought that, once formed, seemed obvious all along. Of course she'd lead the fight against these guards, and they'd win, because they had to. She could do it.

Dija had finished and had rolled back over to hand her the piece of white plastic they had been using as an erasable writing surface.

"There are five or six more that might work, but these twenty have direct experience with some kind of hand-to-hand combat, even if it was mostly glorified calisthenics. It's the best I can do," Dija looked at Ralla, trying to judge her reaction. Ralla studied the names, twelve men and eight women. It would have to do.

"Thank you, Di," Ralla said, flipping the plastic over to the other side. She started sketching a floor plan of their ballroom prison. "This is what I want you to do."

Thankfully, the guards merely dismissed the strategic rearrangement of people as the usual shuffling around that always followed dinner. Even better, there was a guard change before they lowered the lights, so the new guards didn't notice that the people near the doors were different then they were the night before, and looked a whole lot healthier.

Ralla had counted on a force of twenty people with some sort of training. As word spread what they were doing, and it spread quickly, her twenty became close to a hundred. She turned away close to two hundred more. It seemed that too many days with little food and no showers had pushed everyone to a new level of urgency. She worried that the even the ones who did make the cut were a little too enthusiastic about her plan, no matter how hard she harped on the risks.

The plan was simple, though: An initial wave of her and her twenty "soldiers" would take down the guards; the second wave would follow after to overwhelm the soldiers outside.

Ralla thought back to her speech to her soldiers. She had repeated it, almost verbatim, so that everyone in the initial waves understood.

"You are not to kill *anyone* unless it is in self-defense. Manipulation of facts created this unknowing army of fanatics, but these people were no different than anyone from the *Uni*. I know some of you want revenge, but your anger is *not* against these young men. They, personally, have not harmed you. We will let them live as that is the right thing to do. The people who kept us here will be punished, but killing these guards is unnecessary and not who we are as citizens of the *Universalis*."

Her words worked on most, but the logic was lost on others. She hoped she or someone else could stop those few from doing anything rash. In the meantime, she couldn't exactly be choosy when it came to those willing for violence.

Ralla's new spot was directly under the bank of light switches. The guards had controlled the lights during Ralla's first days, but in yet another victory in her war of rule attrition, they had relinquished control of the lights to their prisoners. For the past few nights, her people had turned off two-thirds of the lights each night to sleep. Tonight, Ralla was the one who turned them off. She sat in the twilight of the fake evening, more awake and alive than she had felt in years. Ten of her soldiers surrounded her, all within arm's length. Dija sat near the other door, with the ten other members of the first wave. Di had wanted to fight, but Ralla had insisted she didn't. Not least because people looked to Dija as Ralla's main lieutenant, but also because the girl looked to be made of paper and seemed to weigh little more than the same.

Enough time had passed for their eyes to adjust to the dim light. She could just make out Dija down the long length of wall. Ralla made an exaggerated head nod, which Di mimicked. They both simultaneously reached out and tapped their not-sleeping army. One by one the prisoners-turned-soldiers rolled or turned to look at Ralla. In a move that looked like she was stretching against the wall behind her, she raised her hands. She saw Dija do the same.

It all seemed to happen at once. Ralla slapped a hand down on the carpet. Simultaneously, she and twenty others leapt from their sleeping positions, and made the few strides to the unknowing soldiers faster than anyone thought possible. As she passed the light switches, she flipped them on. As her group impacted the shocked guards, half the room stood and rushed towards the doors.

The four guards were incapacitated before any of them realized they were being attacked. No sooner had they hit the ground than dozens of fists and feet swarmed their incapacitated bodies. And just as quickly as their ragtag assault had started, it started going horribly wrong. The pressure of the mass of the rioting crowd forced Ralla's shock troops into the hallway before they had a chance to regroup as planned and arm themselves.

It didn't matter. By the time the soldiers in the hallway, most asleep, figured out they were being overrun, they were covered in a horde of angry prisoners. Ralla herself had been carried into the hallway with the flow. She found herself face to face with one of the officers, whose panic-stricken look was not one concerned with his command or task, but of absolute fear for his life. The crowd kept coming; more and more people filled the hallway outside the ballroom, spreading in each direction. Ralla was stuck in between the swelling masses. She spotted Dija, who looked elated.

"I hit one!" she yelled, waving a fist. Ralla couldn't help but smile, but it faded quickly as the simple attack savagely spiraled into outright chaos. The push into the hallway was relentless. More and more people tried to flee their prison. Ralla saw one of her commandos with a pistol. They made eye contact, and she motioned for the gun, which he handed over.

The noise it made as she fired it toward the ceiling was louder than anything she had ever heard. Her ears rang so loudly she couldn't hear anything for several minutes. It had the desired effect, though; everyone froze long enough to look in her direction.

"We are leaving this place," she shouted, her voice sounding distant in her head. "But we need to be organized. I want Teams A, B, and C out in the hallway. Everyone else, please stay where you are or move back inside, just for a few more minutes." There were many faces furious to have to re-enter their prison, but enough did so that she could organize her fighters.

A few dozen of her team had fired weapons before, either in a simulator or as a hobby. This was her Team C. They were part of the 100-person push, and now stepped forward to confiscate every weapon they could find. There were more than enough, so four men from the initial assault crew got sidearms. They hefted them and pointed them like they had seen in vids.

The real soldiers, bloodied and battered, were being tied up in the hallway according to plan. The officer she seen a moment earlier was pleading with a gaunt man from Team C. She realized everyone looked a little gaunt, but this man even more so. His pleading was intense, near tears, upset in a way she would never had expected of a soldier. The gaunt man told him to be quiet, and poked at him with his rifle. Ralla stepped over just as the officer burst into tears.

"*Please, please! My brother!!!*" He pointed vigorously towards the crowd still stuffing the doorway. Her stomach sank. Many in the crowd faced inwards and were looking down. She strode over, the eyes of everyone in the hallway on her. She pushed people aside, the sick welling up inside her. When she got to the center of the mob, what remained of the guard was nearly unrecognizable as a person.

She looked back at the officer, who got up slowly, then ran over when his captors didn't try to stop him. He fell to his knees and grabbed his brother's corpse, blood soiling his khaki and jade uniform. Sobbing was the only sound as quiet spread from the circle to the crowd beyond.

Ralla felt her own tears come and did everything she could to fight them back. Not here. Not now. Not with all these people. She watched the officer, no older than her, cradle his younger brother's corpse. His tears created tiny clean spots in the blood on the mangled face. She couldn't stop it; her tears flowed. Her breathing sped up, her teeth clenched. These were not tears of sadness, or even remorse, though she was sure that would come later. No, these weren't the emotions afire within her.

Dija had forced her way to Ralla's side, and now looked at her questioningly, focusing on her wet cheeks. Ralla looked around to her soldiers, who looked back at her with the same questioning look shared with Dija. They were all good people. She knew all their names. The men and women still inside the ballroom, good people to a one. These weren't people who would kill. Not without extreme pressures and stress. This boy had died because of her and not because of her. He died because of the situation, and that wasn't anyone in this hallway's fault, or this prison. Everyone had been frozen by Ralla's tears. Dija asked the question they were all thinking.

"Are you all right?" she whispered, her voice carrying in the silence.

Ralla sniffed once, and fiercely wiped her eyes with the back of her hand. Through gritted teeth, she growled,

"No. I'm *pissed*."

Checking the charge on her gun, she started off down the long empty hallway. And the thunder and the fury followed.

The communicator vibrated in the pocket of Thom's coveralls. He tapped it and placed it to his ear.

"Thom, it's Tegit. Huth filled me in, what's been going on since you left?"

Thom filled him in on their progress so far, and the massive war fleet being built in the bow of the ship.

"You were right to get charges up there." His voice was wet, punctuated by coughs that were wetter still. "We should make that our priority. If they hit the *Uni* with that many ships..."

"Are you OK? We weren't sure you'd wake up."

"I took a few bad hits when we first tied on, past that I don't know. I don't think I can walk."

"OK, we'll figure it out. I assume Huth told you about our other objective."

"Yeah. I can't say I'm surprised." Even in his condition, the annoyance in his voice was obvious. "How much more time do you need?"

"We were going to go for another hour, and then start kicking in some doors."

Thom dropped the communicator away from his ear. There was a new sound, a deep rumble. Thom realized it had been there for a few moments, but now had gotten loud enough to be noticed. He looked over at Cern, who had noticed it as well. He brought the communicator back up to hear Tegit in the middle of a sentence.

"Sergeant, there's something going on up here. I'll contact you in a moment." Thom clicked the communicator off. They were about a quarter of the way down the port side of the ship. After finding nothing on a few of the interior corridors, they had come back out into the concourse area to find a live terminal. They could feel the deep rumble in the deckplates, as if half the engines had been set to full forward, the other full reverse, but there had been no change in the motion of the ship. What they could make out of the actual sound, they heard more of as they passed open hatches towards the inside of the ship.

"Did you ever watch nature vids in school?" Cern asked.

"No."

"We had to watch these vids from back when there was land. There were these wide open spaces with land as far as you could see. Like being on the bottom but having sky instead of ocean. There were these animals that would run together in big packs, like schools of fish. I remember some of the vids would have the cameras right down there with them, and you could hear their feet on the ground. That's what this sounds like."

"I don't think they have animals on board, Cern."

" I mean it sounds like a whole lot of people running."

"OK..."

"I mean a *lot* of people."

Thom stepped through the hatch and drew his sidearm. Cern did the same. The corridor was a narrow one, cutting across what looked to have been an older model cruise ship, one of several on this side of the concourse. They could see the far end of the hallway, tiny in the distance. They cautiously made their way, checking each intersecting corridor. The rumble was getting louder. In the center of the once-cruise ship was a wider passage that ran lengthwise. Thom peeked around the corner and his eyes went wide.

It was a good thing she saw him when she did. If it weren't for the fact that he was on her mind, she wouldn't have even registered his face. It took her army nearly the entire distance from when she saw him to the intersection where he stood before they came to a halt. Even still, the people in the back were jostling to keep moving. When it finally seemed like they were going to stop, Thom stepped out of the side corridor, beaming.

"What are you doing here?" Ralla asked, jogging up to him. Her smile was making her eyes do that squinty thing. Thom felt a burst of adrenaline as he saw her arms start to go up as if to hug him.

Then Cern stepped out into the main corridor.

"Cern!" she said, her voice a mixture of emotions Thom couldn't read. Her arms dropped to her side. "How... what are you... How did you get here?" she sputtered, hugging Cern lightly.

"We snuck on board. I came to rescue you," he said, kissing her hard on the mouth. Thom bristled.

"I brought an extra suit," Thom said, and immediately regretted it. Ralla pulled away from Cern long enough to nod an acknowledgement that he had said something, and then Cern went back to kissing her. She stepped back.

"Did you guys see the shipyard thing?" she asked. They nodded. "Was there still a big sub down the end?"

"Yeah, half the size of the *Uni*'s entire dockyard," Cern said, his eyes locked on Ralla.

"OK, good. We're going to take it."

"OK. Wait, what?" Thom said, still distracted by everything. This hadn't gone nearly as he'd hoped. As if annoyed at their slow uptake, she waved an arm at the impatiently waiting army of dirty, angry civilians that had so far gone unnoticed by Thom and Cern. "Oh," Thom said, still trying to catch up.

"But thank you for your suit," she said, patting him almost patronizingly on the arm. On the last pat, she squeezed it subtlety and shot him a conspiratorial glance. He was more confused than ever. "Are you guys here alone?"

Like latches on a lock, this question caused everything to click into place in Thom's brain. He pulled the communicator out of his coveralls.

"Lo, Soli, recall at once. Egress in 15. We are leaving. Huth, ready Tegit for transport, Cern and I are coming to get you."

"Are we blown?" Tegit responded, his voice sounding even weaker than before.

Thom looked down the corridor at the thousands of faces that went farther than he could see.

"Not yet, but this place is gonna get loud."

He turned to Ralla, who was giving him a look he had never seen before. She looked... impressed.

"We have an injured man. We're going to need a few minutes to get him to the shipyard."

"Do you want help?"

"I think it would be better if we do it for now. We sort of blend in. Can you give us a few minutes' head start before you wake this place up?"

"Thom..."

"OK, hold on. Here..." Thom reached into Cern's coveralls and removed a communicator. "Take this. We'll keep you updated."

She nodded, flipping the thin communications device over in her hand.

Thom grabbed Cern by the arm and started jogging back the way they had come. The rumble started up before they had made it to the concourse.

Soli and Lo arrived almost at the same time as Cern and Thom, all winded and sweating. The storage bay was still dark. To avoid any mishaps, Thom shouted for Huth as he flipped the breaker for the overheads. They buzzed, casting a dull orange glow on the carcasses of old submarines.

"Cern, grab two more sets of coveralls from the supply closet," Thom barked as they entered.

Tegit was pale, sweating, and in the same place they'd left him. Huth looked worried. There was blood on the deckplates.

"I don't think we can change him into coveralls. I think the suit is the only thing that's keeping some of his bones inside."

"OK, hold on."

Thom weaved his way across the bay to the supply closet just as Cern was exiting.

"I think these will fit them," he said, holding up two pairs of the blue coveralls.

"Change of plans," Thom said, brushing past him.

Lo and Cern, being the strongest of the group, carried Tegit between them as they rushed down the passageway. The sergeant couldn't help but keep his eyes closed, his face a contortion of pain. Thom took point and Soli, with the satchel on his back, took up the rear. They passed two groups of mechanics, who didn't know what to make of the scene of four men in hooded coveralls carrying a bloodied fifth. Each time, Thom yelled out "Emergency, emergency," and their path was cleared.

As they crossed the concourse, after an uneventful elevator trip, the alarms started going off. The ominous angry wail pierced the silence. By the time they had made it to the elevator in the new wall, people started to spill out of cabins above, shouting at or to each other in confusion.

But that was nothing compared to what was happening in the shipyard. It was a full-on firefight, with armed members of Ralla's army on the port side near a bank of elevators and a few hundred *Pop* soldiers dug in on the opposite side of the bay. Ralla's group had excellent cover behind storage containers, but they were pinned down. The elevators continued to open, spilling out more and more people as the word hadn't gotten upstairs that there was no place to go. The doors were not in the line of sight of the *Pop* soldiers, nor were the growing groups of civilians, but that wouldn't last much longer.

More containers and subs blocked direct access to the dug-in *Pop* troops, but Thom was able to lead his team around the edge of the bay towards Ralla's people. He found her crouched behind a pallet of plastic piping, which was doing a fine job absorbing the incoming fire by melting. She slammed a new charge into her pistol as Thom waddled up. It took her a moment to register who it was, his face hidden in the darkness of the coverall's hood. Incoming fire sizzled as it hit the bulkhead behind them.

"You've got your man?"

Thom leaned aside and pointed at Tegit, now on the ground beside a heavily panting Lo and Cern.

"We're pretty well trapped here. If you can hold them, I'll lead a few of my people around to the other side and get in behind them. We can meet up at Big Ugly over there," she said with a motion towards the cruiser-sized sub still resting ominously at the forward end of the bay.

She didn't wait for an answer before moving back to get the attention of her nearby soldiers. Hardly marksmen, they alternately ducked or shot wildly over the heads of the *Pop* soldiers. Thom grabbed her arm, and flashed her a wily smile.

"We got this," he said, turning and catching the eye of Soli. The soldier waddled up, keeping his head down and bringing the satchel with him. Ralla watched as Thom unzipped his oversized coveralls and tossed his hood back, revealing the dark gray-on-black armor of his suit underneath. Ralla's eyebrows went up. The blue cloth fell away as Soli and Thom slipped out of their adopted denim skin. Soli opened the satchel and handed Thom a sidearm and a carbine. Thom couldn't help himself, and gave Ralla a wink as he slapped the side of his helmet, snapping the facemask shut. Soli signified his readiness with a pat on Thom's back, who immediately twisted around as he stood and commenced firing.

At first the *Pop* soldiers didn't know what to make of the two carapaced juggernauts slowly crossing the bay towards them. Then as the impact from the incoming fire peppered their entrenchment behind crates and submarines, they started firing back. Most of the soldiers had energy weapons, whose bolts were effortlessly absorbed.

Soli and Thom, unbothered by the incoming fire, continued to strafe the different clusters of soldiers. When the soldiers realized their weapons had no effect, two heavy rifles were brought out and placed on containers for support. Thom and Soli had made it halfway across the bay when the first of these rounds hit Soli square in the chest. He was knocked off his feet as if yanked, and slid backwards across the deck on his back. Thom dove and rolled, firing across the crate where the shot had come from.

"I'm OK," Soli said over the comm. He sounded like he was gasping for breath. The fun was over. Thom got to his feet and sprinted across the rest of the open bay, spraying fire from the carbine as he went. Jumping on top of the crate, he kicked the rifle gunner in the face. As he went sprawling backwards, the rest of the soldiers got up and ran. Within moments, the shipyard was silent.

Thom looked back across the bay from his perch on the crate. There was a steady stream of people filing from the elevators towards the big sub. Already he could hear the whine of the engines. Soli had gotten up and was checking behind the crates and subs for any stragglers. Oddly disappointed, Thom saw Ralla with her back to him, indicating which of the two ramps people should go up to get onboard.

The elevators held 50-60 people each, and there were three of them. It took a little over 15 minutes to get the rest of the people down into the bay. Ten more for everyone to get onboard the sub they had christened *Reappropriation.* By the time the last of the civilians had made it to the portable stairs accessing the cruiser, Soli, Thom, and Huth started taking fire from above. Some of the more enterprising *Pop* soldiers had gone up to the upper-level gangways and were firing down at them. Cern and Lo were already onboard, carrying the now-unconscious Tegit to the medbay on the *Reap* with the help of a broad-shouldered civilian.

Finally, the shipyard was empty. Thom sealed the hatch and made his way to the bridge. Soli and Lo started to round up people to man some of half a dozen turrets along the spine and keel of their new ship.

The passageways, already narrow on the warship, were made almost impassable as people stood or sat any place they could. By the time he got to the bridge, he could tell there was a problem.

The bridge, such as it was, was barely larger than those on transports he'd piloted. It looked as if the craft could be driven by two people, with a support staff of five for communications, weapons, and engineering. The front seats were filled with two men who looked like they knew what they were doing. Toggles flipped, dials checked much as he would have. The other seats on the bridge were filled with men and women looking like they were trying to figure out what each station did, then actually reading the information given there. Ralla stood in the middle of it all, pointing at dials, giving orders, and trying her best to answer the questions of those around her. She looked in her element, like she had been on this bridge, stuck at the bottom of an enemy sub, countless times before.

She noticed Thom and flashed him a smile, grabbing him by the hand and dragging him into the center of the bridge. She squeezed it before she let it go.

"One problem," she said.

"No water."

"You've done this before."

"Actually..."

Suddenly, she was serious, the brief moment of levity flushed from her face. Thom assumed the same attitude.

"They've sealed us in. We can't open the lock from here."

"Where are the controls?"

"They're on the second level, overlooking the bay. I sent a team there, but they should have gotten the bay open by now."

"Oh."

"Yeah. One of many things I'm going to be upset about later."

"My team and I can get up there, no problem."

"Here's the thing. The crane isn't big enough to move this thing. So the whole yard has to be flooded."

"That's OK, we can swim out."

"All the doors seal when there's water. There were signs everywhere on the way in. They obviously didn't want someone to do what we're doing."

"Or what we did before."

"Or that," Ralla replied.

"So it's a one-way thing. That's fine. We can fight our way to another bay and get one of the transports out."

Ralla leaned forward, ducking her head under the curving permiglass viewscreen, and pointed up towards the upper gangways. She motioned for Thom to do the same. There were soldiers covering the gangways. He got her meaning instantly.

"I still think we can do it."

"No, there's no way you could escape from all that."

"So what do we do now? We can't stay here. Can we blow the doors?"

"No ordnance. The turrets have ammo, but that's not going to get us anywhere," Ralla scratched the side of her head, and tried to comb her dirty hair with her fingers. She turned and looked at Thom's suit. "You said you brought one of those for me."

"Oh, no. No way. I left you behind once—no way I'm doing it again."

Ralla cocked her head to the side and smiled.

"That's so cute of you, but I'm a big girl now and I don't need rescuing," her tone went from mildly patronizing to overtly so.

"I didn't mean..."

"You sort of did, and it's fine. My mother does it. My father does it. Cern does it. I was hoping you wouldn't, but that's OK." She put her hand on the shoulder of the man in the right pilot seat. "When there's enough water to go, you *go*, I don't care what else you see. Follow the route we talked about, and don't go near the meeting place unless you know you're clear."

"Got it," he replied.

Ralla stepped past Thom without a glance, and headed back into the ship. Thom, deflated but not ready to desist, chased after her. They ended up in the ship's med bay, a cramped room with three metal beds and cabinets of supplies. Tegit was unconscious in the center bed, being attended by no less than five people, each taking authority over a different injury. Cern didn't notice Ralla's entrance, but he did when she scooped the black satchel from the floor.

"What are you doing?" Cern asked.

"Someone needs to flood the bay. Their soldiers are under orders not to kill me. I'm the only one that can stay behind."

"Stay be...what? What are you talking about?"

"Ralla," Thom cut in. "Please let one of us go instead."

She opened the bag and started remove pieces of the suit. She slid into the armor, her blouse causing odd bulkiness in the underfabric.

"I need to do this, Thom," she said, using him as support as she slid off her shoes and put on the armor's boots. "I need to do it for these people, but more than that I need to do it for me." Her eyes showed something Thom hadn't seen before, as if she were a different person. Resolve was there, of course, but she seemed older, somehow. She said nothing else, but her eyes kept speaking.

"Ralla..." he said, his voice softer, no longer trying to argue, but trying to say something else. Trying to sum up everything that had happened, everything he'd thought over the past months. She looked up at him and her expression showed that she seemed to understand. He tapped the comm on the back of his hand. "Lo, what's the status on our turrets?"

"I've got volunteers in each one, and Soli and I are giving them instructions the best we can. The equipment is pretty similar to ours."

"So we're good to go?"

"Similar. I can't say they won't lock up or explode or... I don't know. Uh oh. I shouldn't have said that, now everyone is looking at me funny," his big voice sounding surprisingly bashful.

"Lo, in about three minutes I'm going to need you to slag it."

"Slag what?"

"Everything."

"We'll be ready."

Thom focused back on Ralla, as she struggled with the armor's gloves. He was surprised Cern hadn't said anything, and when Thom looked over at him, the taller man was shaking and looked ready to explode. His face had flushed with blood and emotion.

"STOP!" he shouted. Everyone in the room froze. When they realized he wasn't talking to them, Tegit's "doctors" went back to their charge, cutting away at the underfabric of his armor and poking at wounds in ways that made Thom queasy. "Ralla, you must stop this craziness. You aren't a warrior. What do you know about armored suits and guns? Who do you think you are?! You're just, you're just, you're..."

He looked ready to pop. Without warning or provocation, Tegit's nearest physician turned with a syringe and jabbed it into Cern's leg. The big man snapped his head towards the attack, then crumpled to the floor, syringe still stuck in his thigh. The physician casually turned back and continued his work on his patient. Ralla stooped to pick up a rifle, pistol, and two charges of explosives.

"Can you help me with the helmet?" Ralla said, as if she were asking him to zip up a dress. The stretchy underfabric conformed to her petite frame, but the covering armor pieces rubbed and clattered against each other. He fitted the helmet and they walked back to where they had entered the sub, stepping over and around people. Pausing at the lock, they could see through the small porthole the rolling stairs still pressed against the hull outside.

"Are you sure they won't kill you?"

"I'm sure they won't kill me more than I'm sure they won't kill you."

"Huh?"

"As sure as I can be."

"You can't know. Let me come with you."

"No. If you don't understand why I need to do this then please just let me go because you care about me and I'm telling you this is something I have to do."

"I was in pretty bad shape when I left you the last time."

"I figured you might be. Maybe you can think of this time as me leaving you."

"That doesn't help."

"Are these suits that good, or were you just showing off before?"

"Both."

"OK," she said. She checked the charges on her carbine and sidearm, then looked back up at Thom, his face bracketed by the retracted helmet, much as hers was to him.

"I'm going to come back for you."

"Oh, don't start that again."

"Ralla..."

"We'll talk about it later." She fumbled for the button to seal the helmet, then thought better of it. Grabbing Thom's shoulders, she pulled herself up and kissed him. The helmets clunked against each other. As awkward as it was, standing there in front of the lock, armor holding them apart, Thom pulled her towards him. All that was unsaid was said unsaid.

Neither moved, but for the kiss. Then Ralla dropped from her toes and pulled away from him, still holding his arm. Thom couldn't let go of her. She gently placed his arm from her side to his. His mouth opened to say what they both wanted to say, but she stopped him.

"Later," she said, hitting the button on the helmet, her tone indecipherable. When it snapped down it made her jump. For a moment, through the helmet, Thom could see she was far more nervous than she had let on. She took his gloved hand in hers, and gave it a squeeze. Reaching around her hand, Thom activated his comm.

"Lo. Light it up."

From deep within the *Reap*, the unmistakable sound of heavy gunfire emanated from all around them. The turrets on the top and bottom of the ship reverberated through the corridors and the deckplates themselves. The people crowded in the passageways of the ship, startled, let out a few screams, many yells, and covered their ears from the sound. Ralla and Thom stood at the lock, oblivious to it all. Thom pounded the door release, which hissed as its pressure seal deflated. The door pivoted outwards.

The walls and floor of the bay were lit red and yellow as the weapons of the *Reappropriation* launched their salvos into everything at the far end of the bay. The guns made short work of subs, containers, and hatches, punching torso sized holes into everything they could see. In the enclosed space, the sound was deafening. Soldiers lying prone on the upper levels, ready to snipe, now fled back to the main part of the ship.

Sealing his own helmet, Thom gave Ralla one more look, his heart in his throat. He stepped out onto the landing of the rolling stairs. Dropping to one knee, he raised his carbine to add his own music to the symphony of noise. He was sure Ralla looked back once as she got to the elevator. Then she was gone.

Neither saw Cern limp back towards the medbay.

A handful of soldiers scattered from the hallway as she exited the elevator. The scene caused her to smile. She fired a few times after them with the rifle, then continued towards the control room. It was empty, dark except for alarm lights pulsing for attention. Floor-to-ceiling windows bowed out, showing a panoramic—if a bit vertigo-inducing—view of the entire bay.

Rolling chairs with consoles attached sat dormant, awaiting activation. She sealed the door with a blast from the pistol, then dropped into the middle chair and coasted towards the window. The cruiser's light cannons were turning the small attack craft and the hanging decks above into burning and falling hunks of metal and plastic. Smoke was billowing out of several cargo containers, accumulating high above in the expansive curved ceiling of the bay.

Ralla tapped the console, which immediately lit up with warnings of the smoke and damage. She scrolled through the menus and found the section she needed. Tapping the screen, she watched the floor of the bay start to slide open; seawater started pouring in. Klaxons screamed their warnings, loud enough for Ralla to hear even though the suit. The flooding happened rapidly, the floor of the bay almost immediately disappeared under water, and the parking struts of the cruiser were quickly halfway submerged. Chest height, she thought to herself. That was fast. A new sound came through the helmet. As her brain registered what it was, she was on her feet with the rifle raised. The door trembled as someone rammed it repeatedly. For the moment, it held.

Tossing the rifle and the pistol into the chair, Ralla started stripping out of the suit. It came off quickly, and the noise of the room pained her ears. The alarms, the shouting from behind the door, the metal-on-metal clang as the battering ram impacted the door, not to mention the continued destruction that bled through the windows from out in the shipyard.

She rolled the rifle and explosives up into a bundle, and used the pistol to shoot out one of the windows. A wall of sound hit her as if it was physical. Acrid smoke burnt her nostrils. Far below, the *Reap* had just started to float free. She wondered if Thom was watching from the now-sealed door. She tossed the bundle out the window, and watched it fall the three stories to the churning water below. The seawater had dropped the ambient temperature, and a cool breeze cut into her rumpled indigo blouse. She waved goodbye as the *Reap* started to slide below the surface, still firing into the rafters.

Turning to watch as the soldiers finally broke through the door, she felt pure fear for the first time. She had been wrong; they were going to kill her. It was unmistakable on their faces. For the second time in her life, Ralla watched a rifle as it connected with her face.

Thom returned Ralla's wave, knowing she would never see it. Water covered the window, and he could just make out the edge of the bay doors as the *Reap* sank away from the *Population.* He tapped his comm.

"Now."

Two dozen charges of high explosive cut through two engines, several inner and one outer bulkhead, four freshwater tanks, three elevators, and a tiny bundle of otherwise sturdy armor.

The explosions could be felt as tiny tremors to the people on board the rapidly accelerating *Reappropriation.* Most didn't notice it. Thom rested his head against the lock, and sighed

PART 3

PART 3

I

Thom Vargas stood at attention at the front of the room, but they spoke as if he wasn't there. Back-and-forth comments were shot right past him, growing louder with every retort. Proctor Jills raised his left hand, and almost immediately the room was silent. Awbee glared at Thom from the opposite corner. Cern, seated next to her, did the same.

"Mr. Vargas. Is it true that you deceived the Council in order to mount a rescue of Ms. Gattley? A venture you knew we would never approve?"

"Yes."

He wasn't sure what answer they were expecting to hear, but half the Council erupted in shouts of condemnation. Jills silenced them again.

"Obviously, you failed. A majority of this Council would see you locked up for what you've done. Before we go that far, I think it only fair you tell us yourself what casualties resulted from your ruse."

"I was told Sergeant Tegit is likely to survive, though it's doubtful he'll be walking anytime soon."

"And how many ships were lost?" Larr asked after a glance from Jills. The glance put Thom on edge. These two were setting him up for something. Something bad.

"Well, probably none. We still have the coordinates where we left the shuttle. I'm sure it's still there."

The room was still hostile, Thom could feel it, but they were listening to him.

"Mr. Vargas," Larr continued in his usual smarmy voice, "the Council, and the ship at large, is only aware that you returned with a few hostages. Can you tell us, what else did you return with?"

"Well, it was more than a few. We rescued at least 3,000 people."

The members of the Council were visibly shocked. They looked to Jills for verification.

"He is correct," Jills confirmed. "We have hidden the actual numbers from the ship for fear it would cause a run on supplies. We're dealing with it. I'll need you to talk to your constituents directly and let them know that there is plenty of food for them and the returning residents. Go on, Mr. Vargas. What else?"

"You mean the sub?"

"Sub?" asked one of the several Council members Thom didn't know.

"A brand new cruiser, Eccee-class, not fully complete but with most of her armament intact," Larr answered. Thom felt that some of the once-hostile Councilmembers were now looking at him in a new and different light. It made him squirm. He tugged at his black uniform. "While your personal mission was a failure, Lieutenant Vargas, what else did you do with your time on the *Population*?"

"Well, we're pretty sure we crippled three of their engines and caused enough flooding that they'll have to use the other engines just to pump out the water. They had come to a dead stop and were listing pretty bad to starboard as we escaped."

"And you're sure no one followed you?" Jills asked. Thom had relaxed, seeing friendly eyes around most of the room.

"Even with the rather poor equipment on the cruiser, we're confident we were not followed. Yes, sir."

"Mr. Vargas," Jills said, rising to his feet. The other Councilmembers, apparently caught off guard, quickly did the same. "While your subterfuge in getting us to approve your mission was dishonest and irresponsible, your actions have had a stunningly positive result. I am not saying that the ends justify the means, but we are at war, and I would be amiss if I didn't recognize a powerful and effective leader. You led your team into hostile territory, returned with minimal casualties, and did significant harm to the enemy. In light of this, and your previous history of actions, I would like to recommend to the Council your promotion to the rank of Commander, with duties to be determined by this Council at a later date. Second?"

"Second," Larr said immediately.

"Vote?" Jills asked the room. Hands went up around the table. Clearly a majority.

"So said. Commander Vargas, would you please approach to accept the insignia of your rank?"

In a daze, Thom walked around the Council table to Proctor Jills. Later, he would remember there was clapping. Not from everyone.

The pain woke her. Throbbing pain, pulsing with each heartbeat, dragging her towards consciousness. She futilely resisted, finally succumbing, arriving at wakefulness with eyes closed and a face in agony. Grimacing in pain caused the corners of her vision to jab white as her damaged tissues shouted hostility. Gasping in anguish, she sat bolt upright in bed.

Either she was blind, or the room was pitch black. For the moment, Ralla was able to step around her pain and focus on the new problem. She was in a bed; she could feel the tattered blanket and the rough material of the cushion under her. The edges were metal. A cot. It was against a wall of cold metal. Following the wall, she slowly worked her way around the space. It was a tiny room, no longer than the cot, not much wider, either. A cell. Her shin discovered a toilet along the other wall, with a sink. The water tasted faintly of salt, but seemed fresh enough.

Cupping some of the cold water in her hands, she pressed it gingerly against her face. Delicately, she touched the damaged right cheek with the pads of her fingers. She knew it was swollen and bruised; the real question was if the bone underneath was broken. Ralla tried to smile slightly, just to move the muscles. The pain was excruciating, but everything still moved. So it was bad, but maybe not too bad.

The left side of her face was fine, so she was pretty sure there was just no light. Even as a kid she had left a shade open in her room to let some of the light from the Yard in. Her mother had slept with the shades fully drawn, in blackness like this. Ralla could never figure that out. The water had felt good, so she held some more against her face.

The metal door was rough with rust that flaked off in her hands. It was locked, so she banged on it. To her surprise, a dead bolt clicked, and a crack of light entered her cell. It was not much brighter in the space beyond, but to her wide open irises it was like daylight, making her squint. This created a whole new wash of pain from her damaged face, but she fought it back.

The man in the doorway was dressed as a soldier, but wasn't one that had been guarding her people in their makeshift prison. He looked serious, but so much so it was as if he was hiding nervousness. His rifle was at his hip, finger on the trigger, pointed right at her. He looked her up and down, seemed to linger on her face, then started to close the door again.

"Wait!" she said, grabbing the edge of the door. Fear broke through the soldier's facade. He staggered backwards and readied his weapon.

"Step back! Now!" he shouted. Ralla tensed and stepped slowly back into her cell, pulling the door more open as she did so.

"I'm not going to do anything to you, soldier. I'm no trouble. I just want to talk to your Governor. That's all. He knows me. We've spoken before."

"Let go of the door. I don't care who knows you. Let go of the door," the soldier said, nearly tripping over his words he was trying to get them out so quickly.

"OK, I can do that. Just please pass the word up that I'd like to talk to Governor Oppai."

Ralla released the door from her fingertips and it swung shut, clanging against the frame. Blackness.

Shuffling across the floor, she lay back on the musty cot and found herself so consumed by thought that she momentarily forgot her pain.

It could have been hours or minutes, but the sound of the door unlocking again woke Ralla instantly. She was upright and sitting on the edge of the bed by the time the door finished opening. Squinting again in the comparatively bright light, the pain had no time to make itself known before her mind was racing. Oppai stood in the doorway, backlit by the room beyond. He seemed frozen there, black shadow casting black shadow.

"Governor, let me first say..."

"No. I don't plan on letting you say anything. You are responsible, directly or indirectly, for the deaths of dozens of my people. Your unsuccessful escape, however vain, caused havoc throughout the ship. That you are alive now should alarm you. You live only until the ship is repaired and I will give my people what they want: the villain. You did this. You tried to destroy the ship just as I told them you would. When they have finished repairs, I'm going to have you executed in front of them all. And they will scream your name as they watch you die."

Ralla's mind paid cursory attention to his words, but moved on rapidly. Why is he here at all, she thought. Why would he come down here if he was just going to let me rot and then kill me? There was something more to this.

"You failed, by the way. You are the only survivor. We had no choice but to destroy the sub your people stole. They're all dead."

That was it. He was livid and trying to conceal it. Livid that she had bested him. That they had bested him. Which meant he was lying. They had gotten away. Otherwise he wouldn't be angry, he'd be gloating. Perfect.

"Governor Oppai..."

"No tears for your friends? You're colder than I thought."

"I can give you something to save your people. All our people."

Oppai paused, searching her damaged face.

"Anything you say now would just be to save yourself. You have every reason to lie and none to tell the truth."

She had hooked him. He was curious, but didn't want to admit it. She looked past him at the guard, who was doing his best to make it seem like he wasn't listening.

"Guard," Oppai said, not taking his eyes off Ralla. "Give me your sidearm and leave the brig." The soldier did as instructed, his exit made known by a metallic clunk of a door she couldn't see. Oppai and Ralla were alone.

He still eyed her with a mix of hatred and distrust, but the sidearm remained at his side.

"Speak."

"OK, first I have to tell you what my mother has been working on for the past few decades."

The meeting had continued, though Thom could barely pay attention. For his failure, they had promoted him. He would have to explain to them his only goal had been to rescue Ralla and for that most important of endeavors, he hadn't succeeded. He wasn't a leader. Tegit was the leader. Thom was merely a tagalong. Sure the team had looked to him when Tegit was knocked out, but that was just because he had been on the *Pop* before. He would explain what the situation was, politely turn down the promotion, and that would be that.

Proctor Jills motioned for him to stay after the meeting concluded. Larr and Awbee stayed as well. The latter didn't even try to conceal her contempt for Thom.

"Will you join us at the table?" Jills said to him. He obliged, uncomfortably sliding into one of the high-backed chairs. Awbee stood at the end of the table nearest the door.

"Proctor Jills," Thom said. "If I could just have a moment to..."

Jills waved him off.

"Later. Awbee, if you would please brief Commander Vargas."

"You realize this is the second time this coward has left my daughter behind. And you promote him for that?"

"Awbee, having gotten to know your daughter well in the years she's spent on and around the Council, I find it hard to believe anyone would be able to leave her anywhere she didn't want to be left. Now, if you would bring Thom up to speed. The sooner we get moving, the better."

Annoyed, and with one final cutting glance at Thom, Awbee tapped the table angrily with her finger. In all the times Thom had been in the Council room, the tabletop had appeared to be a reflective black glass. It was in fact a display, a fancier version of the one in the Command bunker. Before him was a generated image of their blue world as seen from space. The image zoomed in on the n-pole, though Thom realized that it could have been the s-pole or any other edge of the planet. There was no frame of reference.

"Do you remember what I told you the last time I was here?"

"I... what do you mean?"

Awbee sighed and took a moment to gather her thoughts or calm her annoyance.

"I'll start again. Our world is healing itself. From the timeline of the universe, it's happening with extreme rapidity. From the timeline of us, perhaps not as much." She looked at Jills, who nodded for her to continue. "Did my daughter mention to you, or have you noticed, the state of this ship?"

"Yes. She told me she'd tried to get something in the *Daily* about the ship falling apart. She had mentioned it a few times."

"My daughter is a little too observant sometimes, though in this case she didn't know how right she was. There were and are strict orders not to discuss it outside of the Council, but I wouldn't be surprised if Mrakas had pushed her on, or even started her on the path. It doesn't matter. The ship is, as my daughter discovered, falling apart. The *Uni* and *Population* were thrown together with the speed and build quality only the imminent end of the world could bring. Our elders survived, as do we, but these boats were never meant to last this long. We can keep patching and repairing, but when it comes down to it, the Council and I don't feel the ship can last another 30 years. We would have been able to convert the ship to a more permanent version of what we have now, as in a seabed base. But as you can imagine, that would never work with our current state of war with the *Population*. As it is, we thought our domes would give us a more permanent solution. Unfortunately, we can't build them fast enough or large enough to house our entire population. And as you know, they haven't been as secure against discovery as we'd hoped."

"You've come up with a way to speed up the recovery," Thom interrupted, just figuring it out.

For the first time, Awbee seemed impressed with him.

"We think so." She tapped the table and the image zoomed in again, showing a few icebergs floating on the endless sea. "The problem is multi-fold. As you can see, the water is cold enough near the pole that ice does form. Since we've been making records, we've seen a steady increase in the volume of ice formed, and the quantity of icebergs. The problem is, without anything to tether them, they float off with the current."

She paused and reached over for a glass one of the Councilmen had left on the table. There was a small amount of water in the bottom. Holding the glass by the top, Awbee moved it in a small circle. "With no land mass, the water covering the world acts like the water swirling in this glass. The currents are fastest at the equator, and decrease in speed slightly as you move north or south. At the very pole, the water moves very little, but any ice that forms quickly gets spun down and away from the pole into warmer water and promptly melts. Without ice, there is nowhere for the water to go. No ice, no land."

Thom nodded. "So, you want to tether them or something? Like fishing, with a net maybe?"

"Sort of. We're going to grow them," Awbee answered, with obvious pride.

"Sorry?"

"We need to accelerate the process. Over time there will be enough ice that it will lump together on its own and hopefully form its own ice cap. We can't wait that long, so we're going to grow our own ice cap." She tapped the table once again, and the image zoomed in closer, eventually dropping below the surface, revealing the craggy undersea landscape. As they watched, a circle formed just above the sea floor. The circle filled in towards its center, tapering upwards until it formed what looked like an upside-down funnel with a gray and black lattice pattern. The center of the funnel then grew rapidly upwards towards the surface. The camera followed, breaking out into the rendered sunlight, showing the top of the cylinder surrounded by a small iceberg. Water surged from the top of the tube, spraying out into a mist, which fell on the top of the berg. Thom looked up, eyebrows raised.

"Keep watching," Awbee said, motioning back towards the table. His eyes returned to see time speed up. The iceberg grew quickly. The tube grew vertically as additional pieces appeared at its top. The camera zoomed out, revealing the growing ice cap. It pulled back further, showing the entire planet. Dots of brown started to appear on the surface. The dots grew, forming islands. The islands grew and touched. Delicate tendrils of brown reached for each other, becoming continents. Soon it resembled the world he recognized from posters on the school walls as a child. He looked up in awe.

"How long would this take?"

"What you just saw? Decades, if not centuries. There are too many variables to be sure."

"And all that from just the one tower?"

"Oh, no. No no no. One tower wouldn't affect anything. No, we're talking about one tower to start the process. As we are able to create more of the material the towers are built of, we'll build more. We'll need thousands to affect any real change, but this one," she said tapping the image. "This first one is the most important. This is the seed. The others don't have to be as strong or as large. This one is the focal point of the entire process. Everything grows from here. We're calling it the Fountain. It has to be placed at a very specific spot, where the currents are the weakest. After that, we just need time."

"How much time?"

"Months if we're lucky. Years if we're not."

Thom rubbed the back of his right hand absently as he thought it over. He could feel the mood in the room had markedly changed. Seeing the possibilities laid out before them, the glimmer of hope, it had softened them all.

"What about the radiation?"

"Good question. Once the iceberg gets large enough, we go up significantly on the tower. Way up. Instead of spraying super cold water on the snow, we're going to spray it much higher into the atmosphere. Some will land on the iceberg, some the sea, but some of the moisture will stay in the atmosphere and come down elsewhere as rain. By that point we'll have other, smaller towers doing most of the growing work. The spray from the Fountain will hopefully accelerate the natural dilution that is already occurring."

"Do we really have enough metal to make something that tall?"

"It's not metal. You know those suits you took to fail to rescue my daughter?" And like that, her edge had returned. "That's the material we're making the tower out of. That's what we developed it for. The suits were what some of the techs did with the scraps. We make it here."

"Make it?"

Awbee deferred to Jills, who shook his head. Thom accepted being left in the dark.

"So what is it you want me to do? Guard this tower?"

"Not exactly." Jills replied. "Let me stress, this is the most important endeavor for the future of our species since this ship was built. I can't oversell this. Even without the nuisance of the *Pop*, this ship won't survive long enough for any of us to see the world heal itself. Without this ship, it's likely our species won't survive. It has taken us seven years to create enough material for the Fountain. We can keep making more for the extensions and the satellite fountains, but the amount needed is a fraction of what the main unit needs. If we lose it, that's it. We won't have time to make another."

Thom nodded somberly. Self-doubt started to work its way past the hope-filled haze, poking at his consciousness.

"Your mission, Commander Vargas, is to take the cruiser you appropriated, along with several vessels of our budding fleet, and razz the enemy. Attack their installations. Steal their supplies. Capture their transports. Anything and everything. But *away* from the n-pole. We need you to keep their attention as far from us as you can. If we're discovered and they attack us again, we'll do our best to hold them off. But worst case here, if they take us out and the Fountain, that's it for our entire species."

The self-doubt dispersed across the surface of his mind like oil on water. "Sir, I'm not sure..."

Jills raised his palm, cutting Thom off in mid sentence.

"Thank you, Doctor. Mr. Larr, would you and Awbee please give us the room?" The room emptied and Jills walked to the balcony overlooking the Yard. After a moment, Thom joined him. The air circulating the space was fresh and smelled strongly of vegetation. "I can see it on your face. You don't understand why I've picked you."

"Honestly, no, sir."

"Honesty is good. Keep answering me honestly. Because if you lie to me again like you did before your last mission, I'll lock you in the brig till you rot. Now, honestly, who do you feel is the most famous living person on this ship?"

Thom searched the Proctor's face for signs of a trick.

"This isn't vanity Thom, answer the question."

"Mrakas Gattley."

"Of course. Even more so than the Captain, as he would also admit. OK, and who do you think is the most devious. Harder, I know, as you haven't spent too much time here."

"Councilman Larr?"

"Very astute."

"I thought he was your friend."

"As much as anyone is, I suppose," Jills replied absently. "OK, who's in charge of every armed warrior on this vessel?"

"You?"

"Sure, eventually, but before that?"

"Captain Sarras."

"Right. Now answer me this. Why aren't the most famous and beloved person, the most devious and cunning person, nor the most well-armed person running this ship?"

"Ummm..."

"Thom, look, I am very good at what I do. I'm not that smart, certainly not half as smart as Doctor Gattley. I'm not well loved, not very devious, and I certainly don't have my own army. OK, well, I do, but they're following the position, not me. My skill is seeing talent and using that talent. I don't mean in a deceitful, manipulative way. It's knowing how to get everyone who works for me to do what they do best, at their best. So when I ask you to take command of our pirate fleet, know that I see you as the best man for the job *because* you'll be good at it. I know it. That's what I do."

"That is kind of you, sir, but..."

"I knew your father, Thom," Jills continued as if he hadn't heard him. "In my days before the Council I was a rep for the Mechanists Union. I got to know a lot of the mechanics on my beat. Many of them helped get me elected the first time, putting up posters, going cabin to cabin talking to people. Can I tell you something, Thom? Your father was a drunk. A drunk and a screw up and if he was half as smart as he thought he was, he would have put down the drink long before he lost your mother, before he watched his career evaporate, and before he poisoned himself to death."

Thom seethed and tensed, clenching his fists.

"Hit me if you want, but what I'm telling you is the truth. And I'm telling you so you can see our world as it is, not as he forced you to see it. In your mind you're still the fisherman that gets drunk with his buddies. Guess what? You're not. Haven't been in a long time. The moment you chose to rescue

Ralla the first time, that was it. You started on a path that has led you here. And in case you don't realize it, you are now one of the most powerful men on this ship, Commander. You are in charge of your own fleet and report directly to and have the ear of the Proctor of the Council. So if you still think that there is no advancement in this life, I hate to break it to you, son, but you're wrong."

Thom turned and gripped the railing, the force of what Jills said causing his head to spin. For a moment, he couldn't catch his breath. The truth washed over him. They stood there in silence while voices from the floor far below drifted up, the words unintelligible. The artificial breeze rustled the green vines on the walls near the balcony. Thom turned back to face Jills, his eyes moist.

"Thom, I wish I could give you some time to think it over and find your place in all of this. But that is something I can't give you. The one thing I can give you is time to go do the thing you should be dreading the most: Telling Mrakas that he won't get to see his daughter before he dies."

Jills put his hand on Thom's shoulder and motioned towards the door.

"I was a really good fisherman."

"You'll be a better Commander."

III

Oppai tapped the pistol absentmindedly against the door frame, making a metallic clink with no apparent rhythm.

"How sure are your scientists that this will work?" he asked.

"Very sure. Please believe me. We won't need to fight for resources much longer. We'll have *land*. We'll be able to grow things, live outside. Don't you see, we can start all over." Ralla didn't bother to mask the pleading in her voice.

"I do see. It's all very interesting. Unlimited land, for everyone."

"Well, maybe not at first, but over the years I don't see why not. As the ice caps are rebuilt, more and more land will become available."

Ralla was sure he looked interested. He had been lost in thought halfway through her speech about the Fountain, but she was sure he believed her.

"Where is this initial tower going to be built?"

"I'm not sure. I wasn't briefed on that part of the project," Ralla lied. He studied her for a moment, then nodded slowly. "We can contact my ship. They'll fill you in on the details."

Oppai jolted out of his daze.

"What do you mean? How can we contact your ship?"

"We can send a signal out on a frequency they'll be monitoring. They'll be able to send back whatever information you want." Ralla tried to hide her enthusiasm. Could this really be the beginning of the peace between the two ships? She forced herself not to get too excited.

"What's the frequency?"

"I'll need to show you. I don't know the name of the equipment but I'll know it when I see it." Also a lie, but it was a worth a try to get out of the cell.

"OK, but remember," he said, tapping the gun more forcefully against the door.

They left the brig and wound their way up towards the front of the ship. The hallways were deserted. Even in the main concourse had only scattered foot traffic. Ralla tried to ask the Governor about it, but he paid no attention.

The bridge had a similar layout to the one on the *Uni*: Banks of computers with manned stations along the sides. Large wheels and levers made up the forward-most wall, with two young pilots driving the ship. Closer inspection revealed differences. Many screens were off or visibly damaged. Many of the working screens seemed several generations behind what currently outfitted the *Uni*. The center of the room held a large table, similar to what was on the *Uni* bridge, but this one didn't seem to have an embedded video display. What Ralla assumed was the Officer of the Watch saluted Oppai as they entered. Not seeing a Captain made Ralla wonder what time it was.

"OK, where is it?" the Governor said, motioning towards one of the communications terminals. She quickly located the one she needed and pointed to it.

"Set that at 24.8 and I can send a message."

"We'll send a recorded message, thank you. I'm not that stupid." Headsets with microphones were scattered on the surface of the communications terminal. The crewman stationed there slid aside, allowing Oppai free reign over the equipment. "Here," he said, handing her one of the headsets. "Record your message."

Ralla took the set, and nodded that she was ready.

"*Universalis*, this is Councilwoman Ralla Gattley. I am being held prisoner onboard the *Population*." The Officer of the Watch shot Oppai a glance but the Governor ignored him. "I have convinced Governor Oppai of our desire for peace. I have explained to him the outline of our Fountain project to show there is no longer a need for conflict and that our two peoples can finally join as one. He is interested, and would like to see more of our research. Please respond on this channel." Ralla removed the headset and placed it on the table. "Now we wait."

The crewmember reached awkwardly around Oppai to the terminal behind him. "Message encoded and ready for transmission," he said.

"Go," the Governor said immediately. "Make note of the time. I'm sure they're smart enough to delay their response, but you never know. Maybe they'll be stupid enough to give away their distance."

It was almost two hours before they started receiving a response. Ralla had sat on the floor leaning against one of the several disused terminals and was nearly asleep. It was several more minutes before they had enough of the message buffered to start it. A pulse of excitement and surprise bolted through her as she heard Thom's voice.

"*Population,* this is Commander Thom Vargas of the *Universalis.*" Commander? Ralla thought. "We are happy to hear that Councilwoman Gattley is alive, and would like to arrange for her release. We would like to assure you that the Fountain project is real. Data on said project will follow this transmission. We would be very interested in the prospect of peace, though final terms will have to be negotiated in person. We await your response."

Lines of data slowly started to fill the screen closest to the transceiver.

"Peace indeed," Oppai said.

Ralla uneasily got to her feet, not sure what to make of Oppai's expression as he looked over the incoming data. After a few moments, the Governor placed on a headset and keyed the recorder.

"*Universalis*, this is Governor Oppai of the great ship *Population*. No terms of peace will be discussed. Any attempt to rescue Miss Gattley will result in her immediate execution. Any attack on this vessel will result in her immediate execution. We will continue our campaign of reclaiming our domes and facilities. We will not allow your doomsday weapon to be built. We will find out where you are building it, and after we destroy it we will destroy *you*." Oppai made eye contact with Ralla. "Crewman, send when encoded."

"Yes, sir." There was pride in the man's voice.

Ralla sunk back down to the floor in horror. Her own emotions had clouded her judgment. In her desire to make peace, she had completely misread Oppai. Again. Of course he wouldn't negotiate. There was nothing to negotiate. He stood to lose everything, to gain nothing. Such was the shock, she barely noticed being dragged back to her cell.

"No way. The deal's off," Thom said as definitively as he could. They had just listened to the return message in the Council Chambers. Larr and Jills sat silently, watching him.

Larr had just instructed him to be ready to leave with his fleet within the next 24 hours.

"Commander Vargas," Larr said in his usual chilling tone. "There is no deal. You are an Officer in our fleet and will do as you're instructed. We require you to use the ships at our disposal to distract the *Pop* while we ready the Fountain."

"And the moment I do, they kill Ralla."

"I don't see how Councilwoman Gattley is any of your concern."

"Don't see... are you insane? He just said he'll *kill her* if we attack. *I'll be attacking.* How is that not exactly my concern?"

"There's a bigger issue here, Thom," Jills broke in, motioning for Larr to remain silent. "I understand you have a friendship with Miss Gattley. I understand that you feel responsible for her current situation."

"I am responsible."

"But the fact is, there's a larger matter to address."

"Yeah, yeah, your Fountain."

"Not my Fountain, our Fountain. Every person on this ship and on the *Pop*'s Fountain. This is about the future, Thom, and if Ralla were here, she would agree. We can't let her life get in the way of the survival of our entire species."

"I'm not an idiot."

"I'm not saying you are."

"No, you are. What you have to understand is that I've left her behind twice, and now you want me to kill her. How can I live with that? How do you expect me to live with that?"

"Command is hard choices, Mr. Vargas," Larr said flatly.

"I agree," Thom said, standing abruptly and leaving the room.

Maybe it was habit, or some deep repressed desire, but Thom walked in nearly a direct line to the bar. The hand painted sign "The Landing" seemed oddly inviting, homey. It seemed like it had been ages since he had been here last, but it was all the same. His friends were at the bar, well into their third round judging by the empty glasses. If they were upset he hadn't talked to any of them in weeks, none showed it. Their welcome was warm and genuine.

After a few pats on the back, the time apart seemed forgotten. He settled down on a stool, watching the bartender slowly fill up a tall glass with foamy amber liquid. His friends jokingly pulled at his uniform, its fit and condition a sharp contrast to their own. The sound of the alcohol filling the glass was all he could hear. Around him his mates jostled each other in response to some story or joke he hadn't heard. The other patrons in the bar did their usual best to ignore his little gang. The foam crested the top of the glass ever so slightly, and a finger sized portion started a long slow descent down the side of the glass. The light from the overheads caught the bubbles inside, making the beverage appear to glow.

Sliding back from his reverie, he saw that the glasses of his friends were all full, and they were looking to toast his return. He took the glass in his hand, the liquid inside chilling it. He caught a whiff from the constantly bursting tiny bubbles of foam.

"We heard you captured an enemy sub with a bunch of refugees on it," Olly said with only a slight slur of his words.

"Did you kill any of them while you were over there? I heard they killed a bunch of people in our domes," Yully said, looking for confirmation. He had gained some weight, mostly muscle on his small frame.

"Are you back for a while?" Hett asked, his beard now reduced to a mere line along his jaw. The questions seemed to come at once, or maybe hours apart.

"Come on, Thom, what's next?"

The drink was almost to his lips, his eyes focused on the foam. Then he looked past the foam across the top of the glass at his friends. Wide-eyed and a little drunk, they were waiting for some response from him. It hadn't even occurred to them he hadn't said a word since he sat down.

And all at once, like a dream, he saw where he was. On a bar stool. In the bar. Below the Basket. On the *Uni*. In the ocean. On the world. In his mind he saw the world. The solid blue sphere hung in the black of space. Then, slowly, like in the graphic he had seen, the water started to peel away. As if the land below was tearing through, ripping the azure surface skin. The brown grew larger and larger. Soon entire continents marred the pristine blue surface with their turbid, waste-like, jagged forms. But then these too changed. The tawny scars of land succumbing to a new color. Green color. Randomly at first, then spreading and swarming recklessly, swaths of green reaching out with their tendrils of life over every continent.

His friends had gone silent and were looking at him quizzically. The glass poised so close to his lips, the smell of it in his nose. Then it started to move, gradually lowering back down to the bar. A bit of the foam spilling over the side and down over his thumb.

Thom stood, handing over enough credits to the bartender for a night of rounds for his slack-jawed friends. Thom started for the door.

"Thom?" Olly asked, all joviality gone. "Are you all right? Where are you going?"

"To kill her."

IV

The bridge of the *Reappropriation* had changed since last he saw it. New equipment had replaced the inferior *Pop*-installed devices. There were other terminals squeezed into the corners for better monitoring of the other ships in the fleet. Six officers crowded the bridge, and over 150 elsewhere throughout manned weapons, engines, and any number of other vital systems.

Two squads of marines led by Soli and Lo had ready rooms near fast-fill locks on either side of the ship. Nearby were two sleek new short-range shuttles embedded in the hull. The exterior bristled with upgraded guns. Two dozen torpedo ports, their flat exterior doors masking the destruction held within, lined every side of the ship. In the stern, a small bay above the propellers held six mini-subs waiting for action. Docking clamps released, the *Reap* floated above the darkened, silt-covered *Universalis*.

Thom couldn't see them, but saw on the monitors at the rear of the bridge the four corvette-class attack subs, six converted transports now highly armed torpedo boats, and a dozen mini-sub fighters all forming up with the *Reap* as it readied for its official maiden voyage. Every ship knew its assignment, every person on every ship knew the mission. All knew the risks. Thom had trained many of the pilots now spread out in the sea around him. Others came highly recommended. The first leg of their patrol was three straight days south. It would be a long haul for those in the minis, even with regular breaks docked aboard one of the larger subs. He motioned towards his comm officer.

"This is Commander Vargas. Our boards are green and we are ready to go." He clicked the mic to mute for a moment. His impulse was to tell them what he was feeling. To let them share in his fear, his dread, his knowledge. But it didn't seem right. They were all feeling that already—they didn't need that from him. He turned the mic back on. "The importance of our mission, of our success, cannot be understated. No less than the lives of everyone on board the ship below us, and countless more in far away domes, are relying on us. But you know that. Let me tell you what I know. Our enemy is underequipped, under trained, and spread thin. But that doesn't mean they won't fight. We will be successful because of you. I know how hard you have trained, and I know how outstanding each of you is at the job you are doing. If I wasn't so sure, trust that you wouldn't be here to do it. We will approach each conflict with caution, but deliver with precision and might. We will hit them hard, and then retreat. My goal is to return to the *Universalis* with every one of you. That, above all, is our goal. We must do widespread damage, but our damage per location can be minor. We are the greatest fighting force ever assembled in this sea. History will write of us as heroes and warriors. Right now, we are just people. Let's do our job, then celebrate with our feet on land, arms to the sky, backs to the sea."

There was silence as he clicked off the mic. Then off in the distance, down the corridors, then on the bridge itself: applause. He closed his eyes and cringed as he thought of Ralla, and how proud she'd be of him at that moment.

"I'm sorry," he said to her. Then to the pilot, "Take us out, ensign."

For what must have been the first week, Ralla barely left the cot. She was so ashamed of what she had done, she couldn't bring herself to eat or even move. Sometime during the second week, there were brief flashes of realization that she had to do what she had done. That anyone would have jumped at the chance to bring peace. But these flashes were just that, and within moments the depression would settle back in, knowing what she had cost her people.

At least she thought it was her second week in this cell. That was just a hazy guess, though. Every surface she tried to mark to indicate days had been too hard to mar. Eventually she tore the sheets, but they had changed them twice since she had been there. If the constant darkness at first had hampered her perception of time, the constant light now completely destroyed it. But two weeks felt right somehow.

The guards rotated often. To her surprise, one of the guards had slid a book into her cell. It was old, bound, and seemed to be real paper. The cover crackled when she opened it. It must have been a family heirloom. While she would have rather just slept, this was clearly important to someone, and she treated it with the respect it deserved. She finished it quickly. It was a fairly mediocre story about time travelling adventurers causing havoc during famous moments in history. Not something she would have normally read, but it did take her mind off things.

She kept the book hidden when guards opened her door to leave food. After several days (weeks? hours?) one guard—a middle-aged woman with long braided hair and a particularly mean grimace—came in with food and took the sheets off the bed. She tossed them outside, then flipped the thin mattress cushion over. Ralla had hidden the book under her clothes.

The guard seemed to have figured this out as she came over and brusquely grabbed at her. Book found, she stormed out of the cell. But as the door shut, there was a brief moment of eye contact where the guard looked down at the book in her hand, then at Ralla, and flashed a kind smile. Another book appeared under her food tray a few days later, this time an illustrated short novel. A different guard picked that up a few days later, a nervous young man with short hair.

To fill time, Ralla remembered a trick her father had told her about from when he was in the war. After a particularly bad battle, his sub had become damaged and crashed into the seabed. Trapped in the cockpit with no power and few rations, he could do nothing but watch the battle unfold and hope for rescue. It took three days. To stave off boredom, the elder Gattley had imagined himself walking through the ship. Every hallway, every cabin he had seen. From the textures of the walls to the conditions of the carpet, he walked around and around in his mind.

Ralla started doing the same the best she could. She pictured herself on the floor of the Yard, her favorite place on the ship. The thick soft grass cradling her like a living bed of green. The picosun providing the light of midday. Beside her lay Thom, and suddenly it was no longer a thought exercise but a memory. They had been walking after a great meal of words and vegetables. She had just said something that had made him mad. They laid in silence for minutes before he spoke.

"I don't know why you think I'm some kind of leader. That's not me. That's you."

His compliment caught her off guard, and it took her a moment to respond.

"I'm flattered, but I'm not much of a leader either. My dad is, for sure, but I'm just stepping into his shoes. When the time comes for a real election, we'll see what the District thinks."

"Well, I'd vote for you."

"Then maybe we'll just have to move you forward so you can be in my District."

They laughed lightly and awkwardly, both reading into her statement more than she had said. After the silence that followed, he said something even sweeter.

"Seriously, I trust your instincts. I've seen what you can pull together in the past few months. You're a natural at this. I wish I had half the brains you do."

She reached over and gave his arm a squeeze.

The grayish decayed cell slid back in around her, and like that, she got over herself. Had her father been there, or Proctor Jills, it'd be a tough case to say they wouldn't have done the same thing she had. Oppai was a charmer and a fantastic liar. Maybe they would have seen through his ruse, but probably not.

In her mind she thanked Thom for being his usual supporting self, even if he was a hemi away.

With renewed vigor, Ralla rolled out of bed and stood in the middle of her cell and began a new daily routine. First she exercised. Then she meditated on possible scenarios. She was still biding her time. But now it was with a purpose.

Running silent didn't mean they had to actually remain silent on board the ships, but often they did. Normal procedure was to cruise quietly along the edge of a thermal layer. The *Reap* towed an arrow-shaped sensor device that sank below or floated above the layer, relaying data to the techs on board. If an enemy craft was detected by it or one of the minisubs at the edges of the fleet, the information was relayed by laser to all the other ships. Instructions were given to stop, descend, or rise depending on how close the ship was, and where. But so far they had gone undetected.

Their first target was a mining dome the *Pop* had set up recently. It had been discovered by accident by a scouting ship looking for new mining locations for the *Uni*. It was tiny dome, without much room for personnel. A convoy of transports arrived every week, and departed within 12 hours. If their timing was right, the *Reap* and the fleet should arrive just before the convoy arrived.

The stealthy minis, not much larger than their single pilot occupants, ducked below the layer to have a peek. They reappeared above the layer a few minutes later to report the convoy was already docked, and seemed to be making preparations to leave.

Thom looked around the bridge at his crew. They waited for his instructions. As he knew they would, his thoughts went to Ralla. Knowing she would want him to do what he was about to do gave no comfort. He apologized to her again in his head.

"All craft, report status," he said. The comm officer relayed the message. In the close quarters of the bridge, he could hear each craft in the fleet respond through the officer's headphones.

"All craft report green boards and are ready for combat."

"Fleet to Combat One. Begin descent and attack on my orders."

Around him his crew busied themselves at their consoles, relaying orders and modifying aspects of the ship. After a few moments, he received a nod from his second in command.

"Go," Thom barked.

He felt the *Reap* lurch as water was taken into its ballast tanks. Out the viewscreen, the few craft of the fleet he could see in the dim light started to descend. The small fighter craft, with their smaller ballast tanks, were pivoting vertical to gather speed as they launched the first wave.

The *Reap* passed the invisible thermal layer and suddenly the sensor screens lit up with the activity and noise from the dome below. There were a few patrol craft lazily making their rounds within sight of the dome. The convoy—really just a series of transport subs linked together—had just set off. The clear dome lit up the surrounding seafloor with an amber glare.

The patrol craft took far too long to realize what was happening, and were disabled by the fast-diving minis before they had a chance to react. The transport did what any poorly trained crew would do. They sped up, futilely trying to escape. All this did was dramatically increase their signature on the sensors. The transport sub in the lead, the only one with a crew, labored against its heavy train of ore-laden trailers. After a moment they detached themselves, rocketing forward, the instant removal of mass increasing the engine's effectiveness tenfold. Two of Thom's corvettes had entered the fray at the point, sending out grapples, and started towing the ore train back towards the *Reap*.

The transport hadn't gotten far before it was pounced on by two more minis. The engines were knocked out first, and the sub slowly came to a stop.

"Assault teams. Go," Thom said, watching the action on the sensor monitors. Thom could feel the *Reap* shudder slightly, its buoyancy changing as the two shuttles detached from the hull, diving rapidly towards the dome below. Cameras along the keel zoomed in on the action, and Thom watched as the heavily armed assault teams subdued the staff of the dome. His assault teams went about systematically destroying every piece of equipment they could find. The staff was herded into the small lifeboat attached to the top of the living quarters. Thom didn't see it happen, but knew the plan was for charges to be thrown down the open mine shaft, while others were sent down the conveyor belt deep into the mine.

It was all over in minutes. Soli signaled that he and his team were returning. There had been little to salvage. No sooner had the shuttles detached and started their return than flashes of explosions could be seen from the center of the dome. Water burst up from underneath the equipment, flooding the dome to at least waist height. The lights flickered out, cloaking the event in darkness. All that remained were the small emergency lights on the lifeboat, trapped inside a partially flooded dome. Thom had the comm officer send the recall command, and the ships formed up and rose away from the ruin they had caused. Around him his crew seemed elated. He wished he could have shared their joy.

Ten minutes later, it was like they were never there. The fleet ascended above the thermal layer and set out for their next target. With his second in command in charge of the bridge, and by extension the fleet, Thom headed down towards the back of the ship. He wasn't sure if he'd ever get used to the constricted corridors of the *Reap*. Two people had to turn sideways to pass each other. Worse, wallplates were still missing in places, leaving exposed tangles of pipes and wires that threatened to snag, burn, or electrocute anyone who traversed the hallway. He got to the ready room where Soli and Lo's teams were stowing their gear. Soli hopped on one foot as he struggled to remove one of his boots. Thom offered a hand of support, Soli took a shoulder.

"I take it everything went OK?" he asked the marine.

"No resistance."

"None?"

"None. We walked in and everyone immediately put down their tools and whatnot and sat on the ground."

"That's it?"

"They looked pretty ragged, to be honest. When we put them all in the lifeboat, they looked..."

"Scared?"

"No. Disappointed."

"What?"

"Wait a sec. Lo, come here. Tell the Commander what you told me."

Lo was combing his hair, having already put on his civilian clothes. He wove his way between the rest of the dressing/undressing marines, his grace belying his mass.

"The management guy?" he asked Soli. The other marine nodded. "There was this one guy, seemed more like the manager of the place than one of the workers. He was watching over everyone as we rounded them up. Not in a bad way, kind of like how parents do with their kids, you know?

He asked to be the last one in and when it was just him outside the lifeboat, he asked me if we had any food."

"For him?" Thom asked.

"I don't think so. It seemed like he was asking for his whole crew. It was really weird."

"Did you give him anything?" Thom asked. The marines looked at each other awkwardly.

"We gave them what rations we had," Lo answered almost sheepishly. "It seemed like the right thing to do."

Thom stood silently for a moment, and the marines grew concerned.

"Look, if it's a problem, next time..." Soli began.

"Next time *is* the problem." Thom replied. "You absolutely did the right thing. On the next run, if the same thing happens, let me know. After everyone is subdued and the place is clear, I think we can spare a few minutes to find out what's going on."

"What do you think?" Lo asked. Thom noticed the rest of the marines had stopped and were listening in on the conversation. Thom changed his tone and spoke to them all.

"When Ralla and I were on the *Pop* the people we met were very friendly. A real close-knit group. Closer, I'd say, than we are on the *Uni*. Many of them just had this blind hatred of us. No doubt spurred on by their leader. But now I wonder if there's a few cracks in that hull. Above all, protect yourselves and your squadmates. But do your best to treat the *Pop* civilians as well as possible. I'll see about having the cooks siphon off some of our supplies, even if it means we have to RTB a few weeks early for resupply. For the good we'll be spreading, I think it will be worth it."

"Got it," Soli replied.

"Make sure all your men are running on the same layer."

"Don't worry. We were all talking about it on the way back. To be honest, we're kind of freaked out about the whole thing. It's not like we're going after soldiers here."

"Understood. Thank you, gentlemen."

"Commander," they said in unison. Thom uncomfortably returned their salute.

V

The cell door slammed open, but Ralla was already awake, so the dramatic effect was wasted. Oppai's entrance, however, did surprise her. He was fuming. Ralla, having been meditating on her bed, leaned forward to peer out the door at the guards. They looked terrified. Not good.

"Get up!" Oppai barked. Ralla unfolded her legs and did as instructed. The Governor grabbed her arm abruptly and marched her out of the cell and up through the corridors of the ship. She'd been given an ill-fitting jumpsuit after repeatedly complaining about the rankness of her clothing. She kept tripping on the pant legs, causing Oppai to yank her along impatiently. The guards outside the Governor's cabin opened the doors for them, but Oppai froze unexpectedly as they entered. It wasn't until she peered around him that she saw why. There were a dozen men in normal clothing clustered in front of the wood conference table. They turned to look at Oppai, but their eyes slid to Ralla. Oppai didn't seem to have expected them.

"What do you want?" he asked dismissively.

"This couldn't wait, Governor," said a tall, portly man with graying temples and a short brown beard. He stood in the middle of the group. "Perhaps your... pet project can remain seated for a few minutes while we discuss more... *pressing* matters?"

Oppai dragged Ralla towards the couches and gave her a shove. She tried to remain standing, but tripped on her coveralls. Oppai joined the others, all of whom had their noses buried in papers on the table. Ralla only caught occasional word or snippet—"ration situation," "dire"—but the occasional glances they cut her said more than words ever could.

It seemed too perfect. As if Oppai wanted her to hear what they were saying. It certainly wasn't the first time he'd tried to trick her. But his anger at seeing these men seemed genuine, like a child being denied a cookie.

Eww, she thought, I'm the cookie.

Ralla resisted the urge to dismiss Oppai, or underestimate him even slightly. Even if the situation on this ship was bad, he was still an unpredictable threat.

Oppai stood up straight, then said yet another thing Ralla couldn't make out. The message was clear, though; the other men filed out of the room post haste. A few eyed her as they left. She knew a lot of emotions could be faked, but no one could fake fear that well. Certainly not that many of them.

"Clever. I bet your friends think they're very clever," Oppai said, looking out at the shipyard outside the windows. From what she could see, it seemed fine.

"Pardon?"

"I've had four mines go dark on me these past weeks. Tried contacting them. No response. I don't suppose you know anything about this?"

Tentatively, Ralla stood and made her way towards the table. Scattered across it were dozens of printouts of graphs and long series of numbers. Ralla took a moment to realize he had asked a question. She held her arms out in front of her, the long sleeves covering her hands.

"How would I know anything about your mines?"

"We gave your people explicit instructions. I said any attack would result in your death. So they did it all quiet. No distress messages, just darkness."

Ralla felt a wash of panic, but forced it to subside. Why would he have brought her up here to kill her? The cell would have sufficed. The mess would certainly be easier to clean up. His tone made her nervous, though.

"What do you want, Governor? I've been locked in that cell for, what, a month? I have no idea. I have no idea what you're talking about, and honestly, I don't care." She played the part of exhausted prisoner, going so far as to droop her shoulders and bow her head.

Head bowed, her eyes darted around the room searching for anything that could be used as a weapon. With nothing to do in her cell but exercise she was toned into the best shape of her life. Ralla had always felt she was a little soft around the edges, but now she could see muscles making new curves. Oppai was bigger, though, and then there were the guards outside. She doubted she'd be able to force Oppai to the balcony before he struggled free or called for help. Patience, Ralla thought. For the moment, he was buying her act.

"Fine. If they're moving on our mines..."

Our mines, Ralla thought.

"Then we're going to strike. Now. Tell me where this silo thing is."

"I told you, I don't know."

"I'm sure you do.. You've obviously been involved in the planning. You've obviously had access to all the data. Would you have me believe that the Princess of the *Universalis*..."

"I'm *not* the..."

"You will tell me!" he screamed, and as quickly as the storm brewed in his eyes, it subsided. "I see imprisonment has done nothing for your demeanor, so I have a new plan. Let's call it... escalation. Your life is about to become much, much worse. And when you're finally broken, Miss Gattley, you will tell me what I need to know. It's that easy. In the meantime,

I'm going to step up my attacks on your people. I won't let them just take what is ours. Have fun in the Sewers."

His smile made her nervous.

On her ship, they called it the Bilge. It was a series of connected compartments that ran the length of the keel: above the multi-layer carbon outer hull, and below the bottom-most decks. Any water that washed in with an arriving sub, or was spilled above decks, eventually, through a series of tubes and channels, ended up down in the Bilge. The water brought with it all the grime and ooze it had picked up along the way. On the *Uni*, a team of techs kept colonies of microbes to break down the nastiness. Eventually the water was recycled, desalinated, and used as part of the rather sizable amount of fresh water hydrating the Garden.

On the *Pop*, there was no such program. Worse, it seemed like much of their wastewater emptied here as well. The water, such as it was, made its way from compartment to compartment through holes in the bulkheads towards the stern. Presumably, it was then pumped out into the sea. This left solid waste, along with all manner of other unidentifiable filth, to accumulate slowly in the chambers. She could smell it from two levels up, and they hadn't even opened the locks to the stairs. *Nausea* didn't fully describe her repulsion.

As the soldiers opened the hatch to the dark foulness, she vomited. Two guards had brought her down; neither seemed friendly. If suits existed to protect those unlucky enough to clean the humid nastiness, Ralla wasn't given one. Instead, she was given a hose half the thickness of her arm and a partial face mask.

Stepping down from the entrance platform, she immediately sank into a knee-high mass of churning, slimy brown waste. She vomited again, sadly making the area no less revolting.

Feeble orange lights hung from the ceiling, casting barely enough light to let her see what she was doing. Of this, she was thankful. By the look of the hastily patched-together bulkhead behind her, it seemed like this was the forward-most compartment behind the shipyard. Looking aft, she could see all the lights, slowly swaying with the ship, stretching into the distance, blurring to a solid line. As she struggled to get some slack, the dull ache in her slowly healing shoulder erupted into piercing pain.

So she stood there, death grip on the hose, shaking in the muck and the stink and the echoing gurgle.

Ralla closed her eyes. Forced away the thoughts of what was pressing against her legs. Forced away the pungent stench, the clammy cold, and the sting of her wound.

Then she was sitting in the thick grass of the Yard floor. The picosun was at its most intense, bright and warm. Spread chaotically before her were papers filled with charts and tables, like what she had seen in Oppai's office.

No, not there. Here, in the Yard. With...

Thom lay on his back, beside her, hands behind his head looking as relaxed as Ralla had ever seen him. He looked asleep, though she knew he wasn't. At least, he hadn't been when this had really happened, which seemed so long before. He had said something right before this moment, but now

Ralla had forgotten what it was. The air smelled of cut grass and half a dozen different types of flowers.

The papers were from some committee she was on, and she pushed them away in disgust. This, she had done before. Or was it just then? The sound caused Thom to turn his head and open his eyes, squinting in the bright light. His expression asked the question.

"I can't do it, Thom. I just can't."

"Do what?"

"This. All of this," she said, her arm sweeping in front of her. "I'm not smart enough for this stuff."

Thom expression soured.

"Why do you say that?"

"Because I'm not. I know I'm not. Look, Thom, it's not that big of a deal."

"Yes, it is."

"No, I'm not smart like my mom, I'm not born for bureaucracy like my father. It's OK, I'm OK with that. It's just..."

"I don't get where *that*'s coming from."

Ralla flashed to homework as a kid, her mother getting upset when she couldn't figure out a math problem. She remembered how her father would insist she'd be able to understand something, and then when she didn't get it immediately, he'd gently move on, giving up in everything but the words.

"My dad..."

"Is what? What makes you think he's good at this?"

"Because he is."

"Sorry, Ralla. I know I'm coming at this from a way different angle, but I learned a long time ago that parents are nothing but the people who gave us life. They don't have extraordinary powers. They're just normal people."

"Not my parents."

"Was your dad around a lot when you were a growing up?"

"Some, yeah. He taught me a lot of the things we didn't learn in school."

"And when he wasn't there, how do you know he wasn't struggling with all of this just as much you are?"

"Well..." Ralla trailed off. Thom had a point. It wasn't likely, but it wasn't impossible.

Thom propped himself on one arm.

"Ralla, look at me. You are the smartest person I know. You more capable of figuring things out and doing, well, anything, than anyone I've ever met. If you can't do whatever all this dreck is, no one can. And anyone who seems otherwise is faking."

She wanted to kiss him then more than anything. No one had ever told her that before. He was so sincere in his words, so without hesitation in her ability. So much more so than she was.

As much as she wanted to fall on him and kiss him on the lips, she didn't want anything to ruin this friendship. He meant more to her than anyone. He was such a mess sometimes, but when he wasn't...

Tomorrow was dinner with Cern, and she realized that more than anything she would rather just stay here with Thom forever. The thought was terrifying, not because of Thom, but what that meant about Cern. Ralla felt confused, but somehow hopeful. She looked back at Thom with a different set of eyes.

Thom had rolled onto his back again, eyes closed, but his words continued to echo in her ears. The papers scattered before her no longer appeared a daunting, insurmountable task. Now they were just a task. Like any other. Maybe challenging, but doable. It was like a switch had been flipped in her brain. She could do this. Why not?

Ralla did something that she hadn't done the first time. She turned and laid down, her head on Thom's chest, his arm around her. She could smell him, then, that incredible smell of his.

Above her, the picosun started to fade, its color shifting to a faded weak orange. The warmth on her skin disappeared, the dank washing over her in a rush.

But it didn't matter. The horror was gone, the stench no longer overwhelming. Ahead of her was a job, nothing more. One that others on this ship had certainly done before her. Ralla activated the hose.

Ten hours later, after the two guards had returned their charge to her cell and after a long detour in an industrial washroom, they sat in their barracks and argued.

One was convinced that right before the tiny blond woman had turned on the hose, for a brief moment, she had actually smiled.

They had lost one of the modified transport subs in a raid on a dome the previous week. One of the dome's patrol subs had lost its port engine, spiraling out of control, and colliding with the transport. Both subs imploded instantly, killing twelve. In agony, Thom wrote to the parents of the dead.

Two days later, a mini accidently clipped a torpedo distracted by countermeasures, vaporizing both of them.

The *Reap* had received a few hits, but the hull had taken little damage. The crew, though, was a different story. There wasn't anyone on board lacking a bruise or gash from being knocked around, or just from navigating the narrow passageways. The *Reap* fleet had been on the hunt for close to a month, and morale was low. Fatigued and battered, Thom signaled the *Uni* on the longcomm. They were cutting their first patrol short and were returning to rearm, repair, and relax. The response took longer than expected, and surprised him and confused his comm officer. The *Uni* was at location Alpha, approach with caution.

Alpha was the codename for the Fountain build site. Thom was the only one in the fleet that knew where it was. The *Uni* was ahead of schedule, and had not only freed itself from its hiding place, but had already moved north for the build. Thom instructed the Navigator to head north in a zigzag route, stopping frequently and jumping layers on a regular basis. Commands were relayed to the fleet, and they set off. Muscles groaning in protest, Thom left his command chair and made his way back to his tiny quarters, looking forward to the first real sleep he'd gotten in weeks. The trip to the *Uni* would take over a week, and he thought he might sleep the whole way.

His shoes were off before the door to his cabin had shut. He didn't even bother taking off his clothes before collapsing onto the thin cushion that covered his fold-down wall bed.

His feet dangled over the end. As tired as he was, sleep didn't take him. His mind was still going, snapping from thought to thought, from responsibility to responsibility. He imagined himself taking hold of his brain and steering it towards something relaxing.

Thom's first thought was of a celebration. It had been just over a month after the *Uni* had buried itself in hiding. The major damage had been taken care of, and people were cautiously optimistic that they weren't, at that moment, going to die. And that was all they needed to celebrate. Ralla had invited him and his friends to come out with her and hers. There was a small dance club midway up the port side of the Garden. It was not his idea of a good time, nor his scene, but his boys were excited to try out a new place and meet some new women. The music was loud, it was dark, and it had taken them forever to get in the door and find Ralla. He wasn't surprised she had a booth towards the back. Drunken, sweaty dancers packed the place wall to wall.

After his third drink, though, everything was good. He was able to lean back in the booth and look out at his friends dancing with Ralla's. It was an odd sight, Olly towering over the others on the dance floor, doing a decent job dancing with one of Ralla's petit brunette friends. She came up to his chest. Hett's beard dripped with sweat but neither he nor anyone else, it seemed, noticed or cared. Perhaps the most amazing transformation was Yullsin. His skilled, fluid dance moves held the attention of not one but two of Ralla's friends. Even Ralla, alternately dancing with no one and dancing with everyone, seemed oblivious to anything outside of this room, this beat, this moment. Thom wished then, as he did now, so much time and space later, that he could freeze that moment and not leave. Everyone happy.

Ralla moved her body to the beat, dragging her hands up her body, into her hair, and then tossing it around. The curls bounced to their own tempo. She eyed him seductively, beckoning him out onto the floor. He shook his head with a smile, and raised his half-full glass to her. She pouted, and he laughed, the sound lost in the music. With a pounce, she was in the booth with him, tugging at his clothes.

"Come on. Aren't you having any fun?" Ralla shouted in his ear. He could still barely hear her.

"Of course. I'm just not much of a dancer. Trust me: I'm having a great time."

He was. His friends, who had known him longer than anyone, hadn't given a second thought to him being in the booth. Ralla slid back out, her hair covering her face. She started talking to her friends, ear by ear, and as she did their eyes darted over towards him.

"Uh oh," he said aloud, though no one could hear it.

They turned on him en masse, crawling across the booth, Ralla in the lead with a mischievous smile on her face. Once dragged to the floor, he stood motionless, a mock frown on his face. As a group they had surrounded him, a knot of calm in the undulations of the dance floor.

Then, with a crack, his hands went up, a smile spread wide, and he danced. They cheered.

It was an odd feeling, being surrounded by so many people, yet forced to be alone with his thoughts. He looked down at Ralla, her curls now twisting around as she shook her head to the beat, and realized that even if she could hear him, there was no way he could describe how he felt. It's not that she had wanted him out on the floor with them. It's not that he felt any more a part of the group in their midst than he did in the booth. It was because it had seemed to her that he was moping about in the booth, and it looked like he wasn't having a good time. Without being able to explain it, he could see how it would look like that. And that thought had driven her to drag him out. She wouldn't let him mope, even when he said it was fine. She didn't give up on him.

Thom knew there was no way to explain that to someone who'd had a life of inclusion. But that little moment had meant more to him than he could have put into words. When she looked up at him and smiled, he smiled back. That was the best he could do. He felt something then, and barely wanted to admit it to himself. But right there, from that moment, he would have done anything for her.

So as he wearily hung onto the last vestiges of consciousness, his thoughts went again to rescue. If she was alive, and there was an opportunity, any opportunity, he would get her out. As it so often did, his next thoughts went to how best to create that opportunity. Plans within plans within plans.

Thom dreamed of drums. The music and festivities in the club had spread to the deck of the Garden and Basket. Thousands drunkenly danced and poorly sang while music roared. People cheered from the balconies, stomping their feet in rhythm with the melody. He could see the huge drums in the center of the crowd. The pounding, the pounding, the pounding of the drums no longer matched the pounding of the thousands of feet. The music had changed, but no one noticed. It became dissonant, harsh. Around him the celebration continued, a nightmarish cacophony of sound against sound. Rising above it, a new strike on the biggest drum. It sounded different. Odd. Less a bang and more of a...

It wasn't music. Those weren't drums. He snapped awake. The alarm klaxon was unlike the one on the *Uni*, a sound he'd known by heart since childhood. Everyone onboard did. He looked down at himself, still dressed. The door to his cabin had barely hit its stops by the time he was halfway down the corridor, hopping as he put on his shoes.

Another explosion shook the ship, knocking him sideways into the bulkhead. An open panel tore his shirt as he fell to a skidding stop. Another explosion lifted him bodily from the deck, smashing him down and knocking the wind from him. The clamor of panic echoed through the corridors. By the time he made it to the bridge, his senior officers had arrived and were taking over their posts. One glance at the sensors showed how much trouble they were in.

The *Pop* patrol fleet easily equaled their numbers, but most of their ships were larger. As people shouted cries for orders, more explosions rocked the ship. The fear in the voices, the cries for help on the comm, the discord and chaos of it all crushed down upon Thom.

He wasn't sure how long it took, no more than one break in the wailing klaxon, but his mind focused—filtering away, piece by piece, all the unnecessary sounds and stimuli. Suddenly there was nothing but his comm officer, asking for commands to relay to the fleet.

"Defense pattern Oval 1. Weapons free," Thom said calmly. The officer, only a few years out of school, looked relieved at getting an order. The next sound Thom heard was his weapons officer. "Focus fire on the command ship," Thom said, tapping the sensor screen in front of him, selecting the largest vessel and placing it in red rotating brackets. "All offensive weapons open fire." The weapons officer nodded and relayed the message. After a moment's pause the hull shuddered as the heavy cannons fired in unison. The thin, long projectiles lanced out, their heat and speed vaporizing the water in front of them. The sensor screen visually represented the sounds of impacts on the enemy hull. Several of the enemy craft broke off their attack to cover their main ship. "Torpedo boats, area-of-effect fire between *Reap* and enemy fleet." His orders were instantly relayed.

The voice of the officer of the deck filtered its way through to Thom's brain next.

"We have flooding on Decks 1, 2, and 4, and injuries reported throughout."

"Get Soli to take charge of the damage crews, using whatever men he has free. Anybody that can still man their station is to do so. We can patch up the cuts and scrapes later."

No sooner had the words left his mouth than a series of rapid explosions sounded through the hull. Outside the viewscreen the dark green-blue world lit up as the volley from the torpedo boats created a wall of steam and bubbles and fire between the two fleets. All craft beyond the wall temporarily disappeared.

"Blow ballast. Get us above the layer. All craft follow. Formation Delta Z-Down."

Screaming air burst into the tanks and the *Reap* leapt vertically. Any conversation was impossible in the noise, the ship wailing in protest at the sudden movement. Everyone braced themselves the best they could. The fleet always traveled close to the layer for this very scenario, and had run countless drills during their transit. Thom could see around him everyone settling down. This was routine. They had done all this before. Maybe not with a real enemy, but the motions were the same. He hoped the men and women on the other ships were feeling something similar.

The steam wall lasted less than a minute, but it was long enough for the fleet to get above the layer and return to neutral buoyancy. The piercing whistle of air was replaced by deep gurgles as the ballast tanks partially refilled with water. The other ships formed up around the *Reap*. The pilot tipped the big ship forward, and instinctively Thom's right hand shot up to press against the ceiling to steady himself. The view out the viewscreen messed with the mind, barely changing as the deck angled more and more. The sensors showed the rest of the fleet, already minus several craft, forming an inverted "V" with the *Reap* at its point. The tilt continued, and soon Thom needed to brace himself against his console with his left hand. He could hear objects falling forward on the bridge. Mugs and pens clattered towards the bow. A tablet slid from the central table, crashing forward into the viewscreen and shattering.

Then he saw them. The enemy fleet had taken the respite in combat to form up. As he had hoped, they showed a lack of experience. The smaller ships formed a shell around the largest ship. In their commander's mind, a protective shell. They had kept neutral buoyancy, and were rising to meet the *Reap* by pitching up towards them. The ships faced each other head on, but the *Reap* was uphill. Thom didn't bother to wait for them to clear the layer.

"All craft, full volley. Target 1."

His order made it to the fleet almost instantly. The cannons on the *Reap* fired first, their steaming lines not forming so much as appearing fully formed. They impacted the lead ships first, passing through the light escort subs as if they weren't there, leaving imploded bubbles in their stead. The projectiles hit the main enemy ship in a tight grouping, punching a hole clear through the outer hull and pulling a rush of seawater in with it.

On either side of the *Reap*, the remaining corvettes fired their rockets—slower projectiles with much more sizeable warheads. Their solid fuel vaporized the water behind them, leaving huge rising white contrails. The barrage hit the forward-most craft, the impacts each firing off a shaped charge, sending molten metal through a tiny hole in the hull, melting everything in a cone away from the impact site. Two more subs started sinking immediately.

The torpedo subs, on the outer tips of the "V," loosed their weapons last. They fired a mix of slow-moving but massive high-explosive and area-of-effect ordinance. The HE's exploded near and between the remaining enemy craft. Huge white spheres expanded outwards from the explosions. The resulting shockwaves crumpled the hulls of the small scout subs already trying to flee the carnage. The AOE torpedoes took care of the incoming shots fired off by the enemy small subs in their panic.

"Back us off, ensign."

The pilot reversed the engines, sliding them up and backwards away from the crippled enemy fleet. The remaining small subs that had surrounded the enemy command ship had turned and fled down and away from the fight, having never crossed the layer.

Thom could hear excitement in the voices of his crew, but he knew it wasn't over. He stared out the viewscreen, down across the murky expanse, past the wreckage of the smaller ships, locking his eyes on the still advancing command sub. It was half-again as large as the *Reap*, a relic of the last war. Thom had never seen one outside of old vids. The considerable damage to its hull was visible even at this distance. Bubbles streamed from holes peppered across the bow, drifting upwards towards the *Reap*. The hole punched by the main *Reap* cannons was large enough that light leaked out. Water no longer seemed to be rushing in, evidence that the emergency locks still worked.

"Fire again."

"Cannons are reloading, sir."

"Fire again, dammit."

"Ten seconds, Commander."

"Ensign, flank speed to stern, *NOW*."

The officer did as instructed, throwing Thom forward across the central table. The "V" rapidly elongated as the *Reap* tried to gain distance. The lumbering enemy craft finally cleared the layer, and warnings of weapons lock buzzed ominously. The old sub had none of the advanced weaponry of the *Reap*. No cannons or rockets, just old-fashioned torpedoes and a lot of them. They were still close enough to watch as a dozen outer doors slid aside, revealing the rounded heads of the weapons beyond.

"Torpedo subs, AOE!" he shouted, knowing it was too late.

With bursts of compressed air, the enemy torpedoes launched in sequence. Almost simultaneously, the cannons on the *Reap* punched another ultimately meaningless hole in the front of the enemy hull. The torpedoes fanned outwards, pre-programmed to attack different targets.

"Blow ballast, evasive maneuvers and countermeasures!" His cool had gone; he hoped his panic wasn't too apparent.

The craft lurched upwards and backwards, but it wasn't enough. With only a few seconds needed to close the distance, all dozen torpedoes found their mark. Two of the three remaining corvettes disappeared in a puff of steam and fire. Three of the torpedo subs did the same. The remaining craft either dodged the weapon, or took a non-lethal hit. Four of the torpedoes had been designated for the *Reap*. One was confused by the countermeasures and powered harmlessly away. Another bounced off the hull, a dud. The other two impacted along the keel, just below the bridge. Thom was punched downwards and smashed face-first onto the central table, cracking the glass and destroying the interface. The rest of the bridge crew, all strapped in, got knocked around but avoided serious injury.

Flooding alarms added their disharmony to the din. Flat on his stomach, blood obscuring one eye, Thom stared out the front viewscreen and watched as the holes in the enemy sub went dark, the interior lights winking out. It started to sink below the layer, sliding out of view and into the gloom.

"Report!"

It had been two solid days in her cell since she had finished work on the sewers, and Ralla wasn't convinced she'd ever get the smell out of her hair. The long tepid showers every evening helped some, but her hair had clumped into a tangled nest of nastiness.

Once past the initial rankness of the job, the work itself hadn't been too bad. Grueling, for sure, but the hose did most of the work. She thought fondly of the final moment near the stern, when she looked back up the length of the ship, standing at the farthest point from where she had been the first day. Every chamber clean, the overwhelming nature of the job became an emotional moment of accomplishment. It had been the hardest weeks of her life, but having survived... no, thrived at the worst Oppai could throw at her, she felt strong. Stronger than she had in her entire life.

Well, emotionally strong. She was pretty sure she had slept for at least a day straight after she had finished, and even now every part of her body ached. But inside, despite her surroundings and situation, she was actually, surprisingly, happy.

So when the guards came the next day, she was more curious about her next task than fearful. But the fear would come, and quickly.

The two guards, the same that had chaperoned her to and from the sewers, said nothing during their long walk aft. They took two different elevators. Ralla almost expected to arrive near where the sewer ended in some sort of cruel joke to clean it all over again but backwards. Instead, they entered a tall, wide corridor that ran the width of the ship. Ralla had never seen it, but it was clear what it was for, having been in a similar corridor on the *Uni*. It was the main passageway that connected all the entrances to the multiple engine rooms housing the ship's propulsion drives. They walked across to the port side, passing the floor-to-ceiling doors that she knew could slide open to reveal the generators and motors, one for each propeller. Each motor and generator had its own room, sealed from the others in case of attack or malfunction. Twice they passed open doors, and the heat and racket from the machinery washed across them. The engine rooms were bathed in light, bright enough that the engineers could see every part of their motorized burdens.

But it was the end of the hall that had her worried, and the impending doom grew with every step. The last engine room had been sealed off, a crude lock fashioned into the welded plates that sealed up the rest of the entrance. Something gave her a deep, almost visceral, feeling of danger.

Outside the lock was a middle-aged man with receding, greasy hair. He had a nervous presence about him, and Ralla could see why. As they approached, he stepped away from the lock as if it meant him personal harm. He looked her up and down disapprovingly.

"I told him I wasn't going to be a party to her murder," he said, jabbing a bony finger at one of her guards. The guards said nothing, but the engineer could tell by their expressions not to press the matter. He addressed Ralla, looking at her directly for the first time. "I told the Governor this was no place for a woman. I told him you'd just get in the way and when you got yourself killed, you'd probably take out an entire shift."

Ralla wanted to take what this weaselly man was saying as a challenge, but she couldn't take her eyes off the improvised lock. Whatever they were trying to contain inside was bad.

This guy knew it, even the guards knew it. Only the threat of the two goons and their weapons kept her from running.

"Do you understand?" the man asked. She realized she hadn't been listening. Before she could say "no," the guards had grabbed her arms and were moving her towards the entrance. It was then, through the small transparent panel in the lock, that she could see a tiny bit of what was beyond. Her breathing sped up, and as they pushed her bodily into the small chamber, it had become gasps of near panic.

The first door sealed behind her, but it took some time for the lock to cycle. The pressure grew, popping her ears twice. She continued to gasp, the artificial atmo becoming thicker and thicker. The air gripped every inch of her body.

The inner lock cycled, grinding open. Ice-cold water rushed in, numbing her feet, while the heat and pressure of the air made her cough violently. She recovered, and forced herself to look out at the space.

The generator and motor were actually running, defying all logic and safety. The water lapped up against the generator, suggesting impending death by electrocution. A dozen weary workers had paused from their various jobs to stare at her. Two were trying to keep a bilge pump going; the rest were toiling away at the most horrifying task Ralla had ever seen.

It seemed the entire outer and inner hull had been blown out in an explosion. A barricade of metal panels had been hurriedly welded together in an attempt to seal off the engine room from the ocean beyond. On the *Uni*, this was a temporary measure so dry suited engineers could rebuild the hull. That didn't seem to be the case here. They had over-pressurized the room so it could be drained and still use the propulsion unit. The stunning disregard for safety was appalling enough, but it was much worse than that. The pressure was capable of so much. The ocean was still getting in, one tiny crack and pinhole at a time. The entire wall seemed in imminent verge of collapse. The water on the floor was just the most obvious part of an entire situation that bordered on total catastrophe.

It was a waking nightmare. If all or even part of the wall fell, either the violent pressure change would kill everyone in the room instantly or they'd drown. If the water level got too high, they'd be electrocuted. The room felt of death.

All her energy, her pride, her optimism from the previous days was gone. Oppai had won. Every fear from her childhood formed fully and physically into a menacing wall of welded steel and dripping water. She closed her eyes, not wanting to see the other workers look at her with their defeated, lifeless faces. She clenched her fist to bang it against the door. It was time to give up. Anything to be out of this room. To be anywhere else. The fear absorbed her. Panic like she had never known. It was as if Oppai's hands were in her chest, trying to pull her inside out.

Everything she was wanted to bang on the door and surrender. Everything engrained into her to fear for her entire life lay before her in this room. These men would die. Something would happen and they'd die, and she'd die, in the worst way imaginable.

But her hand didn't move. Her clenched fist remained pressed against the door. For a moment she was in the transport with Thom after they had escaped the dome, what seemed like years earlier. As the water filled up, she remembered the feeling of panic as they flooded the stricken sub. She felt like she was going to drown, the suit irrelevant. Thom had held her close then. Held her against him. He must have been scared too. They barely knew each other then. She felt his body against hers now. The water around her feet, cold like it was then. They had flooded the sub to get free. They had faced death to face life. Oppai couldn't win now. Not now. Not ever. And in that moment, he didn't.

Ralla's eyes snapped open, burning with determination. They were all still looking at her. In their faces she saw her fear. The same terror that came with knowing death was looming above them, all around them. She stepped out of the lock into the engine room, the water lapping up against her calves. She ignored it. The workers each wore different clothes, but they all had one thing she needed.

"Give me some boots, and let's get started."

VI

The familiar sights, sounds, and smells of the *Universalis* were small comfort for Thom, the crew of the *Reappropriation*, and its surviving support fleet. There was a small gathering of family members when they arrived, but those who had gotten bad news in the days previous were absent.

Thom accepted hugs from his friends and made his way to the Garden. Eerre seemed to sense his mood, and offered him a hand on the shoulder and a hearty meal in silence. Thom hugged him when he finished, then went to his cabin. He was almost surprised to see it exactly as he had left it. It was all his, but seemed so foreign. The bed was just as unmade as he had left it, though that seemed like someone else. His clothes were in piles on the floor, dropped there when someone else packed for the *Reap*. His someone else's towel hung from the shower door. On his someone else's bed he sat down and cried his own tears, and those for someone else.

Thom met Proctor Jills in the Council chambers that evening, as requested. They stood in silence on the balcony, overlooking the Yard. It was obvious that Thom had been crying, but Jills didn't mention it.

"Come with me. I want to show you something," Jills finally said.

"What?"

"Something that will make you feel better."

They left the chambers and entered a stairwell adjacent to the elevators, the style and aesthetic trappings of the carpeted corridors replaced by the stairwell's stark industrial design. They went up.

The stairway straightened out and arched away from them, following the curve of the hull above. Soon they were in the Spine, and Jills turned towards the bow. The raw latticework began to give way to partially finished walls, then old, but unworn, carpet. Ahead was an open space, dim compared to the harsh lighting of the hallway.

After they stepped through, Jills closed the door to the hallway and for a moment they were in darkness. It took Thom's eyes a moment to adjust. The room was perfectly round, with a waist-high wall. Above them was a transparent dome, showing the sea around them, all the way up to the surface far above. Sunlight trickled down, giving just enough light to see.

"I've never been up here before."

"I hadn't either, until a few weeks ago," Jills replied taking in the view himself. "This was originally designed to be the Council's meeting chambers. Apparently they didn't like it. Turns out some people don't like to look out into the open like this."

"It's also pretty exposed."

"That would be the other reason. Here, look out the starboard side."

In the dim, his face close to the glass, Thom could see a dark, unnatural shape in the distance, just at the edge of what was visible. It was perfectly straight, rising up from the seafloor out of sight, up past the ship, all the way to the surface.

"When we approached we came from the other side of the *Uni*."

"I know."

"I guess I hadn't thought you'd have made much progress. Is there ice growth?"

"Some. Things are proceeding a little slower up there than Dr. Gattley had hoped, but they are proceeding."

"Has anyone been to the surface? Has anyone walked on it yet?"

"Are you volunteering?"

"I... I don't know. Maybe." This one dark vertical line in the distance had turned him into a schoolboy. The wonder of it, seeing the Fountain—the actual thing—with his own eyes. There was so much hope.

"They're still taking readings. Seems like the radiation levels are pretty good this far north. We can ask Awbee later, but her last report said that in a few weeks, depending on winds, we may be able to risk someone going topside for a few hours. Maybe even a day."

"Topside," Thom let the word hang in the air. They stood in silence for several minutes.

Knowing it would ruin the mood, Jills brought Thom back to reality.

"I'm sorry you lost so many men," he said quietly. Thom's excitement slid from his face as the reality of it all returned to him.

"There was nothing I could do."

"I agree. But you see," Jills said, motioning out towards the Fountain.

"I 'saw' before I came up here. Doesn't change anything."

"I suppose not, in some ways."

They stood awkwardly for a few more minutes.

"They're telling me it will be a week or more to repair your ship," said Jills finally. "I'd like for you to take some time and relax. Eat well. You can afford it now. I need you to be at your best when you go back out. We all do."

Thom said nothing.

"The dockyard should have a few more subs to fill in your numbers. We have two other patrols that are going to be out at the same time. This is the most crucial time. We need to protect the Fountain at all costs. Thom," Jills said, turning to face him. "Do I need to be any more clear? Our individual lives mean nothing in the face of the Fountain. Without it, we all die. Our species dies."

"I know. You told me already. I get it and I'm sure for some people that would make it easier. Make it so they could file it away, compartmentalize it. But I can't. I've tried. I told those men, my men, that I'd get them all back safely, and I was wrong. So don't lecture me on the fate of our people, Proctor Jills. I seem to understand the fate of people better than you."

Jills opened his mouth to speak, but Thom cut him off.

"I'll be ready when my ship is. This is just harder than you seem to realize. How many of the people we're killing would switch to our side if they knew what we were doing? If they knew we weren't the enemy?"

"No, Thom, that's where you're wrong. They *are* the enemy. They're trying to kill you. Trying to destroy this ship and the Fountain. If we could get them all to see the error in their ways, that would be great. But despite your wishful thinking, that's not going to be accomplished with a friendly message and a few food packs. I will mourn every death we cause, but not now. Now we must be vigilant, otherwise it won't matter that we felt guilt because we won't be alive to feel remorse. Does that make sense, Commander?"

Thom said nothing.

"There's one other thing. Three hours ago we received another transmission from Governor Oppai. It was the usual mad vitriol, but it also seemed to suggest that his pursuit of the Fountain is becoming an obsession. He gave us an ultimatum, instructing us to disclose its location, or he would kill Ralla Gattley."

Thom spun to face Jills.

"She's still alive?"

"We don't know for sure. He at least wants us to think so. His voice sounded desperate. I responded myself. I told him that under no terms would we divulge the location of the Fountain, and if approached by any ship, we would strike it down with lethal force."

"You killed her."

"If she was still alive, yes, you are probably right. So it seems I'm not as removed from the death as you seem to think."

"What was their response?"

"We're expecting it within the hour. Mrakas has insisted he hear it when it comes in, and despite my, and all his doctors', better judgment, he remains indefatigable."

"If things go wrong, it's going to kill him."

"I think he knows that."

It was worse than she had feared, and was only going to get worse still. On the second day laboring in the decaying engine room, two of her fellow workers had been killed. The ship had taken a sudden turn and the water in the room sloshed around, causing the generator to short. Their deaths were instantaneous. Ralla and the rest of the crew were hanging from crude, temporary scaffolding trying to weld over weak spots when it happened. They hung in the darkness and the silence for over an hour before someone on the outside tripped the breakers for the section. The smell of burnt flesh permeated the poorly ventilated space. Ralla wasn't the only one who vomited.

Two days later, a microfissure erupted, causing panic as the water levels rose rapidly. This time, someone cut the breaker before the water reached the generator, and they worked under the lights of the welding torches for eight hours trying to get the wall sealed. By the time they finished, the water was to Ralla's ribs.

The other hours and days, living under the constant fear of death, were spent hauling sheets of metal that weighed more than Ralla herself. The emaciated workers fared little better than she did. She was sure someone Thom's size could have hauled one of the sheets with only minor difficulty. It took her and two workers, and usually a fourth.

She had tried, at first, to find out more about her fellow inmates, but they were laconic. It seemed like they were prisoners, like her, but were not *Uni* natives. They had all been surprised when she had told them where she was from. Soon, though, the brutality of the job removed any chance or desire to talk. Even at the end of the shift, or during the short breaks for food, they were all too exhausted to speak. They spent their days working, then returned to their respective cabins or cells and slept until their next shift. There was a "B" team that came in when her "A" team wasn't there, but so little work was accomplished, she was sure they were even fewer in number.

She had hoped the routine of repeated, long-term exposure to panic and fear would abate it somewhat, but it didn't. Days blurred away to periods of panic and periods of sleep. There was no joy at the end of a shift, only the slight reduction of terror, but knowing it would return in just a few hours put a limit on how good even that could feel. Then the morning would come. With it, the long walk to the rear of the ship, figuring this would be the day something would slip, something would tear, some little thing would go wrong, and it would be her life, or that of one of her fellow workers.

Every day, every hour, every new leak, every crackle of energy from the generator, every pound of pressure on her skin, every degree of heat, everything a slice in her resolve against Oppai. She knew it. It was a matter of time. He would win.

They came at the worst time. It was at the end of a particularly grueling shift. She was caked in sweat and grime. Her eyes burned from the arcs of the welders. It took her a while to realize the two guards weren't walking her back to her cell. Her heart sank. Ralla knew where they were going, and when she was dumped unceremoniously in Oppai's cabin, she swallowed her pride and fixed herself a drink.

The Governor was visibly livid, seated in a chair at the long table. Around him stood several of the men she had seen before, looking even more agitated than the last time she'd seen them. The one with the beard poked Oppai in the chest. She couldn't hear what they were saying, and didn't care. So she finished her drink, then made another. A knife lay near one of the bottles, which she slipped excitedly into her coveralls. Her heart sank as she realized that she had no strength left to do anything with it. But maybe one good shot. She had that in her. She could do that. She walked calmly towards the table, making out the end of the conversation. The bearded man barked at Oppai.

"Do you understand? This was your idea. Your idea from the beginning, and we went along. Either you fix this, or we will. You understand?" he said, poking Oppai in the chest a final time. With that last poke, Oppai's demeanor changed. He had been seething quietly in his chair. Now, he looked almost calm. Ralla felt a chill. Something was wrong. She put her drink down on the table, the sound causing everyone to turn.

Oppai stood, fingertips on the table.

"Get out," he said, staring at Ralla, but clearly talking to everyone else. His half smile started her adrenaline pumping. She envisioned getting out the knife, and the sweep she would need to get his neck. It was a short blade, but she could do it.

The men, unsure if they should follow his instructions, eventually filed out. As the guard outside reached in to close the door, Oppai nodded at him, and the guard nodded back. The signal was unmistakable.

Oppai pushed pages down the table at Ralla; one made it far enough to be stopped by her glass. They were similar to the one he railed about weeks earlier. There were zeros in column after column. Some were map printouts, with red marks over installation after installation. She couldn't help but smile.

He backhanded her across the face; she hadn't even seen him move from the end of the table. After weeks of grinding in the hotbox below, though, the belt cleared her mind. The real, immediate pain was like ice against the skin. She was slow to bring her face back around, but when she did, it wore a look of weary defiance. The smile returned. Oppai's arm swung back for another strike, but she was ready for it. Ducking, she swung her right fist up into his stomach, connecting and causing him to stagger backwards. Leaping like an animal, she knocked him to the ground. They landed hard on the floor as Ralla, in one motion, took the knife from her pocket and slashed towards his throat.

But he had recovered and deflected it, grabbing her wrist in the process. She swung with her left, and he grabbed it as well. The weeks of labor had exhausted her, and as she struggled to free herself, she found she had no more strength to fight. Adrenaline could only go so far. His hand crushed down on her wrist, and the knife fell to the floor, a bubble of red on his chin its only victim. She was spent and she knew it. Oppai, fueled by anger, retaliated with vigor. In one fluid athletic motion, he pushed her off, spun her limp body around, and held her arms behind her. He smashed her face down onto the table.

Oppai grabbed a handful of the scattered pages, and smeared them against her face.

"You see this?!" he screamed. "This is one of my mining facilities. It was lost a month ago. You see this?!" he asked, grabbing another handful and pressing her face hard between the pages and the table. "This is a convoy that went missing, losing three weeks' worth of materials." He dragged her along the table, her face sweeping up stray pages as it moved. They stopped in front of a group of maps. From her sidelong viewpoint, they were just blue pages. "Every one of these stations is *gone*, and it's *your* fault. Your ship is taking everything from me. And if they were quiet about it before, they aren't anymore. This morning one of my fleets came back decimated. A result of an unprovoked attack by your people. I guess they don't value your life as much as you hoped they would."

"You know, Governor," she said, the pressure and the table slurring her words. "I don't know if you really believe this crap you're spewing, but I know I don't care anymore."

Oppai tossed her to the ground and strode over to the shelves of timeworn books. From the top shelf, he brought down an antique globe. It must have been made from before the floods, as it showed the pristine land masses she knew from her school years. For a moment, she was back in the schoolroom talking to the girl she had thought of as a young her. The reverie was short lived. Oppai slammed the globe down on the table above her, then hauled her up to look at it. He grabbed her head, and made her look at the globe.

"Show me where the weapon is. *SHOW ME!*"

Ralla looked away. He shook her violently. It was too much. The labor, and the dread, and the heat for so many weeks. It proved too much. She just wanted him *gone*. She let her eyes dart towards the globe. Just for a second. They fell on the pole. It was nearly involuntary, and she looked away immediately.

Oppai released her and without the support she fell to the ground. He laughed as he walked towards the doors.

"Thank you, Ms. Gattley. Guards," he said opening the doors wide. "Bring her to the bridge."

As the guards approached, Ralla had a brief moment to herself, in awe of what she'd done. Of what it would mean to her people, her ship. Her eyes moved slowly up from the floor, up the thick and blocky table support, up the rippled enameled edge, up the brass stand of the globe, and finally to the cracked and tarnished sphere itself. Her eyes locked on where her eyes had flashed a moment before. At the pole.

The s-pole.

OK, mom, she thought. I just bought you a month. Maybe more. Make it work.

Mrakas Gattley's cabin was well lit, as usual. The amber tones of the wood floor and white walls contrasted sharply with the obvious and pervasive tone of the people in the room. There were over a dozen. Two were nurses, tasked with keeping their sick charge alive. Then there was Awbee, uncharacteristically doting at her former husband's side. Cern and Larr stood off near the balcony, watching in silence. The rest were aides, milling about, talking on communicators, checking notes. The Captain stood rigidly by the door. As Jills and Thom entered, there was a moment's pause as the energy shifted towards the Proctor. Aides asked him rapid-fire questions, then darted off to make more calls. Thom expected at least a scowl from Cern or Awbee, but got neither. In fact, he got no recognition at all. In the bed, propped up on two thick pillows, were the living remains of Mrakas Gattley. His sallow, ravaged body a mere husk of what it had been. His eyes darted from person to person, eerily alive as the carcass around them decayed into oblivion.

One of the aides got Jills' attention; the Proctor acknowledged, and stepped into the center of the room. The various conversations silenced.

"Mrakas," Jills said with a nod. The eyes on the elder statesman closed, and his head dipped with the barest of nods. "We have little doubt what this message will contain, so please prepare yourself. The computer has finished compiling it, so I'll have the techs play it if everyone is ready."

Around the room there were somber nods. With a crackle, the highly compressed voice of Governor Oppai filled the room. Thom looked for speakers, but could see none.

"I have only done what I have had to do," the disembodied voice chastised. "I have only done what you have forced me to do. I have asked you to back off, and you have not. I have asked you to end hostile actions against the people of the *Population*, and you have not. Well," the voice dropped away, and in its place there were the sounds of a short struggle. Clothes rustling as one person struggled against captors. The voice that returned was still Oppai, but it was different. It lacked the polished sounds of someone giving a speech. There was an edge to it, anger. "Say something," Oppai growled. The terminal weariness in Ralla's voice cut Thom viciously. Whatever thrill he momentarily had hearing her voice, the pain in it, and what was surely about to happen, filled him with impotent anguish.

"Please don't do this. It's not too late for peace," she said. Awbee gripped the pale hand of Mrakas.

"Peace to your people means the subjugation of mine. The people of this ship don't want it, and neither do I. We will fight until there is no more threat from the great ship *Universalis*. And now that threat comes in the form of a tremendous doomsday weapon, designed to drain our seas and wipe out everything we have spent decades building."

"No. That's not..." Ralla's voice grew more distant as her unseen and unheard captors pulled her away from the microphone. They could hear her still struggling in the background.

"Ralla here has given me the location of your weapon, and now we will destroy it."

In the distance, just loud enough to make out, Ralla shouted one final thing.

"They're coming from the northern hemi!" There were more sounds of a struggle.

"And to show you I am serious..."

A scream of terror chilled the room, followed by a single gunshot.

"Ralla Gattley is dead. This is the way you choose it. I..."

Jills signaled the audio dead. Each person handled it differently. Jills and Larr looked somber, their faces ones of pity towards the Gattleys. Cern was in shock, and stumbled back to lean against the balcony's railing. Awbee buried her face in her husband's chest.

Thom, though, showed neither pain nor anguish. His face looked puzzled. The only one to notice was Mrakas, and they made eye contact. It was as if, in that moment, a shared secret passed between them. With a tiny motion of his head, Gattley got Thom to the bedside. A pale hand slid from under the covers, and loosely gripped Thom's forearm. The skin felt plasticy to Thom. A gentle tug was all Mrakas could manage, but he got Thom to lean in.

"She's not dead. You know it, too. Get her back for me. For us."

Mrakas let go of Thom, and let go of life, sinking back into the deep of his pillows and beyond.

Awbee cleared the room with a single glace. The hard-edged scientist had disappeared. In her place was a woman who had married a man who had died. Cern fled to deal with his grief. Jills corralled the Captain, Larr, and Thom into the Council Chambers. They had all heard Mrakas's last words, but didn't speak of it.

"Either there will be time to deal with Ralla's death later, or there won't be. Either way we can't spare a moment now." Jills said after taking his usual seat. "Ralla's outburst of how close they are is a dire sign."

"I don't believe that's what she meant at all," said Larr, already recovered from what had happened in the other room. "No, I think Miss Gattley is far cleverer than I gave her credit for."

"Explain."

"Well, of course they'd be coming from the northern hemisphere. There's no other way to *get* to the n-pole. This isn't useful information, really. We'd already be at full alert. Besides, we've got scouts spread throughout the hemisphere; we'd see them coming from a day away. So the timing of their attack wouldn't really matter. Hours or days, we'd be just as ready. Ralla must have known that she'd only be able to get out a short sentence. No, I think she did something rather heroic."

"You think she lied to them."

"I do. If we were at the s-pole, such information *would* be useful, letting us know we had some time, a reasonably known amount of time, to fortify our defenses. So somehow she sent them to the wrong pole, and this was her way of telling us. Clever girl. Such a shame."

Jills pondered the new information.

"Either way, I don't think it changes much. All she's done, if you're right, is buy us a little more time. Captain, I'm temporarily re-tasking personnel and marines to assist with the Fountain project."

"As long as I can get them back when the unpleasantness starts," the Captain replied.

"Of course. This is our 'All Hands' moment, gentlemen. Miss Gattley has given her life for us. Let's not let it be in vain."

The meeting broke up, but Thom remained, staring at the table.

"Thom," Jills said, after gathering up some pads. "I know this has been a rough few hours, but please don't take what Mrakas said as anything more than the wishful hopes of a dying man."

Thom looked up, as if he hadn't heard what had been said. Jills moved to the seat next to Thom.

"This is it, Commander. The fleet we've cobbled together is the last of the ships we'll be able to build. Even if you can capture more mining facilities, we just don't have the time. We have two smaller fleets patrolling southwest and northwest of our bearing, but at best they'll only slow down the *Pop* fleet. We need you now more than ever to raze their domes and convoys, and if you encounter the *Pop*, to attack and retreat, attack and retreat, all the way back up here."

Jills entered some commands into the table surface, and a blue globe appeared on its surface.

"It might buy us a few more days, and a few days may make all the difference," he continued. "If Ralla did buy us the month it would take for the *Pop* to get from the northern hemisphere to the s-pole and back up here, then we may have a chance. From what Awbee has told me, it's possible by that time the grown berg will be big enough to stay put on its own. If it is, and we lose the Fountain, then there's a chance, a tiny chance that the berg will start the new cap on its own. Not soon enough for any of us to see it, but maybe the children of whoever survives this fight will. It's really just a few days that might make the difference. We need you to be those few days, Thom. And then, when the *Pop* makes its final push against us, we'll all fight here, together. OK?"

"I've got some time before I need to depart, right?"

"No more than a day, I'd hope."

"Then consider me off your clock for that time. Something's bugging me about that transmission, and I think Mrakas heard it too. He just died before he could tell anyone what it was. If I can't figure it out by the time I need to leave, then so be it. But if I'm right, if Mrakas was right, and she's alive, then we owe her—*I* owe her—something."

"Thom. If that ship gets within half a hemisphere of the Fountain, we're going to do everything we can do blow it out of the sea. You understand that, right? It doesn't matter if she's alive; there is nothing we can do."

"A day," Thom replied, and left without waiting for approval.

It took only three hours. Thom found Koin in his workshop, teasing a piece of carbonweave with pliers and a torch into some particular shape. He had noticed Thom's entrance, but said nothing. Thom waited patiently for him to finish. After several moments, the carbonweave, blackened from the constant heat, bent how Koin wanted it, and the tech seemed pleased.

"What can I do for you, Thom? Sorry... Commander?"

"I'm not here on official ship business, so if you have something important to do, please don't let me keep you from it."

"Well, that's just polite of you to say. Don't worry about me. I pretty much live in here now. And with the production ramped up on the, um, *project*?"

"Project is fine."

"...I actually don't have a lot to do. Most of the hard work is being done upstairs by the industry boys. I'm playing around with a new kind of ablative armor for the hull. We'd need a lot more carbonweave than we have now, but it's something anyway. What can I do for you?"

Thom filled him in on the audio cast, and his and Mrakas's feeling that something wasn't right. He told him of Mrakas dying. The tech seemed upset.

"That's too bad. Mrakas Gattley was a good man. Though, I guess we've all been expecting this for a while now. They couldn't exactly keep his health a secret when he'd be walking the halls. I just wish I could have done something for him. But, you know, I'm good at things, not people. People's a different department," he said with a forced smile. "Let's hear this audio."

Thom keyed into console on the table, and within a few moments the audio filled the lab. When it was finished, Koin played it again, this time leaning back in his chair, pondering.

"Well, I can't say for sure, but you guys have a sharp set of ears."

"What do you mean?"

"Well, there's something missing, though I can't be positive."

"What's missing? Seriously, it just sounded off to me, and I don't know why. If Mr. Gattley did, it died with him."

"Listen to it again."

Koin selected the gunshot portion using the console. The audio ran from the gunshot to when Oppai started speaking, then looped back. It played several times before Koin stopped it again. Thom still had a blank look on his face.

"Listen to the other sounds in the background. All the equipment hum? I'd bet a week's pay they were on the bridge. Ours sounds exactly the same. The only other place that would sound like that would be the mainframe room, and I can't think of why they'd be in there. I've never even been to ours, and I'm a tech. So if their bridge sounds like ours, how much would you assume its consoles and metal and all sorts of other official looking things are pretty much the same?"

"When I was on the *Pop* it sure didn't seem like they had the resources to change much in the looks department."

"Good. And they were standing close, right? You can hear her struggle as they bring her towards the mic. You can hear her voice as she gets pulled away from wherever the microphone was. Maybe on his head, or held in his hand. So we hear the gunshot, and then..."

"Him speaking." It took a moment, but understanding swept across his face. "Just his voice."

"Exactly. If they were that close, why can't you hear her slump to the ground. Sorry, that's morbid. But really? You can hear them roughing her up, why not her hitting the deck after being shot? Are the guards really still holding her? And why no bullet sound? It was obvious it was a projectile weapon from the sound. We would have heard the bullet, after it easily passed through her, hit something on the other side. But that's not the most interesting part," Koin said, a smile edging up the corners of his mouth. "Listen towards the end."

He cued up the last few sentences of the cast. Oppai was rambling about vengeance. Using the console, Koin tweaked the audio. Oppai's voice became muffled, muted. The background noise became louder. It was unmistakable.

"She's still fighting them," Thom said, convinced.

"That sure sounds like the exact same angry struggle from the first part. If the audio continued, I bet we would have heard her make some sort of noise. I bet that's why it ends where it does. Like I said, I can't be positive. There are a lot of unknowns and assumptions here. But without proof otherwise, I don't see why it's not possible that..."

"Ralla could still be alive."

Back in her cell, Ralla did the best she could to sleep. Her ears rang from the noise of the gunshot, and her jaw hurt where Oppai had crushed it against the table. Both wrists were bruised from where the guards had held her. She was, however, still alive and in better shape than the guard she had bitten.

Ralla wasn't surprised when they came to get her for work the next day, though there hadn't been breakfast or dinner.

She settled back into the grind of welding and fear. But when the time came for the guards to take them back to their respective sleeping areas, they didn't come. Instead the "B" team arrived, half her team's number and even more emaciated. While all were tired, they couldn't stop working. The water level was rising too quickly. Worse, the engines were driving hard, making it too loud to hear and nearly too hot to breathe.

The strain on the hull torqued their wall of death, and new leaks and cracks were forming by the second. Ralla toiled into the night with the combined and exhausted crews. It didn't occur to her until hours later that everyone she knew had every reason to believe she was dead. She thought of Thom, of her father, her mother, even Cern. Her fellow laborers seemed resigned to work and die here. But in the tiny parts of her brain not occupied by stress, fear, exhaustion, and the task at hand, she was now more resigned than ever to escape, by any means necessary. This room was a bad place to die. She'd rather die trying to escape. What did it matter if she did? She was already dead.

VII

They were eight days out by the time they reached their first target. It was a huge farming dome, one of the first casualties of the *Pop*'s aggression. Nearly the size of the Garden itself, the low, wide dome glowed in the darkness from much distance.

The new *Reap* fleet was a fraction of the size of its former self: a single corvette, four torpedo subs, but more than a dozen small attack subs. The corvette had been modified with mounting harnesses so the attack sub pilots wouldn't have to queue up for the *Reap*'s own tiny docking bay to land and use the facilities.

As a fleet, they didn't bother with their usual caution as they approached the dome. It was clear there were no other ships around, so they dropped in from the layer above and descended to the dome en masse. There was no defense. After getting inside, Soli signaled immediately.

"Commander, I think you should come down here."

"What's the situation, Soli?"

"Thom..."

It wasn't just hearing his first name, it was the tone in Soli's voice that sent a chill up Thom's spine.

"OK, I'm headed down."

There were two unarmed scout subs docked in the *Reap*'s bay. They were highly modified versions of the sub Thom and Ralla had stolen months earlier. The descent was quick, as was the docking. Other than the mechanicals of the lock, there was silence as the door cycled open. The looks on the faces of the marines that greeted him were ominous. So was the smell. The thick, humid stench hit him with almost physical force. He vomited immediately, and clearly wasn't the first.

The dome was roughly circular, with a pinched-out section at the front for the main lock, where Thom had entered. Unlike most of the domes he'd seen, this one had a very low ceiling, heavily braced and covered with lights. It was overly bright. Used to the subdued lighting on the sub, Thom squinted uncomfortably. The floor was nearly all farming space, with squat, one-story buildings in the center for the small community that resided here. Embedded in the floor were massive scrubbers to keep the oxygen/carbon dioxide mixture correct for plant and planter. Designed to work for a small group of farmers and all the crops they tended, they hadn't worked for the opposite. Everywhere were corpses. Thousands.

On every pathway through and around the divided farming zones were bodies. Most were huddled together. Others slumped across the grates of the scrubbers in a misguided last attempt to cling to life. Large swaths of crops had been torn up to give all the refugees places to stay. It seemed at some point the equilibrium had been broken. No one had thought, or perhaps known how, to reset the scrubbers. Without the constant conversion of oxygen from the plants, and the scrubbers designed to supply mostly carbon dioxide, asphyxiation was inevitable.

Thom didn't know how long ago the place had died, but it was long enough that the bodies hadn't decomposed too badly, yet enough time had passed for the air to somewhat get back to normal. A visibly disturbed Soli looked at Thom for orders.

"Do a sweep, make sure there aren't any survivors holed up somewhere. Then get back to the ship."

"What happened?" Soli asked rhetorically. Thom shook his head, staring out at the gruesome scene.

He didn't tell the squad their next target was also a farming dome, and he feared it wouldn't be any different.

Sometime in the early hours of the second straight day of working, they had sealed enough of the major leaks to be able to rest. They were led back to their berths, and Ralla collapsed onto her cot entering a deep, dreamless sleep.

She did little over the next several days other than eat and sleep. Her body was slow to recover, and with little else to do, sleep was the best option. After a week, she was finally brought back to the engine room, and oddly, didn't fear it. She couldn't decide if her strength was returning or she simply couldn't be beaten down any more. She leaned toward strength, because in her free time she had devised a plan for escape.

Ralla was the last to arrive, and in the noise of the room, the crew greeted one another in the sullen sign language they seemed to have invented. New materials lay on the floor for the team to use to reinforce the walls, the outer hull layer seemingly secure for now. This would be a big step. For the first time they would be laboring to get ahead of the problem instead of continually playing catch up. Ralla knew that in a week or so, the ship would be starting a search pattern, looking for a Fountain that wasn't there. The walls would be under tremendous stress at that point. With no way to communicate all of this to her crewmates, she just pushed on with the work. She wondered if she'd have another run in with Oppai once he figured out she had lied to him.

No one noticed when she sliced off a sliver of metal from a sheet, and slid it into her pocket.

The next dome was better. There had been a shortage of food, but few deaths. They hadn't pulled up the crops any more than they had to. The air was stale, but livable. None of techs on the *Uni* or in the dome were alive when the scrubbers were originally built, but as a group they figured out how to reset them. When the fresh, clean air started to circulate, the roughly 4,000 people in the dome cheered. Later, when Soli and his marines tried to leave, there was a small riot. The meager rations they passed out did little to assuage the tide. They pledged to send more food when they could, and promised they wouldn't forget the refugees. Both potentially hollow promises.

After several days of wrangling, Thom was able to convince the Council to divert two heavy transports to shuttle food to this dome and any others that contained survivors. The longcomm process was infuriating, each response taking over an hour to receive and decode.

The second *Reap* fleet zigzagged its way down the world, stopping at dome after dome, each overpopulated with the refugees of the militarized *Pop*. Thousands and thousands of inhabitants, stranded in domes never meant to hold large numbers of people. They found two more domes that were morgues, two others where food riots had taken the lives of hundreds.

Oddly, none believed they were from the *Uni*. All seemed to feel that the war had gotten so bad that their Governor had had no choice but to leave them behind. Or that the evil people on the *Uni* had destroyed the transports that surely would have come. There were dozens of variations of "*Uni* bad, *Pop* good." The marines' uniforms wore no insignia, which was perhaps for the best. No doubt, many of the refugees would have reacted differently faced with a blatant symbol of their enemy. Thom instructed Soli to have his men mention their home causally, judge the response, and then follow up if necessary. They encountered little violence, more exhausted disbelief.

After three weeks, they reached the e-zero line equidistant from n- and s-poles and spread out along it. The other, smaller, fleets sent by the *Uni* did the same around the world. They formed a blockade stretching around the waist of the planet, each sub separated by vast distances. Messages were relayed to the *Reap* over the following days: ships announcing they had taken position on the layer, external sensors deployed. In areas where it was deep enough to have a second thermal layer, specific ships with additional towed sensor arrays were positioned. Now, all they could do was wait. Wait for the inevitable noise of the massive ship *Population* screaming north, bent on destruction.

For the next week and a half, Thom barely left the bridge. His beard grew long, his hair ratty. Meals were brought to him. The central table's screen had been fixed, but the protective glass surface still wore the cracks Thom's body had created. Thom sat in his command chair, slept in the chair, and only left to use the head adjacent to the bridge. He watched the sensors. He watched the data relayed by the rest of the ships spread around the world, all now under his command. There was silence on the ship and silence in the sea.

His relentless vigil concerned his crew. Soli tried to break through his shell, but his efforts were lost. Thom had become a man obsessed. To the eyes of the men and women under his command, it was a tireless pursuit by their commander. His fixation troubled them, but inspired them. Word spread quickly throughout the fleet. A feeling of rigid determination replaced the anxiety of the wait. Quietly, the obsession spread. Their leader's resolve pushed them, motivated them to be ever alert. Showed them all, without words, what was at stake.

As he sat, part of Thom's brain registered the data, registered the sensors, registered the crew milling around him. Deeper, though, his mind was occupied by his real mission. No matter what happened in the next few weeks, he was going to rescue Ralla. Everything else was a distraction.

Eight days after they had taken up station at e-zero, a panicked message from a torpedo sub three days east relayed in. They had engaged the *Population*, and were fleeing north. Immediately, coordinates were spread to the entire fleet. A staging area was calculated far enough north that the majority of the fleet could assemble before the first attack on the enemy. Every ship in the fleet was faster than the *Pop*, even when it was running at full speed. Regardless, they were going to end up far closer to the *Uni* than anyone was comfortable. Thom stoically twirled his finger in the air, his operations officer understanding the silent order.

Far below, the powerful engines of the *Reap*, silent for over a week, began their long spool up. The sound rose gradually from low whine to fevered pitch, all their energies waiting to be unleashed on the sea.

Around the ship, the crew braced themselves. The ops officer watched his board light up green, then turned and nodded to Thom. Without glancing over, Thom pointed forward with the same fingers. The officer flipped a series of toggles, and instructing the techs in the engine room to throw the levers that engaged the propellers. The *Reap* launched forward as if struck, gathering speed like it never had before. Speed increased, faster and faster. Water forced aside by the bow rushed violently around the ship, the cavitations sounding like a waterfall crashing against the hull. Thom rose from his seat and gripped the table with both hands, glaring intently out at the blackness.

Ralla was sure the guards didn't know what to do with them. Her team had finished the inner wall of the engine room, and as far as they could tell it was holding. The search had lasted about a week, the engine load and occasional violent turns a noticeable giveaway. Then they were off, the engines driving under maximum power. The guards would forget about them for a few days, leaving them all in their cells. Then they'd round them up and dump them in the engine room, but there was nothing to do. Some of the guards were visibly conflicted, though Ralla wasn't sure if this was a good thing or a very bad thing. During the days in the engine room, Ralla and her crewmates rested or played games with homemade playing pieces. The expected retribution from Oppai hadn't come. Yet.

She was in her cell when the explosions began reverberating angrily through the hull. For a moment, her excitement mixed with fear as she worried this was the final assault on the Fountain. But she thought better of it; there was no way the *Pop* was fast enough to be at the n-pole this quickly. This could only mean the *Uni* was launching a preemptive attack. It was time to act.

She started banging on her cell door like a woman possessed. With all the acting ability she could muster, Ralla screamed in terror and cried out for help. It didn't take long before a guard appeared at her door. Her heart sank. It was young man who had picked up the illustrated novel weeks earlier. He seemed genuinely concerned. Ralla pretended to faint, crashing into the bed. The lock clicked and the door started to slide open. There was no hesitation. Ralla sprang on the man before the door was fully open. Surprise and fear gripped his face as Ralla placed the sharpened sliver of metal against the man's throat.

"I'm sorry. I truly am, but I need to go. Please take your sidearm and place it on the ground beside you."

The young man cautiously did as asked. Ralla blindly reached for it, keeping her eyes on the guard, with her other hand poised to slice. The sidearm was heavy, an older projectile weapon like Oppai had used to shoot at her on the bridge. She rolled off the guard and pointed the sidearm at his chest.

"OK, get in the cell."

"Please, miss, I'm not..."

"Shut up. Get in the cell," she barked at him. Ralla felt sorry for him, but her resolve somehow stayed. The young man walked slowly back into the cell, and she shut the door behind him.

The main area of the brig was a round room, with a dozen cells around the circumference. Only one guard had been on duty at a time that she had seen. Her escorts to the engine room weren't a part of the regular rotation, and with any luck they wouldn't come looking for her anytime soon.

There were no other prisoners, but across a small passageway outside was another cell block, and here she found two of her team from down below. They were shocked to see her, and reluctant to leave.

"There have to be places you can hide on this ship. Go now, or stay in here to die. The ship's under attack."

They nodded reluctant agreement and scampered out of the brig and down the passageway without a word. They look so thin and fragile, Ralla thought, realizing she probably looked no better.

The brig exited onto a wide hallway, the utilitarian design attesting to its military origins. She had always gone right towards the elevators to get down to the engine room. There was little else that way, so she went left. The dull booming continued as weapons exploded near or against the hull. The lack of alarms or rushing crowds puzzled her.

Stairs brought her up and away from the main hallway, and a flexible connector tube put her into a carpeted, wallpapered, residential ship. Brass light fixtures shed warm light. The third door she tried was unlocked, the cabin empty. She locked the door and looked around.

The cabin was similar to those found throughout the *Uni*, and like the one she and Thom had showered in months earlier. This one, though, had age. Frayed carpet and sheets hung limply. Layers of dust implied years of vacancy. She sat on the bed and allowed herself a moment to think and relax. The weapons fire was less frequent, and had been growing more distant for several minutes.

The cabin had a shower unit, and, after a few minutes of dirty sputtering, clean hot water. There was even soap. She did her best to wash her hair, but it was a lost cause. Weeks of washing with no shampoo, and the constant grime from the work in the engine room, had conspired to knot her hair into a matted mess. When she was finished with her shower, invigorated and cleaner than she had been for months, she located scissors in the cabinet above the fold-down sink.

Without a second thought, she sheared her scalp. Her hair had grown long, longer than it had been in years. Despite that, she was elated to see it pile in the sink. Snip after snip, more of the visual representation of what Oppai had done to her left her body. It was freeing. She flushed the discarded evidence of the past few months down the toilet, and took a moment to see her new self in the mirror. The short blond fuzz made her look younger, yet meaner. Her cheeks were gaunt. She'd always despised their cherubic cuteness, and now her father's taught cheekbones had replaced them. She looked not underfed, but wiry. Tilting her shoulder down, she decided her scar was coming in nicely, not a blemish, but a trophy. As water dripped onto the floor, she saw the gun resting on the lid of the toilet. Into the mirror she smiled, delighting in the conspicuous menace.

Ralla stepped out of the bathroom in search of clothing. The closet had men's and women's jumpsuits, different shades of green and blue. It shocked her that two people could live in such a confined space. Both inhabitants were clearly much larger than Ralla. A belt and some rolling up of sleeves and pant legs helped, but anything more than a casual glance and it wouldn't hold up. She looked like a little girl trying to fit into Daddy's uniform. So be it. One solid sneer and the average person would probably shy away from making any comment.

She tucked the sidearm into one of the cavernous pockets of the dark blue suit and left. It had been less than half an hour since she had broken out of her cell.

Ralla had almost free reign of the ship. The few people that she saw were military, and all were preoccupied with getting ready for battle. The main shipyard was swarming with activity, and any hopes of sabotage there dashed quickly. The engine rooms were a similar story. There were additional guards posted at all the doors, something she hadn't seen on any of her trips there before. She had no idea how to get to any of the various weapons bays, and while her costume was convincing, she didn't want to push it.

So that left something more subtle, but potentially more damaging. What would be her worst fear given a saboteur on the *Uni*? Methodically, she went from lock to lock, crosshatch to crosshatch, watertight door to watertight door, and every one she was able to open, she opened, disabled, and jammed into place. With any luck, a few well-placed hits from the *Uni* would sink the *Population* for good.

Something, though, was nibbling at the back of her brain. It took most of the day before it finally congealed into a fully formed thought. As she braced herself against the floor to wedge a dislodged wallplate into the tracks of an exterior lock, she noticed how much the floor was vibrating. She had been on the ship long enough to tell when the engines were running hard, or when they were idle. Now though, as she placed her other hand on the deck to be sure, the whole ship vibrated more than she had ever felt. The engines were driving inordinately hard, well past the point of safety, she was sure.

The *Pop* arrived early. Impossibly early. More than half of Thom's fleet was still spread across the entire hemisphere. The few ships he had available attacked, but it was a futile effort. The *Pop* blew past them as if they weren't there. Thom issued a regroup order for the local ships, and a retreat order for the rest of the fleet. Best they make for the *Uni* than waste time coming here. By the time he got the *Reap* turned around the *Pop* had opened up a substantial lead. He ordered engines run past flank speed, but it had little effect. At this velocity, torpedoes were useless. At this distance, cannons were no better than knocking on the hull with a hammer. Even beyond emergency speed, the *Reap* gained on the *Pop* so slowly his techs couldn't be sure they'd get back into weapons range before the *Pop* was in range of the *Uni*. Even if he could get closer, the power drain of the main guns would slow them back down out of range after a few shots.

This was a disaster. Nothing short of absolute failure. Thom took little consolation in the fact that there was no way to have known the *Pop* could maintain this sort of speed. He ordered the faster ships in the fleet to return to the *Uni* as quickly as they could. Sensor screens showed the smaller ships on his flanks start to pull ahead.

"She's buttoned up tight, sir," Thom sensor officer reported. "If they have any additional ships, they're all still inside."

"Send a report to the *Uni*. We have failed to engage the *Population*. Currently in pursuit. All attempts at disablement have failed. ETA, 36 hours." Thom's comm officer acknowledged and sent the message. That was it. All he could do now was sit in his chair and watch. Watch his one official task hang before him, untouchable and unstoppable. Watch his chance to rescue Ralla slip away. Watch the *Population*, a juggernaut of fear and anger and destruction.

But so close! He could take one of the scout subs. They would be easily fast enough to get him to the *Pop* and he could try to sneak aboard. He'd done it before. Even as he imagined it, he knew how foolish it was. No, for the moment his place was here, with his crew and his fleet.

They'd be ready, though, and he'd be ready. As soon as the *Pop* slowed down, he'd tear the back of that ship off.

If it slowed down.

VIII

They had been expecting a response from the *Universalis* for hours. The prolonged silence turned out to be by design, as no sooner had they received and decoded the return message from the *Uni* than the great citysub showed up on the *Reap*'s sensor screens. The *Uni* had maneuvered into a parallel course with the *Pop*. Running as hard as the *Uni* was, the *Pop* was still gaining fast and coming up on their starboard side.

The *Uni* must have immediately left their station near the Fountain after receiving Thom's message. The obvious last-ditch effort was ominous. Thom could do nothing but watch the monitors as the ships inched within weapons range of one another. Out the front viewport the turbulence and cavitations caused by the *Pop*'s building-sized propellers churned the water, obscuring everything else. It had been a bumpy and nauseating day, but Thom was adamant they stay in position so they could surprise the *Pop* from behind. Small dots on the sensors revealed the remaining ships in his fleet as they left the leeward protection of the *Pop*.

The *Population* suddenly slowed as the cavernous shipyard doors opened, freeing dozens of ships from its hold. Already at speed, the attack force broke into three groups. The first spread out in defensive positions, the second towards the *Uni* itself. The third group broke off to starboard, accelerating directly towards n-pole.

With the slowing, the *Reap* was finally in cannon range. Thom didn't hesitate.

"All batteries fire. Target propellers."

The cannons started slinging their projectiles towards the rear of the enemy ship. The turbulence caused nearly all of the slugs to miss their target, impacting the hull and causing disappointingly little damage.

"Keep firing!" Thom shouted; the ship shook violently from the wake and now the cannons as they let off their ordnance. "Get us below the wake, ensign," he said, regaining his composure. "Pull us up underneath."

The *Reap* dove, entering smooth water and finally able to slide in under the *Pop*. The speed of the water past the enemy's hull was still enough to knock the cannon projectiles off course. At this distance, the gunners were trying to hit targets half the size of a fist from a platform moving in three dimensions. As of yet, none had found their mark, but a substantial peppering of the rear hull was mildly satisfying. Ahead, his goal was in sight: the gaping, brightly lit cavern of the *Population*'s shipyard. He was close.

Then the fighters were on them.

Ralla jabbed her knuckles into the soldier's bare throat. Gasping for air, he stumbled back, tripping and falling to the deck. Ralla was on him in an instant, removing his weapons and pressing his own rifle to his chin.

"Get off this ship or you'll die," she growled, her tone as menacing as she could make it. He looked confused. "I've sabotaged the ship. One good hit and she'll sink. I suggest you flee." She pushed off him and stood up. "Now," she barked, waving the gun towards the lifeboats nearby.

The soldier got up slowly and staggered away, still massaging his throat and coughing. Ralla could tell that he had no intention of getting on the lifeboat, but he was unarmed. Maybe if the ship did start to sink, he'd come to the realization sooner than others.

Ralla had watched the shipyard empty in an extraordinary display of controlled chaos. The subs were lined up, ready to slide into the water as soon as the vast lock doors slid open. As they split open down the middle, water rushed inwards, carrying equipment and containers aft with the flow, all crashing against the rear bulkhead of the shipyard. Ship after ship slid into the murky water and powered out of sight.

Ralla immediately went into overdrive, going as quickly as she could from door to door, destroying them in whatever fashion she could. She had carelessly assumed there were so few people aboard that she could go about her malevolence unfettered. While pulling out the pneumatic hoses for one particularly large lock, though, a soldier had come around a corner and caught her. She had made the distance to him in four leaping strides, and was at his throat before he could blink.

Now armed with multiple weapons and ammo, she was almost ready to make her way toward the engine rooms. She had already figured how to disable the ship, but her first stop was back to the shipyard. Racks of rockets and torpedoes sat unguarded on the floor. A rocket, roughly the size of her forearm, would be more than enough to destroy one of the engines. There was room in the baggy jumpsuit for at least two. Then she'd just have to figure out how to disable the other engines. One problem at a time, she thought to herself. Maybe with a bit of luck, the engine rooms would be empty. Or she could empty them, guns blazing with rockets spilling from her uniform. The visual amused her.

The tiny *Pop* attack subs were too fast for the *Reap* to hit—the large cannons too slow to track, the torpedoes too easy to dodge. The close-in rockets were having some success, but the crew was having difficulty aiming with the ship heaving around so much. The dorsal cannons continued to bombard the stern of *Pop*, each salvo rocking the smaller sub to port. The enemy attack subs battered the *Reap* with their rockets, each pass ripping away more and more armor.

Above them, the *Pop* had opened side hatches, revealing cannons and torpedo tubes of its own. The drag slowed them considerably, and the *Reap* got noticeably closer to the open shipyard. Almost there, Thom thought.

The *Pop* was still closing the distance on the *Uni* quickly. It would be a few minutes before the stern of the *Uni* was alongside the bow of the *Pop*. That didn't stop the former from launching torpedoes. Thom watched as the tiny dots left the starboard side of the home ship and track slowly across the divide. While still in the no-man's-land between the ships, they winked out of existence as the *Pop* launched a screen of defensive rockets. The concussions reverberated through the *Reap*'s hull.

Thom's sub had reached the midpoint of the *Pop*, and continued attacks on the stern were becoming futile.

"Cannons, target *Population* defenses. Continue firing," he ordered. There was a slight pause as the cannons turned, and then the now-familiar boom and rattle of the cannons resumed. The shipyard was close enough that he could clearly see the glow off to the right out the viewscreen. Time to go.

He opened his mouth to order Soli to the bridge, when the comm officer anxiously interrupted him.

"Sir, urgent message from the *Universalis*. We're to accelerate ahead and engage the break-off *Pop* fleet. Target is likely the Fountain. They must be stopped at all costs."

Dammit, Thom thought. So close. He had stupidly thought the other subs were going to try to flank the *Uni*. Clearly not. This was the closest he was going to get to the *Pop*. At the rate they were closing, it was likely the two citysubs would destroy each other long before he'd be able to get back. Now had to be the time.

"Ensign, get me..." the young comm officer turned in his seat, eyes full of fear. He could tell, they all could tell, that there weren't many ways for this battle to turn out well. Even if they saved the Fountain, the likelihood of the *Universalis* surviving the encounter was fairly low.

And then it occurred to him: if the two citysubs were destroyed, whoever was left would have to piece civilization back together. That person should be Ralla, but it was going to be him. It would have to be. He was the highest-ranking person not on the *Uni*. He had the respect and command of the fleet, at least whatever would be left of it. Him. It filled him with cold fear, but it was too obvious not to be true. This is what Jills was talking about. He must have seen this possibility. This near inevitability. No more fantasies.

Thom looked out of the viewscreen at the lit rectangle in the bottom of the hull of the *Population*, and said goodbye to Ralla for the last time.

The ensign was waiting as patiently as possible, squirming only slightly in his seat. The shipyard presented an easy final target. Thom made a quick mental calculation of time, power, and possible damage to the *Pop*. It would feel cathartic, he thought, to leave some final bit of destruction.

"Cannons," Thom began, envisioning the swath of destruction the cannon fire would do on the unprotected innards of the ship. But it would be a symbolic tantrum at best. All their ships were gone, no critical systems were nearby, and any fires or damage would be inconsequential to the greater goal.

The greater goal.

"Cease fire, divert all power to engines. Everything but sensors. We'll drive in the dark," he ordered. The ops officer paused to make sure Thom was serious, then did as commanded. The lights dimmed, then went out. The subtle breeze of recirculated air diminished to stagnation. The sensor screen cast a dull glow over the darkened bridge. There was a noticeable jump in the *Reap*'s speed. After a few moments, the shipyard slid out of view. A few moments after that, the bow of the *Pop*. Then the *Uni*, and soon they were in the open sea. Behind them, the small attack subs struggled to keep up, but soon broke off in search of easier targets.

Ahead, a small fleet of ships bore down on the Fountain at a rate just slightly slower than the *Reap*. The fight raged on behind, battle fleets slugging it out, everyone onboard surely counting down the minutes before the tremendous cannons along each craft's sides got in range and the real deathblows began.

No sooner had the *Uni* faded from the sensor screens than the trailing craft of the Fountain attack fleet came up on the sensors. Out of range of the rockets, lacking the power for the cannons, and moving too quickly for the torpedoes, they were helpless to do anything. However, they were gaining. Soon the rest of the fleet was within sensor range.

"Weapons, are we going to be able to power up the cannons in time before they get in range of the Fountain?" he asked. The weapons officer used a pencil on the metal of his console to make some calculations. He turned and shook his head.

"If we power up the cannons now, they'll pull out of range. If we wait till we're right on them, it's looking like they'll be at the outer edge of their own torpedo range."

"If we get close enough for rockets?"

"We risk damage to ourselves at that range and these speeds."

"So be it. Get us in range, ensign," he said to the pilot. The rockets didn't require power to launch, and were manually loaded.

They were on the trailing sub in moments, the barrage of rockets lanced forth from the bow of the *Reap* in an angry swarm. The rear of the enemy sub imploded, a fiery bubble of air escaping towards the surface as the sub started to sink and slow. Two more subs were quickly dispatched in the same way. That left four. These seemed to have noticed the advancing *Reap* from their stern, and spread out.

"How long before the lead ship is in range of the Fountain?" Thom asked.

"Ninety seconds," came the reply from the sensor officer.

Not enough time. The front gunners took out another sub; its lifeless hulk tumbled into the *Reap* and scraped deafeningly along the hull.

Three.

"Gunners report ammunition running low."

"Keep firing."

They inched closer to the next target. Thom could see the subs through the inky, greenish water just as they entered the *Reap*'s weapons range. A suicide mission, he thought. They're prepared to die for their cause, ignoring the advancing threat behind them. He looked around at his bridge crew. Fine. So are we, he resolved. With a burst of escaped air, the next sub crumpled from the attack and started to fall into the deep. None of the gunners from the starboard side of the ship fired in the last volley. A bad sign.

Two.

"Sixty seconds"

There was no way to know the exact range of the torpedoes. Any estimate could be way off. If they fired now that would be it.

The second-to-last sub came into range. Dual propellers at its outer corners churned up bubbles, as they pushed their little sub past speeds never intended by its designers. The port gunners opened up, and pinprick explosions hammered the rear of the sub. At least one rocket made it past the outer armor. The propellers stopped, and the sub listed unhealthily to port. It passed so close to the *Reap* that Thom could see into the cockpit as they raced by, a flooded mix of seawater and blood. At least the violent compression had killed them quickly.

One.

"Thirty seconds."

The wait was intolerable. They crept toward the last sub at an impossibly slow pace. In the distance, past the silhouette of the enemy sub, the dark, singular pillar of the Fountain emerged. They had run out of time.

The port gunners opened up, but only a handful of rockets sped towards the target. They splayed across the stern, a pathetic slap on the armored hull. Then, suddenly, the sub started to list to starboard, sliding into the path of the *Reap*. One propeller damaged, the crew tried to maintain course, while the now-much-faster *Reap* rapidly closed.

"Rocket ammo depleted. Orders, sir?" his weapons officer asked. There was no hesitation,

"Ram it."

Thom took his seat and strapped in. It was too late for evasive maneuvers, but the enemy sub tried anyway. The front tip of the *Reap* connected with the enemy sub at its rear right corner, crushing it like paper. The force spun the front of the enemy sub up and back, slamming the top against the oncoming *Reap* bow. Still powering at full speed, the *Reap* violently pushed past the sub, the latter scraping along the bow, across the bridge viewscreen, and up and away into their wake and the sea.

Done.

"Pilot, bring us about and get us back to the fight."

The pilot complied immediately, swinging the cruiser wide and around, rolling to port as he did so to tighten the turning radius. No one had time to celebrate their victory.

"Commander, weapons contact. Torpedo in the water," the sensor officer said, not trying to hide his panic.

"What? From where?"

"Not sure, sir. It looks like... it looks like we only disabled that last sub. They got a shot off."

"Countermeasures!"

"Fired... No effect commander. Weapon has no guidance."

A dummy. The techs had shown him and the torpedo crews how to replace the extensive guidance package in a normal torpedo with additional explosives. It would only go in a straight line, but it would blow big when it got there.

"Bearing?" Maybe they'd get lucky and it would miss.

"Impact with the Fountain in 20 seconds."

"Pilot, alter your turn. Get us between the Fountain and that torpedo. Sound collision."

"Sir," he replied. With that one syllable, he acknowledged the command and voiced the fear all were feeling. He pulled the wheel harder, and the metal in the ship groaned under the strain. The collision alarm wail pierced all other noise. Every person on the ship looked at the deck, the bulkheads, the ceiling, waiting. Waiting for death or water or both.

The torpedo detonated just aft of the main dorsal cannon, instantly killing everyone there and crushing decks and bulkheads. Water forced inwards at speeds impossible to avoid. Emergency hatches slammed shut around the ship, trapping crewmembers but thwarting the water in its ferocious crusade against the air. As far forward as the bridge and as far back as the engine room, the broken spine of the ship crushed inward, severing bulkheads, communication and control conduits, pipes, and power lines. Half the ship lost power instantly. The compression blew out most of the crew's eardrums. Those nearest the impact lucky enough not to drown fell to the floor bleeding as their internal organs liquefied from the blunt force of the air.

Thom didn't have to touch his screaming ears to know that both were oozing blood. Orange emergency lights offered the barest of illumination; more came from the green water pressing against the viewscreen. Cracks spidered out from the impact of the last sub. Around him, Thom's bridge crew were injured, but alive. They had been strapped in. He knew others wouldn't have been.

"Damage report!" Thom yelled, the sound of his own voice hollow and distant in his ears. Soli stumbled onto the bridge, covered in blood. A vicious gash crossed his forehead. Thom was out of his seat and to him before Soli could wave him off. Thom checked him over; disturbingly most of the blood didn't seem to be his.

"Get down to the medbay," Thom shouted again. Soli, in a daze, turned and staggered off.

Thom turned back to see his bridge crew, bloodied but not beaten, trying to make sense of the situation.

"Sections 8, 9, 12, and 13 on Decks 1, 2, and 3 are flooded. Emergency locks are holding. Reports of extensive damage all along Deck 1. Fire in multiple compartments. Power is out across most of ship. I'm seeing cascading failures across all systems," In the dim light and the ringing, Thom was having a hard time figuring out who was talking. From his right, someone else spoke.

"Casualty reports coming in from all along Decks 1 and 2. Injuries reported..." Thom cut the voice off.

"I don't care about injuries, I want fire crews to gear up and get those fires out. I don't care who's bleeding; if those fires spread..." He didn't want to contemplate the consequences enough to finish that sentence. "Can you get the engine room?"

"No, sir."

"Pilot, do you still have control?" There was a moment of silence, then:

"Yes, I think so."

"Get us back to the fight, ensign."

"Sir?"

"We can be dead here or dead there. We haven't won just because we took a beating."

"Yes, sir." He could feel everyone on the bridge calming down as training again took hold.

"I want damage control teams on Decks 1 and 2 to fix anything they can shore up."

"Medbay is reporting being overrun with injuries."

"Tell them that if they were good enough to walk there, they're good enough to walk back to their stations."

"Relayed, sir."

"They can hate me later," he said, barely able to hear himself say it. He could have yelled it for all he knew.

Thom could feel the *Reap* start to accelerate. Worrying creaks and groans echoed through the ship loud enough to hear even through damaged ears. Worse was the grinding. It sounded like one of the prop shafts had dislodged and was trying to abrade itself to nothing. It was causing a harsh and disquieting trembling in the deck. The ship was dying around them, but it limped along, as if knowing it had one final mission.

Minutes passed. Around him the bridge crew continued to relay information and assistance to damage parties around the ship. Thom stepped off the bridge to look down the corridor. Lights winked on and off as electricity arced somewhere, making a short-lived connection and supplying power to some other area of the ship. The shadows held bodies. He stepped back onto the bridge.

There was no way to tell how long the sensor officer had been calling him, but the urgency in his voice made Thom's blood run cold.

"Commander, look!"

On the sensor screen, Thom saw his worst fears: the *Population* was undeterred, still on a direct course to the Fountain. Racing alongside but losing ground was the *Universalis*. It had started to turn to starboard, into the path of the other sub. It was impossible to see what untold amount of damage had been done in the short time the *Reap* had been away. All that could be seen was the *Uni*, more than half of its bulk still forward of the *Pop*, sacrificing itself in a terminal attempt to stop the unrelenting enemy citysub.

The scene unfolded in slow motion, the *Uni* turning and slightly rolling almost leisurely it seemed into the path of the *Pop*. There were no sudden moves with such mass. No last-minute saves. But the mangled *Reap* charged towards them both like a child rushing to come between fighting parents.

In the green, brackish gloom, the contours of the titans became just visible as the two ships finally met. Thom heard gasps as they helplessly watched the collision.

The impact was agonizingly slow at first, the bow of the *Pop* piercing the upper hull of the *Uni*, the latter's angle odd due to the severity of its turn. The *Pop* slid upwards, ripping away hull plating with an ease and savagery no weapon could duplicate. Light burst forth around the wound as the gash became deep enough to penetrate the inner hull. Colossal bubbles of air leapt from the edges between the two subs as water rushed in, killing everyone and everything in the Yard with cold unrelenting pressure. The laceration continued, tearing more and more hull away from the wounded ship.

The bow of the *Pop,* like a knife, continued to rend the spine of the *Uni.* The gaping wound progressed aft past the Yard, and despite a desperate "No!" from one of Thom's crew, opened up the long roof of the Garden. The bow of the once mighty *Universalis* sank rapidly. The deluge continued as air and water struggled to get past each other.

Then, with a final shudder, the ships separated. One seemed unharmed, the other mortally wounded, plummeting towards the sea floor. As they pulled apart, the extent of the damage was revealed to the helpless crew of the *Reap.* The breach torn in the *Uni*'s hull was twice the width of the *Reap,* and ran the length of the Yard and about a third of the Garden. As it continued its mortal tilt downwards, the *Reap* crew could see in, down the cliff-like walls and hanging gardens of the Garden and Yard for the few moments the lights remained on. Then, after a few flickers, the lights across the entire ship winked out and it sank, pitch black, into the darkness.

No one said a word. The *Population* loomed ahead of them. Its pace had slowed considerably, but it was inexorable.

"Are weapons back up?" Thom said, trying not to let the shock of what he had seen overwhelm him.

"Negative."

Thom knew immediately what must be done, but it took him a moment to be able to say it.

"Abandon ship." There was no response. "I said *abandon ship!*"

"Sir? Yes, sir. Yes, sir!" came the delayed response. There was shuffling in the dim light as the bridge crew freed themselves from their chairs. Thom reached forward to the central table, its internal lighting dark, never to be lit again.

On the side, underneath a protective cover, was a button only he was allowed to press. It clicked precisely under the weight of his finger. Triple redundant and isolated wires became excited with electrons for the first, and last, time. Every room and corridor on the *Reappropriation* simultaneously erupted in a noise no crewmember had ever heard in action, yet still knew by heart: the rapid double blat alarm to abandon ship. They'd been trained from childhood to recognize the sound and act immediately and decisively. All knew intuitively where the nearest escape hatch or lifeboat was, and what to do when they got there. The well trained and weary, battle-hardened crew of the *Reap* feverishly but adeptly made their way past the dead bodies, picking up and carrying the live ones to the lifeboats all around the ship.

The bridge crew was the last to leave. Ahead, the *Population*'s torn-up bow looked like menacing razor-sharp teeth filling the viewscreen, ready to devour them. As his bridge crew filed towards the door, Thom made his way forward to the pilot's chair. They seemed reluctant to leave without him. To the dissonant tune of the earsplitting siren he saluted them, and they him, in a silent showing of mutual respect. Thom pulled back on the controls, tilting the *Reappropriation* up towards the gaping maw of the *Population*.

IX

There was nothing else to do. The controls were set, the lifeboats were away. It was likely there were wounded crewmembers still onboard, but nothing could be done for them now. There was no time.

He patted the table gently and told it "Thank you."

Then he was off. Normally, he could have made it to the rear lock in under three minutes at a good run. He knew he had less than two. He did it in one. The upward angle of the ship aided his movements down it, despite the treacherous leaps of faith over collapsed girders and bulging bulkheads.

Everything in the rear lock was in disarray, having slid back against the exterior doors. Dollies, racks, gear, and drysuits piled against the one thing he needed: a scout sub. Thom slid down the deck, joining the detritus, shoving aside containers of food lying on the lid of the cockpit. He looked around for any weapons, but saw none.

The escort sub had a remote connection to the lock door, and as soon as the cockpit was sealed, he enabled it. Despite all the damage to the ship, the pressure was holding enough that the water didn't rush in as the door slid open. He fell back, though, in a stomach-churning drop out the back of the sub. The *Reap* seemed to climb away from him, up towards the black cloud that was the *Population*.

Thom guessed at the time of impact and counted down silently in his head. He got to nine before his comparatively little *Reap* embedded itself into the front of the *Pop*, looking like a piece of errant food stuck in the gaping maw of some massive beast. Disappointingly, there was no explosion. Three of the four propellers still churned and the sub wasn't moving, so he hoped at the very least his beloved ship had bought him some time by slightly slowing the *Pop*. At best, he figured he'd have twenty minutes before it ran down the Fountain.

Thom throttled up and dove down and away from the ship. As he reached maximum speed, he pulled back up again. His aim was perfect.

It had taken Ralla far too long to fight her way down to the shipyard. Door after door had been sealed shut, perhaps in an attempt to keep her occupied, or perhaps as a precaution against the battle being waged outside. Getting knocked off her feet every few moments as torpedoes impacted the hull didn't help. She knew no one torpedo would cripple the ship, but each one still caused her heart to jump a little. By the time she made it down to the floor, nothing was where it was when she had seen it from above. The constant barrage, and one tremendous jolt that felt like a collision, had rearranged, dislodged, or broken anything that wasn't an integral part of the ship itself. The jolt had worried her, but the ship hadn't slowed or turned, so she figured they hadn't run down the Fountain. There was still time.

She had found her rockets. As she figured, only two fit in her coveralls, and her hands were full with a pistol and the rifle she taken from the soldier two decks above.

She had made her way up some scaffolding to the next level, the doors on her level blocked with debris. Another jolt knocked her to the deck, which was the only reason she was looking back towards the bay where she noticed something moving through the open lock in the floor. It was a light. It quickly grew brighter, then it was there. Only in the moment before it hit the surface did she realize what it was.

A dart-like escort sub, travelling at full speed and at a steep angle, broke the plane of the water, bursting forth like an explosion, momentarily airborne. It sailed through the air, passing over the edge of the lock before gravity took hold and smashed it down to the deck. It ground to a halt, water cascading from the hull and vaporizing as it hit a floor hot from abrasion. The canopy popped open, and Ralla was equally surprised and unsurprised to see Thom crawl out, bearded, bloodied, and furious.

Ralla shouted to him, but he didn't hear. She scampered down the scaffolding, nearly breaking her leg as she slipped towards the bottom. Maybe that got his attention, maybe it was her awkward limp, or maybe it was the sheer volume of her screaming. He turned, and she could see the caked blood on his ears. The look on his face when he saw Ralla told her everything she needed to know, had wanted to know, had hoped to know for months. She jumped into his arms and they kissed.

Ralla let herself slide back into reality, and slide down from his arms to stand on the deck. He refused to let her go. Thom looked down onto the top of her head, eyeing the blond, fuzzy lack of hair. Her eyes looked up at him and she shrugged. In turn, Ralla tugged on his ratty beard, and he shrugged. They shared a smile, but it faded from his face as his eyes focused on their surroundings.

368 | U N D E R S E A

"We need to get to the engine room," she said. He looked confused and touched his ear with his finger. "We need to get to the engine room," she shouted, and held up one of the rockets. He nodded and looked around. They found four more rockets and climbed their way out of the shipyard.

Sprinting, they made it to the rear of the ship, down some elevators, and to the corridors that led to the engine bays in little time. They came tearing around the corner only to skid to a stop half a dozen paces away from two guards. Somehow, the men had stayed at their posts during the fight. Thom could hear Ralla talking, but couldn't make it out. Finally she raised the pistol at them, and Thom took that as his cue to raise the rockets up over his head and howl with an animalistic rage bordering on insanity.

The guards scattered.

"There are six engines," she shouted at him, pointing. "You take the first three, I'll take the other three. That last one is personal."

Thom nodded as she ran off. He made it to the first door and realized they had a problem. It was sealed, and the door commands did nothing. They were locked out. He looked down the corridor and saw that Ralla had come to the same realization. She jogged over to him.

"Think these things will blow open one of the doors?" she yelled, holding up one of the rockets.

"It's worth a try," he tried not to yell.

Ralla placed a rocket against the lock's small window and ran to the other end of the corridor. Sighting down the rifle, Ralla nailed the rocket after two shots. The resulting explosion wasn't huge, but it was loud even to Thom. What mattered, though, was that it had blown the window open, and they were able to reach in and open the lock using the emergency release.

Ralla entered to detonate the engine while Thom set up their next two charges on the remaining starboard-side engine room doors. As he placed the rockets, he couldn't help but notice that the last engine room on the far end of the corridor had a full lock for some reason.

What was obvious was their now diminished capacity to inflict harm on the engines. There was little chance of making back to the shipyard for more explosives. They'd have to get to the bridge and try to get control of the ship. Or more likely, die trying. It was odd, but under the fear and the panic there was comfort being here with her. Whether they died or not, at least he was here with her, and they were in this together. The thought shook him, though. Here they were, potentially minutes away from the end of the species, and he couldn't get his mind off this girl. He forced himself to focus, and felt the explosion of her rocket more than heard it.

Ralla came out of the engine room followed by a billow of smoke. She handed him the pistol, then pointed towards the farthest engine room, the one with the full, and rather haphazard, lock. He nodded more in acknowledgement than understanding and watched her jog down the corridor.

As Ralla entered the farthest lock, Thom detonated his two rockets with six shots. After getting the first door open, he wedged a rocket under the round engine bell and stepped out into the hallway to shoot it. It took him half the clip, but it finally went off, taking the bell with it, and causing the entire apparatus to grind to a halt. It was surprisingly cathartic. The next one felt even better. Then he started across the ship to the far bay, only then realizing Ralla hadn't appeared yet.

What if she was yelling for him?

He sprinted down to the last bay. The outer lock was jammed open, but the inner was sealed shut. Ralla was in the window banging on it, screaming. Behind her was water. Everywhere. Now he felt the terror he hadn't felt on his own ship or in any battle. Worse fear than he had ever felt in his life.

The electronic lock controls did nothing. He lifted up the pistol and showed it to her. Through her own terror she nodded and moved away from the door. The water was up to her crawling up her body rapidly. Thom stepped back, hands shaking, and emptied the clip into the window. Now there were holes in it, but it stayed put. Bracing himself against the walls of the lock, he kicked at it. The tiny window, not much larger than his boot, finally gave way with an unsatisfying pop. Ralla came back to the window and stuck her head through.

"Don't do that," Thom said, "grab the emergency release."

"There isn't one!"

"What? How could there not be a..."

"There isn't one; we were kept in here as prisoners, so there's no release on this side. Are you sure there isn't one over there?"

Thom frantically searched the door and the walls for any kind of manual lever. He looked up, eyes wide. Water started to spill over the edge of the window, the level of water up to Ralla's shoulders. She was oddly calm.

"Look, Thom, even if you figured out a way to open this lock, we'd flood the whole ship. Get to the bridge, save the Fountain. I won't let you kill all these people just to save me."

"What people? Ralla, they're all gone. Haven't you seen? There aren't any people here. They're all in our domes. Thousands of them. All of them. I've seen them with my own eyes. There is no one left on this ship *to* kill."

Thom grabbed the edge of the window, braced his feet against the wall of the lock, and stared to pull. There was no movement. Water was spilling out of half the window now, and Ralla had to lift her chin to breathe above the water. Thom pulled harder. The edges of the window cut into his fingers. His blood mixed with the water. He kept pulling. Now there was less than a quarter of the window left that gushing wasn't cold, rushing liquid.

"Thom, I..."

Twisting metal and a scream cut off her words. Something had given way in the back of the bay, and a tidal wave of water had rushed forward. What little air Ralla had was gone, the bay completely filled with water. Thom pulled with his arms, pushed with his legs, the adrenaline surging though his veins. Out of the water came a head as Ralla forced through the hole in a futile attempt to get air. The water squirted past her, filling her mouth and nose, not allowing her to escape from its grasp. She gave up, and Thom felt her cold hand on his as he continued to pull. There was no way he was going to leave. This was it. He wasn't going to leave her again. Not to die like this, so close. Her hand relaxed, and slid away from his. Thom screamed. It was anguish at first, but it became a scream of rage.

Suddenly, with a snap the door gave way. Thom flushed into the hallway on a wave of water.

Now the sea, with its hand in the flooded bay, began its relentless attack on the *Population*.

Ralla's limp body shot out into the corridor, crumpling against a wall, lifeless. Thom struggled to drag her from the current. He hadn't moved her far before she started coughing. He dropped to her side as the water lapped at their feet. Opening her eyes, she saw him crouched over her, and closed them again, a half smile on her face. She was shivering badly, and her skin was a pale, ghostly blue. But as the water lapped around her head, she snapped awake, instantly alert. They both looked at the lock-sized hose of water flooding the back of the ship.

"We need to go. Now," she said, adrenaline temporarily driving her mind and body past her touch with death. They got up and started running. "That whole wall could give way. I helped cobble it together. It's not great."

They made it to the elevators and got out at the main concourse. It was a clear run past the hanging gardens and abandoned food stalls to the shipyard wall. From there it was just a few flights of stairs and a corridor to the bridge. They hadn't taken two steps when a loud bang knocked them off their feet. "That would be the wall," she said flatly.

With low-pitched moan, the floor started to tilt down at the stern. Suddenly, they weren't on the floor of the concourse; they were at the bottom of a hill that looked like the concourse.

"Go. We need to go," she said, pushing him along. He gave up trying to help her and just tried to keep up.

The slope began to get worse. The rear of the boat was sinking, and fast. A garbage can rolled toward them. Then a table. Then a stampede of chairs and rotten fruit. The creaking in the former boats lining the space mimicked those

Thom heard on the *Reap* only minutes before, but exponentially louder and deeper.

They ran up a path that wove in and around decorative grassy knolls and overgrown bushes, slowing their progress. Windows burst high above, showering them with glass as the frames contorted, the entire sub warping and bending under the strain. Plants and soil fell from their gardens, pelting Thom and Ralla with dirt. Legs burning with the strain, they kept at as close to a run as they could manage. To their right, an entire food stall tumbled past, rolling down the concourse, only to flatten itself against the aft wall. Everything had become a projectile. Behind them, water had found its way through and was pooling in the aft corners of the concourse.

Thom and Ralla fought their way forward and up, dodging the debris avalanche as they went. They climbed past the public terminals where they had sat months before, finally reaching the remaining food stalls. Trays piled on the inside of the stalls, waiting to be free and become airborne. The increasing angle had forced Thom and Ralla onto all fours, the looming shipyard wall now more a ceiling. Behind them the sea churned loudly, chasing and eating its way towards them.

After climbing two nearly vertical stairwells, they made it onto the curving corridor that led to the bridge as the bodies of two *Pop* officers slid past them. Blood seeped through their uniforms.

The boat's incline passed 50 degrees, and another body slid towards them. It was the Captain. Having lost her rifle to the water in the engine room, Ralla braced herself and took the sidearm from Thom. She checked the clip and motioned for them to continue. Thom made the mistake of looking back as the body of the Captain picked up speed and fell, tumbling to a bulkhead ten stories below. He looked over at Ralla, but she had no intention of looking down, the determination on her face more sure than Thom had ever seen. They climbed forward, shuffling along using the "V" of the floor and wall as best they could. Eventually, the curve and angle of the ship allowed them to use the wall as the deck, and they broke into a lopsided run. As they neared the bridge, two more bodies lay sprawled against the deck. The doors to Oppai's chambers were open. Ralla peaked around the corner and saw down through the cabin, the far wall littered with books, broken bottles, and glasses. Farther was the shipyard. To her amazement, the lock in the shipyard floor was still open, a cascade of water filling the bay. Turning, she looked up into the bridge.

Oppai stood near the front, bracing himself between the main table and the pilot's chair. Behind him, filling the viewscreen, was the textured dark of the Fountain. They were moments from collision. Oppai locked eyes with Ralla, an eerie smile on his face. Thom pushed off from the actual deck, grabbing the far doorframe and swinging himself up onto the bridge, lying with his back against the wall. Ralla leapt up and did the same on the near side. Oppai did nothing to stop them.

As he sat up and reached for the table, Oppai produced a pistol. Thom rolled under the consoles just as Oppai fired at him. He yelled in pain as the bullet embedded itself in his right arm. Ralla fired back, hitting Oppai in the shoulder. He tumbled forward as Ralla shot again, hitting him in the leg. He fell over the table, hitting the rear wall of the bridge where Thom had just been. His battered leg dangled over the doorframe, hanging in space, the next wall below him the wall of water creeping up the shipyard. Thom used his good arm and the edges of the consoles to pull himself upwards towards the ever-rising bow. Oppai was dazed by his fall, but recovered quickly.

"Stop!" Oppai screamed. Ralla had kept the gun trained on him, but in holding it towards him, she hadn't notice how close his feet were. His foot jolted out and knocked her hand upwards. She fired again, the bullet embedding itself harmlessly in the wall. She struggled to roll towards him to get a better shot, but he sat up and brought his pistol to bear. At point blank range he shot the gun from her hand, taking three of her fingers with it. She cried out in agony as blood spurted across bridge.

Thom had made it to the pilot's chair, and glanced at the controls. The throttle and steering were destroyed. The bow thrusters had been jammed to fire down, the aft thrusters up, in an attempt to fight the buoyancy variance between the two halves. The ship was still creeping forward with enough mass that impact with the Fountain would still be catastrophic. At her yell, he spun around in his chair.

"We're still moving forward," Oppai said, as if reading Thom's mind. The Governor trained his weapon on Thom, hopping slightly on his good leg while bracing himself against the table in front of him. Ralla, her face contorted in pain, tried to move towards him, but he swung the gun towards her. "It may be slow, but it will be enough. The mass of this ship will fold your Fountain like a twig. My people will be safe. I've won."

"Your people?" Thom replied, fighting the nausea as he looked down past Oppai into the shipyard so far below. "You've killed your people."

"You've killed all our people," said Ralla. Oppai, for a moment, looked confused.

"Your people died in those domes. The ones you left there. They died. There wasn't enough food or air. You killed them."

"You're lying."

"I saw them. I tried to help them. Every dome I could, I brought food, I helped them fix the circs. I saved your people, you maniac. The ones you tried to kill."

"No. I did what I had to do to save them."

"No, you killed them and you've killed us all," Ralla spat. "That Fountain is the only chance our entire species has of survival and you've destroyed it."

"No," Thom said flatly, "He hasn't."

Without turning around, Thom jerked his elbow back into the bow thruster control. They instantly reversed direction, downward thrust replaced by upward thrust, and with all the air still in the bow, the ship roared towards near vertical. Thom fell forward onto the edge of the table. The *Population*, attempting to stand nearly on end, shook Oppai off balance. He dropped the gun in a futile effort to grab hold of something, but his fingers found no purchase. Ralla swung herself out over the drop, kicking out at Oppai's good leg. He toppled towards her, grabbing frantically at her baggy blue jumpsuit. But he slipped past her and fell out the door, across the hallway, tumbling down through his cabin, past his balcony, smashing through the windows, finally plunging to his death in the dark seething water dozens of stories below.

With only one hand and most of her weight hanging over the void, Ralla was in a bad way. She struggled to pull herself back up. Thom jumped to the consoles and climbed his way down towards Ralla, oblivious to the pain in his own arm.

"Hang on!" he shouted down.

He dropped to the wall beside her, grabbing her good arm with his. They locked eyes for a moment before Ralla's darted past him and into the distance.

"What is *that*?!!"

The citysub *Population* collided with the underside of the newly formed n-pole icecap, forcing countless tons of ice and snow to blast upwards. The ice tore away at the hull, clawing at it, devouring bracing, panels, and bulkheads. The tremendous power of the remaining engines, coupled with momentum and the buoyancy of the front half of the ship, shot the sub up through the icepack and upward. For a brief moment, the newly desiccant and eviscerated bow reached towards the bare sun. It hung for an instant, then toppled over, snapping the ship in half.

The ship hadn't been perfectly vertical, and now the corpse of one of the two largest beasts the planet had ever seen slammed down and beached itself on the island of ice. Deck upon deck collapsed under its own weight, the sub's ovoid shape sagging outward like a compressed balloon. Girders, forcibly relieved of their charge, snapped outward in compound fractures, piercing the hull in thousands of places. Tears sliced open along the sides, shredding the hull and exposing bulkheads to sunlight for the first time in generations.

The ice sank slightly under the weight, ocean water washing across its surface. But slowly it rose back, the water freezing in the cold air making the floating ice mountain stronger, bigger. The force of the impact had driven the island southward. The Fountain bent and gave, as it was designed to do, but didn't break. With the slowness of the great mass that surrounded it, the Fountain righted itself. Snow from its top continued to fall onto the island of ice and its peculiar new inhabitant, a bloated black carcass of steel and composite.

Time passed. Steel creaked. Panels popped. Mostly, there was silence.

Onto the mutilated bow walked Thom and Ralla, bandaged and bloodied. Around them, the carnage of the citysub *Population* lay strewn across the snowy fields. In the distance, around the base of the Fountain, were small hills. The sun shone bright. More snow fell.

"And you're sure it's safe?" Ralla asked quietly, her bandaged hand clutched to her chest.

"Compared to what?" Thom replied. She squinted at the sun and hugged him with her good arm. She didn't let go, nor did he.

"It's beautiful."

Thom could think of nothing to say, so he pulled her tighter.

"After what you saw, do you think there's anyone alive on the *Universalis*?"

"Ralla, I think there are people alive everywhere."

They looked out across the island, out across the sea.

"Then I guess we have some work to do."

—

This book is dedicated to:
Dennis, an incredible editor, and even better friend.
Carrie and Lauren, for their insight.
and
My parents, for always encouraging my creativity.

All my thanks. All my love.

Geoffrey Morrison is a privateer writer and editor based in Los Angeles. You can find out more about him and his writing at geoffreymorrison.com, or follow him on Twitter @techwritergeoff.

The cover was designed and illustrated by the brilliant Clara Moon, claramoon.com.

The spine and back cover was designed by Betty Abrantes, abrantesdesign.com

The sans-serif font used on the cover, title page, headers and elsewhere is called Telegrafico, designed by ficod, ficod.deviantart.com.

2280915R00193

Printed in Great Britain
by Amazon.co.uk, Ltd.,
Marston Gate.